DARK FARM

DEAN RAVEN

939 Publishing

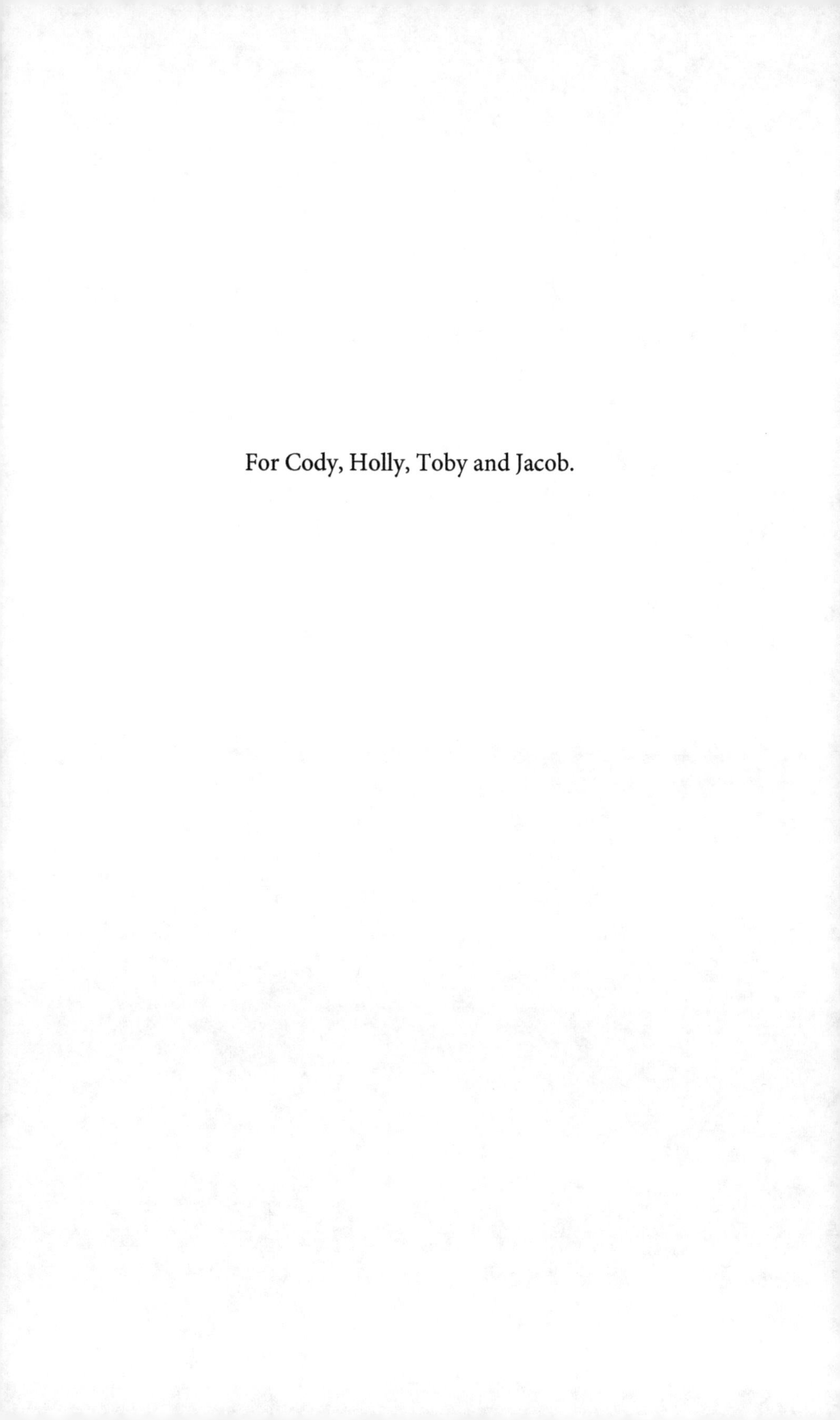

For Cody, Holly, Toby and Jacob.

TABLE OF CONTENTS

1

The buzzard

WHEN MORGAN CAUGHT sight of the buzzard rising above the crest of the hill, he broke into a run.

"Got it!" he barked into his phone.

The bird had its eye fixed on something below. *It's the red*, he thought with a nod. *It sees it. Or smells it. Probably both.*

The buzzard dipped, and at the same time Morgan's boot slipped on a rock, his legs flew out from under him and he sat with a painful jolt in the icy creek.

"Damn it!" he cursed, rolling onto his knees.

Pulling his phone out of the stream, he shook off the water and placed it against his ear. "You still there?"

A voice crackled, "Yessir."

Morgan pushed himself to his feet, grunting in pain as his bad knee buckled under the weight of his body. Sam Morgan, Director of Strategic Capability at the National Security Office, was only forty-three years old, but on days like this, with the weather cold and damp and his war wounds playing up, he felt sixty.

"I'll be there in five," he barked. "Secure the site till I get there. No one gets close. Is that clear?"

He brushed mud first off one leg, then the other. There was no reply.

"I said is that clear?" Pulling the phone from his ear, he moved it close to his mouth. "If anyone gets within twenty feet of that thing, I will make him disappear. Is *that* clear?"

He listened again. Nothing. Not even a crackle.

Grunting in frustration, shoving the phone in his pocket, he squinted up at the clouds, searching again for the buzzard. It floated into sight on an updraft, its eyes fixed on the same spot below.

With a grin of acknowledgement, Morgan took off in that direction.

"Hold on! Sam!"

Glancing over his shoulder, Morgan saw Grieves splashing through the water. He stopped and waited for her to catch up.

Cleopatra Grieves was a few years younger than Morgan, tall and heavy-set, dressed in the same dark blue suit and black boots. A Principal Investigation Officer in the NSO's London office, Grieves had worked with Morgan for just on six years, and there was no one he trusted more. In her younger days she'd been a Jamaican national amateur bodybuilder, but after giving up competitive bodybuilding her body had given up too. She was still the strongest person Morgan knew, but her stamina left a lot to be desired.

"Took your time," he smiled as she approached and bent forward with hands on knees. He watched as she caught her breath. "You should get that bladder looked at."

"Looks like you stopped for a swim," Grieves shot back, looking him up and down. "How's the water?"

He clapped his hands on his friend's shoulders. "If we didn't have a bloodbath to get to, I'd show you," he said with a playful shove towards the creek.

Grieves' face lit up. "So that's what they found, was it? A body?"

Morgan's expression revealed nothing.

"Bodies?"

"Amongst other things," he said, walking off.

He felt bad for keeping their mission secret from his colleague, but he was under strict orders not to reveal anything to anyone. Yesterday he was ordered to the NSO laboratories in Kent, where senior officials and defence personnel leaned over a table gawking at something dead and deformed. It was human, but only remotely so. The brief said it was found by the side of a disused road in the Six Hills, near the northern village of Quorn. Approaching the table, Morgan felt the gorge rise in his throat. He'd read sealed files about doomsday cults and secret societies, witness statements about alleged encounters with ghosts, goblins, aliens and other nasties (all carefully covered up and explained away so the general public could go on with their comfortable, blinkered lives) – but this was the first time he'd come face-to-face with something so obviously not of this world.

Grieves came up alongside him. "This isn't about no terrorist training camps, is it Sam?"

"Did I say it was?"

"From the look on your face, I'm starting to think invaders from outer space."

Morgan opened his hands. "I don't know what they found, to be honest, Cleo. I just know two civilians are down and the thing that massacred them has been contained."

"The thing? Don't tell me it's a werewolf! It's a werewolf, isn't it? I always knew they were real."

"We'll see. Soon enough. Have you had breakfast yet?"

"Ah … yeah. What's that got to do with the price of bacon and eggs?"

"Is that what you had?"

"Mmm. With French toast, fried mushies and a quickie on the side."

Morgan shook his head. "Cooked breakfast. On a week day. My wives complained if I asked them to pass me the box of Coco Pops."

"Next time find an ugly one. That's my advice. You always go for the lookers. You need one's gonna work to keep you happy, not the other way round."

Morgan laughed. "I'm telling Liv what you said. Come on, Cleo, let's speed this up." He made a play-punch at Grieves' bulging belly. "Too bad about the greasy breakfast. I hope it tastes as good on the way up!"

THE TWO OFFICERS strode into the clearing. A half dozen soldiers were standing at attention, each fitted out in a dark blue uniform, black helmet and black boots. They were holding assault rifles against their bodies, their faces taut with excitement. The soldier at the far end was doing her best to control a German Shepherd, which barked and growled and strained at its leash to get at whatever was on the other side of a campers' tent further along the clearing.

"Shut that dog up," ordered Morgan.

The soldier knew better than to talk back, but the look on her face showed Morgan she was helpless to control it.

He approached the animal and moved the back of his hand towards its nose, trying to calm it down. The trick never failed – Morgan's parents were breeders and trainers of Dobermans, and from the time he was in nappies he'd been surrounded by them. But this time the dog was unaffected. Morgan stared at it as it continued barking and snarling at something unseen and unheard. Like the buzzard, the dog sensed something no human could sense, and it wasn't about to be distracted by trivial human gimmicks like the hand-in-front-of-the-nose trick.

Vaguely insulted by the dog's disobedience, Morgan strode up the line, shouting, "Who found it?"

Two men, standing shoulder to shoulder, raised their hands.

Morgan stepped towards them. Their boots and uniforms were muddy, and one man had dirt smeared across his face.

Morgan turned first to one, then to the other. They looked terrified. He could feel his heart thumping against his chest. Even after six years as a senior officer in special ops, he still got a rush from the power he held over some of the country's most elite soldiers.

"No you didn't," he returned calmly.

The hands dropped.

"What are we doing here?" Morgan asked one of them, moving his nose close to the soldier's face.

"Searching out suspected terrorist training camps, sir."

"Did we find them?"

The man was in his thirties, with a short neck and muscular face. A long scar ran from his temple to the corner of his mouth. He looked the type to get into bar fights because he knew he would win. But now he just blinked. Morgan could read his thoughts, could almost see his brain scrambling to figure out what it was his superior wanted him to say.

"Negative, sir."

He moved his attention to the other man. "And you, soldier." Without turning his head, he pointed towards the green polyester camping tent. "What's that?"

The soldier glanced at the cabin-shaped tent, dropped his eyes to the red mess on the ground around it. He gulped. "Nothing, sir."

"What do you mean, 'Nothing, sir'? How can you see nothing?"

"No … terrorists, sir."

"If you didn't see terrorists, what did you see?"

The man was now in a cold sweat. "The marsh. A bird. A … dead rabbit?"

Morgan stared into the man's face. He had close-set eyes, a runny nose and a weak chin. He seemed to have the start or the end of a cold.

"Fall back to the trail," he ordered. He stepped back. "All of you!"

The men hurried away with a collective murmur of relief.

"Come on, Cleo."

Morgan went to inspect the tent, which was flapping in the wind like a wounded bird. There was no other sign of life. The opening was turned away from the clearing, and as Morgan approached it he spied a bloodied head. It was a brown-haired, red-bearded man, lying flat on his back, surrounded by more blood than Morgan had ever seen in one place. The ground was disturbed all around him; there'd been one helluva fight. The rotten, rusty smell of death crept up Morgan's nose and into his throat.

Grieves joined him. "Christ in heaven!" she cried. "What the bloody hell did that?"

Morgan crouched next to the man, who was dressed in beige trousers and a two-toned grey-and-green fishing jacket. He looked to be in his mid-thirties; pudgy body, pockmarked face, crooked teeth, dirty fingernails – a pretty typical male for this part of the country. But what had been done to him was far from typical. It looked like his head had been bashed against a rock, which was now lodged in the back of his cranium. Whatever had killed him had torn away his clothes so it could mutilate him – judging from the volume and spread of the blood, in a demented frenzy of violence.

"There's no organs," observed Grieves, a hand covering her mouth and nose. She leaned over Morgan's shoulder and peered inside the empty cavity. "What's happened to all the organs?"

Morgan stroked his chin. The mutilation reminded him of bodies he'd seen in Afghanistan: in bombed houses, in shallow graves, in ditches by the side of the road. He thought he'd seen the last of that kind of thing.

"Still thinking werewolves," muttered Grieves, stepping away.

Climbing to his feet, Morgan went up to the tent and pulled aside the door flap. The polyester walls, the ground, the bedding – it seemed even the air itself – were red with blood. In a corner of the tent lay the crumpled body of a blond boy in a blue-striped shirt and black jeans, his body battered and broken. As Morgan approached, he could see the boy's head was also bashed in. A bloodied rock lay next to the body.

"Dear Lord," breathed Grieves at the door. "Same as the old man."

Morgan looked at her. "What's your assessment, Cleo?"

At first she shrugged helplessly, her eyes glued to the butchered boy. But she quickly gathered her wits, pulled back her shoulders and glanced around.

"Righto. Daddy hears a noise, goes to investigate, is attacked. Fight ensues. Boy told to stay in the tent, or else runs inside for safety when he sees what's happening to his old man."

She turned back to the man, tapping a finger against her chin. Her eyes followed the trail of blood that led across the grass towards a bank of bushes. "Either one large assailant who killed quick then mutilated, or multiple attackers killing simultaneously. The latter would be my guess."

Morgan edged past her. "Come on, Cleo, there's more to see."

He followed the blood trail to the bushes, where what looked like a strand of small intestine was hanging off a branch. He saw now why the dog was ignoring its training. This carnage was something no training could prepare it for. Something savage and inhuman had entered this lonely clearing and committed an unspeakable crime, and it evoked the dog's primal instincts. The wolf in it had sensed the hunt and the kill, and it either feared it or longed to join it.

The bushes ran along a bank of mud, which sloped down to a creek. The soil of the embankment was disturbed where the two soldiers had clambered down earlier. Morgan spied footsteps close to the water, but there were so many of them it was hard to tell whether they belonged to the soldiers, the campers or the assailants. Some of the footsteps led towards a tumble of boulders that formed the start of a cove, where the creek dog-legged abruptly before heading towards the sea.

After taking a few deep breaths to expel the smell of death from his lungs, Morgan half walked, half slipped down the bank. Grieves was close behind. They reached the water together, held onto each other to steady themselves, saw the foot at the same time.

Sticking out from behind a boulder, it looked like a normal man's foot: hairy toes, yellowed nails, the skin wrinkled and white from too much time in the water.

The toes curled. Morgan almost jumped out of his skin.

"He's alive," breathed Grieves.

"Something they neglected to tell me."

Morgan felt queasy. He'd always hated feet.

"Is it another one of them campers?" Grieves asked.

Morgan had already been warned it wasn't a camper. He moved towards the boulders, and as his eyes locked on the body lying in the bloody water, his muscles tensed. Despite the morning chill, he felt a rise of wet heat within his body. Sweat squeezed through the pores in his arms and chest and face, and he could also feel it in the wetness of his underarms and crotch. The thing in the lab had been dead, and he knew from long experience that death can do strange things to bodies. But this one was different. It looked like a person turned inside out, then squeezed and pulled and shaped into something from a nightmare. It was wearing grey pants and had a metal ring locked around its neck. The blood of the campers had stained its face and body and trousers, and the surrounding water was the colour of rust.

Grieves placed a hand on his shoulder. "Jesus Christ Almighty, Sam! What the hell is that?" She craned her neck forward. "How can that be –"

Morgan leaned closer to the monstrosity, trying to make sense of its misshapen proportions. "How can it be what?"

Grieves was breathing heavily. "Alive."

He glanced at her. "You okay, Cleo?"

When she continued gaping, he turned his attention back to the thing. It stared up at them, its head jerking with involuntary spasms. It seemed to be pleading with its bloodshot eyes, which bulged from hollowed-out sockets in its bulbous skull. It had no hair, no ears, no eyelids, and its nose was a sunken, cancerous scab.

Morgan shook the disgust from his head. They had a job to do, and he couldn't let questions or emotions get in the way of their mission. There would be plenty of time for that once they bagged it, got it back to the lab, and found out more about what the hell it was.

"Doesn't look like our single large assailant, does it?"

Grieves shook her head.

He looked around. "We need to find whatever else was working with it. I don't think this one is going anywhere in a hurry."

As if on cue, a noise began on the other side of the rocks.

Morgan straightened. "Do you hear that?"

It was a squelching sound, like the noise a child might make when sucking on a popsicle. A dread crept up Morgan's spine. Probably the campers' dog, he told himself – though this was unlike any noise he ever heard a dog make.

The thing in the water could hear it too. "Goo, gwoo, ooo," it gurgled, turning its red eyes to the rocks. Its rubbery lips began opening and closing with a horrible pucking sound. One skeletal arm waved in the air, while the other arm, thick and twisted like the trunk of a tree, splashed in the bloody water.

Morgan drew his pistol. Holding it in both hands, he crept around the rocks to the sheltered cove. Here, the creek degenerated into a swamp. The water was brown and stagnant, everything in it dead and dank with rot. The buzzard was circling overhead, and he saw now it wasn't the campers the bird had its eyes fixed on.

Standing ankle-deep in mud, its back to him, was what looked like a gargantuan woman. She had shoulder-length hair, colourless, wet and matted. There were pink patches on her scalp where it appeared clumps of hair had been wrenched out. Her naked body was green and bloated, her skin scarred by boils and welts. Some of the wounds had split open and the exposed flesh oozed with yellow pus.

As Morgan stared in shock, the woman froze. She seemed to have sensed someone was behind her. With an animal snarl, she half-turned her head, then shuffled in a circle to face him.

Morgan almost dropped his gun. The thing – which wasn't a woman – not really, not any more – leered at him through puffy eyes as it strained to see who or what was there.

But the thing's hideous appearance wasn't the worst of it. That wasn't what turned Morgan's stomach and made his legs buckle. That wasn't what made the world as he knew it go spinning away, leaving him stranded in a place where horrific nightmares had crept from the safety of sleep and entered the world of the living. What he couldn't pull his eyes away from was the red, dripping ball in the thing's hands, the ball the thing had been sucking on: a ball that had ponytails that ended in pink polka dot ribbons.

2

You came

YLAN'S FIRST THOUGHT when he peered through the window was: Why have they dragged me to this dump? But when he pushed into the shop and the bell tinkled, he couldn't help but smile. The bell was a grinning metal skull hanging from a twisted wire noose.

"Cool, hey?" chirped Mike behind him – which was enough to immediately make it uncool.

Dylan glanced around. Quorn Fine Arts and Antiquities was a dim and musty dungeon, crammed with dark furniture, dated paintings, yellowed books, fluted glassware and other assorted junk. A dozen or so clocks ticked and tocked in the darkness, adding to the stifling sense of a bygone age.

Dust tickled Dylan's nose and he sneezed fast and hard, sending more dust into the air. Rubbing his nose on his sleeve, his eyes landed on a stuffed fox, its glass eyes on the lookout for its next meal. Behind the fox was a mouldy ferret that was destined to spend eternity with its teeth buried in a rat.

His father dropped a heavy hand on his shoulder. "This way," he said to his wife, moving Dylan aside like a hat stand.

Dylan glanced at his mother, who was having one of her moods. She'd dressed in a plain grey sack, pulled in at the waist by a black belt, the outfit completed by an over-sized blue denim jacket. Her brown hair was held back with an elastic band and tucked behind her ears. Her face was pale and expressionless as she stared past Mike, past the jumble of merchandise, through the shop walls, to something on the other side. She'd spent all morning in bed, and her eyes looked like they wished they were back there.

Mike was compensating by being annoyingly cheerful. It was the only tool in his toolbox and he could always be relied upon to bring it out when someone was feeling down. It never worked, but he seemed to believe the universe depended on him maintaining a state of emotional equilibrium to keep their dysfunctional family from imploding.

Trailing behind them, Dylan was startled by the sight of a skinny youth with collar-length black hair and pimply white skin scowling at him. It took him a second to realise it was his reflection in a mirror. The boy in the glass was dressed all in black and looked as weary and morose as his mother. His lip was curled, his eyes half-closed. Dylan hardly recognised himself.

Dropping his eyes, he turned away, unnerved by the encounter and wishing suddenly, like his mother, that he was back home in bed.

Suddenly his father cried, "Voilà!" and did an improvised tap dance. He ended with his open hand pointing at a dusty sideboard that looked as if it had seen better days. His mouth opened in a huge grin.

"Is that …?" began Lauren, her eyes coming back into focus.

Mike nodded with the enthusiasm of a pre-schooler.

"All the way out here?"

He lifted his shoulders.

"It's not really Hepplewhite. Must be repro."

"You're the expert."

Lauren, all business now, went to inspect it. "Looks authentic." She pulled open a drawer, which was lined with a square of paper printed with strawberries.

Brought to life by this sudden reminder of her past, she waved Dylan over. "Come and see what your father's found."

Dylan slouched towards her. Sometimes he resented her mood swings even more than her depression. At least when she was depressed, he knew how to take care of her; they were allies in their misery; they understood each other. When she was on a high, she tried to act like his mother, and that never worked out well. Not after all those years they'd spent apart – all those lost, unhappy, resentful years of being little more than strangers.

Lauren had pulled open every drawer, and was now on her hands and knees, checking underneath it.

Mike folded his arms. "Mr Waite assured me it's Hepplewhite. I said you'd know straight away if it wasn't. He almost bit my head off when I said that." He glanced around. "– bit my kneecaps off, more like it," he corrected with a smile.

Dylan watched as his mother stroked a large dent near the bottom right corner. The sideboard was evoking memories of something, a thing or place from happier times. The movement of her fingers seemed like something personal, something he shouldn't be watching, but he couldn't drag his eyes away.

"Happy Anniversary!" cried Mike, raising his hands.

Lauren half smiled. "This is incredible," she gushed, pushing herself to her feet. "It's not in bad condition, considering. Nothing that can't be restored."

"I asked Mr Waite to keep his eye out, and this is what he came up with."

"It's like my grandmother's. I haven't seen one close to it since she died."

"I remember. Her pride and joy."

"Can we afford it? This is an expensive piece."

"You can't put a price on memories." He coughed into his fist. "By the way, we're having baked beans on toast for dinner for the next six months."

Dylan, bored by their conversation, fell into an armchair, sending another cloud of dust puffing into the air. Leaning forward, he choked and sputtered as the dust settled in his lungs. When the fit was over, he reached out and grabbed the nearest distraction: a greenish-brown statue. Sliding down in his seat, he raised the statue above his head, turned it around and upside down, held it at a distance and squinted at it.

The statue was carved from a single block of stone and felt cold to the touch. It was in the shape of a bloated monster, a maggoty blob with large, ugly pustules covering its lumpy body. It had eight fat, arm-like appendages, four on each side. Four eyes sat above a huge flabby mouth. The thing was squatting on a black pillar, hunched forward, two of its arms resting over its bulging belly. Its black eyes bored into Dylan as if it knew him and hated him. Dylan stroked its cold head.

Behind him, unheard and unseen, a white-haired figure in a rumpled brown suit emerged from the back office. The man was short and thin, with rounded shoulders, a moon face and receding hairline. His brow was thick and arched, his ancient skin mottled and scored with deep lines and furrows. His green eyes were set deep inside his skull.

At the counter, the man collected a ceremonial knife with a gold, jewel-studded handle and long, curved blade. The knife was heavy and seemed to weigh him down as he approached the armchair.

Preoccupied with the statue, Dylan didn't notice him. The man stopped beside him.

"Who do we have here?"

Dylan jumped in fright. "Jesus Christ! Give me a heart attack, why don't you?"

"Mr Waite!" cried Mike. "Hi! That's just Dylan."

Dylan went back to playing with the statue, making it walk along the arm of the chair. "Just me, just Mr Nobody," he said under his breath.

"Lauren," said Mike, joining his wife, "this is Wilfred Waite."

Wilfred ignored them. He was peering down at Dylan, his eyes like marbles, a smile tugging at his thin purple lips. In fact, everyone was looking at Dylan, at his amateur puppet show.

"You came," declared Wilfred.

His breath stank like something had died and rotted in his lungs. Dylan glanced up at him. The whites of his eyes were tinged with yellow, the skin around them so dark it was almost black. His face and hands were brown with liver spots, and there were scabs on his forehead that reminded Dylan of the fungus that grows on fallen trees. In old Bert's words, the shopkeeper looked like death warmed up.

"Yessir, here we are," chirped Mike. "Today's the big day."

"Not you," snapped Wilfred, hardly bothering to turn his head. "Your boy." He lowered his voice to a hoarse whisper and said to Dylan, "I knew you would come."

Dylan cringed at the old man's creepiness, at the uncomfortable proximity of his bent body and the stench of mothballs and stale sweat that came off his clothes. He turned to his father with a mute plea for help, but Mike looked as confused as he was.

"Your boy," said Wilfred Waite, turning to Mike at last, "is the spitting image of me when I was a lad."

"A century ago," muttered Dylan.

"Dylan!" scolded his mother.

But Wilfred was nonplussed. "Two, to be exact," he corrected.

He eyed the statue, and said in a voice that was almost a chant, "Flesh that is yours shall Z'garh Khrl'ur bestow. Inside you Kragn dwells, and to Kragn shall you return."

Dylan frowned at the old man's words. He pushed himself up in the chair.

"You have excellent taste, young man," continued Wilfred. "That is the great Kragn Z'garh Khrl'ur."

"The great what?" He turned over the price tag. "Twelve hundred bucks?"

"It's an antiquity."

"It's grotesque," said Mike.

"What's it supposed to be?" asked Lauren.

"Kragn is The One Who Came Before," explained Wilfred, hobbling towards a display cabinet. He lifted the glass top and placed the knife inside. "Z'garh Khrl'ur bides His time in serene contemplation, served by the Eternal Priests, awaiting the day of reckoning when He will tire of His divine benevolence and initiate the Reclamation."

"What's that?" asked Dylan.

"What's what?"

"The Reclamation."

"The Reclamation? It's means reclaiming."

"Yeah – duh … but what's this thing wanting to reclaim?"

Wilfred straightened his back. "Everything."

Dylan smirked at the old man's melodramatic tone. There was the glow of fever in his green-yellow eyes, and he was telling the story of this monster as if he actually believed it.

He sniffed the statue's head. It smelt like stale seaweed. "What does its name mean?"

"Clever child," purred Wilfred. "The name does have meaning, though it goes without saying it has no equivalent in any earthly language. The closest interpretation of Z'garh Khrl'ur would be 'Bringer of the Dark'."

"That doesn't sound so scary."

"It's a promise, boy, not a threat."

When Dylan looked at him questioningly, he closed the lid of the display cabinet and returned to the armchair.

"Kragn ruled the sublime order before this false universe began," he explained. "He despises what has become, and when He so chooses, shall return time, space, matter and energy to the order of Before. In the darkness that preceded the dawn of our delusive reality lies Kragn's glory and our salvation."

"You're saying this thing lived before the Big Bang?"

Wilfred closed his eyes.

"That's stupid. There was nothing before the Big Bang."

The old man's eyes shot open. "The only stupidity is ignorance and fear, boy. There was indeed another reality – the only true reality – a perfect order surpassing anything now in existence within this turgid mess you call the universe." He glared down at Dylan, trembling with mania. "Greater than your puny mind could ever conceive of, greater than any human mind can conceive, where reality was dark order and Kragn reigned supreme above all."

"That's enough chatter, Dylan," interrupted his father, patting the sideboard. "We better make tracks before it starts raining again. Are we ready?" he asked Lauren.

"Assuming for a moment that was true," resumed Dylan, enjoying the debate he felt he was winning, "nothing could have survived the Big Bang. It was, like, a gazillion degrees."

"You sound so certain for someone so young."

"It's science."

Wilfred smiled at him, revealing crooked brown teeth. "No, it's magic."

"Now you're taking the piss," said Dylan, waving the statue in his face.

"Put that thing down," said Mike. "Before you break it and I have to pay for it."

Dylan ignored him. "If this thing is almighty enough to destroy the universe, what's it doing 'biding its time' or whatever you said it was doing?"

"Biding time is what we all must do if we are to achieve our deepest desires. Of course, I wouldn't expect a mere child to understand that. Mr Gates," sang Wilfred, surrendering the fight, "I trust you will be treating the lovely wife to a special dinner tonight?"

Mike pulled his eyes away from his insolent son. "Only the best for the best."

"Twenty-five years, if I recall correctly."

"You have a good memory, Mr Waite."

"That's silver. Would I be correct in hazarding a guess you'll be dining silver service?"

"Good suggestion. Never thought of that."

"Somewhere local?"

"Maybe. We'll have to see."

Dylan, angry the old man was now ignoring him, said, "They're going to Café Mellow."

"Dylan!" barked his father. "It's supposed to be a secret!"

"Mike, please," breathed Lauren, placing a hand on his arm. "I already knew. He's not spoiling anything."

"I don't … arrgh!" Mike turned back to the sideboard. "Get up, Dylan," he grunted over his shoulder. "We better get this thing in the truck, or we'll be late for the secret dinner I've been planning for the past two months!"

Dylan pushed himself out of the armchair, statue in hand, and stood with rounded shoulders as his father accompanied Wilfred to the counter and completed the sale. He continued watching as his father returned to the sideboard. His mother went to the other end to help him lift it.

Mike straightened. "Dylan, are you just gonna stand there and let your mother drag this thing out of the shop?"

He gave a small shrug.

"Put that thing down and get over here."

"How about we all help?" suggested Lauren.

Dylan stood stroking the statue of Kragn, intrigued by the notion that something might have existed before this universe began. And there were people around who believed it had found its way into our reality.

Wilfred sidled up to him. "The restaurant," he murmured, taking the statue from him and dropping it into the armchair. "Did you mean Café Merlot?"

3

Home is where the sideboard is

"LIFT!"

Kane heaved and grunted as he helped his father carry the sideboard from the front door to the dining room. They sure used a lot of wood in the good old days, he was thinking. The thing felt like it was filled with lead. They staggered into the dining room, lowered it to the carpet, lifted it again, pushed it against the wall.

"Hey wait, shift it down a bit … No, no, too far; has to be in line with the picture … No, wait, back again."

"Dad!" cried Kane, stretching his back. "It's fine where it is!"

"A job done well is a job done for good."

As usual, his dad was making no sense. "Well, old man, the job is good and done."

"Do as you're told, slacker."

Kane spread his legs and placed his fists on his hips. This was Kane Gates as Superman, his signature pose after putting out a fire or helping a cat down from a tree … or refusing to do what he was told.

"Fine, then," Mike conceded. "Your mother will probably want it moved anyway. Thanks, Kane. Your assistance was much appreciated."

He went to the door to the living room. "Thanks, Dylan!"

The TV remote control rose above the back of the sofa. The volume grew louder.

"What I wanna know," a man's voice was saying, "is why anyone would steal a two-hundred-year-old corpse."

Intrigued, Kane went to see what his brother was watching.

"This follows an earlier incident last month," came the voice of a woman, "when the body of a recent car crash victim, whose name police have refused to disclose, also disappeared."

On the screen, a black-haired woman in a pale blue suit was standing near an open grave in a wild, weed-strewn part of a cemetery. The camera zoomed in on her face. "The police are asking anyone who knows anything about this highly unusual crime to ring Crimestoppers immediately. This is Janice Zhao, First News."

"If that thing turns up in my locker," joked Kane, smiling down at his brother, "those deadbeats at the station are gonna fry!"

Dylan looked corpse-like himself: eyes closed, face white, body thin as a rake, dressed all in black.

"Wouldn't put it past those idiots," Kane explained. "They've done worse to other trainees, I hear."

When Dylan failed to respond, he shrugged and went back to his father. "Come on, old timer," he said, clapping him on the back, "let's go get some refreshments."

They went to the kitchen, where Kane grabbed two Cokes from the fridge.

"Here … catch!" he called out, tossing a can to his father.

"Wha–?" Mike was leaning over a design brief he'd left on the table, and turned a second too late. The can hit his arm and fell with a bang to the floor.

He scooped it up, shook it furiously, tossed it back to Kane. "You can have that one."

Catching it like a football, Kane lobbed it back. "No, you have it."

Mike fumbled with the can. "Kane, old man, I insist," he countered, returning the throw.

"Dad!" cried Kane, frustrated by his father's annoying habit of turning everything into a competition. "Just put it back in the fridge if you don't want it!" He threw it back.

"No, son, it's yours. I insist."

Shaking the can again, Mike stepped closer, held it out, and pulled the tab. Frothy Coke spurted out, soaking Kane's shirt.

"Goddamnit!" he bellowed, leaping back. "You're a juvenile delinquent!" Pulling the cold shirt away from his chest, he pointed at the floor. "Look at the mess you made!"

"Your mother will clean it up."

"It's her special day, jerk!"

Mike grabbed a tea towel and dropped it on the floor. He used his foot to mop up the mess.

"There. All clean. Another job well done." He kicked the wet tea towel towards the laundry room. "Which reminds me: you found your brother a job yet?"

Kane dropped his chin to his chest. He'd been waiting for this. His father thought if you said something enough times, the universe would somehow make it happen.

"There's not much call for couch potatoes in the fire department," he said, heading to the laundry room for a towel.

"They must need cleaners or something."

"Now you mention it, you should see the state of the crappers. All those guys."

"Kane!"

"Come on, Dad, lighten up."

"You need to look after him."

Kane groaned. He stood at the door, dabbing a towel at his wet shirt front, thinking: No way I want that loser bumming me out at work. He can go clean toilets somewhere else.

"It's what brothers do."

Kane glanced up. "Are you sure we're brothers? Dylan looks a lot like the butcher. Mr Seligman, not the one with googly eyes."

"Not funny."

"I'm just saying …"

"Dylan needs a damn job!"

"Then you give him a damn job!"

Mike picked up one of his designs and waved it at him. "My work is highly technical."

"He's an artist. How hard can it be to do what you do?"

"This requires precision. An eye for detail. He doesn't have the discipline for it."

"How does that make it my problem?"

Dylan's voice flew in from the living room: "You know, I may be a couch potato who's only fit for cleaning bogs, but I'm not deaf!"

LAUREN SAT STARING at herself in the dresser mirror. Mike was down-stairs, taking his time getting ready as usual. Sometimes she thought she must be the only woman in the world who got ready faster than her husband. Fortunately, Laura liked having time to herself. It helped her marshal the tiny reserves of energy she had left inside her body and mind, so she could go on fooling the world into believing she was still a part of it. And Mike's clowning and exuberance could be so draining.

She picked up a frame from the dressing table, an oak frame with the word 'Family' inlaid in silver across the top. The photo came from better times, when she and Mike were in their thirties and had three young sons. The five of them were standing on the beach at Harristown, their smiles wide and white, the jetty stretching to infinity behind them. Whoever had taken the picture had gotten the framing wrong – their legs were missing and half the picture was sky – but this was Lauren's favourite photo. In it, they looked as happy as any family possibly could.

It was hard to believe more than five years had passed since that day. Time flew by like leaves in a stream, and each day it became that tiny bit harder to remember what it felt like to have so much happiness and so few cares; how it felt to hold Oliver in her arms and watch him as he grew into the amazing person she knew he was destined to be.

A shadow appeared in the mirror. She turned in her seat to find Dylan standing in the doorway, holding one hand behind his back.

"Dad here?"

Lauren smiled at him, thinking how much he looked like his father: black hair, blue eyes, narrow chin, straight nose and full lips – the French genes in the family. Kane had a predominance of Celtic genes and looked more like her: brown hair, brown eyes, square face, broad nose and strong mouth. Yet personality-wise it was the opposite. Dylan was quiet and thoughtful like her, whereas Mike and Kane were peas in a pod: outgoing, funny and popular.

"I think he's in his office."

As Dylan stood awkwardly in the doorway, she had a sudden flash of him as a twelve-year-old, when he stood in the same spot the morning they packed him off to Briarwood to live with his grandparents. It was the day after Oliver's respirator had been turned off, and the house was as cold and hushed as a mausoleum. Dylan had stared at her, worried and alone, a frightened boy who probably wanted more than anything to have a hug from his mother. But all she could remember thinking was: I wish he'd go away; his need is suffocating me; and worst of all: he was there; he might have done something to stop this from happening. It was an unpleasant memory, the thoughts wrong and unfair; but now she was better, a better person, able to face and own her mistakes – now she was taking the right kind of pills.

He stepped into the room. "I got you a present."

Laura glanced down at his hand, hardly believing her ears. Dylan was holding out a small box.

Her face went hot. "Dylan …"

Returning the photo to the dresser, she allowed her son to place the box in her palm. She opened it. Inside was a silver pendant and chain – an antique, by the look of it. At first, Laura thought the pendant was an angel, but on closer inspection it looked more like a dragon. Or perhaps a wasp.

She studied the curious design. The artist had not fashioned it to look like anything specific. From different angles, it took on different forms – whatever your imagination wanted it to be. "It's … lovely."

"Old man at the store said to give it to you."

"Dylan," she laughed, "you could at least try and pretend you chose it yourself!"

"He said it was your twenty-fifth anniversary and you had to wear silver tonight, or else it's bad luck."

"Well, we wouldn't want that, would we?"

Placing the chain around her neck, she checked herself in the mirror. Now it was on, it definitely looked like an angel.

"Dylan, you are the most honest person I know." She turned back to him. "That's why I don't worry about you the way your father does." She reached out and took his hand, which was soft and warm. "You know he says the things he does because he cares about you, don't you?"

Dylan shifted his weight to his other leg.

"Good things happen to good people. Don't ever forget that." She repeated it, slowly this time. "Good things happen to good people."

"That's what Bert used to say," he reminded her.

"Ah, of course," she smiled. "I thought I'd heard it somewhere." She squeezed his hand. "You miss him, don't you?"

He shrugged awkwardly.

"Last time I spoke with your grandfather, he told me you made him feel like a youngster again. He loved having you there, taking you to his old haunts, playing his prog rock. He said prog rock must be in your genes, you loved it so much."

"He was crazy – in a good way," Dylan rushed to add. "Drove grandma wild with his stories about sea monsters and flying saucers."

"Ah yes, he told me those too. I had many a sleepless night when I was a child. He made them sound so real. I think he half-believed them himself."

"Really? I thought maybe it was just cos he's old."

"He had some pretty bad things happen to him during the war. PTSD does funny things to people."

"Do you think that's why he's losing his marbles now?"

Lauren stared at Dylan's hand, the hand she hadn't held for five years, not since their tragedy ruined everything. "Who knows?"

"He's not the same."

She leaned towards him. "He *is* the same … it's just, his health and age are getting in the way of his mind."

"But he won't get any better … will he?" He looked down. "I already know the answer."

"He's got bloody Alzheimer's, so no, we need to prepare for the worst." The comment came from Mike, who was standing in the doorway fiddling with his tie.

Dylan slipped his hand away.

"What's that lump of metal around your neck, Loz?"

"It's from Dylan," answered Lauren. "Lovely, isn't it? It's for good luck."

"Nice," said Mike, nodding at Dylan with eyebrows raised. "Did you make it yourself?"

Dylan brushed past him.

"Hope it's not hot," he added under his breath.

"Michael!" scolded Lauren. "Why do you always have to say things like that?"

"What? He's an artist, isn't he? Be good if he made something he could sell. Maybe make a living. Is that too much to ask?"

She turned back to the mirror, clasping the pendant. Dylan may not have made it – or even bought it – but that didn't make it any less special. It showed he was rejoining the world of the normal, noticing special occasions, thinking of others, having an actual conversation with her. After all these years of grieving and healing, he was beginning to forgive her. Now all she had to do was forgive herself.

"Are we ready yet?" asked Mike, grabbing his jacket from the bed. He spun around. "Come on, Loz, chop, chop! If you don't hurry up, they'll give away the booking."

Kane paused at the door to his brother's bedroom. His heart was pounding and an animal urge was pushing him to spin around, run downstairs, jump on his bike and race to the quarry and back. He really needed to let off steam before calling January; the thought of the upcoming conversation was making his head spin. But he felt guilty over what he'd said about Dylan, what Dylan had heard, and his father's words – that he needed to go and say sorry to his brother for being such a blockhead – were ringing in his ears. Down inside, he knew an apology was the right thing to do, but it wasn't within his natural disposition to apologise. Apologies were for the weak, and Kane despised weakness.

Sighing with resignation, he raised his hand, held it in the air, listened against the door for a second, then knocked – two raps, followed by three, repeated.

Without waiting for a reply, he pushed in.

Dylan was sitting on the bed, his back against the wall, a laptop propped on his legs. He didn't look up, but Kane saw a crease appear between his eyebrows.

"Hey, Dylan," he called out, sounding more cheerful than he felt.

At first Dylan ignored him. Then he opened his mouth and said, "What?"

"Just seeing what you're up to."

"You haven't come in here in years."

"Haven't had any reason to. Not since we were kids."

"We're not kids anymore."

"Yeah, I know that."

There was an awkward silence.

"Yep," Kane continued, "we're all growed up and stuff."

"So what's the special occasion?"

Kane folded his arms. He was feeling strangely nervous. There was something weird about Dylan lately, a darkness of mood that was different from the shy churlishness he'd shown in the days following his return from Briarwood.

Dylan glanced up. "You better not be here to lecture me."

"Downstairs," began Kane, deciding it was best to get straight to the point. "The crack about cleaning toilets. I didn't mean it to sound … y'know …"

Dylan began typing. "Is that it?"

"… nasty."

His brother went back to ignoring him.

"Dad's worried about you," added Kane, approaching the bed. "It may not seem so, but he is."

Dylan squinted at the laptop.

"What are you up to?"

He closed the cover.

"That story on the news … grave robbers. Weird, hey?"

His brother stared at him.

"Some real freaks out there, I tell ya."

"Is that it?"

Kane shrugged. "Yeah. Suppose. Just wanted to say I'm sorry, set things straight."

It was Dylan's turn to shrug.

"So, what you doing?"

No answer.

"Artsy stuff? Dad said you're pretty good at it."

"Artsy stuff? Do you even know what that means?"

"Show me. Dad said it was like comics … I'm into comics."

"It's not like comics."

"Well, show me."

"Look, Kane, don't pretend you're interested in my life. You've done your brotherly duty. Now go back and report to Dad I'm as lazy and bad tempered as ever."

"Dylan …"

"Go on."

"I just wanna –"

"Get out!"

"Show me –"

"Get out!"

"Don't be –"

"Get outta my damn room!"

The outburst made Kane's face throb. "Why do you always have to be such a dick?"

"Get – the hell – out!"

He spun around and tramped away. "I knew this was a waste of time. Why do I listen to the old man?"

The door slammed. Dylan was alone.

Reopening the screen, he stared at an old woodcut showing a dozen men in loincloths worshipping a statue of Kragn. This Kragn was the size of a house, its eight arms flung open, its fat face turned to the sky. Its mouth was like a cave, the black eyes almost bursting out of their sockets. It looked even grosser and fatter and lumpier than the statue in the antiques store. Rather than a primal god, it made Dylan think of a disgusting, disease-carrying grub.

Staring intently at the picture, he began to feel queasy. The screen went in and out of focus; the lights flickered and dimmed; he felt like throwing up.

Squeezing his eyes shut, he muttered, "His flesh is your flesh is His flesh is your flesh –"

His head jerked up. He thought he'd heard laughter coming from the other side of the door.

"Who's there?" he called out. There was no answer. "Kane, is that you?" Silence. "Kane?"

The lights turned yellow, and Dylan felt another wave of nausea, this one starting in his head before ballooning in his stomach. Suddenly his mind flew back to earlier that afternoon, to the strange dim shop where weird old Wilfred Waite was standing amongst the antiques and trash like a goblin priest of the underworld. What was it he said about Kragn?

As if on cue, Wilfred opened his mouth and began the chant.

"Flesh that is yours shall Z'garh Khrl'ur bestow," Dylan repeated, his eyes staring at the screen. "Inside you Kragn dwells, and to Kragn shall you return."

4

Bad news morning

KANE WOKE WITH a start. It was still dark, but those damn rats were at it again. He listened as they scampered across the ceiling. Then he waited for that other noise to start. Right, there it was: the infernal scratching and gnawing.

Pulling the pillow over his head, he pressed it against his ears. When that made no difference, he flung open the bedside drawer, grabbed a balled-up pair of socks and threw it at the ceiling.

The socks dropped to the bureau, landing on his BMX trophies. One fell to the floor with a clatter, and the rats went quiet. For a few moments there was blissful silence. Then, just as Kane was nodding off, the scratching started up again.

He lifted his head. The clock radio showed six-thirteen. Five hours sleep – nowhere near enough for a trainee with physicals to pass. Fortunately, he wasn't due at the station till four, and he had nothing to do before then but relax, fuel up his body, push some weights, and go for a ride.

He rolled onto his back and lay staring at the ceiling, at the spot where the rats were hard at work doing whatever it was they felt compelled to do every morning. He put his hands behind his head. The breakup with January hadn't gone well last night; hadn't gone well at all. She claimed she wasn't getting too serious, but she was. It was the same thing time and time again: psycho girls throwing themselves at him, pretending they'd forgotten him saying (loud and clear!) that he was leaving town as soon as his training was over; each one conveniently blind to the absurdity of getting tied down when there was so much uncertainty in his future. He scratched his ear. It was a smart move breaking up by text message. Cleaner that way: no drawn-out emotions to deal with – and he wouldn't be tempted to spend the night with

January, the way he did the last time he told her he wanted to break up.

Leaning over, he switched on his phone. Eleven missed phone calls, five voicemails and twenty-three text messages. And yep, all from January. Flattering, he thought with a smile, though he was determined not to start the day on a downer by reading or listening to them.

"Girls!" he complained to the rats in the ceiling.

Throwing off the blankets, he bounced out of bed and stumbled to the window.

The day was a grey square against the black wall. Kane placed his hands on the sill and gazed out at the charcoal sky and drizzling rain. The clouds had settled on the ground, and the houses and paddocks across the road were barely visible. These were the days when it was great to be a fireman.

As he watched, a dog crept out of the bushes and splashed through a puddle to the McLeods' letterbox, where it cocked its leg. It was Gary, the friendliest Jack Russell on the block, if not the planet. Kane smiled and tapped his finger on the glass, trying to catch the dog's attention. With a quick look around, it went back the way it had come.

Kane stumbled to the door, yawning and scratching between his legs. Not such a great day to be single, he thought as he glanced back at his empty bed.

Pulling on his bathrobe, he crossed the hallway. The door to his parents' room was open, so he went over and peeked inside. The bed hadn't been slept in.

"You little devils!" he cried at the empty room, smiling and shaking his head. "That's a turnip for the books," he added to himself as he walked off.

He carried his smile into the shower. As the hot water ran down his body, swirling around his feet and steaming up the glass, he broke into song:

"Do you like beans and tomatoes?

Carrots raw, sugar cane? – Kane, Kane.

Is it fried eggs and bacon?

No, it's cornflakes again!"

He wondered if Mike and Lauren were up yet, what they would be ordering for breakfast. Something hot and full of fat and sugar, he hoped. His parents had been through some tough times lately and they deserved some pampering. In fact, Kane was surprised their marriage had survived past their honeymoon, considering how different they were to begin with. It was good to see them being irresponsible and staying out all night. It reminded him of himself.

After dressing, on his way to the stairs, he stopped outside his brother's room. He still felt bad about what he'd said last night, but reminded himself that Dylan had behaved badly too. Even worse, he told himself, seeing as how Kane had only been joking around. He'd gone to apologise, and Dylan completely over-reacted. Went psycho, in fact. It was clear to Kane, standing there at the dawn of a new day, that it was best if they stayed away from each other from now on, and only interacted when absolutely necessary. This family reunion had been a failed experiment. Too much time had passed. What's more, they had almost opposite personalities and temperaments; there was no such thing as common ground between them, no shared interests, despite what his father wanted to believe.

Pushing the memory of last night from his mind, he went down the stairs. In the kitchen he filled his bowl with cornflakes and added three spoonsful of sugar. When Kane was a boy, when Mike was struggling to get his new business off the ground, the family had subsisted on cheap staples like cornflakes, with dinners generally comprising McDonalds or the standard dish of mashed potatoes, cabbage, peas and cheap cuts of meat. Since getting into the fire service, Kane had given up the McDonalds and carb-heavy meals in favour of a caveman diet, but he was still addicted to the sweet, syrupy crunchiness of cornflakes in the morning.

In the living room, he sat on the edge of the sofa, balanced the bowl on his knee, and went back to his game of solitaire from last night. It was a distraction from the January thing, a way to resist the urge to read her text messages and listen to her voicemails. Plenty of time for reading and listening and responding once January had cooled down, when there was more of a chance for a mature conversation, rather than having to deal with her usual demanding, crying and emotional manipulation.

His phone buzzed. Without thinking, he reached for it, and the bowl slipped from his knee and fell to the carpet, splashing milk and cornflakes everywhere.

"Damn it!"

Kane grabbed the phone. No, it wasn't another message from January, just a reminder of thirty percent off from the health food store he once bought protein powder from.

Tossing the phone on the sofa, he knelt on the carpet and used his hands to scoop cornflakes back into the bowl. He was almost finished when he heard a car slowing down outside.

He glanced up. Lights appeared as the car drove up the driveway. It crunched on gravel and stopped close to the house. The engine shut off, and Kane heard two car doors shut.

"Great timing," he said to the mess on the carpet, wiping his hands clean over the bowl.

Scurrying to the laundry, he grabbed a towel, ran back and dropped it on the wet patch. Then he sat back on the sofa, folded his arms and listened to footsteps approaching the front door.

He smiled to himself, trying to think of something smart-aleck to say to his dad. This was a once-in-a-lifetime chance to turn the tables and get Mike back for all those mornings he gave Kane a hard time for staying out all night. But everything he came up with sounded obscene or incestuous. The best he could manage was: "What time do you call this?" – which was pretty lame when he thought about it.

When a knock sounded at the door, his heart leapt into his mouth. He sat forward. Why were they knocking? Oh no, he thought: Mike must have lost his keys. He could be such an airhead sometimes.

His knees began shaking. Then how did they drive home? And why didn't Mike use the spare key under the pot plant?

Kane glanced at his watch. It was too early for door-to-door sellers or Mormons. It was too early for anyone.

His phone buzzed again, and he snatched it up, thinking it might provide an explanation. But it was only the first of today's pleading/abusive messages from January. *U BASTARD!! I HAVENT SELPT ALL NITE!* this one read.

The knock sounded again, louder this time. Putting down the

phone, Kane got up, crept to the window and peered through the curtains.

Standing on the porch were two strangers: a man and a woman, both dressed in black suits.

Kane stared at them. The man was burly, youngish and blond; the woman tall and skinny, with grey-streaked hair tied in a tight bun. They were looking straight ahead, as if they were robots with X-ray vision and could see through the door.

Kane glanced at the ceiling, at the place where his parents' empty bed stood. In that moment, time froze, and a sense of unreality fell on him like a blanket. He felt like an actor in a stage play, an actor who'd forgotten his lines and was waiting for someone to prompt him from the wings.

An instant later, the lines came.

He felt like throwing up. Surely this couldn't be –? There's no way they …

Kane shook the ridiculous notion from his head. It was their anniversary last night. Their twenty-fifth. They drank too much and made a spur-of-the-moment decision to stay at a hotel instead of driving all the way home. They were sensible, like parents are supposed to be. He pictured Mike and Lauren sitting up in a king-sized bed in matching fluffy white robes, enjoying bacon and eggs with orange juice and fresh-brewed coffee. Mike was a cheapskate; he'd be putting off their departure till right on check-out time.

These people were here about Tuesday's barn fire, he told himself, nodding at their sensible decision to interview him. It was clearly a case of arson. Kane's truck was the first on the scene, and it was only natural they would come to get a statement on what he saw when he arrived at the blaze.

All this passed through Kane's mind in a flash. He glanced around the room: at the bowl of cornflakes on the coffee table; at the TV screen; at his mother's awful lava vase; at the unfinished game of solitaire. Please, he thought, staring at the towel on the floor; please let it be about the fire.

A voice called out, "Is anyone home?"

Leaving the window, Kane went to the door, took hold of the knob. He squeezed it until his knuckles turned white, then, with an effort, turned it and pulled open the door.

The strangers exchanged glances, as if they hadn't expected anyone to be home. Then the woman fixed him with a dead stare. He could see the rims of her contact lenses. He turned to the man, who was staring past him into the house. Why wasn't anyone saying anything?

"Good morning, sir," the woman said at last. "I'm Detective Young. This is Detective Weisenbach. Is this the home of Michael and Lauren Gates?"

Kane's mouth felt like he'd swallowed a bowlful of cardboard. "Uh … yes, that's right. Is this about the fire?"

The woman frowned at him.

"The fire on Tuesday," he urged. "The barn."

The man swallowed. From the corner of his eye, Kane saw his Adam's apple bounce. He glared at him, thinking: Damnit, will somebody say something? – and then a noise sounded behind him.

He spun around. Dylan was standing at the top of the stairs, wearing Batman boxer shorts and a white singlet, his face as pale as the moon, his black hair dangling in his eyes. He was squinting against the light, his arms folded against the cold. The voices must have woken him.

"Who is it?" he asked in a croaky voice.

Kane opened his mouth. Behind him, the woman began to speak.

5

Killing time

KANE RAN TO the smoking building and dropped to his knees before the closed door. He could hear the cackle of a fire, and listened hard to find out what it was trying to tell him. Wisps of smoke were seeping from the building, but he couldn't feel any heat. He tried to remember his training, which had taught him to dig into his feelings, thoughts and senses, put them all together, and visualise what the fire was doing – but his brain was too busy interpreting what it was seeing to be able to listen to what was inside him.

He glanced over his shoulder as two others joined him, dressed, like him, in full gear. Nodding at them, he jumped to his feet, kicked open the door, and peered into the darkness. The fire wasn't in that room, just cardboard boxes and a lot of smoke. Kane waved through his two companions and watched as, heads down, they rushed inside.

He was about to follow when his heart rate trebled. It felt like a machine gun was going off in his chest. He tensed his muscles, breathed hard, tried by a force of will to make his heart slow, but the staccato went on and on. Darkness suddenly ballooned in his head, and for a second he thought he would faint.

The feeling soon waned, but as the darkness fell away, all thoughts drained from his head. While he stood there, paralysed with fear, terrified he might be having an aneurysm or heart attack, an explosion sounded inside the building. The door slammed shut.

Kane staggered back. That wasn't supposed to happen! His mind flew into a panic. Should he attempt to rescue them? Wouldn't that be suicide? If they were alive, they would have come out by now.

"What the hell do you call that?"

An officer wearing a dark blue suit was coming up behind him, stomping through puddles of water, his face red and shiny with rage.

Before Kane could get out a word, the man hit his shoulder with his open palm.

"Those two are dead. You know that, don't you?"

"I –"

"You just killed two people!"

The man's words lit a flare of anger in his chest.

"I was looking for the fire."

"You were looking for shit!"

"There was only smoke!"

"And what have you been taught about that?"

Kane's mind went blank again.

"Well?"

"They – they went in too fast!"

"You waved them in!"

"Well, that doesn't mean –"

"You waved them in!"

"It's not my –"

"I didn't see anyone else waving them in!"

"It's not my fault they're stupid!"

"Whose fault is it then?"

Kane looked dumbly at him.

"You're responsible for their deaths!"

"They're grown men!"

"You're a team! You're supposed to look out for each other!"

An image of his father scolding him about Dylan flashed in his mind, and his heart began racing again.

Shaking with fury, he yelled, "Why doesn't everyone shut the hell up about how responsible I'm supposed to be?"

"Because you're a dangerous little hothead!"

That was it. Kane ripped off his helmet. He was so furious he was seeing stars. "I didn't sign up for this shit!" he shouted in the man's face.

Shoving the helmet into his chest, he took off back to the station.

The two trainees appeared from the alley next to the building.

"Sorry, sir," said the tall, pimply-faced one. "We really stuffed that up. Can we do it again?"

A GOLDEN-BROWN PICKUP truck rolled along the dirt road, stopped near a cliff, then reversed until the tray was facing the ocean.

The door opened, and out stretched Kane's legs. His boots hit the ground. Pushing himself away from the seat, Kane leaned against the truck and stared down at the dirt. He had no will or energy to go any further. He was still wearing his fire pants and had stripped down to a white t-shirt, which was wet under both arms. There was another spot of wetness in the middle of his chest.

After a minute, he pushed himself off the truck and went around to the tray. Lowering the tailgate, he jumped up and sat contemplating the ocean. The waves were grey and cold under a heavy blanket of cloud. Where they hit the reef, the water was white and choppy. Beyond the reef, far out at sea, was a tanker, which from this distance appeared as a charcoal blob balanced on the horizon. Kane imagined what it would be like to stand on the bow and feel the swell of the waves as they lifted and dropped the enormous ship and everything on it. Pretty much what I feel now, was his thought.

He recalled the panic attack he had earlier. It was like nothing he'd ever felt before, and it terrified him. Though Google told him it was psychological, most likely a reaction to stress, a part of him still worried it was something worse: a bubble of weakness in his heart or his head that one day, when he was exerting himself at work, or in the gym, or on his bike, would return to claim him. The Gates' curse, come to take its latest victim.

Shaking his head, he turned his eyes to the land, to the long pale curve of coast. In the distance, the old cannery stood like a ruined city near the water's edge. As the land approached his truck, the cliffs rose, then fell away to a small beach, a favourite recreation spot for his family in happier times. Where his truck was parked now was the place his father always parked – close to the narrow track that led down to the water.

In the sea below, a man was bodysurfing. The figure raced a wave, caught it, disappeared into the break, then reappeared with arms flailing. Despite the despair that seemed to fill every space inside him, Kane's mouth turned up in a smile. Years ago, his father and he would race the waves together, just like that, and end up with lungs full of water, just like that. On these occasions, his mother and two younger brothers would sit on the beach and watch them intently, not interested in their antics, but afraid the two fools would drown if they took their eyes off them. "Be careful!" his mother would cry, well aware they couldn't hear her. "You'll kill yourselves out there!"

Now they were both dead.

'A frenzied knife attack by unknown assailants' was the official verdict. Probably a gang of dope fiends, high on ice, after cash for their next fix, he'd heard someone conjecture in the corridor of the police station. It appeared Mike and Lauren had been ambushed behind the Café Merlot, their bodies found at first light in a nearby alley, their pockets emptied, all money and jewellery gone. The investigating officer said they were just in the wrong place at the wrong time – victims of a botched robbery that got out of control – their standard lines when they didn't know what the hell had happened.

Kane couldn't accept it was simply a case of bad luck. Surely there must be more to this than bad timing? Two people with eighty-five years of life between them had been slaughtered. Obliterated from the face of the earth. In the space of a few violent seconds. For a couple of hundred dollars' worth of cash and trinkets. And before that, his youngest brother, Oliver: killed in a tragic fall. What had his family done to deserve all this death?

Tears flooded his eyes and rolled down his cheeks. Wiping them away with both hands, Kane took a huge breath, like he was trying to inhale the ocean. I came here to remember the good times, he told himself, not dwell on the unfairness of the universe. To get his parents' screams out of his mind, he forced himself to listen to the squawking of gulls and the whoosh of the waves, to feel the coldness of the salt air as he drew it into his body, held it in his lungs, then blew it out warm and infused with his DNA, sharing it with the world, with the beach, the water and the man below.

The man below. Kane suddenly realised that, while he'd been lost in thought, the bodysurfer had vanished. He sat upright, glanced about in alarm, then caught sight of him close to the reef, head bobbing up and down as he searched for the next wave.

Leaping from the tray, Kane locked his truck and took off down the trail. When he reached the sand, he pulled off his boots and socks, stripped down to boxer shorts, raced to the water and dived into an incoming wave. The water shocked him, went up his nostrils, made him forget everything but the ice that was burrowing into his skin and flooding into his veins.

He swam out to the bodysurfer, an athletic redhead about his own age.

"How's it going?" he yelled, as they bobbed together in the swell.

The man nodded, then swam out to sea, kicking water in his face.

Kane followed him. "Here it comes!" he cried.

Together they raced the swell. The man caught it and rode the wave towards shore. Kane, treading water, watched him.

After a while, the man swam back, smiling with big teeth, cocky after his win. He came at Kane, leapt on him, and pushed him under.

Kane flailed and swallowed a mouthful of salty water. He fought back, forcing the man to choke on his own mouthful of salty water. The two splashed and grappled and dunked each other, yelling and laughing like teenagers, until the man shouted, "A big one!" and let him go.

This time, they caught the wave together. They rode it shoulder to shoulder all the way to the shore.

There, the man sprang to his feet and took off up the beach, stopping to collect a towel and a pile of clothes, before racing towards the trail Kane had come down.

Kane stood at the water's edge, watching as he disappeared from view. He was shivering so much his teeth clattered. Now the man had gone, he felt an overwhelming sadness, an ache in his chest, feeling the stranger's disappearance as yet another loss: something else to mourn. He kicked at the water, kicked it away from him, as if he held it responsible for the man's decision to leave. He'd hoped their game would go on for longer. It had been a welcome distraction, a slice of life in the midst of all this death and depression. Now Kane was alone, the only person on the beach.

He turned back to the ocean. The waves seemed to go on forever, a rolling canvas that would never stop, not until the sun burnt out, or all water on the planet evaporated and there was nothing left but rocks and sand. In its vast solitude, in the heavy breath of the waves, there was something almost supernatural about this place. For a moment, Kane imagined he was the last person alive, the lone survivor of an apocalypse that had wiped out all humanity. What kind of disaster was it? He tried to recall. Contagion? Nuclear blast? Zombie rising? He couldn't make himself believe in any of those. Perhaps everyone had simply vanished – just like his parents, but on a global scale.

Skulking up the beach, he got dressed, dropped to the sand and lay on his back, wet and shivering, staring at the sky. The clouds were darkening, descending, threatening to suffocate him. As the sun slipped over the horizon, the temperature began dropping fast, but Kane hardly noticed it. He was stressing about tomorrow's appointment with the funeral director. It would mark the commencement of the 'death circus', the period when people would expect him to make arrangements, welcome unwelcome guests, and be ringmaster to his parents' farewell performance. He would have to be strong, and engage with the world, and make decisions, when all he wanted to do was take to the Six Hills for the next month and wait for all this despair and distress to pass.

But when three gulls came sailing over the cliff, crying out to each other like jubilant teenagers, they reminded him that life went on, and he was a part of it. More than that, his father had charged him with a mission, something that overnight had changed from an annoying Dad-thing to a vocation; he needed to look after his brother.

Rain began to fall, the drops hitting his face like torpedoes of ice, washing the salt from his eyes and his lips. Shortly after, the first of the evening's fishers came plodding down the beach with their rods and buckets, telling each other, in raised voices, stories of the fish they had yet to catch.

Their voices brought Kane back to the now. With a heavy sigh, he got up, brushed the sand off himself, turned, and climbed the trail back to his truck.

6

Land of the dead

BY THE TIME Kane got home, the house was dark. He switched on the light and poked his head into the living room. The first thing he saw was a black lump in the corner.

"Jesus Christ!" he cried, a hand flying up to his chest. "You scared the crap outta me!"

Dylan was sitting with his knees pulled up to his chin, his hair hanging in front of his face like a curtain. It trembled as he breathed.

"What are you doing?"

No response.

"Dylan!"

"Walking the dog."

"Don't be an idiot." Then, to fill the silence: "We don't own a dog."

Dylan pulled his knees in closer.

"You're creeping me out, Dylan. Even more than usual."

He didn't move.

"You eaten yet?"

"Not hungry."

Entering the room, Kane went up and stood over him.

"You've gotta eat, kid. You didn't have much meat on your bones to begin with."

Dylan seemed to be holding his breath. His hair had stopped trembling. It reminded Kane of the days before Oliver died, when one of their games at the leisure centre was to swim to the bottom of the pool and see who could hold his breath the longest. (Surprisingly, it was usually Dylan.)

"How about pizza?"

It was like he was talking to a rock.

"Dylan!"

"How about getting outta my face?"

"Come on, don't be a baby!"

In a burst of violence, Dylan leapt to his feet. His eyes like bullets, he brushed past Kane and headed for the stairs.

"Where are you going? Dylan?"

Kane stood frowning at his brother's back, kept staring long after Dylan had disappeared up the stairs. *What should I do? What should I do? What should I do?* his brain kept demanding. It had been asking the same question all the way here. One minute the answer would be: *Dylan's almost eighteen; he's old enough to look after himself; I should take off and start a new life.* The next minute he'd be thinking: *I'm responsible for him; I'm responsible for the house; it's what Dad would have wanted.*

Crossing to the bottom of the stairs, he rested his elbow on the bannister. Kane had never even had to take care of himself, let alone a sullen, lazy adolescent. There was always his father behind him to push and pay: his BMX bikes; the deposit for his truck; the decision to join the fire service; a cosy house full of food and everything else needed to satisfy his wants and needs – these were things that just happened. After Oliver died, when Dylan went to live with their grandparents, Mike had spoilt him rotten, giving in to every juvenile demand and tantrum. It was over-compensation for the loss of his brothers and the neglect by his sedated and unresponsive mother, and he took full advantage of it. When Lauren recovered enough to notice him, she spoilt him too. Thanks to their concern and generosity, Kane had no idea how to be a responsible adult. He only knew how to be a free agent, taking whatever was offered, carried along by his desires and the tide of circumstance, doing whatever it was he felt like doing at the time.

He stared up the stairs. *That was the old Kane,* he told himself. *I'll soon be a fully-fledged firefighter, responsible and accountable for protecting life and property, saving people's lives by putting my own life in danger. That needs focus and commitment.* And whatever happens from here on in, he reminded himself, *I'm now the adult in this household, the sole breadwinner, the only one with a hope in hell of keeping the house going. I need to control my temper and stop being so* immature and self-centred – stop being a hothead. The thought terrified him.

Bending under the weight of responsibility, he took the stairs slowly, two at a time. He pushed into Dylan's room. It was dark and stuffy, like the sheets hadn't been washed or the window opened in five years.

"Me again," he announced. "What's it gonna be? – chicken or supreme?"

Dylan was face down on the bed, one arm over his head, the other by his side.

"Pizza," Kane explained. "Barbecue chicken or pepperoni with cheese and lotsa red and green shit on it, on some kinda dough. Round and flat like a Frisbee. Ring a bell? Or I could get fish and chips. Nothing beats the classics. What's yer poison, guvnor?"

Dylan ignored him.

"Fish and chips then?"

Silence.

"Pizza?"

Still no reply.

"Dylan!"

Dylan didn't move.

"Christ almighty! As if I don't have enough crap to deal with at work!"

He waited to see if the outburst had made any impression on his brother. It hadn't. Now he lost his temper for real. "Fine. Starve to death, for all I care. Make it four out of five."

Wincing at his insensitivity, Kane stood staring at the back of his brother's head, debating with himself whether to leave him in peace, or go and shake some sense into him … perhaps rub his back and reassure him everything would turn out fine? What would Mike do? Probably yell at him some more, then go get his mother.

In the end, Kane did what his stomach told him: he left to get pizza.

DYLAN TUGGED AT the iron gates, even though it was obvious they were locked. He rattled them in frustration, then, alarmed the clanging noise would invite attention, strode quickly away, his hands shoved in his pockets.

Yellow lights threw a sulphurous sheen across the road. A storm last night had stripped the last of the leaves from the trees, and they were blowing along the sidewalk like a tiny army. They were the only sign of life.

Turning a corner, Dylan made his way down the narrow side street that separated the graveyard from a factory that made cardboard boxes. It was as dark as a trench down here. Pulling his hands from his pockets, he blew warm air into them, then rubbed them together.

At a spot where an ancient yew tree spread its branches over the cemetery wall, Dylan stopped and glanced to his left and right, then up at the warehouse windows. They were blank. He turned his attention to the cemetery wall, which was built from huge blocks of stone, mossy with age. He could see the wall was not built to be breached. This was going to be tough.

Standing on his toes, he wrapped his fingers around an overhanging branch. The bark was rough on his soft hands, and he could already feel the uncomfortable strain in his arms – and this was before he even transferred his weight to them. Dylan knew he was in no physical condition to scale this wall. He hadn't exerted his muscles or lungs since phys ed classes at school (and even those he'd mostly managed to wriggle his way out of), but a masochistic urge pressed him to try. If he ripped his arms from their sockets or smashed his head open on the paving stones, at least that would be better than going home defeated, where his smug, interfering, useless brother waited to shove pizza down his throat.

Fighting against the pull of gravity, he walked his feet up the wall and hooked his legs over the top. He felt the blood rush to his head, felt his head throb, his face go hot. After a sudden panic he might be trapped in that position, he inched his hands along the branch to get his body closer to his feet, then, using a series of twisting and pulling motions, managed to get his whole body up on the wall.

Shaking his arms back into their sockets, Dylan coughed out a laugh. When he looked down at the street below, which from here seemed like five metres away, a shot of adrenaline sizzled through his loins. It felt like he'd achieved a superhuman feat, something that last week he wouldn't even have contemplated trying.

On the other side of the wall lay the land of the dead. As Dylan sat catching his breath, contemplating the dark tombstones that rose from the ground like crooked teeth, he marvelled at how peaceful it felt up here on the wall, looking down on all the people at rest below. There were so many of them – a veritable city. And none of them had any cares, or impossible dreams, or worries about what the future might bring. Wars, famine, loss, catastrophe: none of that mattered to them. The things that matter belong to the living. In that moment, it almost seemed to Dylan that life is the tragedy, death the natural state of being.

Earlier, after Kane left the house, Dylan got up, took his father's Honda Civic, and drove to the funeral parlour. He had no real plan, nothing in particular he was intending to do; he just felt an urge to be close to his parents. The parlour was closed, of course. He had a passing thought of breaking in (it was unlikely there would be much security), but then came a new idea: he would go and be with Oliver. Oliver had already been in the ground for five long years, and now his folks were on their way to join him. If Dylan didn't think too carefully about it, he could almost feel relieved that his loss would be Oliver's gain.

So now here he was, breaking into a graveyard like some kind of ghoul.

Recovered at last from the climb, he slid his legs off the wall and dropped to the grass. How bizarre it felt to be standing in a locked cemetery after dark, with nothing but cracked and crumbling gravestones for company. If something were to happen – if, say, the dead were to begin clawing their way out of their graves – there would be no one to save him, no easy way out. He was walled in and helpless.

A chill trickled down the back of his neck. There might be monsters, zombies or grave robbers hiding behind these trees and headstones, nightmarish beings that only crept out of the mausoleums and hidden caves once the gates were locked, when the land was returned to the dead. Dylan half wished there were. It would smash down the walls of this absurd, pointless world he was forced to exist in, clear away the smugness and unfairness and open the door to something new and dangerous – a danger he could face head-on, not one that happened behind his back to the people he cared about and depended on.

He figured from the general state of neglect and decay that he was in one of the older parts of the cemetery. Crouching near a headstone, he read the inscription.

In affectionate remembrance of Daniel Worthing, beloved husband of Abby. Died Mansfield Bridge, 8th March 1837. Aged 46 years. "In sure and certain hope of the Resurrection to eternal life."

Yep, definitely old. It came to Dylan that this might be the place where the grave was disturbed the other night and the corpse stolen. The body still hadn't been recovered, as far as he knew, which meant the grave robber was still at large. A panic struck him that a night watchman might come along, mistake him for the culprit and call the police – but of course, he had no shovels or accomplices, so the most they could charge him with was unlawful entry. And he wasn't even sure that what he was doing was unlawful.

Getting to his feet, staring down at the grave, he wondered if anyone remembered or still mourned for Daniel Worthing. Probably not. Unless you were famous, or your corpse stolen, you were quickly forgotten. Plots like this were nothing more than a waste of space, a tourist attraction at best.

Putting the negative thoughts aside, he made his way between the gravestones, heading up the hill towards his brother's plot.

It took him a while to find it. He'd only been here on a handful of occasions, the last time about two years ago when his grandfather brought him back to Quorn for a visit during one of his mother's false recoveries. The visit had been a failure; she'd already relapsed before they arrived. But good old Bert did his best to turn the disaster into something memorable. He took Dylan to Jacob's End to show him the blight on the land, the dead fish and birds in the bay, and see if they could catch a glimpse of any sea monsters. (They didn't.) They filled up on pub food, Bert let him take a few sips of Guinness, and then they went off to see Oliver, both happily dulled by drink. He recalled Oliver's plaque was near one of the rose gardens, on the other side of a summer house. He remembered the summer house because it was where Bert stopped to take a leak while Dylan kept lookout on the path.

And there it was, just as he remembered it (though without poor old Bert fumbling with his fly as a funeral procession makes its way up the hill towards him).

Next was the rose garden, then Oliver's grave. Dylan approached it and stared down at the bronze plate.

In memory of our son and brother, Oliver Gates. Gone too soon. Aged 6 young years. Always loved, always remembered.

Kneeling on the wet grass, he brushed away dirt. The plaque was cold, the metal tarnished. Dylan knew there was nothing of his brother here: not his spirit, not any traces left of his ashes. He had hoped that by being here he would feel Oliver's presence, that his grave would evoke memories of some of the good times they had together, but all he felt was a slab of cold metal buried in a carpet of grass. A vast emptiness opened up inside him at the thought that all this had been a waste of time and effort.

"Who can resist the sweetness of its breath, the weight of its fist lodged deep in your belly?" came a voice behind him.

Dylan fell back, his lungs in his throat. The shock of a voice in this place of death had been like a sledgehammer to his stomach. And now the owner of the voice was upon him. It was the old man from the antiques store: Wilfred Waite.

Dylan got to his feet. Wilfred was dressed in a rust-coloured over-coat and red woollen scarf, a burgundy fedora, with matching ribbon and feather, sitting on his too-large head. On his feet were white running shoes. His haggard face wore a look of feverish excitement, his green eyes blazing at Dylan from their black sockets.

"What are you doing here?"

"Who can say no to its desperate allure …?"

"How did you get in?"

"… the promise of its intoxicating secrets?"

"What are you crapping on about?"

Wilfred showed his brown teeth. "The scent. Of a thousand graves."

Dylan gaped at him.

"Didn't your grown-ups ever tell you it's rude to stare?"

"What. Are you. Doing here?"

"I came to see you, Dylan Gates."

"You came to … What? How did you know I'd be here?"

"There's no time to waste."

"Have you been stalking me?" Dylan glanced around, suddenly afraid he was locked in a graveyard with a lunatic.

"My assistant is driving around the block," Wilfred continued, "waiting for my call. It wouldn't be wise for people to see us here. Too many prying eyes in this accursed town," he muttered to himself. "I won't let them ruin everything, not this time."

"Get lost, creepo."

Wilfred rubbed his hands together. "It's time to go, boy. Time to begin putting the wheels in motion. We have been charged with a momentous mission, you and I, a change for which the world is ill-prepared."

"I don't … What are you doing here?"

"The stars and planets have moved into alignment, as the prophet Zubrasa foretold. The time is come."

Dylan looked the small, bent, frail man up and down. He reminded him of a bobblehead Hobbit he'd seen at Killer Gamez. Harmless. Probably wandered in through a gate that had been left open.

He returned to his brother's plaque.

"Don't turn your back on me, rude little cur!"

When Dylan ignored him, Wilfred said in a more conciliatory tone, "Listen to me, boy. You, I have the great privilege to relay, are the Chosen One. The most favoured of the gods. Do I need to say it any plainer? Does any of what I am saying penetrate your thick skull?" He didn't wait for a reply. "The Great Old Ones, in their infinite wisdom, have deigned to honour Dylan Gates with the role of emissary. Isn't that ludicrous? And ironic, you must admit. Just as your pathetic life was descending further and deeper into tedium – as if that were even possible – here entereth the sublime immortals to deliver you from your miserable, meaningless existence."

Dylan sputtered an involuntary laugh. "Crazy old codger," he murmured, half turning his head.

"You would do well to accept. The divine demand obedience. I have been charged with delivering you to them, to receive their blessings and throw open the doors for their glorious return. The very fate of existence rests in your unworthy hands."

Dylan placed his hands on his brother's plaque. The grass was wet. The tree above him rustled in the wind. He could hear the old man's breath rattling in his lungs. Wilfred had fallen silent, having worn himself out with his monologue.

Unable to resist, Dylan turned around to see what he was doing.

Wilfred was gazing down the hill at the lights of the town. "Turn your eyes to the slush of humanity," he pronounced, gesturing at the view. "The crime, the selfishness, the cruelty, the … apathy. The best lack all conviction. The worst are gutless and afraid. Panic and emptiness, that's all that remains." He turned back to Dylan. "The time of man has ground to an ignominious halt. All this we shall now obliterate and remake as the Old Ones demand it. The hour has come, Master Gates. A new order is rising, and we shall rise with it, to sit on the throne of the world for all eternity. Kings will worship us; nations will scramble to serve us; and we shall annihilate them or spare them to serve our needs as we see fit."

"You are one crazy cat," muttered Dylan, hardly believing what he was hearing.

"I am the Lion."

"You're a delusional sociopath."

"I have the power of the ages in my grasp. Now come."

Dylan rubbed his face hard. "Go away," he groaned. Then, once more: "How did you know I'd be here?"

"You would do well not to cross me."

"Were you following me? Are you some kind of pervert?"

Wilfred shook his head in frustration. "Do as I say, stupid boy! Stop wasting my time!"

Dylan leapt to his feet. "Do you understand what's happened to me?"

Wilfred, alarmed by the threat of youthful violence, took a step back. He pressed his hands together. "I do," he said, drawing out the word in an attempt to sound sympathetic. "Your wretched parents, cut down in the prime of their lives by person or persons unknown, now at rest."

"That's right. They're dead."

"And because of their sacrifice, you, young man, are on the threshold of the greatest moment of your life – of any life."

Dylan tugged at his ears. "You're a psycho! My parents were murdered, everything's gone to shit, and you come here trying to – pick me up or something!"

"Gadzooks, boy, stop your pathetic whining. It does my head in." Wilfred raised his hands to the sky. "Why do halfwits always presume death to be the end? They blubber and blather about it till the cows come home. It aggravates me no end. I have no tolerance for annoying halfwits."

"I don't … You –"

"Death is not the finish, you naïve, senseless simian. It's an evolution, a transformation … a bend in the road."

"What are you babbling about? Look around you. These people are dead. D–E–A–dead. They're not going anywhere. Ever!"

"Are you certain about that? Does a maggot comprehend the laws of the universe – that such laws even exist? What if I told you I could show you a world where death is an illusion, a lie?"

"I'd say you're wacko. Everybody dies. Even creepy old men like you."

"I have no intentions of dying."

Dylan threw up his arms.

"I haven't lived all these years and studied the secrets of the ages only to have my efforts turn to dust."

"What am I doing here? I'm arguing with a gargoyle."

A shudder passed through Wilfred's body. "I would not normally abide such monumental rudeness," he warned, containing his anger with an obvious effort. "But I appreciate how your mind is somewhat unhinged at this time by certain inconvenient passings, so I will overlook your insolence. Just this once, mind you."

He took a card from his coat pocket. "After your period of mourning has ended, you must come and pay your respects at my farmhouse. There – if you will permit me," he added with a touch of sarcasm, "I will show you a world where gods walk and the dead share their secrets. You will shuck the skin of a boy and emerge a man, I promise you that."

Stepping closer, he slipped the card into Dylan's pocket. Before Dylan could say anything, he shuffled away, shaking his head and muttering between his teeth.

Dylan pulled out the card. Scribbled in blue ink was an address on Deep Ocean Road, the old road that winds through the Six Hills to the seaside village of Jacob's End. He flipped it over. It was a business card for Quorn Fine Arts and Antiquities.

Tossing the card on the grass, Dylan stared at the bronze plaque, trying once again to feel some connection to his long-dead brother. But he couldn't get Wilfred's words out of his mind. He'd said something about the walking dead. And he raved about gods as if they were his best friends.

Dylan shook his head. The old man was insane. Or a child molester. Or both. It occurred to him Wilfred Waite might be like one of those evil ex-Nazi serial killers who kidnapped young men and did vile experiments on them.

Yet something about the man's words intrigued him. There was a crazy consistency in his ramblings, a logic that suggested he'd thought long and hard about these gods and their plan to take over the world. He seemed to really believe what he was saying. Just like back at the shop.

Dylan rubbed his eyes. Was he so pathetic he was ready to latch onto the first weirdo who came along and offered him a distraction from – what had the old man called it? – his miserable existence?

He picked up the card and slipped it into his back pocket. Then he took it out and tore it in two, and in two again. He threw the pieces over his shoulder. The wind picked them up and blew them back at him.

7

Laid to rest

"T HEY'RE GONE FROM our sight," a woman crooned against Dylan's cheek, "but never from our hearts."

He could tell from the high-pitched voice and the sweet floral scent of her cologne who it was: Kane's stalker ex-girlfriend, January Bell. With a gentle sigh, she wrapped her arms around him and pressed herself against his back, while Dylan stood awkwardly, his arms pinned to his sides. Her breath tickled his ear as she murmured, "I'm here for you, Dylan. And Kane. You're not alone. I'm here for you. Both."

He tried to twist around in the hope she would release him from her suffocating hug. She didn't. In fact, her grip tightened, as if she were worried he might break free, throw himself to the ground and start digging at the graves like an excitable dog. Fortunately, the group around Kane broke apart, and after a wet kiss on his ear, January rushed away to claim him.

Rubbing his ear dry, Dylan watched her take his brother's hands. She looked great, he had to admit. She'd chosen a knee-length midnight-blue taffeta dress that showed off every curve of her body. Her blonde hair was piled on her head, and she was wearing the type of fascinator you might see at a horse race. Kane seemed genuinely pleased to see her, and Dylan wondered whether his brother was stupid enough to fall for her fake sympathy. Watching them – seeing her domineering presence and his brother's little-boy response to her – made his stomach turn.

"An awful tragedy," pronounced old Mr Waldron, startling him. "Just awful. And completely unexpected. But you boys are strong; you'll get through it." His bullfrog face was brown and serious. "Do you think you'll be heading back with Bert and Elizabeth now? Bert – Elizabeth. What happened to them?" he asked, glancing about.

Dylan watched the loose skin under his jaw swing from side to side.

The Waldrons lived down the road and bred llamas. Dylan wondered how Mr Waldron knew his grandparents, who'd probably never seen a llama in their lives.

"They left after the service. Bert wasn't doing too well."

Sighing, Mr Waldron placed a heavy hand on his shoulder. "I'm sorry to hear that, Dylan. I didn't know your grandfather, but your dear mother told me all about his bravery and service. Just know you came from very good stock. Good genes. Strong." He dragged his hand down Dylan's arm. "Come and see Marge and me if you need anything, you hear? Gloves, scarves, a jumper. Nothing is too big or too small. You know where we live. All you have to do is ask." When he saw Dylan's attention drift to his brother, he shook his arm, adding, "Do you hear me, Dylan? I'm being serious here. Dead serious."

"Dead," laughed Dylan.

Mr Waldron removed his hand. Clearly mortified by Dylan's reaction to his unfortunate choice of phrase, he made a quick excuse and went off to find his wife.

Alone again, Dylan turned away from the mourners and stared down at his mother's nameplate. He tried to feel her spirit, or at least evoke some of the memories of her that lived on inside him. Strangely, the only memory that came was the night she accepted his gift, the night she told him that good things happen to good people. The last night of her life. The memory was so strong he could almost see her seated in front of him now, fingering the silver charm he'd given her, staring at him as if seeing him for the first time. Except she wasn't here, not as flesh and blood. Kneeling on the grass, he wondered: Do her remains really fit under that slab of metal? Was any of what made her a human being there, or was it just a pit of ashes for the worms to feast on? Then he thought: Do worms eat ashes?

Before he could think much more on it, his attention was drawn by a voice calling out, "Come on, dear, here he is." It was a large woman in a small black dress, tottering towards him on red stilettos, one hand pulling a fox terrier on a pink leash, the other waving at him. She had on too much rouge and lipstick for a funeral. The floppy black bow on her head bounced against her wavy red hair as she made her way across the grass.

Approaching him, she called breathlessly, "If you need anything – absolutely anything – you'll let me know, won't you, love?"

Dylan climbed to his feet. He tried to recall who she was. Friend of the family? Distant cousin? He stared down at her dog, which seemed a little bored and tired, having sat through the service without a single whimper or bark. It shivered, glanced up at him, then bent down to chew its foot.

"Won't you, Alan?" the woman repeated, moving into his personal space, her face round and earnest.

Dylan backed away. He had no idea who the woman was, and had no desire to find out. To get rid of her, he said, "I'll ring. Soon. I promise."

She pinched his cheek, hurting him. "Good boy," she cooed. "You're such a cutie. Your mother and father were very proud of you. And now they're gazing down on you from a higher plane – a better place: the Garden of Eden; in the bosom of our Lord. And Sorrow leans her drooping head, whilst we, the living, slink towards Paradise, when our faces should instead be turned to the Sun, to the brightness that beckons us as it beckoned to them; if only we should see." She joined him in staring down at the three plaques. "Youth and Beauty, both are dust. Lauren, Michael, Oliver," she read. "Lauren, Michael, Oliver. We remember them; we cherish what was; and we thank the Lord for taking Love to its eternal home, by His side. Love is all that matters, Alan. Higher love; love that soars outside of ourselves; love for others. Love eternal."

Dylan started edging away. "I have to ..." he began, nodding towards his brother.

She took his excuse in her stride. "I'm afraid, young sir, my good self and Louisa must now take our leave and skedaddle. Home to beddy-byes. It's not safe for single girls like us to be out after dark. Is it, darling?" she asked the dog, leaning towards it. "Not with all the goings-on around town lately. Murder," she breathed, turning her face to Dylan. Her eyes narrowed. "Most wilful and foul of sins. Proof positive of Satan's disregard for our Divine Father. We've all been touched by its savage hand: you and me, your brother, Kane, poor Louisa. Our measure is how we embrace it. Death begets Life. Life begets Death. We're part of an endless cycle. Whether by God's hand or the Other's, we all return to Our Lord's embrace in the end. Our paths may differ, our journeys be short or long, but only the destination matters." She patted Dylan's cheek. "Choose your destination, well, Alan Gates. Remember: Life begets Death. Death begets Life. Choose wisely."

With a final sympathetic smile, she tottered away, dragging her dog across the grass.

Dylan watched her as she zig-zagged between the graves, stopping every so often to read an inscription. He still had no idea who she was. She arrived late to the service, creating a minor commotion, and then sat at the back, cradling and petting her dog. He hadn't seen her speak to anyone, apart from him (and, of course, Louisa). It struck him she might be a funeral crasher, a ghoul who drew life from other people's tragedies. Despite the gospel fervour of her speech, he didn't get the sense she was trying to convert him; it seemed more that she wanted to teach him something – something about life, death and grief. Whatever it was, the lesson had gone right over his head.

The woman disappeared behind a mausoleum, and with her departure Dylan felt the encroaching return of his grief. Sometimes when it came, he was able to sit on it, to push it down like clothes being forced into a suitcase; but at other times, the sadness rose like a tsunami and consumed all his thoughts and actions.

He felt a sudden urge to race after the woman and drill her to find out if she had any real answers to his despair. He imagined accompanying her to her tiny flat, to her simple life in which the sadness and tragedy of death meant nothing, where she would heal his sorrow over tea and biscuits. He guessed that, at some point in her life, she'd faced death, faced murder, and stared it down. Now, Dylan told himself, she was on the other side of sorrow, in a place of peace, where she was able to come out and help others get through their tragedy and loss.

Perhaps that was her lesson, he thought. Get over it. Move on.

Her advice brought to mind Wilfred Waite's words. Death is not the end, was his message. It's a bend in the road, a continuation of the journey towards … he hadn't been clear about that part. So who was right? Dylan wasn't religious, but he did have a belief in the unknown – in the practical unknown, not in the notion of an omniscient Creator gazing down on everyone from the clouds. Then again, how realistic were Wilfred's notions of spirits, zombies and cosmic gods? Maybe both of them were crazy – who knows?

Glancing over his shoulder at the funeral party, he saw that Kane and January were now in the summer house, where they sat at the end of a line of mourners waiting to say their goodbyes. With the departure of the scary red-haired woman, the people near Dylan approached him too, uttering their prayers and platitudes. After saying their goodbyes, they trudged away with heads lowered, leaving Dylan alone amongst the graves. Alone except for a single worker, who was collecting the collapsible chairs. He watched as the man stacked the chairs in the back of a buggy, doing his job noisily and efficiently like any good labourer, his energy dizzying after the slow pace and quiet tones of the service. The man was getting on with it, cleaning up, moving on.

A hand landed on his back.

"You okay there?" asked Kane. "You look a bit … green."

Dylan stiffened. His mind screamed at him to shake off his brother's hand, but he wasn't in the mood to start another argument. He just hoped Kane would get the message and leave. At least January wasn't with him. Another bear hug from her would have been the death of him.

"It'll be okay," persisted Kane, though he didn't sound very convincing.

Dylan stared at the writing on his dead brother's plaque. *Always loved, always remembered*, it read.

The words were a lie. No trace remained of Oliver. Except for this stupid epitaph. Always remembered? By whom? The two people who'd kept his memory alive for the past five years were gone. Ashes to ashes, dust to dust … What was the point of the stuff in-between?

"We should go," Kane said, rubbing his back.

So what if all roads lead to heaven? Dylan was thinking. That's what the scary woman hadn't revealed to him: the point of the in-between. If there's a God, and God wants us by His side, why does He put us through so much shit to get there? A vague memory from Sunday school threatened to feed him the answer, but Dylan wasn't here to get answers. He was here to feel bad. That's what funerals are for, isn't it? – to make the aftermath of death worse than the death itself? If you can survive the funeral, then getting over the death is a breeze. It made a crazy kind of sense (as much as anything over the past few days made sense).

"Come on, Dylan."

"I'm not going."

The words came out before he was conscious of them. He just knew he wasn't ready to go back to an empty house full of dead memories, and a brother who wouldn't leave him in peace.

"I'm not going," he said again, to make sure Kane knew he meant it.

"It's getting late."

"I like it here."

Dropping to the grass, he pulled his feet up, crossed his legs, held onto his boots. The grass was cold and damp – he could hardly stop from shivering – but he wasn't about to give Kane the satisfaction of seeing him jump up with a wet patch on his pants.

"Come on, Dylan. Let's go."

He shot his brother an angry glance. "I said I'm staying. Don't you ever listen?"

"For how long?"

He hadn't thought that far ahead. It didn't seem to matter how long – an hour, a week; both seemed plausible.

"Until I feel like leaving," he said, shrugging.

"It's getting dark. They'll be closing the gates soon."

"Then go."

Kane sighed in exasperation. It sounded to Dylan like he was on the verge of crying. "How will you get home, hey?"

That was a good question. Last time Dylan was here, he'd driven himself. This time, stupidly, he came in Kane's truck.

"Hitchhike," he said, to get his brother off his back; though in truth he didn't have any plans beyond the next three minutes.

"Get up, Dylan. Don't be stupid. We can come back tomorrow."

Dylan closed his eyes.

"You're being crazy."

"Yep."

"I'm not leaving without you."

"Then don't. See if I care."

There was a long silence. Dylan opened his eyes. His brother's long shadow was still falling across his family's plots.

Crouching next to him, Kane leaned into his line of vision. "I gotta go," he said. "One last chance. You coming or what?"

I hope he means it, thought Dylan.

Kane hesitated another moment, looked like he was about to say something, then shrugged and stood up.

Dylan braced himself for another explosion of frustration and anger. Instead, there was the jangle of keys. Up at the summer house, January began yelling something at them over the tombstones.

"I don't know why I'm doing this," he heard Kane mutter under his breath. "I must be crazy as he is."

He appeared again, this time with his keys in his hand. "Here," he said, holding them by the ignition key. "Take these, drive yourself home. I'll catch a ride with Janny."

Dylan gaped at him. Had he heard Kane right? His new truck. His baby. Was this some kind of trick? – a bluff? Did Kane really think he was stupid or pathetic enough to fall for a con? He kept his hands on his boots, worried Kane would snatch the keys away if he tried to take them.

"Please, please drive carefully, Dylan. There's not a scratch on her. I couldn't bear to see that first scratch; not today. You'll be careful, won't you?"

Nodding dumbly, Dylan took the keys from his brother's hand. They were warm and felt slightly greasy.

Kane ruffled his hair. "Take it easy, man. I'll see you later on."

And then he was gone.

Dylan released his breath. Mouth open, he picked out the ignition key and stared at it in wonder. The key to his brother's treasured truck. It seemed like a talisman – a sacrifice. The key ring had two ornaments: a silver BMX bike and a red firefighter's helmet. They represented the sum total of Dylan's knowledge of his brother: junior jock turned fireman. And now Kane had revealed something else about himself. As with the red-haired woman, Dylan didn't quite understand what that was, but he knew something had changed, something warming on this cold, damp, depressing afternoon.

Clambering to his feet, he felt the weight of grief slide from his shoulders. This was the best he'd felt since the morning he listened at the top of the stairs as a stranger destroyed his world with a few awful words. He shook the keys to hear them sing, smiled as January's last words faded away, glanced around and found the graveyard empty.

He realised he no longer wanted to stay here all night in the land of the dead. But what to do instead? A movie? A long drive in Kane's precious truck? Dylan knew the brotherly thing to do would be to race home and make sure Kane didn't do anything stupid with cunning old Janny. He stroked the tiny firefighter's helmet. No, that wouldn't work. He couldn't risk January taking Kane back to her place, or whisking him away to some secluded spot where they could be alone. He needed to head her off at the pass. He needed to chase after them, give Kane back his keys and go home with him, as planned. It was the only way to be sure old Janny didn't worm herself back into his life – into both their lives.

Breaking into a run, Dylan wondered whether these were the first steps of his journey to the other side of sorrow.

8

Moving out

DYLAN LEAPT OUT of a nightmare. The room was dark, the wall and door in front of him gone. In their place was the monster that had stalked him in his dream: through the graveyard, up an unlit alley, now into his bedroom. The monster was a hideous mass of brown pustules that ballooned and burst like volcanic mud, each pop releasing what looked like beetles, which spiralled away then flew back, to be reabsorbed into the bubbling flesh. The thing was dragging itself across the carpet, sluggish and deliberate, as if it knew Dylan was trapped in his bed, trapped by its foul corpulence and by his fear.

He watched in terror, his lungs contracting, his throat tightening. As he struggled to draw in air, the thing paused at the bottom of his bed and bugs flew out en masse, swarming towards him, covering his face, crawling into his mouth and ears and nose. He could feel them inching down his throat and windpipe, but his muscles had seized up and he had no ability to cough or run or swat them away. Now they were in his stomach; now in his lungs. He fought to breathe, to move his arms, his legs – to move anything. The beetles crept into his bowels, into his bladder, tickling and itching and hurting him, and still they came, flying out from the monster and crawling into his mouth and ears and nose.

At last Dylan found his muscles and drew a ragged, relieved breath. The monstrosity took this as a sign to begin oozing over the bed, oozing over his legs, dragging its foulness up his body towards his face.

"His flesh is your flesh is His flesh is your flesh," he heard from its cavernous mouth. "And to Kragn shall you return."

DYLAN JERKED AWAKE. It was dark, and he was enveloped in warmth and softness. He raised his head from the pillow, to find the monster gone, the bugs too, the wall and door returned to their rightful place. As he stared wide-eyed into the darkness, the familiar shapes of his room began to emerge: the shelves, the chest of drawers, the toys, the Manga posters on the wall. I'm safe; it wasn't real, he thought with relief, dropping his head back on the pillow.

He got up on his elbows. Where the hell did that awful nightmare come from? It was so vivid and real; he could still feel the bugs inside him, the weight of the thing on his legs, the terror at being unable to move or breathe. Dylan had never had a nightmare like that before – but then, he'd never lost his parents before either. He only wished that were part of the nightmare too.

An insane thought came to him. Maybe it was. Despite the craziness of the idea, he got up and went to check.

At the door to his parents' room, he hesitated before turning on the light, savouring the delusion, the anticipation of finding his parents fast asleep in bed. He smiled at the thought of the barrage of questions he'd get when they awoke with a start. They'd sit up and shade their eyes and screw up their faces at their oddball son as he stood smiling at them in the middle of the night.

When the light went on, Dylan saw the bed was made up and empty, exactly as his mother had left it. Her red scarf was draped across the bedspread, stretched out like a long streak of blood. She'd forgotten it in the push by his father to get to the restaurant in time for their booking.

Going to the bed, he picked it up, brought it to his nose, breathed in the scent of his mother's favourite perfume. The scent was fading, just like her memory. It was her absence Dylan felt now, not her presence. It was like chunks of reality had been gouged out of the air in the places Lauren was supposed to be.

Walking backwards, hitting his back against the wall, he slid down to the carpet. A sense of doom gripped him like a hand around his throat, making it hard to swallow. What was he supposed to do? He was seventeen years old, broke and unemployed. His mother had been his protector, his sole supporter. His father's business paid the bills, put food on the table, provided a safety net while he spent his time figuring out what to do with the rest of his life. With his only living grandfather suffering from Alzheimer's; with his grandmother heading in the same direction; with Kane having his own life, a life as alien to Dylan as that of the llama-loving Waldrons down the road – with everyone deserting him, what was he supposed to do?

Terrified all over again, Dylan stared wide-eyed at the window. It was still dark, but he had no hope of getting back to sleep, not with that monster lurking behind his eyelids, waiting to ram those damn bugs down his throat again.

Pulling his knees up to his chest, looping the red scarf over his neck, he pressed the material hard against his nose and waited for morning.

DYLAN OPENED HIS eyes. He knew straight away where he was: in his parents' room, lying on his side on top of the blankets, where he'd crawled when the floor became too hard on his buttocks. He was in his pyjamas, his mother's scarf still looped around his neck. The clock told him it was just after nine. The room was light, and he could hear the TV at low volume downstairs.

Sitting up, he ran his tongue over his teeth. Cottage cheese came to mind. That's disgusting, he thought, screwing up his nose.

Pushing himself off the bed, he went to the bathroom. Shit, I look like … shit, he thought as he caught sight of his pasty face in the mirror. The black rings under his eyes were scary, not to mention the white crusty bits clinging to the sides of his mouth.

"Grrrross," he groaned, looking away.

Turning on the tap, Dylan splashed cold water on his cheeks, then scrubbed his face hard with a towel. Throwing the towel over the shower curtain rail, he took out his toothbrush, squeezed on blue toothpaste, and turned to face the door. As he brushed, he tried to imagine his mother appearing in the doorway. She'd stood there countless times since he'd been back – at least once a day, watching him, as if she needed to reassure him (and herself) that they were a family and cared about what each other was doing.

His mother refused to appear. All Dylan felt was a vacuum in the doorway and a corresponding vacuum in his chest. Her absence.

As he spat froth into the sink, it struck him that what he'd thought was the TV was actually voices. Drying his mouth, leaving the bathroom, he went to the top of the stairs and bent over the balustrade. Kane was talking in a quiet murmur. Then came another voice, an older man by the sound of it. Unable to make out what they were saying, Dylan went back to the bathroom, rinsed his toothbrush under running water, pushed his hair away from his eyes, and started down the stairs.

Kane was standing in the kitchen, on the far side of the table. He was leaning over an open lever arch file, his forehead creased with concentration. A red-haired man in a blue pin-striped suit was sitting opposite, his back to Dylan, a dark blue briefcase open on the floor next to his leg.

Kane straightened and shook his body like a wet dog. "Oh, hey, Dylan," he piped, catching sight of him. "Sorry, kid, didn't mean to wake you."

"Who's this?"

The man twisted in his seat. He was mid-thirtyish, with a ruddy complexion and copper-coloured beard, wearing blue-framed glasses that matched the colour of his eyes. He leaned towards Dylan, nodding profusely.

"Joel Standish," he announced. "You must be the brother."

Dylan stared at the man's smiling mouth. His top teeth were white and perfect, the bottom ones yellow and crooked. He dressed and held himself like an actor or model, but Dylan guessed he was here about the will. Just like Kane to leave him out of the conversation.

"Why didn't you wake me?"

The man closed his mouth and sank back into the chair. He was clearly used to family conflicts and seemed practised at making himself invisible.

Kane moved around the table. "Dylan," he said, "why don't you sit down? You want a cuppa? I just made some. In the teapot even. Who'da thought?"

Dylan glanced at the documents on the table. He recognised some bank statements, what looked like a legal contract, and an accounts book he remembered from his father's office.

"What's all this?" he asked, his scalp prickling. He was thinking: What does this Joel person want with bank statements? Shouldn't he be handing over a cheque? And why is Kane acting so strangely?

"Well, um …" Kane, unable or unwilling to answer his question, joined him in staring at their guest, who was leaning over the table, pulling the papers towards him.

"Listen, Joel," Kane said once everything was sitting in a neat little pile: "I've got the picture. I'll call you in a few days, if that's okay. See if we can't work something out." He waved his hand at the sympathy cards, which stood randomly amongst the general mess. "Once we've dealt with all this."

"No problemo." Joel smiled at the dirty dishes, dirty glasses, uneaten food and other rubbish, assuming that's what Kane was referring to. "I'll get out of your hair, then fellas."

Dropping the collection of papers into his briefcase, he closed it, shut the clasps, said, "Oops, sorry," opened it and took out the accounts book. He tossed it on the table. "That one's yours."

Closing the briefcase again, Joel pushed back his chair and stood up. He was much taller than he looked sitting down.

"I know this is rough," he said to Kane in a voice that suggested he didn't, "but we'll need to know one way or another by the end of the month."

"Sure," chirped Kane. "Plenty of time," he added, smiling at Dylan.

Joel nodded, and walked around them and out of the kitchen. Kane followed.

Dylan pulled the lever arch file towards him. Bank statements. Letters relating to Mike's business. A tabbed section with mortgage papers. Someone had splashed tea or coffee on the most recent bank statement, then spread it across the page with their fist – a tiny, inconsequential act that made Dylan's head throb. Tears welled and fell on the page, on the stain, and he rubbed the wetness away with his fist, like Mike or Laura had done a week or so ago, like they would never do again.

He heard the front door close. A few moments later, Kane reappeared.

Dylan wiped his eyes on his sleeve. "What's going on?" He jerked his thumb at the chair. "Who was that?"

Kane had dropped the fake cheerfulness. Collecting a plate, he brushed crumbs into the sink, turned on the tap, held the plate under the running water. "Some trouble with the mortgage payments." He wiped the plate with a dirty tea towel. "He's from the bank. Don't worry, I'll sort it out."

"Sort what out?"

Kane put the plate back where he found it. "Nothing for you to worry about."

"What did he mean by the end of the month?"

Kane spun the tea towel in the air like a propellor.

"Do we owe him money?"

"The bank. We owe the bank money."

Dylan stared at him.

"We'll be fine," Kane reassured him, slapping the tea towel against the edge of the table. "Dad had a few accounts outstanding, that's all. I need to go chase them up. Nothing you need to worry about."

His brother was no actor. He lied the same way little boys lie: with his mouth, not with his eyes.

"Come on, Kane, stop bullshitting and tell me the truth."

"The truth. You want the truth." Kane went to the laundry and threw in the dirty tea towel. From the door, he said, "If I told you the mortgage repayments are more than we can afford, what would you say?"

His words hit Dylan like a punch in the stomach. "They're kicking us out?"

Kane came up to him. "No, no, don't jump the gun. I just said there's a big mortgage."

Dylan slid into a chair. Lose the house? How was that possible? How can you lose a house?

A sudden suspicion entered his mind. This was highly convenient for Kane. When their parents were alive, he'd talked endlessly about leaving sleepy, soul-destroying Quorn, and now he had the perfect excuse. He could get a transfer to another station, and then it would be goodbye Quorn and goodbye lazy, no-good brother.

"I'll get a job," he said, standing. "That's all there is to it."

"Dylan –"

"I know I haven't tried very hard before, but …"

"Dylan –"

"I'll start looking right now."

"Dylan!"

"What!"

Kane's face was grey. Dylan had never seen him afraid before. It was like seeing him naked.

"The mortgage is big. When Mum stopped working, they couldn't pay it back. So it's still there. I don't get paid that much. I won't be able to make that much money every month."

Dylan started pacing from the window to the wall. "There's got to be a way. If I get a job –"

"Let's take it one step at a time. I'll scrape together this month's payment and then we'll work something out."

"We could borrow the money," Dylan suggested, stopping by the fridge.

"From who?"

"The bank, of course."

Kane laughed at him. "Borrow money from the bank to pay back the money we owe them?"

"Don't laugh at me! At least I'm trying to think of a solution!"

"There is no solution."

"Don't say that."

"We'll have to sell the house."

Dylan bunched his fists. "I am not leaving this house!"

"Calm down, Dylan. There's worse things than losing a house."

He was so angry he couldn't even look at his brother. Kane seemed to have given up already. How long had he known about this? How long had he kept it from him? Had he already found someplace else to live?

"Look on the bright side," Kane offered. "If we do have to go, it'll be a new start." He swung his arms around. "Maybe I don't wanna stay in this place anyhow, now Mum and Dad are gone. Too many bad memories."

So there it was: the truth, at last.

Dylan stormed past him and out of the kitchen. Bounding up the stairs, he heard Kane calling, "Whaddaya think? Dylan? … Dylan!"

AT HIS PARENTS' bedroom window, he pressed his hands against the glass and glowered at the garden below. Down back was the old treehouse, falling apart with neglect. After Oliver's fall, his mother wanted it torn down, but his father couldn't bring himself to do it. To him, the treehouse was a shrine, not a crime scene. So there it remained over the years, battered by the sun, wind, rain and hail, the odd plank every so often coming loose and falling to the grass below: a dying monument to a dead child.

Over the fence, Mrs Kimmerle was hanging out washing, her face blank with boredom. She wasn't living there when Oliver died, so she didn't have a clue about the significance of the wooden box that was casting its shadow over her garden. Her curse was the opposite of Dylan's: a complete lack of drama. She was a victim of routine, of daily chores that rubbed away the minutes of her life like a polishing cloth rubs away molecules of silver from an old teapot. Yet right now, Dylan would have given anything to swap lives with her, to have the security of a house, the certainty of a pension. He watched with envious eyes as, with slumped shoulders and heavy steps, Mrs Kimmerle went inside to join her boring, flat-faced husband.

He rested his forehead against the cold glass. He'd known this view for most of his life and couldn't imagine anyone else coming in and building their lives here. The garden had been designed by Mike, who'd treated it like an engineering project, with clean lines, neat planting and clipped hedges. He'd been fastidious at weeding, pruning, sweeping and mowing; the garden looked like it belonged in a private estate. So much effort week in and week out – and yet, how long would it be before nature took over and turned Mike's perfect yard into a jungle?

He should have been working to pay off the mortgage, not wasting time out there, sneered a voice in his head.

Dylan shot a glance over his shoulder. The voice had sounded so real it might have come from his brother.

But Dylan knew Kane better than that. He'd never say anything nasty about his father, certainly not to Dylan. He also knew how hard his brother was trying to stay positive, how much he was making an effort to keep things together. At least he did until today.

Anger flared in his chest. What gave Kane the right to pretend everything would be alright, when more and more was being stripped away from them? And why couldn't he stop it from happening? It was becoming clearer that Kane was part of the problem, not the solution.

He looked beyond the yard, beyond the Kimmerles' house, in the direction of Jacob's End. Somewhere between here and there, somewhere along Deep Ocean Road, lived Wilfred Waite. Dylan shook his head. Crazy old fool. Turning up at the cemetery like that. He was probably demented, like Bert, his head filled with stories that made no sense. What had he said? – that Dylan was some kind of chosen one. What exactly did he mean by that?

He scowled down at Mike's perfect garden. If Wilfred had a weird interest in him, could he use it to his advantage? He owned a business, so maybe he could give Dylan a job. Or lend him money. The more he thought about it, the more Wilfred Waite became their best hope for saving the house.

"The shop, the shop, the shop …" he chanted, and pushing himself away from the window, went to make good on his plan.

9

Down on the farm

AFTER DRIVING FOR twenty minutes, Dylan hadn't passed a single car. Not many people use Deep Ocean Road these days. The highway is a lot quicker if you're travelling down to the city, and if you're headed to the ocean, you're better off taking the road to William-stown. There's nothing at Jacob's End but a broken jetty, empty shacks, poisoned water, rotting seaweed and dead fish.

Passing through the Six Hills, Dylan kept a lookout for any road that might lead to Wilfred Waite's house. The old man had said something about living on a farm, but there was any number of turnoffs and trails between here and the ocean that could lead to a farm.

He squeezed the steering wheel till his knuckles went white. What was he doing on this wild goose chase anyway? Chasing a delusion? Wilfred wasn't about to give him a loan or a job. They didn't even know each other until a few days ago, and even then, all they did was bicker. There was sixty years between them, and there wasn't anything they had in common that would entice Wilfred to hand over a suitcase full of cash.

Apart from his delusional interest in me, Dylan thought.

He felt a pang of discomfort. Was he driving out here to take advantage of a senile senior citizen? "Yep," he confirmed out loud, then thought: He wants something from me, he should pay me for it. Nothing wrong with an honest trade, a redistribution of wealth from rich to poor.

Looking at it that way made him feel better. With a crisis to handle, Dylan's focus had switched from grief and despair to the burning question of how to make money. He knew Wilfred Waite was the answer; he just had to work out exactly what it was he was selling.

Before embarking on his drive, Dylan had visited the old man's store. It was closed. The woman in the flower shop next door told him she hadn't seen Mr Waite all week. His hours were sporadic at the best of times, she said, and suggested Dylan call the number on the window. He did, but there was no answer. His calls didn't even go to voicemail.

For the rest of the morning, Dylan tried to immerse himself in a game of Zombie Uprising. But his mind was distracted by the thought of real zombies – and monsters and gods and the weird-looking goblin who believed in them. He rang twice more. Still no pickup. Maybe I'm wrong, he thought as he threw down the phone after the second time; maybe Wilfred Waite was what he appeared to be: a raving lunatic. Or maybe he died.

Eventually he couldn't wait any longer, and jumped in his car. He was just wasting time, sitting in a house that was about to be pulled out from under him. How was a long drive down Deep Ocean Drive any less productive? More to the point, Kane was due home any minute, and Dylan felt ill at the thought of one more minute of his brother's forced cheerfulness and complete and utter incompetence.

His thoughts were interrupted by the sight of a car driving towards him. As it drew closer, Dylan saw there were four teenagers inside, singing their heads off. God knows where they'd been; probably at Jacob's End, fooling around in the abandoned buildings, or smashing whatever windows remained, or spraying graffiti on the warped and crumbling walls. The two couples stared at him as their cars passed, as if challenging him to criticise whatever illegal or immoral things they'd been doing out there.

He checked his phone. Still no call from old man Waite. Did this useless fool really own a business?

Resting the phone on the steering wheel, Dylan switched to a new song: *White Room*. It was Bert's favourite song – a song to smoke pot to, Bert always said. (For medicinal purposes only, of course.) Dylan smiled, wondering what his poor grandfather was doing right now. He didn't want to dwell too much on the answer. Bert's health had gone downhill fast in the past three months. At the funeral, he hardly recognised him. Yet for the past five years they were inseparable. They tinkered with old car engines, listened to sixties' prog rock, scoured car boot sales, went walking and fishing; and through all this, Bert had told him endless stories about his time in the army, how he'd won his medals for gallantry and distinguished conduct, and how he'd uncovered deeply-buried secrets about supernatural goings-on that had been hidden from the general public for decades or even centuries, so people could go on blindly believing their life was everything they thought it was.

Halfway through the song, the car reached the peak of the sixth hill, at which point the country fell away like a landslide. From here to the distant water lay a wasteland. Patches of vegetation clung desperately to the rocky terrain. The sparse trees and bushes, remnants of an ancient forest that had been dead for two centuries, were gnarled and ugly, while dotted across the landscape were tumble-down farmhouses, brown stone barns and the occasional cow or sheep. Deep Ocean Road scratched a line to the ocean, which shimmered with sickly light in the early afternoon sun.

Dylan pulled over and sat for a while contemplating the view. Faced with the vast expanse, he felt his heart sink. To find Wilfred Waite he would have to do one of his least favourite things: he would have to talk to people.

He squinted at Jacob's End, which marked the end of Deep Ocean Road. From this distance it looked almost picturesque: a jumble of wooden shacks and stone cottages clustered around a small bay. A long jetty jutted into the ocean, the water white and frothy where it ran up against the posts. But the image was deceptive. At the beginning of last century, Jacob's End was a thriving fishing community, self-sufficient and well on its way to becoming a regional trade hub. And then something disastrous happened. One night, an invisible poison stole through the village, killing everyone. The water was poisoned too. Dead fish rose from the depths of the bay, wiping out the birds that came to feast on them. Even today, dead fish and birds unlucky enough to have ventured too close to Jacob's End washed up on the beach, where they rotted and stank, ensuring all but the brave and the wilfully destructive stayed well clear of the cursed village.

The poison crept into the land too. The grasslands and fields sur-rounding Jacob's End took on the appearance of frostbite, even though there'd been no frost for three months, and the cows, goats, horses and sheep that fed on the grass grew gaunt and grey. In time everything died. The creeping death continued spreading inland for the next two decades, slow, steady and unstoppable. And then the spread slowed year on year, until today its advance is hardly noticeable.

Gazing out over the plain, it was clear to Dylan something was wrong. The water shimmered with a hue that didn't seem natural: a greasy non-colour that made him queasy if he stared at it for too long. The same hue continued across the land, where it covered the ground like a sickly varnish. And then, a few hundred metres into the plain, the land made an abrupt recovery. The grass came back to life, livestock grazed, and everything seemed normal.

Bert claimed to know what happened at Jacob's End. In his youth he was stationed at army bases around the world, and he told Dylan stories he'd heard of coastal communities that did trade with amphibious beings that lived in vast cities under the sea. In prehistoric times (so the legends went) the beings roamed freely over the land, but after the rise and spread of homo sapiens, they retreated to the water and built their cities and grew their civilisation at a safe distance from the savagery, wars and destruction of the humans. Bert believed the people of Jacob's End made a pact with such beings – and then something went wrong. Something pissed them off, and in retaliation they sent a creeping death from the sea to poison the bay and destroy the village and the surrounding land.

Dylan always took his grandfather's stories with a huge grain of salt. While in the army, Bert was given LSD as part of a covert research program, and so it wasn't surprising he had colourful tales to tell. He was a great storyteller; you had to give him that. (At least he *was*, before dementia crept into his mind like the poison through Jacob's End.)

Thinking about Bert led Dylan to wonder whether Wilfred Waite might be in the early stages of Alzheimer's himself. That could explain his mania for cosmic gods and his fixation on Dylan as some kind of saviour of humankind. Would dementia be a help or a hindrance to the mission? he wondered, tapping his fingers on the steering wheel. It was hard to know.

Sighing, he released the brake and began his descent.

HE ALMOST MISSED the turnoff. The entry was hidden by a tangle of bushes, and it was only at the last minute he saw the broken letterbox and the chipped and faded sign that identified the property as White Horse Farm. White; Waite – was there something in that? Realising he was clutching at straws, Dylan spun the wheel and turned the car down the dirt road.

Not too far along was a metal gate, hung with signs that announced, Private Property and Enter at Own Risk. Dylan stopped the car and pulled on the handbrake. Seeing the gate wasn't locked, he got out and dragged it open.

Getting back into the car, he drove through, and kept on driving towards the farmhouse. The fields on either side of the track were rocky and barren. It was hard to imagine any livestock ever grazing there. Leafless trees clawed at the sky; others, less fortunate, were lying dead on the ground, having succumbed to the ravages of time and the elements. The bones of long-dead animals showed as white mounds against the grey-brown ground.

Dylan had already visited three houses along Deep Ocean Road and was beginning to give up hope. The first two were deserted, the properties crumbling and clearly uninhabited. The third looked not much better, but as he knocked on the door, he thought he heard a small whimper inside. He tried the handle. The door was locked. Peering through a window, he caught a glimpse through a tear in the curtain of ancient furniture, a Turkish rug, framed pictures on the walls, a rat staring back at him from the sofa top (fat and belligerent, not the least bit afraid of him). Surely no one lives here, Dylan told himself. Certainly not a business owner like Wilfred Waite. Guessing at most it was a den for drug dealers or crims on the lam, he went back to his car and pressed on towards Jacob's End.

He expected this muddy road would lead to similar disappointment. Maybe he'd misunderstood what Wilfred had said. Deep Ocean Road led through barren land to fetid water and a deserted village. Why would anyone live out here? There were no amenities and nothing to do. There was only death and decay, its stink carried by the sea breeze across the land from the rotten bay. Wilfred had a business in town, which meant if he lived out here, he'd have to make the half-hour trek to town every time he opened the shop. Wilfred Waite, an octogenarian who seemed to need a driver to get around. It made no sense.

The dirt road wound through the flat land. At last another gate appeared, this one secured by a giant padlock. Dylan parked the car and got out.

Beyond the gate stood an old stone farmhouse, rising to two storeys and looking like it might crumble to rubble the next time someone knocked on the door. Near the house was a wooden barn, while further down the road stood half a dozen mudbrick huts, huddled together like a small village. From there, the dirt track continued through the field until it became indistinguishable from the field itself.

Jumping the gate, Dylan strode towards the house. His boots squelched in the mud, the suction trying to pull them off his feet. As he walked past the barn, he could see at some point in its history it had been converted to a makeshift chapel. The wooden slats were black with age, the tiles on the roof dropping one by one to the ground. A tower rose high into the sky, topped by an empty bell tower.

Further along lay a mangled tractor that looked like it had been melted in a furnace. After that was a stone well. Dylan stopped and peered into the abyss. A foul odour rose from the depths, accompanied by a soft whining. At first Dylan thought it was the wind whistling through the well, like the sound air makes when it's blown through a flute, but then he realised the air was still. Nothing stirred in the yard: not a bird, not an insect, not a fallen leaf. The sky overhead reminded him of Mrs Kimmerle's wet sheets that hung perpetually on her clothes line.

He stared at the farmhouse. The ancient grey-stone building was fronted by a portico, a rotting wooden frame that leaned at a dangerous angle. The upstairs windows were boarded up, and there was a gaping hole in the thatched roof, a hole that might have been caused by a meteorite crashing through the house. Behind the farmhouse rose a small hill, thickly populated by pine trees, providing a backdrop to the property and making it look almost theatrical. The rest of the garden was dead or dormant, no trace remaining of what it must have looked like when the farm was a going concern.

Dylan turned back to the gate. No one lives here, he told himself as he trudged through the mud, fists clenched. Trying to find Wilfred Waite's farmhouse was a fool's errand, a complete waste of time. Now he faced the long drive home, where all that awaited him was a ticking timer and more awkward conversations with his useless brother. Frustrated by failure, he kicked a rock with all his might, and it shot forward and clanged against the twisted metal of the tractor.

That's when he heard the dogs.

THE PARLOUR WAS a place of perpetual twilight, where nothing much had changed in the past hundred years. Above a central stone fireplace hung an oil painting of a severe-looking middle-aged man in black religious robes, sitting on a high-backed chair inside a room not dissimilar to this one. He was the first thing you saw when you entered the room, and you couldn't escape his gaze. His black eyes bored into you as if judging whether you were worthy or wicked enough to enter. On either side of the fireplace were mahogany shelves, stretching all the way to the ceiling, filled with cloth- and leather-bound books that gave the room the impression of an old library, complete with a crust of dust and the fusty smell of mildew. Near the window were an overstuffed green velvet armchair and a tapestried foot stool. A threadbare Victorian-style red-and-black rug, two small oak tables and a floor-standing lamp with burgundy fabric shade and yellow tassels completed the room's furniture.

This afternoon a shaft of milky light, swirling with dust motes and carpet moths, descended from the ratty curtains to a pair of white sneakers. As the dogs commenced their barking, one of the shoes began tapping on the rug.

"Damned hounds," muttered Wilfred. "Arlene!"

Wilfred was seated in the armchair, an ornate ivory telephone hand-set pressed against his ear. "Hold on," he said into the mouthpiece. "Arlene!"

A hag with greenish-grey skin and an onion-shaped head shuffled into the room and stood glancing about with bulging eyes. She was wearing a shapeless olive-green housecoat and purple slippers, which made her feet look enormous. Her hair was grey and patchy, cropped close to her scalp, and she had no eyebrows to speak of. Her nose and ears were abnormally small.

"Feed the hounds," Wilfred ordered without looking at her.

The woman stared at him, her beakish mouth opening and closing, then, without a word, turned in a circle and left the room.

Picking up a rubber mask, Wilfred held it over his mouth and sucked in oxygen from a tank that stood next to his chair.

Dropping the mask in his lap, he lifted the phone to his ear. "So yes, Gideon," he purred, "after an eon of searching, success." He dropped his head back. "Gideon, Gideon, ye of little faith. Of course he was telling the truth. No man can resist these practised hands; you know that. It pains me how you doubt me after all these many years." He nodded. "Yes, back in 'twenty-eight. In Dunwich."

Listening again, he flicked his black tongue across his purple lips.

"En route as we speak, and making all possible haste. I have authorised him to use whatever force is necessary. Or pleasurable," he added with a smile. He squirmed in his seat. "I feel the Spheres tremble, old friend. We are getting close. We are getting very close."

He was interrupted by a knock at the front door.

"Who the deuce can that be?" Into the phone: "Would you please hold a moment?"

Straining his neck towards the door, Wilfred listened hard. When the knock sounded again, a smile stretched across his face.

"My guest has arrived, Gideon. Better late than never. I will call you back once I know more."

He replaced the phone in its cradle. Reaching over the arm of the chair, feeling along the table, he found and picked up a miniature oval portrait of a young man with a round face, white skin, rouged cheeks and long black hair, dressed in a heavy brown coat and white cravat.

He held the pendant close to his face. "You were such a handsome devil," he said to the picture.

10

Communing with the dead

"**M**IKE, OLD CHUM, this is ridiculous."

Kane was leaning over the kitchen table, trying to make sense of his father's accounts. He had the mortgage papers, statements from three bank accounts and tax returns for Mike's business going back five years, and though he'd been going over them for the past hour, the big question still on his mind was why Mike had taken out a second mortgage. He was a self-employed draughtsman, with no office rent or staff to pay, and he always seemed to be working. Often when Kane arrived home late at night, Mike would be locked in his office, the click of his keyboard or the scratch of his pencil the only sounds in the house. It didn't make sense they owed so much on the mortgage. Maybe he was a secret gambler. Keeping a mistress? Gambling with a secret mistress? He shook his head at the documents. Only something outlandish like that would explain the dire state of their finances.

His eyes were grainy and sore, his head like a block of lead. His mind was pounding at him to stop trying to understand something Mike had taken with him to the grave, and his mind, of course, was right. What difference did it make how they got into this mess? The only fact that mattered was that Kane had no way of making the monthly mortgage payments.

In a burst of frustration, he shoved the books and papers away. Flying off the table, they slapped to the floor. Papers scattered across the lino.

Pulling out a chair, Kane dropped into it and sat staring at his hands. They were strong hands, but he'd never felt weaker.

"Don't be a crybaby," he warned himself as anguish and panic began their inevitable rise in him. "Focus. You need to focus."

He didn't know how long he'd been sitting there staring at his hands when he heard the front door open. It slammed shut, and footsteps approached the kitchen. He quickly rubbed his cheeks dry.

Dylan appeared in the doorway, his blue eyes bright in his white face. He stopped short when he saw Kane staring at him.

"Oh – hey," he chirped, glancing at the papers on the floor.

Kane looked him up and down. Dylan's clothes were rumpled and grubby. There was dirt on his face, lines of it running down his cheeks.

"Where have you been?" he asked. "I thought you were still in bed."

Dylan went to the sink and peered down at all the dirty dishes.

"Where were you?"

"Out. On a visit."

"Who with?"

Dylan smirked.

"Have you been out all night?"

As Dylan walked past him to the cupboard, Kane screwed up his nose. "What is that godawful smell?"

Dylan laughed shrilly – an unfamiliar sound from his usually gloomy brother.

"You smell like you've been rolling in manure."

Dylan brushed the dirt off his trousers.

"Don't do that. You're making a mess."

"Chill, brother."

"Chill, brother? Who are you? Shaggy?" He got up. "Where have you been?"

Dylan, smiling to himself, took out the box of cornflakes and went back to the sink. He rinsed a dirty bowl under the tap.

Kane knelt and began collecting the papers and books from the floor. He could hear Dylan behind him, shaking cornflakes into the bowl. The box rustled, then the fridge opened and closed.

"You wouldn't believe me if I told you."

Kane glanced impatiently at him. He was in no mood for his brother's games.

"Go to bed," he ordered, getting to his feet. "You look like you're about to fall over."

Dylan plucked at his shirt, pulled the material to his nose. "I suppose

I do stink a bit."

Kane watched him as he poured milk into the bowl, left the milk on the counter, carried the bowl and a spoon to the table, sat down and began eating. Despite himself, he was curious to know how his brother got this dirty, and why he was so bloody cheerful all of a sudden.

"Were you up all night?"

Dylan nodded.

"Doing what?"

"You wouldn't believe me if I told you."

"Try me."

Kane waited for an explanation, but his brother kept on eating. As he spooned cornflakes into his mouth, he seemed to be enjoying a private memory. He was nodding and smiling and chewing with his mouth open, making loud crunching and smacking noises. Kane knew he knew Kane hated that, but he wasn't about to yell at him and distract him from answering his question.

Slapping the papers down on the table, he crossed to the window and gazed out at the rain. Rising above the Kimmerles' roof were thick clouds, black and angry. Another storm was on its way.

"I've been communing with the dead," Dylan declared to his back, and then went back to his crunching and smacking.

The comment was so weird, it took Kane a while to process it. He realised suddenly that Dylan must be referring to their parents. He must have been out at the cemetery. But all night? He looked again at the state of Dylan's clothes, thinking: What was he doing? – rolling around in the dirt?

"What –"

"There's this wizard," explained Dylan, waving his spoon at him. "Necromancer, he calls himself."

Now Kane was even more confused. Wasn't 'wizard' a code for someone who cooks up drugs in meth labs?

"Wilfred Waite. He's got books and chemicals that do things that are out of this world."

"Drugs? You mean drugs?"

Dylan laughed at him. "No, stupid. Magic."

Kane's next thought was 'magic mushrooms' – but he thought it best to let his brother go on with his explanation, rather than keep jumping in with a bunch of random guesses.

Dylan went back to eating cornflakes and chewing with his mouth open and smiling at his private memory.

"What are you saying, Dylan?"

With mouth full, he said, "I'm saying Wilfred Waite is a warlock, and he's given me a job."

"A what? A warlock? Like a male witch warlock?"

He spooned more cornflakes into his mouth.

"Is that what you're saying? This character is a male witch?"

"Warlock. No one says male witch."

"I don't believe what I'm hearing."

"Told you."

"You're talking about it like it's …" Kane couldn't think of an analogy, so he threw up his hands.

Dylan seemed pleased by his reaction.

"What did you take?"

Now Dylan was the one to look confused.

Kane felt the magma of panic rise inside him. With everything else he had to contend with, a drug-addled brother would be enough to push him over the edge. His mind yelled at him to run – run away from Quorn and Dylan and psycho ex-girlfriends and all these obligations, and do whatever the hell *he* wanted to do, not what his dead parents expected of him. He wasn't a mature, responsible adult; he was a healthy young man, in the prime of his life, and he'd be damned before he let this family tragedy be his personal tragedy.

"I'm going to work," he said, though today was his day off.

"The spells are ancient," Dylan said, beaming at him.

Kane went up to him, a sick anger blurring his vision. "What is this shit about warlocks and spells? What drugs are you on, Dylan?"

The shrill laugh came again.

From his reaction, Kane wasn't sure anymore that this was about drugs. He had no idea what it was about. Time to start the conversation over.

"Who is this person you spent the night with?"

"Mr Waite."

When Kane looked bewildered, he added, "The old guy from the shop we went to – when we bought the sideboardy thing."

Now they were getting somewhere. After they arrived home with the sideboard, Mike told him about the store owner: a doddering gnome with oversized clothes and a voice like tyres on gravel. He said this guy had told them a wacky story about a supernatural monster that wanted to destroy the universe. Afterwards, they had a good old laugh over Dylan's debate with him.

"What's this shopkeeper got to do with anything?"

"He's a necromancer."

"He's the warlock?"

Dylan kept on eating.

"The kind that casts magic spells?"

He nodded.

"Real spells or pretend ones?"

"Real ones."

Kane had a sudden vision of Dylan dancing around a bonfire with a bunch of naked, saggy-skinned old men and women, who got their kicks from enticing impressionable teenagers into their nasty Satan-inspired orgies.

He shook the image from his head. "And?" he asked, though he wasn't sure he wanted to hear more.

Dylan leaned back in his chair. He looked dead tired, but he was also shaking with nervous excitement. "I went to Wilfred's farmhouse, down on Deep Ocean Road. There's an old church there, and old Willie said there were people buried behind it, from when the farm was running last century. We built a fire and did these chants from these old books, and this rumbling came up from the ground. Willie said it was the spirits of the dead. He said he can make out what they say, and I will too when I'm initiated. I had to bury three runes and do rites over the graves – and if I do that enough times, eventually I'll understand what the corpses are saying, same as him."

All Kane could think was: This is worse than drugs.

"He needs an assistant cos he's getting too old. I'm doing it, Kane."

He beamed at Kane, waiting for his reaction.

"Doing what, Dylan? You're talking gibberish."

Dylan made an exasperated face at him.

"You – just said you were talking to dead people."

"No, I said Wilfred was."

"First thing is: that's impossible. Second thing: name me one time a zombie story has ever turned out well."

Dylan smirked at him. "They're not zombies. They're spirits."

"I don't care what they are."

"Zombies are dead bodies," he explained. "Spirits are –"

"I know what spirits are!" Kane felt like he was conversing with a lunatic.

Dylan's face began to darken. "Can't you be excited for me just this once? This is a job. I can get money. For the house. And Wilfred said he'd give me a spell so we never have to worry about money again."

"There's nothing in what you've said to get excited about, Dylan. Seems to me you're either raving mad or a complete idiot."

"Don't talk to me that way."

"You just told me you've been hanging out with a warlock and playing Chinese whispers with dead people. Can you hear yourself?"

"All I hear is my Neanderthal brother thinks everything I do is shit. Nothing's changed around here! Welcome back, Dad!"

Pushing back his chair, Dylan got up and stormed out of the kitchen.

Kane stared at the empty seat, his mind surprisingly calm. At least this was the Dylan he knew. Returning to the window, he gazed out at the sodden garden, trying to draw energy from the greenery and life out there. He was finding it hard to comprehend how his brother could possibly play games with dead people after the trauma they'd just been through. It seemed criminally morbid. Kane had focused on going the opposite way: staying positive, getting on with his life, forging ahead. He was back on track with his training; he'd resisted January's attempts to use the tragedy to get back into his bed; he was trying to figure out what to do about the house. If Dylan was headed down a dark path, there was a risk he would drag them both down.

Leaving the window, he went to the dining room, to his mother's sideboard, and picked up his parents' favourite wedding photo. They were both dressed in white, under a clear blue sky, hugging in a garden of red roses. His mother was gazing lovingly at his father, his father smiling out at him.

"Don't worry, folks," he said to the picture. "I'll get to the bottom of this."

Putting the photo down, he opened a drawer, pulled out a pile of papers, and went through them until he found the bill of sale from Quorn Fine Arts and Antiquities. Then he went to the computer and typed in 'Wilfred Waite'.

DYLAN THREW HIMSELF on the bed. His brain was still popping like fireworks over what had happened last night, but his mood had taken a sudden dive, thanks to his brother's scepticism and pigheadedness. How could he be so naïve? They lived in Quorn, for God's sake! There were probably more Wiccans and magic shops per square mile here than anywhere else in the world. If anyone was being stupid and ignorant, it was Kane.

Despite the thoughts crackling in his head, he quickly fell asleep. But it was a slumber more than a sleep, a dream-memory of the graves behind the chapel at the farm. In the dream, Dylan had his ear against the ground, where something gnarled and black, buried just below the surface, was whispering to him in a guttural voice. He couldn't make out what the thing was saying, but its tone suggested an enticement, a promise of something incredible if he would do it a favour he couldn't yet understand.

Now he was back in his bedroom. He could hear the hiss of pipes, a bird squawking outside his window, something banging in the bowels of the house. The room was full of shadows, though Dylan knew it was still morning.

His mother's voice sounded close to his ear. "Eat your breakfast," she said. "It's your favourite."

He saw Fruit Loops pouring into a bowl. But that was Oliver's favourite breakfast, not his. He heard his baby brother's excited squeal, and knew he was probably in the treehouse, swinging off a branch or climbing towards the sky. He virtually lived up there, high above the rest of the earthlings. He thought it was the next best thing to flying. Oliver was fearless, just like his brother Kane, whereas Dylan was the quiet one in the family: the artist and thinker. The odd one out.

The shadows grew, and now Dylan was in a different room. This one was dark. Maroon velvet curtains covered the windows, which appeared boarded up. A broken chandelier was hanging from the ceiling, swinging like a pendulum. Then he saw them. Ghostly shapes. They started as a grey mist, emerging from cracks in the dirty ceiling and from the edges of the cornices, but as they descended, they materialised into the shapes of people – ugly, twisted, freakish dead people, with hollowed-out eyes and crushed skulls and mouths open in silent screams. They came from the worst-of-the-worst nightmares; but these ones were real. Wilfred had shown him their pictures in his books. He told Dylan they were the key to riches and power, that all he had to do was learn to communicate with them, to speak their language and help them find eternal rest. And in return …

He jerked awake. His heart was pounding, his head throbbing painfully with every beat. His mouth and his eyes were dry, and it felt like a cavern had opened up in his stomach, demanding to be filled.

Rising onto his elbows, he gazed at the window. It was dark outside. The house was silent.

Dropping his head back on the pillow, Dylan closed his eyes and was once again fast asleep.

❚❚

Necromancer's assistant

THE NEXT TIME Dylan woke, it was light outside. Sunlight peeked from the edges of the blinds and he could hear Gary barking at cats. His bedside clock said it was almost midday.

Groggy and weak, he got up and checked his phone. There were sixteen missed calls, all from Wilfred Waite. He smiled. The old man was rude, self-important, loud and demanding, but he wore his narcissism like a cape, and essentially told the rest of the world (Dylan included) that if they didn't like it, they could go to hell. Dylan respected him for that.

He rang Wilfred back.

"Get over here," were the old man's first words. "Why didn't you ring me back? There's work to be done. I haven't spent all these years in preparation, only to have some snivelling milksop come along and ruin everything. If you're aiming to slouch around like a rubber-boned layabout with too much time on your hands and no more sense than a three-toed turkey, I can easily find another brainless dolt to train!"

Dylan opened his mouth to apologise, but Wilfred had already hung up.

He smiled and returned the phone to the bedside table. "Crazy," he said, shaking his head.

Though he could laugh at Wilfred behind his back, he knew better than to test the man's patience. For the next few days, he arrived at the farmhouse on time and did everything he was asked. Initially he baulked at some of the darker rites, the ones involving human bones, animal blood and ancient words he discovered later were the names of demons – but as Wilfred explained: "How do you expect to summon the dead without entering their darkness? The important thing," he added, "is knowing how to find your way back."

In one of these rites, Dylan had to chant the name of a dead wizard while pouring pigs' blood over a burial mound behind the chapel. Apparently, the blood was an offering to the man buried there, in return for which the corpse would ferry the wizard from the underworld to grant Dylan a wish. When nothing happened, Wilfred handed him a shovel and instructed him to dig up the body and pour the blood down its throat. "Uh, maybe next time," Dylan replied, handing back the shovel, and on the drive home tried to convince himself that digging up a corpse and force-feeding it pigs' blood was worth the price of a house.

According to Wilfred, these rites were necessary to prepare Dylan for his role as necromancer's assistant. "The underworld won't accept any old upstart who comes along and whales on their door demanding entry," he told him. "You have to prove yourself worthy."

Dylan was desperate to be found worthy. For the first time in his life he had a purpose, a role he was sure would lead to something, and if he failed at this … well, that didn't bear thinking. Still, he hadn't yet reconciled himself to digging up a rotting corpse and filling its mouth with pigs' blood so he could ask a dead wizard a favour.

He soon learnt, from listening in on Wilfred's phone conversations, that the wizard was searching for a book, one so rare and powerful that the only known copy was sealed away, accessible only by a small circle of trusted scholars. Wilfred was convinced a second copy of the book had come into the possession of one of his enemies in New England.

"Fool!" he heard Wilfred cry one night. "Doesn't he know the Tso-thua spell will open the gate to Flaying Demons if he doesn't mark the ground with the bones of a newly dead child?" He lowered his voice. "Is he dead? – Damnation! Why do the lamebrains have all the luck?"

After a few days of gathering his nerve, Dylan asked him about the book. He steeled himself for an explosion of abuse, and was surprised when Wilfred responded with a rare smile.

"The Necronomicon is not just a book," he explained, waving a jaw bone at him. "It's a repository of power that men have sought and died for for a thousand years. I've uncovered a lost copy through my ingenious detective work, and now our real work begins."

"Is it a spell book?" asked Dylan, at which Wilfred's face collapsed into its usual look of disapproval. "I'm surrounded by imbeciles," he muttered, tottering off.

But he'd only gone to retrieve his laptop computer. "There," he said, shoving it into Dylan's hands. "You may as well further your education, for what it's worth."

On the screen was a black-and-white photo of a large book, resting on a lectern, surrounded by bearded men dressed in button-up overcoats with high collars. The book looked to be bound in thick leather. The photo wasn't particularly clear, but Dylan could make out in bas-relief, in the centre of the book cover, what appeared to be a horned devil. He zoomed in. The devil seemed more alien than the goat- or jackal-based devils he was used to seeing. The caption stated, 'Necronomicon. Arkham University. 1908.'

He clicked on a link and a picture appeared of a lumpy, spherical monster, with fat tentacles and a dozen eyes of differing sizes scattered across its body. It reminded him of the nightmare from earlier that week, the one he guessed was sparked by the statue of Kragn he'd been playing with in Wilfred's shop, though this monster was called Mghorgah. He scrolled down to more images: goat-faced devils, human sacrifices, artists' impressions of unearthly beings flying down on leathery wings from an angry sky.

"Is any of this real?" he asked Wilfred. But his mentor had gone back to packing animal bones into a leather bag.

The next day, when Dylan arrived at the farm, there was no one home. His knock echoed through the empty house. Wilfred didn't answer his phone calls. This was the first time in a week he hadn't seen the wizard, and he had a sudden dread his mentor had died, or lost interest in him, and his adventure was over.

He went to the farmhouse the following day, and the day after that, and still no one answered the door. Wilfred's dogs continued patrolling the grounds, chasing off unwelcome visitors, and he presumed the creepy housekeeper was inside; but for whatever reason, no one would respond to his knocks or answer his phone calls.

His worry deepened. He fell into a depression, his putrid life crowding in on him, reality stabbing at him like a sadist with a pointed stick.

Kane, who'd just returned from a five-day training camp, told him the bank was pressuring him to put the house on the market, and as far as he could tell, there was no alternative. That same day, Joel Standish rang to say there would be no concessions or extensions to the payment deadline and he wanted to make sure the brothers had somewhere to go once the bank foreclosed. Kane didn't even seem concerned: he was caught up with his job and his ongoing problems with January Bell, and this only confirmed in Dylan's mind that without Wilfred Waite, he had no future.

When Wilfred finally rang, he almost exploded with joy. Putting the phone to his ear, he opened his mouth to speak.

Wilfred beat him to it. "It's mine!" he cried.

Dylan knew what he was talking about. "Have you got it?"

"Didn't I say it was mine?"

"Yeah, but …" He sighed. "Don't worry."

"Snyder has secured a vessel."

"A boat?"

It was Wilfred's turn to sigh. "A vessel for the first spell."

"Cool!" breathed Dylan, not really understanding. "Does that mean you need me to come over?"

"Why are you not here now?"

The phone went dead. Dylan tossed it in the air and watched it fly in an arc and land on the bed. He smiled at his laptop, at the picture he was crafting, a picture of a fat, gorilla-like ogre emerging from a demolished mausoleum with a severed arm in its mouth.

"Now," he said, tapping his head against the wall, "the real fun begins."

12

The Messenger

THE BLOATED, NAKED body of a man lay face down on the stainless-steel table, its skin lumpy and discoloured. Dylan stared at the creases in the back of its neck, trying to figure out if the body was real. It looked like it was made of moulded resin – a movie prop, perhaps. He was too scared to touch it to find out.

Wilfred was placing red candles on the floor. So far he hadn't said anything about the corpse.

Dylan turned to him. "Is it –?"

"Don't go lily-livered on me, boy."

He glanced back at the body. "I – uh –"

"Nothing in the Necronomicon is gained without a price."

They were in the makeshift chapel, which was empty apart from the table, a single pew, a wall of storage boxes marked with the name of Wilfred's shop, and five coffins stacked in what was once the chancel. The coffins looked like they'd been piled there in a hurry. Two had broken panels, and there was a trousered leg poking out of one of them, at the end of which was a mummified ankle and a foot in a black sock.

Dylan placed his hands on his head. "Who – is it?" he asked, though he didn't really want to know.

"Nobody. A vagrant."

His stomach turned over. "You didn't …"

"I didn't what?"

Dylan made stabbing gestures in the air.

Wilfred laughed at him. "Snyder works at the hospital." He began lighting the candles.

"Who's Snyder?"

Wilfred squinted at him. "Snyder is a snivelling codfish, with pretensions of being me." He stood with an effort and a groan, and stretched his back till it cracked. "Don't just stand there like a fence post. Come and light these things for me."

Dylan accepted the matches.

"Mr Snyder has somehow succeeded in making connections at all the funeral parlours in these parts. The Devil knows how. No doubt by means nefarious, knowing the way that slithering sewer slug works."

Dylan glanced again at the corpse. "Did he have to pay for it?"

"*I* paid for it. For silence. Far more costly than an over-sized, good-for-nothing sack of guts. Now get to it and light those damn candles."

"I've never seen a dead body." Dylan went closer and peered into the corpse's face. It was a man of about forty, with fat cheeks, a splotchy complexion and dirty blond hair. It looked like he'd lived a rough or unhealthy life. "It's hard to believe this used to be a man. It's like a shell with the crab gone."

He had a sudden sickening thought of his father lying face down on a table like this, the grisly subject for an as-yet-unknown spell. But Mike and Laura were cremated, he reminded himself. Was that a good thing or a bad thing? he wondered. Now they were cremated, he couldn't ask Wilfred to bring them back to life. If he'd known before the funeral that Wilfred was a reanimator, he might have insisted they be embalmed and entombed in a mausoleum, just in case.

Shaking the ridiculous notion from his head, he turned away from the corpse and set about lighting the candles.

"Don't move any of them, or there'll be hell to pay."

He hadn't seen Wilfred perform any reanimations yet, but he was almost certain his subjects would come back broken, like the dead son in 'The Monkey's Paw'. As Wilfred kept reminding him, magic comes with a price, and now that Dylan had journeyed to the other side of sorrow, he was glad he didn't have the choice to bring his parents back from the dead.

"Would you hurry up? We don't have all night."

"What are you planning to do with it? – with him?" Dylan asked.

Wilfred pulled back his narrow shoulders. "I intend to summon Yog-Sothoth."

"I read about that. Isn't it some kind of ancient god?"

"Yog-Sothoth is the key."

"To what?"

"Yog-Sothoth guards the gate."

"The gate?"

"Yog-Sothoth *is* the gate. Past, present and future all are one in Yog-Sothoth."

Dylan watched Wilfred hobble towards the pew, where he'd left a black leather bag with long handles. "Okay. Whatever. So what happens when it gets here?"

"Yog-Sothoth will reveal to me where the Great Old Ones broke through. But first: the spell."

"Ooh, the spell! Cool bananas! Magic time!" Dylan glanced about. "Where's the book? – the Necronomicon? I wanna see it. Is it the one in the picture?"

Opening the bag, Wilfred extracted a pair of wire-rimmed glasses, placed them on his nose, then pulled out and flicked open a notebook. He turned the page, turned another.

"Patience, boy. All in good time."

Dylan went up and peered over his shoulder. The notebook was scrawled from edge to edge with text and symbols. The left page was headed, 'Orium', the right page, 'Sacrium'.

Wilfred shoved him away with surprising strength. "Get away from me, you infernal nuisance! Get back to those damn candles!"

He turned and rummaged in the bag, then glanced around in a temper. "Where in hell did I put those marker pens?"

KANE PULLED UP in the parking spot outside Quorn Fine Arts and Antiquities, turned off the engine, leaned his elbow on the window and stared at the Closed sign in the door.

Leaving the truck, he approached the shop, watching his reflection in the window as he drew closer. What he saw was a tall, well-built figure in blue jeans and a light grey hoodie, someone you could trust had the youth and strength to race into your burning house and emerge with the occupants slung over his shoulder; someone who would go to any lengths to protect his family from those bent on harming or corrupting them.

Placing his hand against the glass, he peered inside. It was too dark to see anything beyond the lamps, books and small tables in the window, but it was quite obvious the shop was empty.

After taking a furtive look up and down the street, he stole into the narrow alley that ran down the right side of the shop. The alley led to a small courtyard, a graveyard for busted furniture, empty packing boxes and general trash. At the rear of the courtyard was a small, ivy-covered garage with the door hanging off its hinges. Weeds as high as his knees grew from between the cracks in the paving.

Kane tried the back door. Locked. Next was the garage. As with the courtyard, the garage was packed with scraps of furniture, empty boxes and trash. There was no room for a car, and judging by the thick layer of dust and the cobwebs hanging from the ceiling and connecting all the junk, no one had been in there in months, perhaps years.

Turning back to the shop, he looked up at the second storey, where there were two windows. And one was open.

Scanning the scene with the eye of a firefighter, he calculated that by climbing onto the fence and pulling himself up the drainpipe, he could make it to the window. There was a small ledge there, which would afford him just enough of a footing to push the window all the way up and climb inside.

Within a few minutes, Kane had executed his plan and was entering the top floor of Wilfred's shop.

He switched on his torch. Half the floor space was taken up by packing cases and second-hand furniture, some plastered with red SOLD stickers. Against the far wall was a small kitchen, beside which stood a square table, two white plastic chairs and, a little further along, a closed door with a male/female sticker on it. To Kane's left was a staircase that led to the shop floor below.

As he approached the head of the stairs, he heard a noise that sent a shiver trickling down his spine. Rats, he thought with disgust. He stared at a stack of crates. More nasty, filthy rats. Unable to help himself, he went to see what they were up to.

The black thing that raised its head and yowled when the light hit it was no rat. It was a cat: a wild, skinny thing, with green eyes, a long tail and matted hair. As Kane played his torch over it, the beast hissed and spat at him, flicking its tail from left to right, hitting the crates on either side. The cat was defending a treasure, a pile of meat and bones that used to be an animal – a bird, by the look of it. There were feathers all over the place. Blood and guts had slipped and dripped down the crate, forming a small pool on the floor.

"Bon appétit," he muttered, and turned back to the stairs.

Behind him, the cat returned to its meal. Crunching bones, chomping on bloody flesh, it purred like a machine, like it was the happiest cat on the planet.

Downstairs, the shop was dark and quiet. It reeked of mildew and dust, the kind of smell you'd expect from the house of a crazy pensioner who lived in flannel pyjamas amongst hoarded newspapers, magazines, bags of old clothes and boxes of accumulated junk. Junk was the right word, Kane thought as he flashed the light around the store. This was the type of rubbish that usually appeared on people's verges – the stuff that was still there when the garbage truck came around.

Slipping behind the counter, he rifled through the drawers. Rubbish again. Not even interesting rubbish. Nothing that suggested zombies or monsters.

At the back of the store was a door that led to a tiny office. Inside the office was a rolltop desk, a brown leather swivel chair and built-in shelves loaded with books. On the wall above the desk was a message board, with so many Post-it notes pinned to it that none of the cork was visible.

Kane switched on the desk lamp. Next to the grubby PC was an A4 sheet of paper, a things-to-do list. Shaking off the pen, he held it under the light.

Things to Do (it was headed):

1) Ring Mr. Stevens – delivery Thursday?
2) London, Sunday 11 a.m. – St James Place – Augustine's Globe, Louis XIV chair, books
3) Snyder – chapel/Friday – reminder *Logan

4) J. St. – transfer rem funds

5) Slithium, antrebella, hooves, glim moss, salamander eyes – ring
    Mad Marvin

More indecipherable crap. Dropping the list on the keyboard, Kane's eye was caught by a single sheet of notepaper, on which were written the words, 'Cafe Merlot', along with the restaurant's address. Under that was his brother's name: DYLAN GATES. The words were underlined so many times, the pen had ripped through the page. When Kane lifted the notepaper and inspected the desk below, he saw the pen had scored deep cuts into the wood.

"Jesus, Dylan," he cursed, running his finger over the marks, "what have you gotten yourself into?"

"YOU UTTER IMBECILE!" snapped Wilfred. "Wrong again! The sign must be done precisely as I described! Can you possibly be any stupider?"

Wilfred and Dylan were standing on either side of the stainless-steel table, hovering over the dead vagrant. The corpse was now on its back, arms by its sides, and it was inscribed from head to toe with symbols from Wilfred's notebook. Scattered on the floor, among the candles spewing yellow smoke, were half a dozen black marker pens.

"I'm trying!" yelled Dylan, squeezing his hands into fists. "We've done it a thousand times! It's not working!"

"Impatient whelp! If you do the sign correctly, it will work! Concentrate while I repeat the spell."

Wilfred closed his eyes and began the chant:

"Per Adonai Eloim, Adonai Jehova,

Adonai Sabaoth, Metraton On Agla Mathon,

verbum pythonicum, mysterium salamandrae,

conventus sylvorum, antra gnomorum,

daemonia Coeli God, Almonsin, Gibor, Jehosua,

Evam, Zariatnatmik. Veni, veni, veni!"

His eyes sprang open and he stared expectantly at the corpse. When he saw nothing had changed, his face creased into a scowl.

Dylan, his head down, was playing with his phone.

"Why aren't you making the sign of Gor?"

Dylan opened a spam email about a sale at an online shoe store. "You've been saying that spell for two hours," he sighed, scrolling through the message. "Hey, they're pretty cool!" he cried. "What do you think, boss?" He raised his phone. "Maybe you should buy them to replace the ones you got blood all over."

"That's how long it takes."

"Huh?"

"That's how long it takes."

"How long what takes?"

"The blasted spell!"

"Oh right: that." He went back to his phone. "Why?"

"What do you mean, 'Why'?"

"Why does the stupid thing take so long?"

"Because if it was simple, every simpleton would be doing it. Now put that thing away and make the blasted sign!"

He watched while Dylan, curling his lip, slipped the phone back into his pocket. He made a half-hearted sign of Gor over the body.

"You've got to wait till I say the spell!"

The minutes ticked by. Wilfred chanted. Dylan made the sign of Gor. He was cold and bored, and his arms felt like they were about to drop off. This was the first time they'd attempted a spell from the Necronomicon and he'd expected a lot more from it. Maybe the book was a dud.

He was gathering the nerve to call it a night when one of the dogs began howling like a wolf. He turned his head towards the sound and was startled by a flash of lightning that lit up the cracks between the shutters. This was quickly followed by a thunderous boom that shook the building, dislodging dust and cobwebs from the ceiling.

"I hear you!" screeched Wilfred, his eyes raised. "I hear you! Hear me too!"

The shutters rattled furiously. Both dogs were now barking and yelping in a frenzy. A door banged over and over again as wind sped around the building.

Suddenly a shutter broke loose and the chill wind came bursting into the nave, hitting Dylan like a wave of ice. Shivering with cold and fear, he stood rooted to the spot, unable to pull his eyes away from Wilfred, who seemed charged with electricity, running up and down the length of the table chanting, "In virtute Hatheg-Kla! In virtute Hatheg-kla!"

Suddenly he stopped.

"Behold!" he cried, spreading his arms over the corpse. "The Messenger doth appear! Look! Look!"

Resting his hands on its stomach, Wilfred turned his wrinkled face to Dylan with boyish glee. "It's here!"

To Dylan's surprise, the corpse was moving; or rather, something inside its bloated belly was moving. Fascinated by the trembling flesh, he leaned in for a closer look.

All of a sudden, the body gave out a loud farting noise, and bubbles of air escaped from its mouth, moving its lips, making it appear like it was trying to talk. The foul smell blew up Dylan's nose, causing him to gag, stagger back and cough so hard he almost threw up.

"Christ!" he cried, his hand pressed over his nose. "What's happening?"

Wilfred was unaffected by the stench. Ignoring Dylan's question, he moved his mouth close to the dead man's ear. "My friend," he murmured, "you have acquitted yourself admirably. Now it is time to open the gate."

Standing erect, he chanted:

"Na'ai-ka'ulh-mi'groh-Yog-Sothoth-a'reyh – Yah!
Na'ai-ka'ulh-mi'groh-Yog-Sothoth-a'reyh – Yah!"

The corpse twitched. Wilfred, encouraged, raised his arms and chanted faster:

"Na'ai-ka'ulh-mi'groh-Yog-Sothoth-a'reyh – Yah!
Na'ai-ka'ulh-mi'groh-Yog-Sothoth-a'reyh – Yah!
Na'ai-ka'ulh-mi'groh-Yog-Sothoth-a'reyh – Yah!"

The wind went on racing through the chapel, rattling the eaves, banging the broken shutter, blowing dust and yellow smoke throughout the room and into Dylan's eyes and mouth. Outside, a deeper sound rumbled, shaking the air, growing louder by the second. Something was coming. The dogs knew it, and had increased their frantic barking and howling.

Abandoning the corpse, Dylan ran to the window and tried to secure the shutter. It pulled with uncommon strength at his hand, refusing to close. It seemed to have a life of its own, a part in this insane ritual.

Glancing over his shoulder, he could see Wilfred was flagging, leaning for support on the table, struggling to continue the chant. Sweat streamed down his face; his limbs trembled. But after a brief rest, he raised his head, raised his hands and started up the chant again, pausing every so often to place his ear against the dead man's stomach to make sure that whatever was happening in there was still happening.

Surely he can't keep this up, thought Dylan. He'll have a heart attack if this goes on much longer.

But on went the chanting. Wilfred was like a man possessed. Veins bulged in his forehead; his beady eyes shone with mania. He seemed to have forgotten Dylan was there.

When the corpse emitted a long burp from its dead lips, Wilfred jumped and yelped with glee.

Then the unbelievable happened. The body sat bolt upright, its eyelids flying open. For a few seconds, the eyes stared ahead in stark terror; then the muscles relaxed, and the corpse fell back and returned to its lifeless state. The wind died, the banging and rumbling subsided, the dogs went quiet. All was still, apart from the dust falling from the ceiling and Wilfred panting and nodding his head over the prostrate figure.

Dylan felt like he'd awoken from a nightmare. He was reminded of his grandfather's stories of LSD-induced visions, and wondered whether that's what had just happened. Had Wilfred spiked his drink? Then he remembered he hadn't drunk anything since arriving at the farm.

"Is it …?" he began, stepping closer.

The corpse started moving again, silencing him. At first it looked like a bunch of snakes squirming together in the dead man's belly; then, very quickly, the movements became violent. The black symbols Wilfred had drawn on it began to smoke and bubble, burning into its skin like brands. To his horror, Dylan heard noises that sounded like bones cracking and organs squelching and bursting.

He backed away, his mind reeling with dread at the thought of what might come next. When his back hit against the wall, he stopped and gaped at what was happening on the table.

The corpse was getting fatter, inflating like a balloon. Whatever was growing inside it squirmed and struggled like it was impatient to break free. As the body grew larger and rounder, the crunching and bursting noises subsided until all Dylan could hear was an awful squishing sound that made him think of jellyfish.

Before long, the corpse was an impossible size, unrecognisable from the man it had once been: a gigantic leathery egg.

All this time, Wilfred had been murmuring to himself, his eyes squeezed shut. His hands were pressed against his chest, and Dylan could see he was holding onto a charm, a charm that had been hanging on a chain behind his shirt.

The inflation slowed. For a while, the thing lay rocking from side to side. Then it stopped. Wilfred opened his eyes.

The corpse jerked. Suddenly it shuddered violently and almost rolled off the table. Wilfred put out his hands to steady it, and the next moment a curved talon broke through where the man's sternum would have been, turned in a half circle, and dragged itself down the skin. The talon clinked as it met the metal of the table, and then the skin peeled like a banana and fell away, revealing something huge and red that bucked and writhed and began to unfurl.

Before Dylan could see what it was, the thing flopped onto the floor on the other side of the table.

Wilfred rushed to investigate, while Dylan, his hands pressed against the wall, listened to whatever was scrambling about in the darkness. He could tell from the ecstatic look on Wilfred's face that the old man wasn't disappointed with the results of his labours.

Soon enough, the creature emerged, rose to its full height and turned, and Dylan could see what had impressed the wizard. It was garnet-red and hairy, the size of a small horse – but more than anything, it resembled a bloated, bloody wasp. Its eight bony legs ended in curved claws, and in place of a face, the monster had a ragged mouth that exploded with squirming red tentacles. A series of black spines ran the length of its body, which ended in a long tail.

As Dylan watched in awe and horror, the creature extended four leathery black wings and flapped them to shake out the creases. Its mouthful of tentacles quivered, and it released an unearthly screech unlike anything Dylan had ever heard before. The noise propelled him to the door, where he stood trembling and panting and rubbing the smoke and dust from his eyes.

Wilfred, however, was standing up to the beast like a superhero or a sacrifice. Holding out the charm – which Dylan could see was a talisman in the shape of a beetle – he cried, "Submit! Submit! I command it! Stand down!"

The thing screeched at him, lurched to the side, and launched itself at the window where Dylan had battled the shutter. The opening was too small for it to squeeze through, but that didn't stop it from trying. After a few attempts to batter the wall with its body, making the entire chapel shudder and creak, it changed tactics and began ripping away the wood with its claws.

"Stop! Stop!" cried Wilfred, holding up the talisman, to no avail.

Before long, the creature had ripped a hole in the wall large enough for it to squeeze through. Twisting its wasp-like body, dragging itself outside, it began climbing up the side of the chapel.

Wilfred rushed to the hole and poked his head through, still holding out the talisman.

"Damnation, it's climbing all the way to the roof." He spun around to Dylan, who was still at the door. "Get out there!" he yelled, waving his arms at him. "Get after it!"

He peered through the hole again. "Get back here!" he shouted, shaking the talisman at the thing.

Pulling his head in, he rushed past Dylan and out the door. Dylan stumbled after him, and together they watched the beast drag itself onto the peaked roof, where it stood silhouetted against the night sky, the tiles it had dislodged dropping to the ground in a succession of clatters.

"What's it doing?" asked Dylan.

"It can't fly on wet wings," Wilfred murmured to himself. "They need to dry."

He was right. The creature's wings were stretched wide on either side of its body, glistening in the light of the gibbous moon. Like a baby bird, it seemed uncertain of its ability to fly, though it was eager to try. One by one it lifted its bony legs, shook the moisture from its wings, stretched its dark-red body towards the stars.

All of a sudden the rotten tiles broke away underfoot, and with a screech, the thing slipped and scrambled and tumbled down the roof, fell through the air and dropped with a thump to the ground. With tiles raining down, it clambered to its feet and bounded away, screaming like a banshee, still flapping its wings.

Wilfred grabbed Dylan's arm hard, pulling him down. "Go after it!" he roared in his ear.

"What?" cried Dylan, jerking his arm away. "Do I look stupid? That's a god! I'm not chasing after a god!"

Wilfred threw up his hands. "How can you be so –? That's not Yog-Sothoth, you fish-brained dolt! It's a Messenger! Now go bring it back!"

Dylan stepped back. "Are you insane? What do you expect me to do with it?"

"Do what I'm paying you for. Now get!"

"You're not paying me anything."

"Get!"

Dylan placed his hands on his head, trying to figure out exactly what Wilfred was expecting him to do. "I'm supposed to catch that thing and drag it back here?"

Wilfred was tapping the talisman against his palm. Shaking his head in annoyance, he glanced up and saw Dylan was still there. "Get!" he barked.

Dylan slipped his hand into his pocket and stroked his phone, trying to gather the nerve to pull it out and call the police. He knew Wilfred would never let him do that, but he also knew the monster was out of control, clearly dangerous, and needed to be stopped.

Dropping the talisman, Wilfred stared at him as if he could read his thoughts. "Very well," he grunted. "You're a fish-brained, hog-livered titmouse, but … have it your way. When you find it, put it down with the powder of Vraith, like I showed you. We'll have to raise another." He flicked the talisman. "After I find out how to make this useless scrap of metal work."

Turning around, he placed his hands on his hips and huffed at the busted chapel. "What a damn mess. Next time, I'll get Snyder to build a cage. Hell and damnation, I'll need another corpse!"

Dylan wracked his brain, trying to remember the Vraith thing. When Wilfred explained it to him, he'd only half attended.

"Why are you still here?" cried Wilfred, shoving him towards his car. "The longer you loaf around, the more people will die."

"Die? What do you mean, die?"

"What do you think I mean? The Messenger has to eat to grow. How else did you think it fulfils its purpose?" His eyes opened wide and he hit the palm of his hand against his forehead. "Of course! That's why it took off. I should have had offerings. Why didn't you remind me to have offal at hand?"

Dylan felt a creeping dread about what he'd gotten himself into. He glanced over his shoulder at the chapel, where the stretched skin of a dead man lay on a mortuary table, his insides having come to life and run off to eat people.

With a shaky voice, not really sure he wanted to know, he asked, "What's its purpose?"

Wilfred sneered at him. "What did you think was the purpose of the Messenger?"

"I thought you wanted to ask it things."

"Ah, my young friend," Wilfred cackled, "the bounds of your imbecility are limitless."

As usual, his insults went right over Dylan's head. "I didn't think people were gonna die."

"They wouldn't have had to, if this damned talisman had worked like that fool said it would. But they will … and they are. Being devoured right now, if our friend is doing its job. So get yourself after it."

Dylan stared helplessly at him. "I – uh –"
Wilfred squinted at him.
"I need …"
"Well? What is it?"
Dylan squirmed. "We've been here for … I need to, um …"
"Spit it out!"
He nodded at the farmhouse. "Can I go bathroom first?"

13

Dragon attack

CLAUDE AND LILA Barry only ever left Jacob's End when they needed to shop for supplies, or when Lila borrowed books from Quorn Public Library. There was nothing else of interest to them in town. They had no family or friends there, and in truth, most people in town thought them rather queer, and weren't shy at gossiping about them in loud whispers as they went about their business. It had been almost two years since that episode at the garage (when Claude was arrested for waving a tyre iron at the incompetent mechanic) and the Quorn Service Station had changed hands since then, but towns like Quorn have a long memory.

The Barrys were one of the oldest families in the county, having lived at Jacob's End for as long as records had been kept. They were here when the blight came a century ago, and after the creeping death had finished its work, the surviving family members drifted back, their entire wealth and history being tied to this tiny village. These days, the Barry clan survived mostly on welfare and lived an isolated life where their only relationships were with each other.

Today, Claude and Lila had been away from home for almost six hours. They were in Quorn for an hour or so, buying groceries and exchanging library books, and left for home at the usual time. But as their old Ford Cortina chugged up the second of the Six Hills, steam began shooting from the bonnet, and the car sputtered and died. It was almost an hour before another car appeared on the road, and then another hour before a tow truck arrived from Quorn. Then there was the long wait at the service station while the car was being fixed.

It was now past sunset and they were on Deep Ocean Road and anxious to get home. Claude glanced at his wife, who was staring straight ahead, her face glowing in the light of the dashboard, her straight blonde hair appearing almost translucent. Her face had weathered well over the years, he was thinking. She looked great for sixty-something. Then again, when there was little to smile or frown about, and when you spent most of every day reading historical romances in bed, leaving your put-upon husband to do all the cleaning and cooking and caring for your son, there wasn't much exertion or wrinkling of the skin to crease a person's face.

"Don't fret, Mother," Claude said, scratching the stubble under his chin. "Ormy will be having his kip. He won't even know we're not there."

Lila turned her head stiffly on her neck. She didn't say a word, but Claude knew that look. She kept her eyes fixed on him long enough to make sure he really did know it.

Ormond Barry recently turned forty-four, but his family had never stopped treating him like a baby. From an early age he had a fascination with the ocean, claiming invisible friends lived out beyond the reef, where the seabed fell away and the water ran deep and black. Most days he could be found at the water's edge, talking to himself in a strange language or listening with his head cocked. His mother took to calling him 'Seachild', and the name persisted to this day, as had Ormy's fascination with the waves and whatever dwelt beneath them.

Until recently, Ormy had accompanied his folks on their visits to Quorn. He didn't like people or noise or change, but there were two things about Quorn he did like. He'd begin the day by enjoying a double chocolate sundae at Daisy's Milk Bar (no nuts or sprinkles if you wanted to have a peaceful drive home), and then, while Lila chose her books and Claude bought supplies from the grocer's and hardware store, Ormy would visit the animal shelter to pet the cats. But a few weeks back, something happened to change all that. A little way out of Jacob's End, on a blank stretch of road in the middle of nowhere, Ormy started whining. By the time they reached the Six Hills, he was wailing and writhing in fear. He wasn't able to say what had terrified him, but from that moment on, nothing – no promise of ice cream or the soft fur or gentle purring of cats – would convince him to leave the safety and comfort of Jacob's End. Lately he'd grown increasingly fond of pottering around the abandoned sheds, mumbling to himself and making friends with the dead birds, so his parents comforted themselves with the knowledge he'd found other interests to occupy his time.

"Don't worry, Ormy," Claude said, as if his son could hear him from all these miles away. "We'll be home soon."

To fill the silence, he switched on the radio. A soft rock-country Christian song came on, and accompanied them as the car motored through the barren landscape, the lone vehicle on this long, dark road. Figuring the song might soothe his wife's nerves, he turned up the volume.

Lila mumbled something.

"Wha?" grunted Claude.

"… on the road," said Lila, leaning forward.

He switched off the radio. His eyes weren't what they used to be, but when he squinted he saw something black blocking the road ahead. He squinted harder. Whatever it was, it was the size of a large car. But it wasn't a car. It was moving like it was alive.

Pressing his foot on the brake, turning the steering wheel, he pulled over.

"What is it?" whispered Lila, her eyes like spotlights.

Claude took his glasses from the glove compartment, put them on, moved his face close to the windscreen. The moon was obscured by cloud, and the headlights didn't quite reach the thing, but from here it looked like a mountain of rocks and branches.

"I don't –" he began, and then the clouds dispersed and moonlight fell upon the road. The thing raised its head.

Lila screamed the way she'd done through the worst parts of her son's birth. Claude was mesmerised by the mass of writhing red tentacles, and it took an enormous effort of will to pull his eyes away and slam the car into gear. Without another look at the thing, he did the quickest three-point turn of his life.

Speeding away, he glanced in the rear-view mirror. The monster was now standing up to its full height, its body a long black silhouette against the charcoal-grey of the evening sky. When it spread out huge leathery wings, his heart rate doubled, and a sudden constriction in his chest made him grunt in pain.

Lila dug her fingernails into his arm. "What's happening?" she shrieked in his face. "What's it doing? What's it doing?"

The thing's head reminded Claude of a sea anemone. A gooey, shiny liquid was dripping from its tentacles to the road, and all he could think about was blood: blood on its mouth; blood on the road; blood on whatever it was eating.

"Don't worry," he assured Lila, prying her fingers from his arm, trying to keep his voice steady. "We're safe. Just have to make it round this corner."

But the monster would prove him a liar. As Claude watched in horror, it began hopping along the road towards them, using its folded wings like crutches. After hopping a few metres, it came to a stop.

The monster receded in the rear-view mirror, Claude staring back at it in disbelief. He shook the steering wheel. "It's stopped!" he yelled with glee. "We made it! We bloody-well made it!"

Lila, who had been staring at him in terror, turned her stare to the road behind them. She choked out a strangled cry.

Claude glanced in the mirror in time to see the thing leaping into the air. Flapping its wings, it rose heavily, fighting against gravity, following the line of the road. Its tail curled beneath its body, and Claude gasped when he saw the tail ended in what appeared to be three giant stingers.

Lila leaned into the back seat, unable to pull her eyes away from the thing. "It's flying!" she cried. "Oh, my Lord, it's flying! What is it? It's flying! It's chasing us! What is it?"

Claude's eyes were locked on the rear-view mirror.

"It's flying! What is it? What is it?"

"Shut up! You're not helping things!"

She dug her nails in his arm again. "What in blazes is it?"

"It's …" It suddenly became clear to him. "… a dragon."

She turned her head. "I can't see it! Where is it? Where is it? I can't see it!"

"Good. It's gone."

Lila pressed her cheek against the window.

"It's gone," Claude repeated, louder this time, nodding in agreement with himself.

Her body went rigid. "No, it's not! It's coming up behind us! It's catching up! … catching up!"

Claude leaned closer to the mirror. There was nothing there.

"It's too fast for this old bomb!"

"You're being hysterical. It's not there. Sit back and shut up."

As usual, she ignored him. "Go faster! Go, go, go, go, go! Go faster!"

"I can't go any faster."

"Put your stupid foot down!"

"What do you think I'm doing?"

"Not enough, as usual." She gasped. "Oh, Lord Jesus! I said go faster!"

Their eyes met. Time froze. With an almighty bang, the roof caved in.

STOPPING THE CAR by the side of the White Horse Farm road, Dylan rested his forearms on the steering wheel. He had no idea where the Messenger was. It could be anywhere by now.

He dug in his pocket and pulled out the talisman Wilfred had given him. It looked like a shiny beetle, with a round body and five asymmetrical legs. The thing was hollow and had some kind of herb or fungus in it that smelt like a swamp. He turned it over, smelt it again, wrinkled his nose. What was he supposed to do with it?

He replayed the conversation with Wilfred in his head.

"This will show you the way," the wizard told him, placing the talisman in his hand.

"How does it work?"

"It shows you the way."

"You already said that. How does it work?"

"You'll see."

"Does it glow or … get hot when I get close?"

"Not to my knowledge."

"What does it do then?"

"How should I know?"

"Because, er … you gave it to me."

"So you assume that means I know how it works? Do I know every-thing? Now be off. You're wasting precious time."

"You said it would lead me to it."

"It will."

"But how?"

Wilfred was getting frustrated with him. "Trust the talisman."

"Trust the talisman?"

"Trust the talisman."

"How can I trust it when I don't know how it works?"

"Just go. Then you can tell *me* how it works."

So off he went.

He shook it. "Lead me to your master," he ordered in Bela Lugosi's voice. The beetle was no more responsive than a piece of costume jewellery. Sighing, he fastened the chain around his neck. Maybe the thing worked better that way.

After waiting a few seconds for any clues to the beast's whereabouts, Dylan shook his head in bewilderment, put the car in gear, and took off again.

A little further down the road, his attention was drawn to the field on his right. He slowed to a stop, lowered the window, leaned into the night and glanced around. There was nothing out there. He hadn't seen or heard anything, and there was nothing to see or hear now. It was an unremarkable tract of land, flat and featureless, no animals or move-ment of any kind evident. But Dylan felt an irresistible urge to turn the car off the road and drive towards the distant rise. The feeling was hard to explain – it was like the craving a starving man might feel on spotting a table laid with plates of hot meat.

His mouth curled into a smile. We're connected, he thought. That's what the talisman does. With a sense of pleasure greater than anything he could ever remember feeling, he turned the car in that direction.

Having surrendered to the craving, Dylan was on a high. He leaned over the steering wheel and pressed his foot hard on the accelerator, and the Honda sped up and jumped and banged as it flew over the uneven ground. Normally this would have terrified him, but right now he had an urge to go even faster, to leave the ground and shoot into the air like a supersonic missile. I'll explode if I don't get to that thing soon, he thought as he egged the car on.

Approaching a wire fence, he held firmly onto the steering wheel, bracing himself for the impact. As the car crashed through, he spied white shapes dotted across the land, and guessed from the crunches as he drove over them that the shapes were bones. Bouncing over bumps and hollows, a sudden vision rose in his mind of the Messenger devouring terrified sheep on the way through. It pinned them down with its razor-sharp talons, spat out corrosive saliva, then sucked up the soup of meat and guts with its tentacled mouth. He could see the image as clear as day, as if it were a memory of something he'd actually witnessed.

To his right, near a broken fence, was a large pile of bones. Dylan jerked the steering wheel in that direction, but the car kept going, sliding across the damp grass, unresponsive to his efforts to correct its motion. He pressed his foot on the brake, spun the wheel, regained control, sped up, and the Honda flew through the opening in the fence, scattering bones and landing with a squeal of metal against the bitumen road. The car bounced on its tyres, bounced again, and came to a stop in the ditch opposite.

He was back on Deep Ocean Road. He looked over his left shoulder, then his right. There, in the middle of the road, was a pile of blood and guts, melted over wool and bones. The Messenger was disturbed, Dylan thought as he backed up the car. Someone came along and it gave chase. I'm close.

He was right. Further along, around a bend in the road, was the Barrys' car.

INSIDE THE CRUSHED Cortina, Lila was cringing under the glove compartment, screeching in terror as the monster banged and tore at the metal above her head. Beside her, Claude was frantically trying to start the stalled car.

"Shut up, shut up, shut up, shut up," he chanted as he turned the key again and again in the ignition. "You're making it madder."

"Don't tell me to shut up," his wife shot back, slapping his knee.

Claude frowned at her. Then a razor-sharp talon broke through the roof, and she started screeching all over again.

"Run!" he yelled, pulling on the handle and pushing his shoulder against the door. But the Messenger had bent the frame of the car. The doors were jammed. They were trapped like kippers in a can.

In a last-ditch effort, Claude tried the ignition again. To his amazement and relief, the engine burst into life. For a moment, he was stunned. He grinned dumbly at his wife.

"Go!" she screeched, slapping him again.

When he slammed his foot on the accelerator, the car took off so fast it felt like there were only two tyres touching the road.

As the vehicle pulled out from beneath it, the Messenger overbalanced, lost its grip on the roof, fell and rolled onto the road. In a flash, it was on its feet, flapping its wings, lifting its bloated body into the air, speeding after them.

Claude watched in the rear-view mirror as it flew low towards them. "Damn thing! … Give up! … Eat sheep!" he muttered. "Leave us the hell alone!"

The monster ignored him. It appeared to have acquired a taste for humans, and was no longer interested in the sheep that stood like silent ghosts in the fields to their left and right.

It didn't take long to catch up to them.

"Hold on," Claude warned his screaming wife, and hugged the steering wheel.

The Messenger slammed into the boot, forcing the front wheels into the air. Sparks flew as the car spun in a half circle and came to a stop.

Smashing through the rear window, it began dragging itself into the car.

DYLAN SPED AFTER them, watched as the Messenger caught the Cortina, slammed on his brakes. The Honda skidded, coming to a stop in the middle of the road.

He gaped in horror at the scene ahead. The monster had grown to three times its original size. Wilfred had warned him the thing was ravenous, but he hadn't said it would grow this fast. How much larger would it get if given the chance? And how much destruction would it cause once it grew so vast nothing could stand in its way? It was called a Messenger, but what kind of message was it carrying besides death and destruction?

Grabbing the flask of red powder from the seat beside him, Dylan pushed open the door, clambered out, and ran towards the Barrys.

He stopped a safe distance away and watched as the Messenger fought to drag its body into the battered car. He couldn't see through the darkened windows, couldn't see how many people were inside the Cortina, but it was obvious the killer was intent on consuming whoever was there. He had to act quickly.

With a trembling hand, he pulled from his pocket a crumpled page of notepaper. "Reyh'a-Yog-Sothoth-groh'mi-ulh'ka-ai'na – Yah! Reyh'a-Yog-Sothoth-groh'mi –" he read in a throaty voice.

The Messenger froze. Responding to Dylan's chant, it began pushing and pulling its hairy body and bony legs out of the car.

Once free and standing on the road, it turned towards him, let out a scream and started advancing. As Dylan watched in awe, it spat out a long stream of saliva.

"Yipes!" he cried, sidestepping the corrosive liquid. Oh shit, he thought, backing away; this damn spell better work or I'm soup.

The Messenger was getting closer.

"Reyh'a-Yog-Sothoth-groh'mi-ulh'ka-ai'na – Yah!" he cried, walking backwards. "Reyh'a-Yog-Sothoth-groh'mi-ulh'ka-ai'na – Yah!"

The spell seemed to be working. The Messenger was faltering, its wings sagging, its legs struggling to pull its fat, hairy abdomen along the bitumen. A succession of long screeches attested to its rage and frustration.

Dylan raised the flask. "Reyh'a-Yog-Sothoth-groh'mi-ulh'ka-ai'na – Yah! Reyh'a-Yog-Sothoth-groh'mi-ulh'ka-ai'na – Yah!"

In a last-ditch effort, the giant wings flapped, the eight legs tensed and sprang, the long red body rose in the air. At the same time, Dylan reached back and threw the flask with all his might. Dropping to the road, covering his head with his arms, he waited for the talons to sink into his back.

He heard the glass smash – a devilish shriek – a sloshing sound as something thick and wet hit the road. Then silence. The smell of fresh meat and offal washed over him.

Slowly he moved his arms away from his eyes. He peered under his armpit. Spread across the road, from where the Messenger had taken off to the heels of his boots, were gobs of blood and chunks of guts and bones: the remains of the dead itinerant and all the animals the Messenger had dissolved and devoured. The stench of it made Dylan gag.

Climbing to his feet, he turned his eyes to the squashed and broken car. Two white faces were pressed against the driver's-side window. Their eyes rolled over the mess on the road, before coming to rest on Dylan.

He shrugged and gave them an awkward wave.

14

Aftermath

ERCHED ON THE edge of the sofa, fists on his knees, Kane moved his gaze from the Dylan on the TV screen to the one kneeling on the carpet next to him. They both looked the same: skinny frame, pale face, blue eyes, long black hair. They were dressed the same, in Dylan's characteristic black long-sleeved top, black jeans and black boots. The main difference was that one Dylan was smiling, while the other was frowning. It was like his brother had been split into the opposing sides of his personality: the angel and the devil.

The serious Dylan, the one on TV, nodded at a microphone. "I got there after it happened," he explained in a deeper-than-normal voice.

The reporter, a young woman in a cream chiffon shirt and textured grey woollen pants, seemed disappointed. "You can't tell us anything about the attack?"

"All I saw was a beat-up car and lotsa blood and stuff."

"You didn't see a flying dragon?" she coaxed.

Dylan shook his head, his eyes wide with innocence. "Looked to me like a case of car versus sheep. They broke through the fence and escaped onto the road, you know. It was a fat mess."

The reporter, nodding, turned to the camera. "Dragon or simple car accident? You decide. This is Kyleen Jenkins, reporting for GTV Nightly News."

Snatching up the remote, Kane turned down the volume. He glared at the back of his brother's head. "Christ, Dylan! What did you do?"

Dylan placed two playing cards together on the coffee table. He was building a house of cards, listening to the news, but not watching it. Kane knew his brother hated having his picture taken, and guessed he had the same aversion to seeing himself on TV.

"Dylan!"

He picked up a ten of spades, held it above two sets of joined cards, slowly lowered it to form a bridge. He picked up another. "Don't knock the table," he warned.

"You almost killed somebody."

"Don't be melodramatic."

"I saw what happened … the car … the –"

"Nothing happened to them. I had the reversal spell. It was all fine."

Kane shook with anger. He'd always known Dylan was stubborn and uncaring, but this was verging on psychopathy.

"I saw the car," he said again, trying not to yell. "That thing almost got them."

"Almost. Didn't. Two different things."

"You need to stop this."

Dylan poked out his tongue. "We've – only – just – begun," he said as he carefully placed two more cards together on top of the bridge.

Unable to sit still any longer, Kane jumped up and paced the room. He couldn't stop thinking about how close Dylan had come to being mixed up in a murder – a double murder. And he was telling him it was nothing to worry about. He bit his lip. Were his brother's bad attitude and foul moods more than adolescent angst? Was he disturbed? Mentally ill?

He'd been planning to save his ace until he had more evidence, but Dylan's blasé attitude was scaring him. He needed to shock a human response out of him.

"I checked into that creep you've been hanging out with," he said from the other side of the room. "There's records of a Wilfred Waite going back to the eighteen-hundreds."

"Told you he was old."

"You're not trying to tell me it's the same dude?"

"Dude?" He fell back with laughter.

Kane went up and stood over him. "Grow up, Dylan. This isn't a joke. I think that guy had something to do with what happened to our parents."

At this, Dylan sat up and took notice. His face twisted into a scowl. "That's a lie."

"You may not believe it, but the police might."

His brother stared up at him, trying to read if he was serious or not. Kane held his gaze.

"Hey, look," Dylan said: "don't go doing anything stupid. Wilfred has the Necronomicon, the most powerful book on the planet. You think he can't defend himself?"

"Stay away from him then."

He returned to the cards. "I can't do that."

"Dylan …"

"We'll be more careful next time."

"What does that even mean?"

Dylan glanced up. "Why would you think Wilfred had something to do with … with the murders?"

"I went to his shop. Looked around. He had the name of the restaurant written down."

"Which restaurant?"

"Which one do you think?"

Dylan stared into space. "Is that it?" he asked at last.

"Isn't that enough?"

"He went to a restaurant. That doesn't mean he murdered anyone."

Kane resisted the urge to tell Dylan his own name was written below the name of the restaurant. It wasn't only that it creeped him out to even think about it; he was also concerned it might have the opposite effect to what he intended. It might make Dylan think he was more important to Wilfred than he really was.

"The guy's a psycho. And he's turning you into one."

Dylan crossed his eyes and wobbled his head.

"Don't be a child."

When his brother ignored him, Kane bumped the table with his leg, demolishing the house of cards.

"Hey! What did you go and do that for?"

Leaning over, he began collecting the scattered cards.

Kane fell into the chair opposite. He didn't know what else to say. He had no authority over Dylan. All he could do was yell and argue, and then watch his train-wreck of a brother throw his life away.

"What would Dad say if he was here? – if he knew you nearly killed somebody?"

Dylan picked up the last of the playing cards. "He's not here. And we won't be either in a few weeks."

"So that's it, hey? You're acting out cos we're losing the house?"

Dylan slammed the cards down on the table. "If that's what you think of me, maybe I'll move out right now!"

"And go where?" asked Kane, leaning forward. "To the farmhouse? To live with a creepy old man who might have had something to do with our parents getting killed?"

"He didn't. They were murdered by randoms."

"Randoms? Who stabs two strangers randomly? Takes their money and drags them into an alley?"

"Wilfred is helping me."

"He's using you."

"He's helping me cast a good luck spell so we can save the house."

"And how's that going? The good luck?" He glanced about the room. "I don't see much good luck happening around here."

Dylan flicked through the pile of cards. He looked spooked, confused, out of smart-alec retorts. Maybe I'm getting through that thick skull at last, thought Kane. Time to go easy on him.

"Listen, Dylan: we got a couple more months on the house."

He glanced up. "How?"

"I sold Mum's jewellery. And … my bikes. And followed up some of Dad's unpaid accounts."

"Your precious BMX bikes?"

"I kept one. You can only ride one at a time, hey?"

Dylan stared at him, his face unreadable.

"So let's sit down and work out a plan. A proper plan … that suits both of us." He got up and went back to the sofa. "Who needs good luck when you've got yourself a plan?"

Dylan didn't look convinced.

"You've gotta give it time, bro. Things'll get better." He picked up the remote and handed it to Dylan. "Brother's choice."

"Good things happen to good people," Dylan said, taking the remote from Kane's hand. "That's the last thing Mum said to me, you know." He turned up the volume, then placed the remote on the coffee table, next to the pile of cards. "So I guess I won't hold my breath."

15

On the trail

P ROFESSOR SIMON ORWELL scratched his fingernail at the hole in his desk. He was having a flashback to the day the hole was made. Three years ago, a bearded student in a beanie, angry at his grade on an exam paper, grabbed the professor's favourite letter opener and tried to stab his hand. People assume history students are bookworms – weak-kneed and indifferent to things that happen in the present – but history, like every other subject, has its share of lunatics.

The professor returned his attention to the newspaper that lay open in front of him. He pushed his reading glasses up his nose.

"You were looking for me, Simon?"

He glanced up. "Arika! Quelle surprise! Mrs Nakajima told me you weren't in today."

Arika was wearing what his students referred to as 'shabby chic': a white lace dress dotted with red flowers, and what he referred to as her 'pixie boots'. With her mahogany hair swept back and her dark olive complexion glowing with youthful vitality, she looked like a study for a painting by Rosetti.

The professor's eyes softened. He was a self-confessed 'crusty old fogey' who was fond of saying he wished the world had stayed in the eighteenth century, before the industrial revolution came along and messed everything up. He had snow-white hair, a long, deeply-lined face, sharp features and heavy-lidded blue eyes that seemed to rebuke everyone and everything around him. But each time his research assistant entered the room, a spark lit up his face and he radiated the warm blush of youth. In the professor's eyes, Arika Livingston represented the best the twenty-first century had to offer.

"My dear girl," he said, taking off his glasses, "you look ravishing. Come on in, before I have all the boys at my door."

Arika, smiling, shook her head at him. He knew she thought him misogynistic, his manners outdated, but he also knew she allowed him his quirks on the basis of his advanced age and burning intellect. Arika was smart, insightful, loyal and driven – exactly the type of daughter he would have hoped for, had he been prone to procreation during his younger years.

"How are you, Arika? Have you seen today's news?"

"No, I –"

"Perhaps you might close the door."

Simon spun the newspaper on the desk and pushed it towards her. He'd circled the article titled, 'Dragon Claim in Car Accident'.

Arika bent over the page. As she read the story, she slid into a seat. The professor sat quietly watching her face.

When she finished, he leaned back in his chair, palms raised. "Exciting, no?"

"A dragon with tentacles around its mouth."

"Grave robbings … a Messenger no less –"

"A *possible* Messenger. Maybe a disoriented bat and a few lost sheep."

Simon frowned. He was rarely excited over anything these days, and wanted desperately for Arika to share his enthusiasm.

"We ignore the signs at our peril," he stated, glancing at his watch.

"Hmmm, the car was crushed. Maybe it rolled."

"It happened outside of Quorn. What do you make of that?"

"Coincidence?" Seeing his earnest face, Arika had a sudden change of mind. "You're right," she said, springing up. "No such thing as coincidence. I better go check it out."

Simon held out a business card. "I have a good feeling about this one, Arika. It's our first real clue."

She took the card.

"The Gates boy. The witness. His address. I couldn't find the address of the couple who were attacked, but I'm sure you will find someone out there to direct you."

"Quorn. That's quite a drive."

"Would you like company?"

"No, you have far too much on. I'll be fine. I'll head out there now."

"Are you certain? I could reschedule a few classes."

"Don't trouble yourself, Simon. I can catch up on my podcasts on the way."

The professor pushed himself to his feet. His arthritis was playing up, but he tried not to show it. There's nothing the young hate more than old people whingeing about their aches and pains.

"Be careful, won't you, Arika? The boy's story contradicts what the occupants of the car claimed. If it *was* a Messenger, he might have been involved in its conjuring."

She gave the professor an evil smile. "Then my thesis will come in handy."

Simon had a moment of confusion.

"You haven't forgotten what my thesis was on?"

He raised a finger in the air. "Ah yes, of course: Truth, Lies and the Inquisition."

She went to the door. "The trick," she said, "is not to leave any marks."

Smiling, the professor collected his glasses and followed Arika out of the office.

Standing at his secretary's desk were a man and a woman, both wearing dark blue suits. Simon watched them as they watched Arika walk down the hallway.

"Sorry to keep you waiting," he said.

His words startled them. "Don't mention it," the man said, spinning around. "I'm Sam Morgan. This is my colleague, Cleo Grieves."

Simon looked him up and down. "National Security Office, was it?"

Morgan smiled at him. "I'm Director of Strategic Capability. Ms Grieves is my lead principal investigations officer."

"Pleased to meet you, Professor," said Grieves.

Simon nodded at her. "That accent," he said; "let me guess. I've been to most places on this planet and I rarely get it wrong." He thought for a moment. "Caribbean … of course. The island … would be … Jamaica."

Grieves smiled at him. "Very good, Professor. Dat's where me roots be."

He turned back to Morgan. "Strategic Capability, did you say? I'm not familiar with that directorate."

"You know about the NSO?"

"I make a point of keeping up with matters of national interest. The public policy of today is the history of tomorrow, I always like to say."

"It's fairly new."

"I don't recall reading about it in the annual report."

"Wow, you really *are* up to speed, aren't you?"

"What is your reporting line? I'd like to look you up."

Morgan stared right through him. "I'm sorry, Professor, we don't have much time. Can we …?" He gestured towards the professor's office.

Simon studied him. Something didn't feel right. The story in the papers didn't warrant a national security agency sending two senior officers to investigate. A phone call was the usual response to unexplained phenomena, and even then, the caller invariably sounded embarrassed and was quick to apologise for wasting his time.

"I understand you're after information regarding the so-called dragon that terrorised two unfortunates the other night."

"I know it's an unlikely story –" began Morgan.

"That it is."

"– but NSO policy is to follow up anything that might involve even the slightest threat to national security."

"Strategic Capability was your directorate?"

Morgan nodded.

"Capability in what, may I ask?"

"The capability to keep our country secure – from any threat, real or perceived."

"Of course. I presume this story fits within the 'perceived threat' category?"

"At this stage."

"So – excuse me for sounding dense – but remind me why you're here?"

"I'm told George University has a world-class reputation in matters of myth and superstition."

"No, you misunderstand. I meant, why you're here in person."

Morgan glanced at Grieves, who had a small smirk on her face. "We were down this way on another call, thought we'd pop in and meet you in person. Always helps to put a name to a face."

"Would you care to follow me? I have a class to take, but we can talk on the way."

The officers followed the professor down the hall.

The School of Historical and Philosophical Studies was housed in the oldest part of George University and the wing was in a state of near dilapidation, university funds being reserved for the more popular and contemporary courses of study. The rooms were poky, the parquet floors scuffed, the plaster walls cracked and peeling in places, but this didn't worry Simon Orwell. He was passionate about anything pre-twentieth century, and never felt more at home than when he was wandering these musty, hallowed halls.

"What was it you thought I might be able to help you with?" he asked as they passed a group of students in vigorous debate over a map of Europe in the Middle Ages.

"Well," Morgan began, "I understand you're an expert in ancient rites and religions."

"I do profess to know a little on the topic."

"As I understand it, you specialise in little-known cults."

"Like you, Mr Morgan, I enjoy playing detective. Popular history makes me yawn. The challenge for me is making known the unknown. So yes, 'little-known cults' as you call them are my specialty."

"Goodo."

"I don't see how this is connected with the incident the other night. Surely that was all a misunderstanding? – concussion, perhaps? Mental disturbance explains a lot of cultish behaviour."

"You would think so. But the couple involved are – for want of a better word – yokels. Limited intelligence. Living on welfare in the boondocks. Their description showed an unusually vivid imagination if it wasn't based on something they witnessed. Strange, I know. We did a search on the net and they ID'd a couple of things they thought might be the culprit. And then we came across your name. One of the things they pointed to was a winged creature that was supposed to have been summoned in ancient rites to clear the land in preparation for the coming of some kind of supernatural deity."

The professor stopped. "A Messenger."

"That's right."

"Why would you suppose it's a Messenger, rather than a more garden-variety dragon?"

Morgan smiled. "I'm not supposing it's anything at all."

"If that were true, you would not be here."

Morgan peered up at him like a penitent child. Professor Orwell stood at almost six foot four, and though bent with age, still towered over his two companions.

"You're right, Professor: there are other factors in this case. But I'm not authorised to discuss them."

Simon's ears pricked up. The officer was probably referring to the recent grave robbings, but he suspected there was more to their investigation than that.

"If you can't be completely forthcoming with me, Mr Morgan, then I don't know how I can be of assistance."

"We just need to know more about Messengers."

"You're not prepared to reveal the other facts that brought you here?"

"I'm afraid I can't."

"Messengers are fictitious creatures," stated the professor, walking on, disinclined to be of any greater assistance.

The officers followed. "Why are they called Messengers? What's their message?"

Simon stopped again. "The term is a little misleading. As you said, they are called to clear the way for the arrival of a deity." When the officers said nothing, he added, "Their role is to kill any living thing in the vicinity that may pose a threat to their god, or the emissaries of the god."

"What would a god need with that kind of protection?" asked Grieves. "I mean, if they're a god …"

The professor turned to her and adopted the tone he used for especially dumb students. "My dear, the gods the ancients worshipped are not gods in the sense you may be familiar with. Some are immortal, but even they can be hurt with the right kinds of rites and implements. The Messengers are their insurance policy." He started off again. "And a test. Only a true follower can summon them. The gods will not present for every trumped-up egomaniac who attempts a summoning spell."

"You talk as if all this is real," commented Morgan.

"Who's to say it isn't?"

"Does that mean you think a Messenger might have attacked that car?"

"No, I don't. If there was ever such a creature, there is no verifiable record of one. Nothing that stands the test of scientific rigour."

"So," said Morgan, "if it wasn't a Messenger, is there anything else it could have been?"

Simon was wearying of the interrogation. He opened his mouth to suggest the officers go back to trawling the net for their intelligence, but instead said, "There are any number of gigantic bat-like creatures and dragons in ancient lore, but again, pure myth, I'm afraid. If such a creature does exist, 'Where has it been hiding all these centuries?' would be my first question."

"Outer space?" suggested Grieves behind them.

Simon smiled at her over his shoulder. "Actually, there *is* an ancient legend about winged creatures flying to Earth from the stars. But I am fairly certain that legend is myth too."

He halted outside a classroom. Inside, a dozen or so young people were sitting at desks, looking bored. Why does every new generation of young people slump more than the last? he asked himself with a shudder of annoyance.

"Well, here we are," he announced, trying not to let his frustrations show. "I'm afraid I haven't been of much use."

"Not at all, Professor," said Morgan. "You've been most helpful in closing the book on this case."

"Hallucinatory mushrooms was it then?"

The officer nodded absently. He didn't seem to get that the professor's question was a joke. He handed him a business card and waved his partner toward the stairs.

"Goodbye, Professor Orwell. And please: if you think of anything more, no matter how outlandish, ring me on that number."

The professor tapped the business card on his thumb as he watched their departing backs.

THE TWO OFFICERS stopped on the pavement outside the university. Morgan pulled out his car keys.

"What do you think, Sam?"

Morgan turned to his friend. "He's very convincing." He glanced up at the brownstone building. The clouds were reflecting off the windows, but he had a feeling the professor was standing at one of them watching them. "And a good liar. Step up the surveillance."

16

The mummy

PUSHING OPEN THE door, Dylan felt like a burglar. Wilfred had given him his own set of keys, but he couldn't shake the feeling he should knock and wait for Arlene, the housekeeper, to let him in. Truth be told, he was scared stiff of the old woman. She was always following him around, eyeing him like a shark in a green housecoat. Stepping into the entry hall, he had the unnerving feeling she was hiding somewhere with a shotgun, waiting to step out and blow his head off.

The place was gloomy as always. And cold – almost as cold as outside. A chopping noise was echoing down the dark corridor, coming from the kitchen at the rear of the house. As Dylan listened, a scream tore through the air.

The chopping went on uninterrupted. Heart thumping, Dylan rushed down the hall, his brain reeling at the thought of what Arlene might be doing back there.

At the door to the kitchen, he paused and peeked into the room. The back door was open, and Dylan could see a trail of blood leading across the paving stones, up the steps, and over the floorboards to where Arlene was standing at the butcher block. She had her back to him, a meat cleaver raised above her head. With a grunt, she brought it down. Her housecoat was obscuring Dylan's view, but he could see she was attacking something large and brown – part of a cow, by the look of it.

Lifting the bloody cleaver again, this time using both hands, she brought it down with all her might. Dylan watched in disgust as she increased her speed, chopping the animal like a machine. Blood and pieces of flesh and bone flew all over the kitchen, turning the bench, the cupboards, the walls, the ceiling and Arlene's green housecoat red.

Suddenly she stopped and stood panting over the table. Dropping the meat cleaver, she went to the sink, turned on the tap and began washing her hands. Dylan could see now that the bloody mess had been the front third of a horse.

He gasped.

At the sound, Arlene froze. A tremor ran through her body, from her pointed head to her unnaturally large feet. Slowly, she turned off the tap, picked up a tea towel and wiped her hands on it.

Dylan stepped away from the kitchen. Pressing his back against the wall, he sidled away as quietly as he could, holding his breath. He could hear the housekeeper's coarse breathing, a rattle as she picked up the meat cleaver, the tread of her shoes on the floorboards.

He gasped again when the blade of the cleaver appeared in the doorway. Then came Arlene's blood-stained hand, then the bloody sleeve of her housecoat, followed by her bug-eyed face and onion-shaped head.

She turned to him without a word, as if she already knew he would be standing there, and for a few moments they faced each other, neither saying a word. Arlene began tapping the cleaver against the wall.

"I didn't –" said Dylan, stepping into the hallway, his hands raised in surrender. "I didn't … I was … I'm here to see Wilfred."

He gaped at the bloody cleaver, at the flecks of blood on the wall, and thought: She's a nutcase; she doesn't know the difference between me and the horse.

Another chilling scream rang out, this time behind him. He realised then that the first scream hadn't come from the kitchen; something was happening in the basement. The scream degenerated into a howl, an awful sound that went on and on, erasing Arlene from his thoughts and propelling his feet back down the hall towards the front door.

I need to get out of this loony bin, he was thinking as he ran. But at the basement door he paused. The howling had receded to a whine, and now he thought he heard Wilfred's voice. He pressed his ear against the door. He couldn't make out what Wilfred was saying, but it sounded like he was talking to someone.

Looking up, Dylan gazed longingly at the front door. Out there, beyond the gloom of the hallway and the blood-spattered kitchen and the mad housekeeper, lay freedom, fresh air and sanity. All he had to do was take a few more steps. But a voice inside his head said: If you leave now, there'll be hell to pay. You were given strict orders to come here today, so get your shit together and do what Wilfred is paying you to do.

"He's not paying me anything," Dylan mumbled, then, with a glance at Arlene, put his shoulder against the basement door.

The housekeeper gave him an uncharacteristic smile and returned to the dead horse.

DOWN IN THE basement, Wilfred was interrogating a mummy. The shrivelled thing, a shrunken skeleton wrapped in crispy black skin, was strapped to a metal rack, naked apart from a sheet covering its lower torso. Laid out on a nearby trolley was an assortment of tools: knives, pliers, bolt cutters, a stun gun, a dentist drill, and other implements you might expect to find in a hospital operating theatre. The mummy was staring at the tray with eyes wide and round.

"Wrong!" barked Wilfred, picking up the stun gun.

He held it against the mummy's neck and pressed the trigger. As the weapon zapped, the mummy arched its back and screamed and struggled against its restraints.

Sighing, Wilfred released his finger from the trigger and inspected the stun gun under the light. As his victim puffed and panted, he waved it before its eyes. "Wonderful toys we have at our disposal these days, wouldn't you say?" he said, zapping the air. "Jonathon would have had fun with these newfangled playthings. He did so love the art of pain."

Laying the weapon aside, he picked up a metal skewer. "This was more Jonathon's style. He had a thing for eyes." He laughed soundlessly at a private memory. "A thing for eyes. I can never pass a shish kebab shop without thinking of the cantankerous old bastard. Now," he said to the mummy, brandishing the skewer like a wand; "one more time, my friend. Tell me: How do I control the Messenger?"

The terrified mummy tried to talk, but without a tongue, all it could manage was, "Uh-guh-gauh."

Dropping the skewer on the trolley, Wilfred swapped it for a pair of bolt cutters.

"Let's shake things up a little," he said. "Take it up a notch or two.

And don't forget, Willem, if I happen to go too far, I can always keep snipping away until you're mincemeat, and then we can start over again. I have all the time in the world, and a cornucopia of tricks to extract the truth."

He positioned the bolt cutters over the mummy's thumb. It struggled and gagged in terror.

"I know, I know: you assumed you were at rest." He moved the cutters to the knuckle. "Don't you know there's no rest for the wicked?"

Using both hands, Wilfred squeezed the bolt cutters. But it was only a ruse. Smiling at the panting mummy, he laid the bolt cutters aside and picked up the skewer again.

The blackened thing bucked its skeletal body in a display of belligerence that belied its defenceless situation. The restraints pulled tight, cutting into its skin, sloughing off flesh, the wounds oozing with reddish-yellow fluid.

"Ooh, that looks painful. If you answer my question, I promise I will end this and send you back to the hell you so deservedly came from."

The mummy stared at him with murderous hatred. It gurgled, "Uh-guh-gauh."

"You do know," returned Wilfred, stroking its bald head with the meat skewer. "You're scared of retribution; I understand that. Yog-Sothoth does not like to be disturbed."

"Uh-guh! Uh-guh!"

"Yes, you do. I saw it in your letters." His eyes turned to stone. "Don't treat me like a fool!"

Throwing the skewer against the wall, Wilfred swiped up the bolt cutters and positioned them over the mummy's forefinger.

"Do you know what I hate even more than being lied to?"

He waited for the mummy to reply. When it didn't, he snipped off the forefinger.

The thing screamed and struggled, the scream turning into a long howl of agony. Wilfred flicked the severed finger at a bucket. He missed, and the finger landed on the dirty floor.

"Being treated like a fool is what. The fools are the ones who dare oppose me, or get in my way. One day, mark my words, all you insignificant gutter slime will fall before me and beg me to throw you a scrap of rotten offal to save your starving carcasses, so you can enjoy another minute of pointless existence." He moved his face closer to the whining mummy. "A fool, am I? Do you think a fool could rise to the throne of the world? Because that's where I'm headed. And do you honestly think I will countenance slugs like you on the day I ascend to my place at the right hand of the gods? I can assure you, I won't. I will ship you off to a special kind of hell you can't even imagine, and smile with unadulterated pleasure at the sounds of your eternal torture and pain. You fear the wrath of Yog-Sothoth? You have no idea what wrath is. But keep on defying me and –"

His monologue was interrupted by the sound of the basement door opening. Glancing up, Wilfred saw black boots and jeans falling down the stairs.

Dylan's face appeared, white and scared.

"What's happening?" he cried.

His eyes took in the gory scene: the stains on Wilfred's butcher's apron, the blood on the floor, the finger next to the bucket.

"Who's screaming?" His eyes landed on the mummy's face. "Jesus Christ! What the hell is that?"

Turning back to the mummy, Wilfred snipped off another finger. The shrunken thing howled.

"Dylan, my boy. Nice to see you. Better late than never." He waved at him. "Come down and meet an old accomplice of mine: Willem Groning. Willem: this is my new protégé, Master Dylan Gates."

The mummy stared imploringly at Dylan. "Ehhr, ehh," it gurgled.

"Is it – dead?"

Wilfred smiled. "He was." He threw the bolt cutters onto the trolley. "And will be again, once he answers my damn question."

Dylan glanced at the severed finger, the bolt cutters covered in blood. He moved up a step. "Whoa, man, this is messed up! Raising dead people so you can torture them … Is this what you wanted the Necronomicon for?"

Wilfred crossed to the bench, where the book in question lay open.

"You ignoramus. I didn't learn the trick of reanimation from the

Necronomicon. How do you think I found the cursed book in the first place?"

"I didn't think –"

"I promised you that soon enough you would talk to the dead, didn't I? Learn their secrets. Exact favours." He waved his hand at the mummy. "Et voici."

"Not like this!"

"How then? Over tea and scones? Can you possibly be any stupider?"

He put on his reading glasses, moved his face close to the page, mouthed something.

"Excellent," he announced, spinning around. Pulling off the glasses, he waggled them at Dylan. "Now then, hold your fool tongue, get down here, and sit in that chair."

At Wilfred's command, Dylan's body went limp. For a few moments he stared slack-jawed; then he trod heavily down the stairs, walked stiffly to the chair next to the torture rack, and dropped into it like a rag doll.

"Good boy. Now, shut those peepers of yours and don't move a muscle until I tell you to."

He watched with satisfaction as Dylan complied. Reaching out both hands, he brushed the hair away from his protégé's face and tucked it behind his ears. "That's better. You youngsters and your beatnik hair. What are your parents thinking? I should get out my shears right here and now." He patted Dylan's head. "Time to have some shut-eye, my young friend. Forget about all this unpleasantness. You will come to see in time that it's a necessary evil. We have to step on a few cockroaches and gut a few rats if we are to clean out our house in preparation for our esteemed guests. Be assured that by the time you awaken, our journey will have moved to its next glorious phase, and you, my boy, will behold the world through very different eyes."

He returned to the trolley and collected the bloody bolt cutters. Clicking them twice, he said, "Don't worry, Willem. We haven't forgotten you."

17

A trip to Quorn

THEIR NAMES WERE written on the letterbox: Michael and Lauren Gates. So quaint, Arika thought with a smile. Only in small villages like Quorn did people still put their names on their letterboxes.

She climbed the steps and knocked on the door. No answer. Placing her ear against the door, she knocked again. Clearly no one was home.

She glanced around. The house stood in a typical country village street, the road narrow and quiet, the blocks wide and tree-filled, some attached to paddocks where horses or sheep grazed. It was a far cry from her own childhood, growing up in Aunt Beatrice's flat in a grubby Newham lane. Probably the most dangerous thing to happen around here was a stubbed toe.

Arika went back down the steps. Though she was sceptical in Simon's office about the sense of making this trip, on the way down she had a change of heart. The eyewitnesses were clear and unwavering about what they saw. Their descriptions were consistent, and though they maintained their attacker was a dragon, they said its face looked like an octopus. That wasn't something you'd expect small town simpletons to make up, even in a place like this, with its pagan roots, history of witch trials and preponderance of modern-day Wiccan covens. The local authorities had said the damage to the car was atypical of a collision with an animal or a common rollover. Arika was certain something supernatural had visited Quorn, and she was determined to find out what it was and how she could track it down.

Slipping through an unlocked gate at the side of the property, she made her way to the first window. The blind was down, but from its position she guessed it was a living or dining room. The next window along opened into the kitchen. Arika placed a hand against the glass and peered into the room. The place was a mess. There were dishes, plates, cups and glasses piled in the sink and on the countertops; more on the table. Pizza boxes. Styrofoam cartons. Cereal boxes. Beer bottles. An overflowing bin. The floor was filthy. She glanced down the path towards the back yard, where the garden was neat and green. Why didn't the state of the kitchen match the outside of the house? Something didn't feel right.

Returning her attention to the kitchen, Arika noticed half a dozen cards on the fridge and the shelf next to it. Squinting, she could make out some of the words. *With deepest sympathy. Sharing in your sorrow. Thinking of you.* A death in the family, it appeared. That might explain the mess.

Voices came from the direction of the street. Creeping back to the gate, Arika peered through the slats. Two boys were walking down the middle of the road, wheeling bicycles, talking in loud voices about a school football match, dissecting the game like they'd probably heard their fathers do about grown-up matches. They were too young to be Dylan Gates, Arika thought; the Gates boy had been driving at the time of the attack. These kids' voices hadn't even broken yet.

She was right: the boys passed the house and kept on walking, their voices fading as they turned the corner and disappeared from view.

Returning to the kitchen window, Arika opened her bag. "This might be it," she said to her Glock, lifting it out. She pointed it at the kitchen, tapping the trigger. "Was he in Quorn, do you think? Maybe he was following the trail of the Messenger, just like us." She lowered the gun. "I'd be surprised," she said, stroking its barrel. "Still, there must be some connection between the Messenger, Quorn and Dark. It's too much of a coincidence to be a coincidence. You think?"

Talking to her gun made Arika feel better. Her father had always talked to his gun, and when young Arika giggled about it, he explained that the best marksman needs to have a close relationship with his weapon. They should be like siblings, looking out for each other, knowing each other's strengths and limitations, so they can act in a split second when the rubber hits the road. It was a story designed to amuse a child, but she'd grown up believing it.

"Glad to see we're on the same page," Arika said, returning the

Glock to her bag.

Convinced the Gates' house was hiding secrets, she headed into the back yard.

KANE DROVE HIS pickup truck into Wilfred Waite's farmyard and parked behind his father's Honda Civic. He was pretty sure his brother hadn't seen him. Not only was Dylan generally oblivious to things happening around him, he would have been waiting with his usual pouty face and childish tantrums if he knew Kane had followed him here with the intent of confronting Wilfred.

Climbing down from his truck, he went up to the gate. There was no one about, so he jumped over it and strode through the mud. The house loomed before him like a prop in a post-apocalyptic movie set. If the Honda hadn't been outside the gate, he wouldn't have believed a business owner and alleged immortal sorcerer like Wilfred Waite could live in such a dump.

Frowning at the broken roof, he heard what sounded like galloping horses. The next moment, two monstrous Rottweilers came hurtling around the corner of the house. Black and hairless, with long limbs, yellow fangs and bloodshot eyes, they barked and snarled at him like hounds from hell.

"Shit!" cried Kane.

For a long moment he stood paralysed with fear, watching the beasts as they advanced on him with murderous intent. Then his muscles kicked into gear, and he turned tail and ran away faster than he would ever have thought possible. This time when he jumped the gate, he barely touched it.

The two dogs slammed into the bars as if they thought they could run straight through them. Dropping to the ground, they rolled in the mud, scrambled about, sprang up and leapt at the gate, barking and snarling in fury.

Kane stared at them, his heartbeat pounding in his ears. Were they … dead? He crouched for a closer look. Enraged by his lack of fear, the dogs threw themselves against the gate. Yellowish froth flew from their jaws and splattered on his jeans. Their breath smelt like maggoty fish heads.

He got up, thinking: Damn fool brother, putting crazy notions in my head.

"You've got some bloody ugly pets!" he yelled at the house as he pulled his phone from his pocket. Then, to himself: "Should get animal control out here before they maim somebody."

He pressed Dylan's number and paced from the gate to the truck and back as he waited for the number to connect. The phone went to voicemail.

"Damn you, Dylan," he cursed, glaring at the farmhouse. "Dylan," he said, "it's me. I'm out front. Tell Waite to come out. I need to talk to him."

Hanging up, he stood staring at the farmhouse door. The dogs went on leaping and barking. Nothing else stirred in the cold morning air. Kane could feel the seconds ticking by on his wristwatch. When it was clear neither Wilfred nor Dylan was coming out, he went back to his truck.

He checked his phone for messages. Nothing. Dylan spent all day on his phone, so it wasn't hard to figure out when he was being ignored.

"Freaks," he muttered, getting in the truck.

Pulling the gear shift into reverse, he spun the wheels in the mud and backed up at speed. The dogs were still leaping and barking, their rage and determination undimmed. Kane had no doubt that, had they breached the gate, they would have chased him all the way back to Quorn.

PARKING IN HIS driveway, he jumped from the truck, slammed the door shut and walked towards the house. He was still fuming about Dylan ignoring him, not to mention how he went straight back to the farm-house after the talk they'd had. It was another nail in the coffin of their fractured relationship, and Kane really wasn't sure what to do next. Give up? Leave Dylan behind to fend for himself? Live his own life as best he could? An old school friend at the funeral had given him that advice, and a second funeral is what this situation with Dylan felt like.

As he bounded up the steps, a young woman rose from the seat near the door.

"Ah – hi – who?" he sputtered, thinking at first it was January.

"Sorry, I didn't mean to scare you."

"You didn't scare me," Kane answered with a smile. "I just … I thought you were somebody else."

"I'm Arika Livingston. I'm a research assistant at George University."

Kane breathed steadily, inhaling her heady perfume as he gazed into her soft brown eyes. It was obvious she wasn't from around here. Her accent was too refined, and her lacy, flowery top over designer jeans wasn't the kind of outfit the daughters of goat and sheep farmers generally wore. She reminded him of a Spanish exchange student he once had a crush on at school.

"I – er … Are you lost?"

"I hope not. Are you Dylan Gates?"

"Dylan?" Kane was confused. Girls never came around asking for Dylan.

"So you're not Dylan." She gestured at the house. "Do the Gates still live here?"

"They do. At least Dylan and me do. I'm Kane."

"Brother?"

"I'm the handsome one."

She folded her arms and stared coldly at him. Kane held her gaze. She refused to look away, as if she were challenging him to give a more suitable answer.

I've got a live one here, Kane thought, energised by the defiance he read in her eyes. And a real looker. Time to turn on the old Gates' charm.

"How long you been waiting here?"

Arika glanced at her watch. "An hour. Give or take." She tossed her head at the seat, where she'd left her tablet. "The tethers of technology. You can work anywhere."

"Tethers?"

She smiled, as if he just confirmed something.

Kane smiled back. "Did you … want to get a drink or something?"

As he said it, he felt his face go warm. It sounded like a cheap pick-up line – which in essence it was.

Arika nodded at the seat, at the bottle of water next to her tablet. "I'm good, thanks. I came to see your brother. Do you know where he is?"

"You're here about the dragon thing?"

"How'd you guess?"

He shrugged. "ESP. Plus there's no other reason somebody who looks like you would come see my little brother. It *is* about the dragon thing, isn't it?"

"Whatever it was those two people saw."

"Are you doing an assignment on whack jobs? Country cretins? The Barrys are all related … inbred, y'know. They probably see pixies and leprechauns and –"

"I'm not a student."

Kane eyed Arika suspiciously. A person doesn't wait around an hour to question an eyewitness about yesterday's crazy news story. Unless she believes it. He was hoping the story would have faded into obscurity by now, yet here was someone about to dredge it all up again.

"I work in the history department. We're doing research into old religions and cults."

He nodded. That kind of made sense. "You believe in monsters then?"

She raised her shoulders. "Call me open-minded. The stories are interesting from a cultural and sociological perspective, whether they're true or not."

"You've looked into a lot of these … stories?"

She glanced at her watch again. "Quite a lot."

"What's your make on it?"

"Look – Kane, is it?" Arika frowned. "I'm enjoying our little chat, but I'd prefer to speak with Dylan."

"He's not here. I was looking for him myself."

"Where is he?"

"Maybe I can fill you in on what happened."

"It doesn't work that way."

"What doesn't?"

"Research."

"What? Is there a rule book?"

She half closed her eyes.

"Dylan told me all about it. A few times. Interesting story. Let me buy you a coffee and I'll tell you what he said."

Her face brightened. "What did he see?"

Kane stood smirking at her.

"Was there anything more than what he told the reporters?"

He shrugged.

"Well?"

"I'm dying for a cuppa. Been driving around for hours. You wouldn't want me sitting in a coffee shop all by myself, like some kind of inbred loser, would you?" He smiled disarmingly.

"Look, I don't have time for this."

"You've been sitting on my porch for an hour. Doesn't sound to me like you're in a hurry to be anywhere else."

"I need to get back to the university, if it's any of your business."

Kane frowned at her. This wasn't going to plan. He wasn't used to girls resisting him, and this only pushed him to work harder to win Arika over. Apart from the obvious benefit, if he could quiz her over the Messenger thing, he'd be able to assess her threat level and take necessary precautions to make sure no mud ended up on his brother.

A surge of desperation rose in him. He struggled to mask it, but he had one of those faces that can be read like a comic. "Just half an hour? I'll make it worth your while. Quorn coffee is as legendary as its dragons."

"Is there more to the story than what he told the reporters?" Arika asked again, this time in a no-nonsense voice.

"Mmn, could be."

Her face hardened. "I don't have time to play games."

"Aw, come on. Don't be so uptight. You're on Quorn time now. Just one drink for the road, and I can let you know what Dylan told me."

"Tell me now, or I'm off. I'll come back when your brother is home."

"He's not around much these days."

"Then it seems I'm wasting my time."

"You seem pretty pushy for … what was it? – a research assistant?"

"And you're pretty stubborn for a … What is it you do?"

"Firefighter," Kane replied, pulling back his shoulders. It felt like he'd drawn aside a curtain on a dating game show to reveal the grand prize. His occupation always impressed the ladies. He was impressed himself, considering how much he'd achieved since starting the training program.

"Ah, of course." She nodded at his body. "I bet the girls around here go wild for the big, strong firefighter with the cheeky grin, hey?"

He folded his arms, pushed out his biceps, smirked a little. "Don't get no complaints."

Turning on her heel, Arika went to collect her tablet and the bottle of water.

"I would appreciate it if you would please tell your brother I called, and ask him to phone me." She lodged the bottle under her arm. "Here's my card."

He took it from her. 'Arika Livingston, Research Assistant, George University' it said, followed by a phone number and email address.

By the time he looked up, Arika was at the bottom of the steps.

"Hey!" he yelled at the back of her head, not really sure what just happened.

She ignored him.

"Arika!"

She turned. It was clear from the look on her face that she wasn't happy.

Kane stared at her in confusion. He had no more tricks up his sleeve, but he knew he couldn't let Arika leave. It was more than a desire to pump her for information – more than a boy-meets-girl thing – more than the fact he hated the thought of skulking inside and spending another afternoon alone in an empty house. His desperation was centred on his life, on the question of how to fight Wilfred Waite's influence over his idiot brother. Arika seemed to know something about freaks and magical monsters – he needed her help.

"Dylan did tell me stuff," he conceded. "Really weird stuff. And … I think he might be in trouble."

Arika didn't respond, but at least she wasn't frowning now. She took a step towards him.

"I could really do with some advice."

18

All about Dylan

MAIN STREET NEVER changes, Kane was thinking as he drove into town. There are always a few cars around, a couple of trucks, some shoppers, a dog tied to a lamp post, a smattering of people with nothing else to do but sit in the village square watching the world go by. Quorn's predictability and its lack of drama were great for young families and senior citizens, but for lively young people like Kane, with their eyes on the world and everything there was to explore in it, being in Quorn was like being kept in a locked room. Since he was twelve, he'd dreamed of escaping, and now, at last, he'd reached the age where he could make it happen.

But as he pulled up in a parking bay outside the Brandywine Grind, he felt the weight of nostalgia on his chest. He knew that once the house was sold, he and Dylan would be moving on. There was nothing to keep them in Quorn – only fading memories and constant reminders of the tragedies that had befallen them here. With persistence, he'd drag Dylan away from the clutches of Wilfred Waite, and then they'd move away to a place where only good things happened and the drama and surprise in their lives didn't come from madmen and monsters. It was a comforting thought … so why was he feeling so down?

While he waited for Arika to park, he went two doors down to Quorn Fine Arts and Antiquities. The closed sign was still in the door, and he doubted the shop had been opened since the last time he was here (when he broke in, he reminded himself with a smile). Wilfred was apparently too busy corrupting his brother to spend time making a living.

In the coffee shop, Kane chose a table in the window and watched as Arika took a seat. She looked about his age – early twenties – with an olive complexion, hazel eyes and dark wavy hair that fell to her shoulders. She was ever alert, her eyes darting around the room. He wondered what was going through her mind. Kane had only ever dated local girls, all from high school, all mired in local family politics and gossip, and Arika seemed as alien to him as the world they were here to discuss.

"Do we order at the counter?" she asked.

He looked around for Frankie, the waiter. "What would you like?"

"I'll get it."

"No, it's my treat."

"I can put it on my expense account."

"I invited you. I'll pay."

Arika got out her purse.

"We'll work out the bill later," said Kane.

He glanced over at the counter, with its steampunk barista machine, small selection of rolls and baked goods, and local pottery, oil paintings and knitted animals for sale. But no Frankie.

Tapping his foot on the tiled floor, he squeezed his hands together under the table. He was trying hard to think of something interesting to say. He suspected that once Arika pumped him for whatever it was he knew, she'd be out of here. Possibly even before the coffee arrived.

"When I was at school," he said, "history was all about kings and queens and Ancient Rome. We never studied monsters and magic."

Arika was staring at the slices and cakes. Was she hungry? Perhaps he should ask her if she wanted something to eat.

"Professor Orwell – Simon," she said, glancing at him, "specialises in cultural history and metaphysics. Most history studies are rote learning, which bores us."

"I used to be able to recite all the English kings and queens without even thinking."

"Impressive."

"I don't think I could do it now, though."

"Not a skill a fireman needs, hey?"

"Nope," he replied, being immune to sarcasm.

Her attention had returned to the counter. Where the hell was Frankie? He usually buzzed around the tables like an old blowfly.

"Who's Professor Orville? Did he send you here?"

"Orwell. Simon Orwell. And yes, he thought the story deserved investigation."

When Kane said nothing, she joined her hands on the table and said, "We're examining ancient legends, how they're created and perpetuated, and how they influence culture going forward. You'd be surprised by how strong some of these beliefs are, and the lengths some people will go to convince themselves they're true. It's one thing for ancient tribes to believe in gods and demons; they didn't know about science, so everything around them must have felt magical. It's a whole nother matter for people today to believe in supernatural entities and magical powers."

"So you're not here chasing monsters?"

Arika smiled. She had very white teeth. "The thing those people described sounds a lot like one of the old legends some people still think is true, and we'd like to examine what influenced them to interpret their experience in that way."

Kane's heartbeat sped up. He was dying to tell Arika what Dylan had told him about that night, but he was scared of what would happen if anyone found out his brother was messing with black magic. He still didn't believe it himself – not totally.

"So you don't believe some kind of monster appeared out of no-where and attacked that car?"

"As a researcher, I have to keep an open mind."

"Sounds like you're saying you maybe do believe it."

"Perhaps."

"I thought you just said people who believe in magic are stupid?"

Her smile this time was softer, more genuine. "I was making the point that the burden of proof these days has to be higher because science has more explanations for the unknown, and more methods for testing claims and outliers."

"Is a dragon an outlier?"

"More like a myth."

"Isn't myth another word for fairy tale?"

"I think of it more like an untested assertion. Neither true nor untrue until evidence confirms one way or the other."

"This so-called dragon isn't a dead myth, though. It's something the Barry's said they saw the other night. Alive."

"Hence the need for evidence one way or another. Hence my open mind. Just because things are buried in time, doesn't mean they couldn't have existed at some point in history. And if that's true, what's to stop them being raised again?"

"Now you're having me on," said Kane, wondering how much Arika knew versus what she'd read in books. "You can't really believe dinosaurs and shit can be resurrected by magic."

"Who said anything about dinosaurs?"

"Dragons, dinosaurs; it's all the same thing, isn't it?"

They were interrupted by Frankie, a yellow-tinged man with limp brown hair and a straggly beard. "Sorry, folks," he said: "diarrhoea. Musta been the curried fish pie. Are you eating? Don't have the curried fish pie is my recommendation."

"Just cappuccino, thanks," said Arika.

"Sure, miss, anything for the lovely lady." He glanced at Kane. "What about you, Sugar?"

Kane pulled a face at Arika. "Sugar … Kane … get it?"

"I got it."

"The usual, thanks," he said to Frankie. Feeling playful, he added, "Hey Frankie, did you ever see Jurassic Park?"

Frankie tapped his pen on his notepad. "U-huh," he drawled, one corner of his mouth pulled down.

"Did you know it's real? They're bringing back T-Rex and stuff."

"No shit," said Frankie. He paused for a second as if waiting for the punch line, then sauntered off. "As if we don't have enough old dinosaurs in Quorn."

At these words, two grey-haired ladies sitting nearby straightened their backs in indignation. As Frankie ground coffee beans, they bent their heads over the table and hissed their disapproval at his joke. Kane watched them, knowing they wouldn't dare say anything to him. The Brandywine Grind was the only place in town that served decent coffee, and no one wanted to make an enemy of the owner's ill-tempered nephew. Not unless you wanted your order to be seasoned with saliva or something worse.

"Okay, Kane," said Arika, "time to fill me in on what your brother told you."

As his name passed over her lips, Kane went warm inside. It felt as if someone had turned up the temperature in the room by ten degrees.

"The creature," he said, leaning closer: "he called it a Messenger."

Arika's mouth fell open. She folded her arms on the table. "He called it a Messenger? How could he know that?"

Kane sat back. He realised that in his first few words he'd already ratted on his brother.

"I don't … Dylan's just a kid. He doesn't know what he's talking about."

"He just happens to know it was a Messenger?"

"He must have read about them on the net."

"He said he arrived after the accident, so how could he even suspect a Messenger?"

Kane stared helplessly at her. He needed to protect his brainless brother as much as possible, but what was the point in dancing around the truth? Arika was of no use to him unless he told her at least some of what he knew about Wilfred's antics.

"Listen," he said, resting his elbows on the table: "if I tell you what Dylan told me, you have to swear not to say anything to anyone."

She was leaning so close now he could feel her breath on his face. There were flecks of green in her hazel eyes, and he could see she was wearing contact lenses. He wondered what she looked like in glasses.

Concentrate! he admonished himself, turning his head to Frankie at the counter to take his mind off his libido.

Arika's face was deadly serious. "I can't promise you that, Kane. It's my job to find out these things and report them to Simon. It's the reason I'm here."

"Then –"

"But what I can promise is that I will keep Dylan's name out of it if at all possible."

"If at all possible."

Kane bit his thumb. He had no reason to trust this woman; they'd met less than an hour ago. She could be a plant, like one of those sexy, dangerous, Soviet spies who were trained to seduce their targets to learn state secrets. If that were the case, she was doing a great job.

Frankie came back with their drinks, setting them down on the table. "Yell if you need anything else," he said. "I'll be out back."

Kane waited until he was gone, and then said to Arika in a low voice, "Dylan is involved with this scary old man who's promised to teach him magic."

She brought her cappuccino to her lips. Kane could see she was edgy with excitement, though she was trying hard not to show it. "Go on," she urged, taking a sip.

"The dude's name is Wilfred Waite, and he says he's two hundred years old, and according to Dylan he's looking for a sorcerer's apprentice, or some shit like that."

"Was it Wilfred Waite who called up the Messenger?"

"That's what Dylan said."

"Was he there when it happened?"

"No," lied Kane. "He was on the road, driving down to the farm, and saw the accident. Waite told him what the thing was."

"Kane, if that thing really was a Messenger, then I can tell you: Dylan is mixed up in something worse than you could ever imagine."

"What do you mean?"

"It takes a ton of bad magic to raise a Messenger. But that's not the worst of it. A Messenger has one reason for existence: to kill everything in sight. Anyone who raises a Messenger is doing it to commit murder."

Kane's mouth went dry. Lifting his cup, he took a long drink. The coffee didn't make any difference. His mouth still felt like cardboard and his mind was still refusing to believe what Arika had just told him. All Dylan had said was that the Messenger was summoned to reveal some cosmic knowledge – to bring a message, as he put it.

Dropping his cup on the saucer with a clang, he said, "That's insane. Dylan's not a killer. He would never do anything like that."

"Maybe he didn't know what Waite was up to."

"Of course he didn't know."

Even as he said the words, he knew he was fooling himself as well as

Arika. Dylan's reaction to the news stories; his response to the demands he stay away from Wilfred: he knew. He may have stopped the thing from killing anything other than a few animals, but he knew all too well what it was. And where was Dylan now? At the farmhouse, with Wilfred. And what was he doing there? Who knew what new horrors they were conjuring to set loose on the world?

"Tell me more about this Messenger thing," he said to Arika.

"What did Dylan tell you about it?"

"Tell me what you know first."

She held his gaze until he looked away. He thought she would wait for him to speak first, but then she said, "The purpose of a Messenger is to clear the land of all life."

"Where did it come from?"

She ran her finger along the rim of her cup. "It was summoned. From … another dimension."

He sputtered a laugh. "You can't be serious."

She took a drink, nodding at him.

"How is that even possible?"

"No one knows. The spell is supposed to be in a book called the Necronomicon. But hardly anyone alive has seen a viable copy, so we don't know for sure."

"Waite has it."

She sucked in breath.

"Waite has the Necrowhatsit."

"Necronomicon," said Arika.

"Dylan said it's a book of magic spells. He said Waite can talk to dead people, and he's after some kind of cosmic knowledge."

Arika stared past him. "Which is why he raised the Messenger."

"I don't get it. If a Messenger only lives to kill, why did Waite summon it?"

"That's not all it does. It's called a Messenger because it precedes the appearance of a god."

"A god? Now you're kidding me!"

"Not a god from a human religion. One from other dimensions of reality."

"Is it …? – I don't even know how to respond to that."

"The Messenger is the herald of Yog-Sothoth, a deity that sits across dimensions and … controls traffic, so to speak."

"Controls traffic."

She nodded.

"Assuming this Yog-dog-god thing really does exist, what would Waite want from something like that?"

"Yog-Sothoth guards the gate between the dimensions and – so the story goes – sees everything. People who summon him usually want great knowledge … and power."

Kane stared at her, feeling curiously weightless.

"Some of his followers believe Yog-Sothoth will reveal to them how to break the seal between the dimensions so they bleed into one another."

Now his stomach was churning, flopping and gurgling. He placed his hands on it to calm it down.

"He could be trying to destroy the world?"

"More likely change it."

"Into what?"

"Into a place where he has power over billions of lives."

"That's madness."

"You wouldn't believe some of the things people have done in the name of these gods."

"*These* gods? There's more than one?"

"A pantheon. If the gate is broken, they could all come flooding in."

Kane shook his head till it hurt. "So the Necro-thingumajig is some kind of key?"

"You could say that. Are you sure Wilfred Waite has it?"

"I'm not sure about anything."

"How about murderous dragons from another dimension?"

"Y'know …" He placed his hands on his head. "No, I'm not even sure about that."

19

Confronting

KANE WATCHED AS a young, short-haired woman wearing a fluffy pink jumper and baggy denim jeans pushed an old-fashioned pram past the coffee shop window. Stopping at the kerb, glancing left and right, she manoeuvred the pram onto the empty road, then pushed it towards an elderly woman, who was seated on a park bench knitting something blue. The mother parked the pram and turned to hug the older woman, and then they sat with heads together, the young woman chatting into the air while the older one knitted away with deft fingers.

"Do you know them?" Arika asked, watching Kane watching them.

"Uh – yeah," he grunted, shrugging. "Not *know* them; just know *about* them. The one with the pram was in my year nine class – Sybil Trudehope. She dropped out the first time she got pregnant, never came back. That's her third, from three different fathers. The old woman used to run the nursery, and now she's having an affair with Vicar Jim at All Saints – he's got chilblains, so it's his socks she's knitting."

"Impressive," smiled Arika.

Kane tapped the side of his head. "All the kings and queens of England," he reminded her.

As they watched, a car swerved into the parking spot alongside the liquor store. A young man got out, went up to the women, and butted into the conversation.

"The uncle of one of her kids," Kane pointed out. "I forget which. He's engaged to the woman who runs the dog grooming salon. He's into comics trading. Last Easter, he won a hot dog eating contest and had to have his stomach pumped."

He looked on as the man waved his arms about, his actions and whatever he was saying bringing frowns of consternation to the faces of the two women. The exchange worried Kane. In the past few weeks, he'd noticed growing incidents of people acting strangely in Quorn: arguing in the street, talking to themselves, looking shifty. There was a growing tension in the normally friendly, relaxed village, and Kane wondered if his parents' murder had anything to do with it. The police had flocked to Handleford and Quorn in the first few days after the attack, perpetuating the sense of fear and unease, but they'd been gone for some time now, and yet there remained a lingering sense of something not quite right.

Arika slipped her laptop from her bag. "Do you think you can –"

"Hey!" cried Kane, half standing. "There's Dylan!"

His brother was cruising down Main Street in his father's white Honda Civic, bent over the steering wheel like he was having trouble seeing the road. He parked the car two doors down, got out, and with head lowered, made his way towards the shop. He continued walking past the window without seeing him.

"Blind git," Kane mumbled, and took off after him.

"Dylan!" he called out. "I've been ringing! What's up with you?"

Dylan was hunched over, a little unsteady on his feet, as if he had a stomach ache or a sore leg. He didn't seem to hear him.

"Dylan!"

He half turned his head, but kept on walking.

Catching up, Kane placed a hand on his brother's shoulder. Dylan jerked away, then spun around to face him.

"What's wrong?" asked Kane.

Dylan glared at him. "Nothing," he replied testily. "Nothing's wrong." Then: "I'm not used to people creeping up on me in the street, is all."

"I wasn't creeping. I called you. You ignored me … as usual."

Dylan sneered at him.

"You okay? You don't look well."

He pulled back his skinny shoulders. "I'm very well. Never better, if you must know."

"You were out at Waite's farm."

Dylan cocked his head. "Nosy bastard. Have you been following me?"

"I've been ringing."

"Yes, well, we've been busy."

"Talking to dead people?"

"How did you guess?"

"Well, come on home. We need to sort a few things out."

His brother looked perplexed; but very quickly a realisation dawned on him.

"Home, did you say?" he shot back. "And which home might that be? The one Daddy lost through his blundering ineptitude and mismanagement? What would be the point in that? Hmm? My place is out at the farm, with Mr Waite, where I have employment and an income and a future. What did you ever give me, besides a headache from your constant whining? Well, listen carefully: this is where it ends. From now on, you will not interfere in my life, or tell me what to do. You will move ahead with your own life, with no more thought for me than you would give to a passing stranger. Stay away from me, if you know what's good for you. Is that clear?"

With a curl of his lip, he turned away, stepped to the antiques store, inserted a key in the lock. A moment later and he was inside, slamming the door behind him. The lock clicked, and Kane was alone.

Arika came up behind him. "Why did you let him go? Did you tell him I needed to talk to him?"

"I've had it!" Kane bellowed in her face. "Up to here!" he added, touching his chin with the back of his hand.

Realising that shouting at Arika was rude and unnecessary, he lowered his voice. "He's lost it. He's … a freak. He's moved in with that – that freak. They deserve each other. I can't deal with him anymore. There's just … He can do whatever he wants from now on. That's it. I'm done."

Throwing an angry glance at the antiques store, he started back to Brandywine.

"Kane," cried Arika, running after him, "what happened?"

"If that moron wants to get mixed up in weird shit, he's welcome to it. I've tried and I've tried and … I don't care what Dad would say. He's a lost cause. There's nothing more I can do. Nothing. Sorry, Dad –

nothing!"

"Kane, come back inside and let's talk about it."

He turned to her, no longer interested in chatting her up or finding out more about gods and aliens. In his eyes, Arika was a part of the warped world Dylan had gotten himself involved in, and he needed to get as far away from it and him and her as possible. He needed to move away from Quorn – tomorrow, if he could manage it.

"Listen," he said. "I told you everything I know. Why don't you go on back to your university? There's nothing here to see, no monsters hiding in the bushes. I told you everything I know. It's over. I'm done with this crap."

He felt bad as he jumped in his truck and reversed, even worse when he glanced up and saw Frankie storming out of Brandywine Grind with his arms in the air, assailing Arika for walking out without paying the bill. But Kane was too enraged and confused to go back. Staring at the speedo, he tried to calm himself by pushing his brother from his mind and plotting his escape from sleepy, depressing, freak-infested Quorn.

ARRIVING HOME WITH a six-pack of beer, Kane didn't notice Arika's car parked on the side of the road. But there she was, back on the porch, just like before.

She didn't say anything, just stood there watching him. He took a seat, pulled out a beer and handed it to her.

Arika sat next to him, accepted the bottle, and tried to twist off the cap. It wasn't that type of bottle.

"Here," offered Kane, holding out a hand.

"I'll do it," she said, and to his horror, placed the bottle cap against her eye socket, like he'd seen some drunk do on YouTube.

"Holy shit!" he cried, but then she laughed and handed the bottle to him.

Kane held it against the edge of the seat and hit the bottle with his palm. The top went spinning away. He gave the bottle back to her, then did the same with his.

They both took a swig.

"This is some weird shit," Kane breathed, shaking his head.

She nodded. "Not everyday weird shit, though. Fanatics trying to raise hell on earth."

"He spends all his time with that creep. How could he, when he knows what Waite might have done to our folks?"

"If Waite does have the Necronomicon, he could be holding a power over your brother."

Kane looked at her. "What kind of power?"

"What was that about your folks?"

He didn't feel inclined to tell her the story right now. "Tell me more about the book. How does it work?"

"The Necronomicon isn't just a book," Arika explained, "it's an energy source … a key to some not very pleasant dimensions. And a magnet for all sorts of crazies."

"What did you mean by a power? Do you think it's the book that's making Dylan act strange?"

"If Waite wants to control him, the Necronomicon would have the kinds of spells he needs to do it."

"But why Dylan? He's a skinny adolescent. Lazy as all hell. Bad tempered. Unreliable. He could have chosen somebody like …" He glanced at Arika, and saw from the look on her face that she knew what he stopped short of saying.

Now he was vulnerable and confused, she seemed to be warming to him. "It could be like hypnotism. The subject needs to be open to suggestion. Not everyone can be hypnotised."

"I need to work out how to break the spell."

Arika took another swallow of beer, then frowned at the label. "Well, I'm not an expert at things like this, but I'd say a good start would be to get your brother away from the mad sorcerer."

"Or steal the book." Kane tapped his bottle on the arm of the seat. "I need to get back out to the farm."

Then he turned to Arika and told her everything.

WHEN HE GOT to the part about the dogs, she said, "What will you do about them?"

"Worried about their welfare?"

"I'm worried about *your* welfare."

Kane felt the blood rush to his face. "I'm a fireman," he asserted. "Trained in search and rescue."

"So if the dogs are stuck up a tree," she smirked, "we'll have it covered."

He placed his empty bottle on the floor, smiling at her little joke. His head jerked up. "Did you say we?"

She placed her empty bottle next to his. "I can help."

Kane shook his head. He should have seen that coming. It was clear as the nose on his face that Arika was the type of person who never took no for an answer. She came all the way out here for a story, and she wasn't going home without one. But her involvement was out of the question. This was a family affair. What Kane was intending to do was dangerous, possibly deadly, probably illegal.

He was explaining this to her when they were distracted by the sound of an approaching car. It was the Honda. Kane watched as the car turned into the driveway, drove up, and ran into the back of his truck.

"What the hell!" he cried.

Taking off, he leapt from the top of the steps and raced towards the car.

Dylan was slumped over the steering wheel, with barely enough strength to lift his head. "Kane," he croaked, pushing open the door. "Help me."

"What? What's wrong?" He glanced around for bruises or blood, before realising Dylan hadn't been driving fast enough to get hurt. "What's wrong?"

Arika came up behind him, phone in hand. "I'm calling an ambulance."

"No, wait."

Kane pulled Dylan off the steering wheel, reached down and unfastened the seatbelt. His brother lolled in the seat, staring at him with heavily-lidded eyes.

"I was looking at him," he murmured. "Then it was me. I wasn't me. It was him."

"Wha?" grunted Kane. "You're not making any sense." He turned to

Arika. "He's not making any sense."

"He locked himself in the basement … so I couldn't get out. But he wasn't strong enough. He went to the shop. I was there."

"Hey, man, hold on. You're babbling."

"You don't understand."

"Cos you're not making any sense."

"I can feel him … still there … inside my head. He's trying to get back in … pushing me out."

"What are you talking about?"

Dylan grabbed his collar, pulling him down. "Wilfred Waite. His body is failing. So he wants mine."

20

Possession

AFTER SEEING DYLAN to bed, Kane joined Arika in the kitchen.

"It's like he's been hypnotised. He's imagining all kinds of things."

Arika was sitting at the table, typing into her tablet. Her jacket was hanging off the back of her chair, and he saw she'd helped herself to another of his beers.

"I'm seeing if there's anything that resembles what your brother described," she said without looking up.

"I've seen those TV shows where people act like idiots. I get hypnotism. But switching bodies? That smacks of paranoid delusions."

"Don't jump to conclusions, Kane. We need evidence."

"I wouldn't be surprised if he's having a nervous breakdown. He's been through so much since … since Oliver died and he was packed off to Briarwood. Our mother was clinically depressed, then old Bert got dementia. Dylan was out there feeling responsible for Oliver, feeling abandoned … blamed. Then Bert. Christ." He sat down. "Or drugs. It could be drugs."

Arika moved her face closer to the screen. "There's plenty of stories about spells that can switch bodies and minds. Here's one from the late nineties. A woman claimed her mother took over her body, and that was her excuse for murdering her. All very convenient. But no actual proof it can be done. No credible witnesses … Ah, demon possession … mm, sounds like a scene from *The Exorcist*. There's some experiments about out-of-body experiences; but that's more illusion. It's not about living in someone else's body, walking around in it … driving a car in it …"

Kane was only half listening. His mind had locked on the positive, on the fact that Dylan had escaped the clutches of the psychopathic Wilfred Waite. "At least he's home," he said. "And he's seen that – that nutcase for what he is. He won't be heading back to the farm in a hurry."

Arika inhaled sharply. With a huff, she reached for her beer. "Nah, that doesn't make sense. Another fairy tale."

"We need to get out of here … now."

"Multiple personality disorder …"

"If I had my way," Kane said, "I'd go out there and burn the place down."

That one caught Arika's attention. She stopped with the beer bottle pressed against her mouth.

He smiled sheepishly. "Forget that last bit."

UPSTAIRS, DYLAN WAS dozing. He was aware of his surroundings, the smell of his dirty socks, the sound of kids yelling outside the window, his brother downstairs with a woman he'd never seen before – but he was also dreaming his mother was in the room across the hall. He could see her in his mind's eye, folding up washing. Her routine was to take the basket of clean clothes upstairs to her bedroom, fold each item, place them in stacks on the bed (shirts on shirts, jeans on jeans, socks in piles according to their colour), then make the rounds of the rooms to deposit each stack in its appointed place. Dylan found a warm comfort in the dream. Even though he knew it wasn't real, he tried to press that knowledge down into the mattress so he could maintain the illusion for longer. Wilfred had taught him the impossible can become possible if you have enough belief, so who's to say, if he concentrated hard enough, his mother wouldn't come breezing into the room? She'd chide him for sleeping in the middle of the afternoon, then hand him his shirts in a neat pile, a little stack of socks balanced on top.

The illusion was drowned in a wave of dizziness. Dylan's eyes flew open and his stomach flip-flopped and spurted acid into his throat. Coughing, he sat up and threw off the sheets.

The room appeared to be buckling, like an earthquake had hit the house. Nausea swelled inside him. He pressed his palms against his eyes.

"Nooo!" he cried. "No way!"

Something was poking around in his head.

"Get out!" he cried at the wall opposite. "Leave me alone!"

But the intruder was insistent. The wall bulged, the furniture dissolved into a blur of colours and shapes … and then the bedroom melted away and Dylan found himself in a dark sitting room. He was slumped in a lumpy armchair facing maroon velvet drapes. Something smelt rotten – the kind of decades-old rotten that infiltrates the walls and carpet and furniture.

"Kane," he whined.

He tried to move, but couldn't seem to locate his muscles. There was a throbbing pain in his fingers, a feeling of pins and needles in his legs, but the rest of his body was as inanimate as the armchair.

Survival instincts kicked in. With a massive effort of will, Dylan found and flexed his biceps, and then, inch by inch, sensation began returning to the rest of his body. He could stretch his fingers, extend his legs, twist his torso, turn his head. He sighed with relief when at last he felt his heart beating weakly in his chest.

"Kane?" he murmured, pushing himself out of the chair. He stood for a moment on wobbly legs, then, stepping jerkily, made his way towards an oval, gilt-framed mirror.

Wilfred Waite stared back at him.

"Kane!"

"TRY BODY SNATCHING."

Arika shook her head. "That'll just come up with movie references." She stared hard at the ceiling. "Oh well, can't hurt."

She typed in the words and pressed Enter.

"On no, look. Hmm, a lot about grave robbers. Nothing about stealing a living body."

"Let me see."

Kane spun the tablet towards him. Arika's mention of grave robbers reminded him of the day of his parents' murder, the afternoon he and his father moved the sideboard into the house. Dylan had been watching the news: a story about a stolen corpse. Kane hadn't thought much of it at the time, but now it seemed an unlikely coincidence that people were ransacking graves at the same time Wilfred was playing around with dead things.

He typed in 'grave robber' and 'news', and they both watched as the screen filled with stories.

"Wow," he breathed, "will you look at that."

Arika took the tablet back. "A two-hundred-year-old sailor," she read. "He would have been dust. There's a recent one" – she pointed at the screen – "only three months old." She read more. "They're all over the place. Strangely enough, they were all men. Seems like the grave robbers around here are a bunch of misogynists."

"Are what?"

She smiled to herself as she kept going through the stories.

"Oh look: there's a woman. Tatiana Aspidov. Defector from the KGB. Died in the fifties. Wow, she was reportedly almost six foot four. Died in suspicious circumstances … poisoned umbrella would be my guess." She sat back. "In most of these cases, the perpetrators tried to hide what they did, so they probably weren't just vandals doing it for kicks."

"Not hard to guess who it was," Kane muttered.

"That's a helluva lot of bodies."

"He must have accomplices. A decrepit old man couldn't dig up all those coffins." A thought hit him. "Please don't tell me Dylan helped him dig up those dudes. No," he reminded himself: "Dylan didn't know him back then. And the kid probably has punier muscles than old man Waite."

"There's a couple stolen from mausoleums," said Arika. "And some from pretty public areas. It looks like he's being selective, or else why would he take chances like that?"

"But why? These are people who've been buried for months. Or years. Decades even. It's not like Waite's resurrecting long-dead girlfriends so he can go out dancing with them."

"Or long-lost boyfriends, noting they were almost all men. We should ask Dylan when he wakes up. The more we know, the better prepared we'll be."

"Prepared? There's no preparation needed. We're getting the hell away from that psycho. This house is getting sold and we're leaving town as quick as it takes to pack."

Arika seemed about to argue with him, then thought better of it. She scrolled down the screen and clicked on another story.

A stair creaked.

Kane's head flew up. "Dylan!" he called out. "That you?"

Footsteps sounded, and his brother appeared in the doorway, squinting against the light.

"How you feeling?" asked Kane.

"Good, good," he replied, clasping his hands in front of him. He glanced at Arika. "Apologies for my behaviour earlier. It was completely out of character. I blame nervous exhaustion from long hours at the store."

Kane frowned at him.

"Mr Waite and I have been working like dogs, cataloguing a shipment of valuable antiques destined for very important clients. We really must pace ourselves from now on."

Kane stood up. "Why are you talking like that?"

In reply, he received an icy stare, which was quickly replaced by a smile. "No rest for the wicked! Those antiques are not about to catalogue themselves." He turned away.

Kane went after him. "Dylan," he said, "you're not going anywhere. You need rest."

"Rest is for children and old men."

He grabbed his arm. "And sick brothers."

"Get your filthy hands off me!"

His eyes blazed with rage; but a moment later a cloud passed over them and he said affably, "I mean, please: go rejoin your friend. Don't make a fuss on my account."

He left the house.

"Dylan, wait!" called Kane, chasing him down the steps.

Throwing open the car door, he jumped inside and locked it.

Kane rapped on the window. "Get out of there, Dylan. Have something to eat or something."

He started the car and reversed, almost running over Kane's foot.

"Hey!" he cried, jumping back. He raced up the road, and when the car came to a halt on the road, placed both hands on the bonnet.

The car reversed further, stopped, then drove around him. Kane watched with fists on hips as it cruised around the corner.

Turning back to the house, he saw Arika standing on the porch. She held up her car keys and jangled them.

"Car chase, anyone?"

"DON'T GET TOO close," Kane warned as they tailed the Honda through the streets of Quorn.

"If we go any slower, we'll be going backwards. I take it your brother doesn't normally drive like a pensioner?"

"You read my mind." He checked his phone for messages. There were none. Shoving the phone back in his pocket, he squinted at Dylan's car and said, "We can't let him see us."

"He won't."

"If we can see him, he can see us."

"He doesn't know what my car looks like."

"It was parked outside the house."

"You're fussing like my Great Aunt Celia. Relax, Kane. I'm a dab hand at this."

He looked at her. "You don't get fazed by much; I'll give you that."

"My father's a private detective. I learnt cool from him."

"For real?"

"He taught me everything I know."

"Wow," said Kane. "Impressive. And here I was, thinking you were just a brainiac."

She glanced at him. "I could show you a thing or two in the ring."

"Is that a promise?"

She didn't bother to respond.

Placing his hands in his lap, he asked, "Was your dad always a PI?"

"When I was a kid, he was navy. We travelled a lot."

"I suppose being a PI is safer than the navy."

"The opposite, actually."

"I thought PIs made their living chasing cheating husbands, sitting outside sleazy motel rooms –"

"My dad is more like a security consultant. If a company – or a government – has a problem, and isn't getting anywhere with the regular avenues, he comes in with his special skills."

"Special skills. Sounds interesting. Is that what he taught you?"

Arika smiled at the road ahead. Kane already knew she was a girl of many talents, and now he was getting an inkling where those talents came from.

"If I can't convince Dylan to come back, maybe I can hire your dad to rough up Waite." He leaned towards her, ghost-bumping her shoulder. "Or maybe you could do it. Rough him up, I mean."

"I don't know where he is."

He looked at her. Her face was like wax.

"My dad's missing."

Kane watched her watching the Honda. "What happened to him?" he asked, then quickly added, "Sorry. That's none of my business. You don't have to tell me."

"No," Arika rushed to reassure him. "You told me your story; it's only fair I tell you mine."

When the Honda turned right, she flicked the indicator and followed it around the corner.

"He took on a job with Simon – Professor Orwell – tracking down a man who was alive at the beginning of last century. Last time we spoke, he said he found a lead, and then he just vanished. Into thin air."

"You've no idea where he went?"

"He never told me what he found. He was pretty confident he was onto something, though. He could be anywhere."

"Did you say he was looking for a guy who lived a century ago?"

"Yeah – his house, not him, of course. He'd be long dead. Simon's research shows this guy travelled all over the world, so my dad could have gone to the North Pole for all I know."

"That's too bad."

"After he went missing, Simon offered me the job as his research assistant."

"That was nice of him."

"It was good to get a paid job." She glanced at him. "I was doing my PhD under the professor … before he met my dad, this was. Simon's an amazing historian. When he told me about the legend of this lost library, I thought if anyone could find it, my dad could. I was probably more desperate than Simon to find those books. Some of them may be the only copy in existence, lost for centuries. Simon never thought of hiring a private detective until I told him what my dad did."

Kane watched her as she stroked the steering wheel with both thumbs. She was probably feeling responsible for hooking up her father with the professor: the precursor to his disappearance. On his part, he couldn't help but be excited by their shared experience of loss – it was the first real connection between them beyond their mutual interest in his brother and the mad sorcerer.

"Every time there's a knock at the door, I think it's him. It drives me crazy."

"Yeah, that knock on the door … I know all about that." He leaned forward. "There. I knew it. He's on his way to that damn farmhouse."

"Want me to catch up?"

"No point."

"I could drive up alongside and run him off the road."

"You've almost got me thinking you're serious."

Her silence told him she probably was.

"Let him go. Can you turn the car around?"

Arika seemed disappointed. "We're not going out there?"

"We're going out there. But not right now."

She turned off the road and slowed to a stop. Staring after Dylan's car, she said, "What's the plan?"

Kane bit his thumb, trying to think. He'd already settled on his goal: put as much distance between Dylan and Wilfred Waite as possible, even if that meant kidnapping his brother and driving non-stop to Cornwall. But he hadn't yet been able to work backwards from there to where they were now.

"Kane?"

"No plan. Not yet." He smiled at her. "How are you with animals?"

21

The body snatcher

DYLAN FLUNG THE book across the room with as much strength as his feeble body could muster. The book flew like a bird and hit the gilt mirror, which crashed to the floor, scattering shards and splinters of glass across the carpet.

He felt scared, angry and helpless. There wasn't anything useful in the books he'd been flicking through. The spell Wilfred used to swap their bodies was from the Necronomicon, Dylan was sure of it, and of course Wilfred hadn't left *that* book lying around.

With an effort, he shuffled across the room, bent over, and picked up a triangle of shattered glass. The wrinkled face of Wilfred Waite peered back at him. The eyes – Wilfred's sunken, black-rimmed eyes – his eyes – were shiny with terror. Dylan stared at the hated face. The more he stared, the greater became his fear that the change was irreversible, that he was fated to live the rest of his days as an octogenarian.

He dropped the glass to the floor and made his way to the day bed. He felt so weary, so like … an old man. It hurt to move, hurt to breathe, hurt to sit on the bed. Falling back with a groan, he closed his eyes and dropped his head to his shoulder.

HE WAS JERKED awake by the sound of a key in the door.

Pushing himself up, Dylan stood on unsteady legs as the door opened. Like in a dream, he saw himself – his body – step into the room.

Wilfred looked down at the books strewn about the floor. "A fine way for a guest to act in his host's home," he scolded, waving a finger at him like an old school teacher.

Dylan hobbled menacingly towards him.

Wilfred folded his arms. "Now that wouldn't be fair, would it? – a healthy young buck like me, against pathetic, crippled old you."

Dylan stopped at a safe distance. He saw cruelty in his eyes, those teenaged eyes that until recently were filled with little more than boredom. In fact, the whole aspect of his stolen body oozed menace. Wilfred's mind had perverted it, turned it into something that looked sinister and nasty. He'd witnessed the sadistic things Wilfred did to his resurrected friend, the torture he seemed to revel in, and knew he wouldn't hesitate to do the same to him if given an excuse.

"Soon as I get out of this body ..." he warned.

"Please," breathed Wilfred, raising his eyes to the ceiling. "No juvenile threats. Look at this sensibly, boy. You didn't appreciate or value this youthful vessel, whereas I do. More than you can ever hope to understand. This body is everything to me: a joy and a pleasure beyond anything *you* ever felt. Accept the inevitable, and be heartened by the knowledge that this mortal frame is destined for greatness. As I told you from the beginning, your body was born to rule, to sit shoulder to shoulder with gods and command a new world order." Wilfred sneered at him. "You don't honestly believe that you – a lazy, obnoxious, ungrateful little whelpling – deserve this body more than I? You're not that simpleminded, are you?"

"You're a lying thief!"

Wilfred crouched and picked up the mirror's gilt frame. He shook his head at it. "This was a gift from my third wife, bless her simple heart. I do miss her steak and kidney pudding. She had a special way with offal, did Bessie." He glanced at Dylan. "I never lied to you, boy. You just heard what you wanted to hear."

"My brother will stop you."

Dropping the frame, Wilfred sprang to his feet. "That log-headed ox? A match against me?" He squeezed his hands into fists. "I'll crush him like a beetle."

Dylan shut his mouth. He knew his threats were getting him nowhere. If anything, he was putting thoughts in Wilfred's head, thoughts that might place his brother in danger. He wasn't certain Kane believed his story about Wilfred and the goings-on at the farm; but that wasn't the point. If Wilfred perceived Kane as a threat – any kind of threat – all he needed was a few seconds when his brother was off guard to plunge a knife in his heart.

Wilfred softened his face. "Believe it or not, Master Dylan, I like you. You helped me at a time when I most needed it. Now it's my turn to help *you*."

Dylan eyed him warily. What had brought on this sudden reversal of mood? Wilfred helped no one but himself.

"I am a valuable person to know. You've done me a great favour, at great personal cost, and I am not one to let a sacrifice like yours go unrewarded. Tell me: what would you like? I am at your disposal; your humble servant. Name your treasure."

"I don't want anything from you."

"Come, now, surely you do. Everyone desires something."

"Give me my body back."

"I have riches squirrelled away all over the world. What's your poison? Wine? Women? Gold?"

"I want my body!"

"I would very much like to continue our collaboration, doing the Great Ones' work. Wouldn't you like that too? In fact, I can help you find your own body, a new vessel to go forth in. You have many more options than I, with your extended gene pool and all. It will be a breeze. And then, perhaps you might join me in my grand adventure, become an immortal, like me: one with the gods."

Dylan was baffled. Despite his fury, he felt himself warming to Wilfred, in the same way he'd read about hostages being drawn towards their captors. Here was Wilfred offering him immortality. How often does that kind of offer come along?

"Perhaps you might choose your log-headed brother. How often have you gazed on his firm musculature in envy and thought how nice it would be to be that strong? He must be a hit with the ladies."

Dylan stared at him, hardly listening. Then the truth hit him, and a blast of hope surged through his weak, aching body.

"Do you think I'm an old fool?" he spat, taking a step towards his enemy. "Just cos I look like one?"

Wilfred picked up one of the books, brushed off some dust, placed it on the lamp table. "I know these are probably not your cup of tea. I can have some of your own brought in … a TV, video player? I don't care for television myself –"

"You won't kill me cos you're scared you'd be killing yourself."

Wilfred shot an evil glance at him. He bent to pick up another book. "In time," he said, flicking over the pages, "I do believe we will grow to become friends again, helpmates as we continue our journey towards enlightenment."

"Kill me, and you might find yourself back in a dead body."

"Stranger things have happened between former associates."

Dylan was growing bolder. He could tell by Wilfred's reaction that he'd hit the nail on the head.

"You're losing hold. I can feel it. You're scared. You can't hold on."

The book dropped to the floor. In a flash, Wilfred had him by the throat.

"Shut that fool mouth! You dare test my patience? I will rip your throat open with my bare hands! I will reach into your lungs and suffocate you while you gasp for every pathetic breath! Pain will visit you as you have never imagined in the worst of your nightmares!"

Shoving him against the wall, Wilfred strengthened his grip on his windpipe. Dylan wheezed as he fought to draw breath. His young face, the dark soul of Wilfred Waite twisting it with anger, bore down on him. He could taste the sweet breath of youth, feel the strands of his own black hair tickling his face. I've miscalculated, he thought. He's killing me right here and now. His eyes watered, blood pounded in his ears like a hammer, the room began to dim.

Drawing back, Wilfred relaxed his hold. Dylan staggered and his arthritic knees gave way. As he fell, Wilfred caught him under the arms and helped him to the day bed.

"Forgive me," he said gently. "I have the foulest temper."

Stepping away from the bed, he gazed down as Dylan, panting and coughing, massaged his bruised throat.

"I appreciate this is an unnerving time for you. You're confused, and you feel the need to strike out at someone. But it's pointless trying to second-guess a man who has lived three lifetimes."

Spinning on his heel, he walked away. "I've enjoyed our little chat, but it's time to go see a man about a spell."

Wilfred paused at the door, turned, and glanced again at the books and glass scattered across the floor. "In my absence, I suggest you clean up this damn mess."

And then he was gone.

Dylan leaned forward, hoping for a chance to escape. But when the key turned in the lock, he fell back, weak and broken. Rubbing his throat, he stared at the window opposite. When he first came to the farmhouse, he assumed the boarded-up windows were to keep intruders out, but now he knew better: they were here to keep things in.

He closed his eyes. His arthritis was playing up, his gastric reflux was worse, and it hurt to swallow, but before long he was asleep, and dreaming he was walking through a deserted city. It was night, and the buildings were all in ruins. There were no lights, only the pale glow of the moon behind a thick blanket of cloud. Dylan wandered through the litter-strewn streets, looking about in wonder. Nothing stirred. He entered a plaza, piled high with broken chunks of concrete from the ruined skyscrapers, and paused to take in the destruction. Around him was life obliterated: broken office furniture, smashed computers, glass, paper and dust. And bones. Lots of them.

Suddenly the clouds parted and the light of the moon fell upon the ruined city. Dylan's eye was caught by a colossal pillar of black stone in the distance, which rose from the rubble and dominated the landscape. As he stared, something grey and gelatinous dragged its obscene bulk up the pillar, settled at the top, and sat there surveying the city. It turned its head and fixed its red eyes on him.

DYLAN LEAPT OUT of sleep. He sat up, his head like lead. How much time had passed? There were no clocks in the room, but his bladder was full and his stomach was crying out for food, so he guessed some time must have passed since Wilfred came to see him.

Pushing himself to his feet, he hobbled to the door and banged on it with his fist.

"Let me out!" he yelped. "I need to piss!"

He listened at the door. The house was silent. He stepped back and raised his voice. "I said I need to use the bathroom!"

Rattling the handle with one hand, he banged on the door with the other. No one came. He was looking around for a vase to use as a chamber pot when a familiar wave of nausea travelled through his body. He squeezed his eyes shut, bent over, pressed his hands against his stomach and dry retched.

As quickly as it came, the nausea receded.

Dylan straightened, glanced around, and to his astonishment saw he was standing beneath turbulent clouds on a grassy knoll. Before him was a flat rock, sheared at an odd angle and etched deeply with what appeared to be a pentagram. Around the perimeter of the pentagram were weird symbols and geometric shapes, chiselled into the stone. A small metal dish sat at the highest end of the altar, and from this dish a red liquid had flowed into the grooves of the pentagram.

His mind buzzing, Dylan held up his hands. They were his own, thin and white. Like the altar, they were stained with blood. Dropping to his knees, he began scrubbing his hands on the grass, then noticed a towel inside a black leather bag to his left. The bag also contained sandalwood-scented handwash and a bottle of Highland Spring water, which he used to clean his hands properly.

Climbing to his feet, drying his hands on his pants, he glanced around, trying to get his bearings. In the distance was Jacob's End. He could tell from the dead land and the glimpses of Deep Ocean Road that he wasn't far from the farmhouse.

Dylan was certain this wasn't another dream. He could hear insects and birds, smell the blood on the altar, feel the ground beneath his feet and a cool breeze on his face. It was all real. He was back in his own body.

His excitement soared. He'd been right: Wilfred wasn't strong enough to hold onto his body for more than a few hours, and Dylan could return at any time. Drunk with relief, he threw out his arms and ran around, feeling, as if for the first time, the joy and strength of being young.

Now to get as far away from this place as possible. He scanned his surroundings for any sign of his car. Where would Wilfred have parked it? The land curved downwards in all directions, but there was no sign of a trail.

As Dylan watched, a head appeared, a small head with straggly ginger hair, and a man with a bony face and rounded shoulders came strolling up the hill. It was Kenny Snyder, Wilfred's acolyte, bodyguard, grave-robber and general fixer. Peering up, Kenny gave Dylan a yellow-toothed smile. He was wearing a brown boiler suit and black leather gloves, and was carrying something baby-sized wrapped in a dirty blue jacket. To Dylan's horror, the shape squirmed, and a tiny hand poked out.

At this, Kenny stopped, his creepy smile dripped away, and he regarded Dylan with narrowed eyes. Dylan sucked in breath. Had the shocked look on his face given him away? He couldn't keep his eyes off the jacket and whatever was squirming inside it – which wasn't something Wilfred would be doing right now. Wilfred would be holding out his arms, eager to get on with whatever it was he was planning to do with the bundle.

Before Dylan could make a move, he was distracted by the sound of a voice – a chant, if he wasn't mistaken. It seemed to be coming from inside his head, then from the surrounding air. The world quivered with each sound.

Pain slammed into his forehead like a brick, and he dropped to his knees, banged his chin on his chest, and knelt on all fours with eyes closed while he waited for the pain to fade. The breeze died; the smells changed; all went quiet. The light behind his eyelids dimmed.

When he lifted his head, his worst fear was realised. He was back in the sitting room, on his knees on the musty green carpet.

He raised his hands, already knowing what he would find. They were brown and scabby and wrinkled.

"Yaaahhh!" he cried, shaking them violently, as if that would make them go away.

Grabbing hold of a brass lamp, pulling on the cord till it ripped from the wall, Dylan raised the lamp over his head and lobbed it at the door. Ignoring his arthritis and gout, he pushed himself to his feet, hobbled to the bookcase, and with an effort, tugged on it and watched with satisfaction as it crashed to the floor. Then, with an invigorating feeling of release, he set about destroying the rest of the room.

22

Rescue squad

DRIVING UP TO the farmhouse gate, Kane parked his truck and looked around. Dylan's car was nowhere in sight.

"It's just how I imagined it," breathed Arika, pushing open the door, unable to pull her eyes away from the dirty, broken house.

"Where could he have gone?" muttered Kane, thumping the steering wheel.

"The car might be hidden," Arika suggested. "There: behind the barn."

"It's not a barn, it's … Hey, hold on," he cried as she swung her legs out. He gestured at the rifle.

Reluctantly, she handed it to him. "You sure you don't want me to do it?"

"He's my brother."

"I'm a better shot than you."

"You think?"

"I think."

"You'd be surprised at the number of savage animals we have to control here in Quorn."

"Three a year, is it?"

Kane got out of the truck. "At least double that."

He checked the rifle, then went up to the gate. He could hear the dogs barking behind the house, and guessed from their savage excitement that they'd heard the truck as it approached the house. Figuring they must be chained or locked up, he climbed over the gate.

Arika came up behind him. She had the strap of her bag looped around her neck and was waving his wrench in the air.

"Don't forget to put that back when you're finished with it."

She followed him over the gate and into the yard. It was getting late and the light was fading, the shadows lengthening. A mist of rain was in the air; probably more would come later, judging by the clouds. Not the best time of day to be entering a spooky old farmhouse to do battle with an evil wizard.

They'd only walked a few paces when one of the dogs came scrambling around the corner of the house.

"Goddamnit!" yelled Kane. "Where did that come from?"

He raised the rifle to his shoulder, aimed at the dog and fired.

The dart hit the Rottweiler in the nose. It yelped, crumpled to the ground, bowled through the mud, bounded to its feet and ran in a circle, howling like a devil. Then, with a pathetic whimper, it took off back to the house.

The other dog wasn't far behind. Before Kane could re-load, it launched itself at him. As he watched in horror, its black body rocketed into the air, soared towards him, and slammed into his chest. The rifle went flying away; he threw out his arms and fell backwards into the mud.

The dog somersaulted, rolled in the mud, jumped up, and was at him in an instant. Kane scrambled back, got his hands on its neck, pushed it back with all his might, then lay staring in terror as it snarled into his face. Its yellow teeth snapped at his nose. Its breath smelt like a sewer. Brown froth dripped from its jaws, splashed on his cheeks and ran into his mouth.

"Gaaahhhh!" he cried as the dog scratched its claws at his chest, trying to propel itself forward. Its muscles were like steel; its head was straining to get closer to him; his arms were weakening.

As the dog's snout made contact with the skin of his nose, he was startled by the sound of a rifle shot. The dog stopped its onslaught, turned its head and snapped and growled at the dart embedded in its flank. Arika then appeared in his line of vision. Raising the rifle butt, she slammed it into the side of the dog's head, and Kane heaved the monster off him. It fell with a splat in the mud, scrambled up, glanced around in confusion, then took off after the other one.

Getting onto his knees, Kane spat on the ground, trying to get the disgusting taste of dog spit out of his mouth. Arika was standing over him, the rifle held army-style against her chest.

"That," he said, wiping his mouth on his sleeve, "is a sight for red-neck eyes." Pushing himself to his feet, he held out his hand. "Doesn't mean you get to keep it."

Arika gave the rifle to him. "Seems to have scared them more than anything," she said, pulling the wrench out of her bag.

"It'll take a while for the drug to work."

"Maybe it doesn't work on the undead."

He looked at her. "You think they're zombie dogs? They sure do smell dead."

She shrugged. "We should get to the house. If they aren't asleep by now, they'll be back."

Kane put in another dart. "Come on then, Rambo."

As they passed the chapel, Kane pointed out the hole in the wall and explained that that was where the Messenger had broken out. There were deep claw marks going up the wall, the roof was broken and there was a smattering of tiles on the ground, indicating the place the monster lost its footing and fell. It was the first time Kane had seen it, and it brought to vivid life the horror his brother had helped unleash on the world.

He went over and had a quick look inside. It was pretty much as Dylan had described it. No one had bothered cleaning up the mess.

"Nothing here," he remarked as Arika joined him.

She leaned into the hole in the wall, checking out the steel table, red wax candles and broken coffins. "Phew, it stinks in there. Hey, what's that?" she asked, pointing at a leathery white-and-black sack on the table. It looked to be spattered with blood and gobs of dried entrails, which reminded Kane of sun-dried tomatoes.

He pulled her away. He knew what it was, but didn't want her getting distracted. Though he'd told her about the raising of the Messenger, his explanation hadn't extended to the fate of the dead itinerant who birthed the monstrosity.

On they went past the well and the twisted piece of farm machinery. In the distance were the huts Dylan had described. In its current state, it was hard to imagine this place as a thriving farming community. The place was like a giant mud pit, most of the vegetation dead, the bushes and trees leafless, their trunks and branches twisted as if writhing in pain. It was clear Wilfred Waite had chosen this spot for its isolation, and Kane wondered again about the horrors the wizard had raised here, far away from the eyes and ears of nosy neighbours.

At the farmhouse porch, he placed his ear against the door. The house was silent, though he thought he heard a low droning noise that might have been coming from a generator.

Standing back, he knocked.

A few seconds passed. No one answered. Kane knocked again, louder this time. Still nothing.

"What now?" asked Arika.

He put his ear to the door. No answer didn't mean there was no one home, but he couldn't let that stop him, not now they'd come this far.

"Is it true firemen have special keys that open any door?" Arika asked as she squinted through the dirt-caked window.

"We do," answered Kane, straightening. Raising a leg, he slammed his heel against the door. The ancient wood splintered and the door flew open, making a house-shaking bang as it hit the wall.

"They're called fire boots."

Stepping over the threshold, Kane found himself in a gloomy antechamber. A dark hall ran down the centre of the house, ending at a closed door. To his left was a small parlour, set up with old-fashioned furniture: fat armchairs, two small tables, an ornate telephone and an ugly floor lamp on a red-and-black rug. Shelves on either side of a central fireplace held dozens of books, which, upon investigation, he saw were mostly medical texts, history books and travel guides.

"Do you think we should be doing this?" asked Arika, glancing around nervously. "Breaking and entering, I mean."

"I doubt Waite will call the cops on us," Kane reassured her, "knowing what we know about the Messenger. If he comes home before we find the book, we'll give him a choice between Dylan and a jail cell. That should do it."

Leaving Arika at the bookshelves, he returned to the foyer. Beyond the parlour was a staircase, the banister worn and shiny from the rubbing of countless hands over untold years. The wooden stairs were scuffed and split and chipped from age and neglect. Dark wood panelling followed the stairs to the second floor, and attached to the panels was a series of oil paintings, each in an ornate gilded frame.

Kane went to check them out. The painting at the foot of the stairs depicted a sallow, long-faced man with flushed cheeks and wavy grey hair, parted in the middle. He was sitting in a shadowed room, wearing a black collarless coat and white ruffled cravat. The nameplate was inscribed: 'Jonathon Dark, Putnam Village, 1688'.

The next painting depicted an older man – probably in his seventies – with the same long, humourless face and receding grey hair. He was wearing a maroon coat and mustard waistcoat, and was seated in a wooden chair overlooking a sickly rural landscape. The nameplate on this one announced the man to be 'James Dark, London, 1761'. One of the first dude's descendants, was Kane's guess. The stairwell was too dark to see much else, but Kane assumed the paintings were further portraits of the Dark clan, becoming more recent as they ascended the stairs.

"Oh my God!" hissed Arika, who'd crept up behind him.

"What?" cried Kane, his heart leaping into his mouth.

"This is it."

"What?"

"The Dark farm."

He glanced at the paintings. "I don't –"

"Jonathon Dark," explained Arika, "is the name of the man my father was hunting."

Kane was confused. It didn't make sense that someone would be looking for a man who'd probably been dead for over three hundred years; until he remembered it was the man's library Arika's father had been searching for.

"Not that Jonathon Dark," Arika added, nodding at the first painting.

"His great great great great grandson?"

"This is his farm. His farm!" She glanced around in awe. "We found his farm." Pulling out her phone, she began taking pictures of the paintings.

"I probably missed a 'great' or two."

"After all this time. I'm –"

The floorboards overhead creaked, and they both froze and raised their eyes to the ceiling. The house stayed silent, as if it were holding its breath.

"You heard that?"

She nodded slowly.

"Maybe we should call the police," Kane ventured, worried that things were starting to get out of hand. "If this is the place your father went missing … Waite could have had something to do with it. Like with my own family. He might have murdered them all. He could … we could …"

"No way," countered Arika, brushing past him on her way to the room on their right. "No police. If something happened to him here, I need to know *now*, not wait for search warrants and all that crap. They'll just get in the way."

Shrugging, he followed her.

The room Arika had entered was set up for formal dining. A sideboard, stacked with china, stretched the length of one wall. The table was long and narrow, the chairs gothic. Two tarnished candelabras, their candles burnt to stubs, were home to spiders and dirt, and judging by all the cobwebs and dust lying thick on every surface, this room hadn't been used in decades.

"Let's check out back," she said. "Then we'll do upstairs."

Kane followed Arika down the hall. He was starting to regret inviting her along. The search had suddenly become about her father and this supposed lost library. What's worse, Arika was a loose cannon who seemed to do whatever she wanted regardless of the consequences.

At the back of the house was the living room. This room looked more lived in and less dusty than the others they'd seen, with brown velvet sofas, brown bookcases, brown paintings on the walls and bric-a-brac everywhere. A huge crystal chandelier dominated the room, and the owner had a fetish for taxidermy judging by the stuffed animals all over the place: a moose head on the wall, an eagle hanging from the ceiling, other birds and small mammals eyeing each other across the room. The place reminded Kane of Wilfred's shop: a warehouse for household junk. There was an air of the nineteenth century about it.

"Simon would have a field day in this place," Arika declared, entering the room. She stroked a stuffed mongoose that was frozen in time in a fight with a snake. "Ooh, more!" she cried, spotting half a dozen books stacked next to a sofa, and went to investigate.

Kane left her and opened the door on the other side of the hall, which led to the kitchen. This was the cleanest room so far. A fat black pot sat on the stove, wisps of steam floating to the ceiling. There was a pie dish on the butcher block, a cookbook open. There's someone home, Kane thought, and his scalp tingled at the realisation someone had heard them enter; someone who let the dogs loose; someone who was no longer here.

Stepping quietly across the floorboards, he paused at the stove, a heavy, ancient thing, fired by coals that radiated a fierce heat. Using a pot holder, he removed the lid and peered inside. It was some kind of stew, with meat and root vegetables bubbling in a reddish-brown gravy. Kane released his breath. For a moment, before lifting the lid, he was worried he'd find a human head or some other body parts cooking away. He wouldn't put it past the fruitcake who lived here.

Crossing to the window, he checked out the back yard, a small paved area fenced off from the rest of the farm. There was an empty washing line and a broken outhouse out there, but no one in sight, and nowhere a person could hide.

"Where are you?" he mouthed, staring at the gate that led out of the yard. Perhaps whoever had been cooking had left that way, which meant they could be anywhere by now. He reminded himself that he and Arika were intruders in the house of a madman, likely a murderer, and Wilfred might feel justified in shooting them on sight if he caught them here. They needed to hurry this up – and watch their backs.

He returned his attention to the kitchen. To his left was a closed door, which, on inspection, he found led to a small laundry. Plaster was peeling off the wall; paint was peeling off the ceiling; a stack of unwashed clothes sat on a sorting table, some of them stained with blood.

Wrinkling his nose, he turned to find Arika standing at the door to the kitchen, staring at the stove. As he crossed the floor to join her, he saw her face change. Her eyes widened, her mouth opened, her arm flew up – she was pointing at something behind him.

He spun around as the pantry door banged open, and out flew a woman with wild orange hair and bulging eyes, her grey face twisted in rage. She was wearing a stained green housecoat, with one purple slipper on her stockinged foot, and she had a gigantic butcher's knife raised above her head. As the woman rushed at Kane, she released a succession of weird shrieks, like she was the one about to be carved into small pieces.

Instinctively, Kane raised the rifle. It hit the descending blade and the knife flew from her grasp, hit the butcher block, and clattered to the floor. Without missing a beat, the woman took hold of the barrel, ripped the rifle from his hands, threw it across the kitchen. Her fingers reached for Kane's face. He grabbed her wrists. Her black fingernails were sharp like talons, and they were locked on his eyes. With surprising strength, she pushed him back, and he tripped over his own foot and they fell to the floor.

The woman was now on top of him, screaming and drooling yellow spit over his face.

"Christ!" yelled Kane. "Not again!"

Grabbing the collar of her coat, Arika tried to drag her off him. The woman turned her head and snarled and snapped like an animal, her pointed teeth looking like they could take off her arm.

"Get it off me!" howled Kane.

Arika retrieved the rifle, aimed it at the woman's back and fired. The dart hit her. Nothing happened.

"Useless crap," she murmured, slamming it down on the counter.

"It doesn't work straight away," Kane reminded her through gritted teeth.

"Oh yeah; course."

Grabbing her bag, she pulled out the wrench and weighed it in her hand. It was a hefty piece of metal, potentially lethal if used with enough force.

"Arika!"

The woman's scaly face was bearing down on Kane, her teeth almost close enough to take off his nose.

Arika stepped up, lifted the wrench above her head with both hands and brought it down between the woman's shoulder blades. The momentum pushed her nose into Kane's face. Fortunately, at that moment, she had her mouth shut, and their lips met in a weird kind of kiss.

Kane sputtered and pushed her back. "What the hell are you doing?" he cried.

Realising more desperate measures were needed, Arika raised the wrench over one shoulder and swung it like a tennis racket, slamming it into the woman's shoulder. There was no discernible reaction. As well as having supernatural strength, the housekeeper seemed impervious to pain.

"Sorry, ma'am," Arika said as she raised the wrench again. "This will hurt me more than it hurts you."

This time she aimed at the side of the woman's head. The wrench came down and hit her cheek with an audible crack, and her hair flew off and skidded across the floor. Arika gasped. The orange hair was a wig. Apart from a few patches of grey hair, the housekeeper was completely bald. What's more, her head was an unnatural shape – like a distorted pear – with a bony ridge running from the top of her head to her spine.

Arika gaped. As before, the woman hardly blinked. It seemed she only had eyes for Kane.

"To hell with this," Arika snarled, and swung the wrench for the fourth and last time. This time she didn't hold back. She put her shoulder into it, the wrench flew down and collided with the woman's head with a sickening crunch, and she fell like a bag of potatoes on the kitchen floor.

Kane sprang up. Backing away, he stared at the housekeeper's body to make sure she was no longer a threat, then turned to Arika.

"You okay? Arika? Hey, Arika."

She was staring in shock at the woman, at her neck, which was bent at an impossible angle.

"I think … I think I killed her."

Kane leaned closer. The woman (if that's what it was) didn't appear to be breathing.

"Don't worry about it," he said. "You did what you had to. We'll work something out."

When Arika said nothing, he added, "Dylan told me about her. She's the housekeeper. He doesn't think she's human."

"Does that make a difference?"

"It's self-defence, whichever way you look at it. She'd have had you next. After eating my face."

Saying the words out loud made Kane's head spin. He'd been too charged with adrenaline to think about it while he was fighting for his life, but eating his face is precisely what the homicidal housekeeper had in mind.

Unable to resist, he hugged Arika hard. "You saved my life," he murmured, tears blurring his eyes. He wasn't exaggerating. If Arika hadn't come with him – hadn't been waiting on his doorstop earlier today – he'd most likely be dead by now; either eaten by the demon dogs or ripped apart by the demon housekeeper.

He felt her body go rigid.

"What the hell –?" she cried.

Kane pulled back. Arika was staring in terror at the dead housekeeper.

He whirled around.

Behind him, the woman's fingers were creeping towards the butcher's knife. As Kane watched, they closed over the handle. She lifted her arm and slammed the blade into the floor, then rolled over, held onto the handle with both hands, and pushed herself to her knees.

Kane and Arika backed away. The woman's head was hanging to one side, but she didn't seem to notice or care. Her eyes bulged like they were about to pop; her lips pulled away from her pointed teeth; three slits on either side of her neck opened and closed as if they were pulling in air.

Climbing to her feet, she jerked the knife out of the floor, raised it high, and charged again at Kane.

He ducked as the knife came down, and it nicked his shoulder. Taking advantage of the momentum of her failed strike, he put one hand on the small of her back, the other on the back of her scaly head, and shoved her hard at the refrigerator. Her head slammed into the metal door and she fell to the floor, dropping the knife once again.

Rushing over, Kane took hold of the refrigerator with both hands and pulled at it with all his might. An ancient, heavy thing, it took a while to begin moving.

Then the housekeeper grabbed his leg with a grip of steel, and he yelped in surprise and tried to shake her off. With her left hand she was reaching blindly for the knife.

Arika was on the other side of the refrigerator in a flash. She kicked away the knife, and together, with a strength born of desperation, they pulled the huge metal box over. It tottered for second, seemed about to drop back, then fell on the housekeeper with a horrible crunch.

The weight of it pinned her to the floor, but it wasn't enough to stop her. Her arms and legs pushed and shoved at the metal as she fought to get the thing off her, her efforts accompanied by a horrific shrieking that sounded more like frustration than pain.

"How can it still be moving?" breathed Arika.

A pool of greenish-black liquid was starting to spread out from under the housekeeper's body, and soon her movements slowed, her arms twitched, her body went limp. Then came an awful stench – like the smell of something dead a long time, a smell you would normally expect from rotting seaweed and maggots bloated from feeding on washed-up fish.

Staring at the growing pool of putrescence, Kane knew Dylan was right. This – thing – wasn't human. He doubted whether it had even been alive – not in the conventional sense.

"Let's get the hell out of here," he said.

"I'm guessing," said Arika, wrinkling her nose at the stinking greenish-black puddle on the floor, "the hell is here to stay."

BACK AT THE staircase, Kane stopped and opened a small door. As he'd guessed, the door led to wooden stairs that descended through darkness to a basement. He was fumbling around for a light switch when he heard the floorboards creak overhead.

This time he knew it wasn't just the settling of an old house.

Pulling her gun from her bag, Arika held it under her chin and crept to the bottom of the stairs.

"Where'd you get that?" Kane whispered loudly.

She didn't answer him. Shaking his head, he followed her up the stairs, reloading his rifle as he went. If it was Wilfred up there, he was prepared to shoot him on sight; in fact, he'd do the same to Dylan – no more arguments, just throw him over his shoulder, load him in the truck and drive.

There were five doors on this floor, four of them open. First they checked the open rooms, looking in closets and under beds and behind the shower curtain and anywhere else a crazed person or thing might be hiding with evil intent. This done, they stood outside the final room.

Kane listened at the keyhole. The room was silent. He tried the handle. It was locked.

He stepped back, pondered a moment whether to call out to whoever or whatever was inside, then decided they needed whatever element of surprise they had left.

"Get ready," he said to Arika, lifting his boot.

ON THE OTHER side of the door, Dylan was having trouble holding the heavy brass lamp above his head. He'd heard the commotion below, the footsteps mounting the stairs, and knew this could be his last chance to escape. Perhaps if he hit Wilfred hard enough, he would shock him out of his body, and then the tables would turn and *he'd* be the one on the landing, safe inside his own skin. He'd lock Wilfred in this room, find and burn the Necronomicon, and end this madness once and for all.

The door flying open took him by surprise. He staggered back, his legs gave way, and the lamp slipped from his hands and crashed to the floor behind him.

He looked up to see his brother standing over him.

"Kane!" he cried, tears streaming from his eyes. "How did you –?

What are you doing here?"

Kane, his face burning with hate, bent down and grabbed him by the collar. He lifted him from the floor.

"Where's my brother?" he demanded.

"Kane," Dylan croaked, "it's me."

Shaking him, Kane lifted him higher. "Listen, you freak: you tell me where Dylan is, or I won't be responsible for your welfare. I know he's here. Tell me now."

Dylan gurgled. "Sme, sme … gane … sme …"

Arika touched his arm. "Kane. That's enough. Put him down."

"I will, when he tells me where Dylan is."

She moved her face into his line of vision. "He already has."

Kane stared in confusion. He must have seen something of Dylan in the scared face and black-rimmed eyes, as a tremor passed through his arms and he lowered Wilfred's body to the floor.

"No way," he said, struggling to breathe. "It's a trick."

"No trick," gasped Dylan, rubbing his throat. He looked up at him. "Where's my Mars Bar?"

It was the punch line to their favourite joke when they were kids: something so stupid and juvenile, only his brother would know it.

Kane dropped to his knees. He couldn't take his eyes off the squat, wrinkled, badly-dressed man who was talking as if he knew him. He felt woozy, like he'd drunk a pint of beer on an empty stomach.

"Dylan," he groaned, shaking his head. "Man … you look like shit!"

23

The basement

THE STAIRCASE DOOR led to a low-ceilinged basement. Pausing on the last step, Kane leaned his elbows on the bannister and gazed around in wonder. The basement had been fitted out as a laboratory, the walls whitewashed, the floor a slab of concrete with deep cracks travelling the length of the room. A row of fluorescent lights, suspended from chains, ran down the centre of the room, throwing a cold white light across the benches, shelves and equipment. Pipes and electrical cables criss-crossed the room and led up through holes into the house.

"What's all this about?" he asked the room as he stepped onto the concrete floor. He screwed up his nose. There was a strong earthy smell about the place, mixed with bitter, mouldy and bleachy smells. The droning sound he heard at the front door was louder down here.

"This is where he mixes potions," answered Dylan behind him.

"Wow," breathed Arika, who was catching her first glimpse of the basement. "This is amazing! Who would have thought –?"

Her eye was caught by the shelves on the other side of the room. "What's all that?" Slipping past them, she went to investigate.

"The guy on the hill must have helped him set this up."

"Snyder," said Dylan. "Snivelling Snyder. He's more like the 2IC. Wilfred's got his henchmen to help around here."

"Is that what he calls them?"

"They do the digging and heavy lifting."

Kane's mind went into alert mode. Kenny Snyder sounded like the type of weasel who'd run away the moment you said, "Boo," but he pictured these henchmen as burly, belligerent characters, probably criminals, not averse to using violence if threatened or given an order by Wilfred.

Dylan sat with a groan on the step. "They're gorillas."

"Thanks for telling me earlier, dude. Come on, we need to hurry this up."

He crossed to the steel table in the centre of the room. Long and rectangular, it had a tap and sink at one end, with hoses leading across the floor to the wall. Kane knew from crime TV what it was: an autopsy table. Near it were a bench and two wooden chairs, along with another table tilted at a forty-five-degree angle. The wall opposite was fitted out with metal shelves, on which were dozens of glass bottles, jars and flasks, some containing frogs, snakes, salamanders and body parts like eyes and tongues, others filled with liquids and plant material that looked like herbs, fungi and woody sticks. Arika was lifting down jars, opening them, peering in, sniffing them, making funny faces at the contents.

"This is ancient stuff," she remarked over her shoulder. "Like, nineteenth century ancient. It probably belonged to Jonathon Dark."

Kane glanced around. "I can't see the book. Dylan?"

Dylan, having caught his breath, pushed himself to his feet and went up to the torture rack. It was hard to believe that only a few hours ago, a terrified mummy had been strapped to it, its eyes pleading with him for help. The rack was now clean, the torture implements put away. Arlene, in addition to her talents as a homicidal fighting machine, had also been a stellar housekeeper.

"It's not here."

Kane turned to him. "How can you say that? You haven't even looked yet."

"It's never left out in the open. I hardly even saw it. Wilfred always worked from notes."

"Damn it! The thing could be anywhere!"

"I already told you that."

Kane went back to the stairs and checked out the garbage piled underneath. It was mostly empty boxes, broken equipment and plastic containers filled with screwed-up paper, rags and used cleaning products. He turned back to the room.

"Which is why we're damn well looking everywhere. You're not staying in that godawful body one minute longer than you need to."

Dylan coughed and sputtered like an old man. "What if it doesn't work?" he gasped at the end of it.

Kane looked at him, and as usual got a little shock. Every time he saw his brother's rumpled clothes and wrinkled face, something heaved in the pit of his stomach.

"Of course it'll work. Arika said the book is the key to getting your body back. So tell me: where's the best place to start?"

"I dunno." Glancing around, Dylan scratched his stubbled chin. "Though …" He squinted into the distance. "There was this one time … Wilfred needed something from the Necronomicon, and he stared at me as though I knew where it was. He didn't go get it, though; just stood there tapping his foot. Then he sent me upstairs to get him tea."

"And?" prompted Kane when Dylan stood staring into space.

"When I got back, the door up there was locked. They didn't let me in for about twenty minutes, and then they had the book."

"They?"

"Snyder was here."

Kane's mouth turned up at the corners. "There's a secret hiding place."

Arika screwed the cap on the jar of toads she'd been sniffing. "Did I hear someone say 'secret hiding place'?"

"It must be where Waite keeps the Necro-book-thingy."

"Any ideas where it might be? Dylan?"

Dylan shrugged.

"We should split up," Arika said, replacing the jar on the shelf. "Take a wall each. There must be a safe – a switch or a latch or some-thing."

"You take that one," Kane said to Dylan, nodding to his right.

"Look for somewhere where there's gaps between the bricks," suggested Arika. "Or maybe some irregularity in the floor."

Kane smiled at them, feeling the buzz of anticipation in his chest. "The book is down here; I'd bet my life on it."

"Kane …" began Dylan.

"I'll look around these shelves," said Arika, returning to the jars and flasks.

"I'll take this wall."

"Kane," Dylan said, louder this time.

Kane went up to him. "I know what you're about to say, bro. But you told us you didn't see it."

"I wasn't really looking."

"You said it's a big book. How could you miss a huge book that radiates evil energy?"

Dylan shook his head.

"And what about Waite always working from notes?"

"Unless he needed the power of the book."

Kane didn't want to hear any more about the book being with Wilfred at the altar on the hill. They needed to get on with the search, before Wilfred or his henchmen returned to find the door busted in and the gooey green remains of the housekeeper seeping through the kitchen floor.

"Focus on the positive, Dylan. The book wasn't there; you said so yourself. It must be here."

"I –"

"And if it's not here, at least we'll know where the bastard is hiding it. And we'll come back when he's home and get it off him then."

"Okay. I suppose you're right."

Kane punched his brother's shoulder; gently, so he didn't break any bones. "Listen, kid, we're not gonna stop till you're out of that disgusting body. I promise. Now we better get on with it, before Waite or some of his gorillas turn up."

They searched every inch of the basement without success.

"This can't be right!" Kane cried, so exasperated he was getting heartburn. He looked Wilfred's body up and down, from his white hair to his white sneakers, feeling his hatred rise, even though he knew it was his brother in those ill-fitting, old-man clothes. "You're a weak old fossil. You use that damn book all the time. It's gotta be somewhere easy to get to."

He bit his thumb, thinking hard. Dylan said it took Wilfred or Kenny about twenty minutes to get the book, so maybe there was a hidden room down here, rather than a safe or secret compartment, which would only take a few minutes to open. He scanned the basement again. A hidden room would most likely open from a wall that faced into the house, rather than out to the yard. That meant one of the walls on either side of the staircase.

In the corner of the basement opposite the stairs was a disused metal laundry basin, dented and rusty with neglect. Kane had checked in and around it earlier, to no avail, and now he went back for another look. The plug hole was choked with matted grey lint, dust and chips of plaster that had fallen from the ceiling. Though the rest of the laboratory was clean and tidy, this corner of the room was caked with dirt and grime. Above and below the basin were cracked white tiles; above them, a light fixture missing the fluorescent tube. A chain hung from the fixture, no doubt taking the place of a light switch. Kane fingered it. That was funny. He hadn't noticed it before, but the last third of the chain was the only thing here not covered with dust.

With a mounting sense of expectation, he tugged on it.

Machinery hummed in the wall. The laundry basin shuddered. As Kane stepped back, the entire tiled section of the wall – roughly a metre-and-a-half square – grated, jerked, then swung towards him on metal hinges, carrying with it the disused basin.

Smiling like a jester, he placed his hand on the wall, bent forward and peered into the darkness.

"What's in there?" asked Arika, squeezing in next to him.

Five stone steps led down to an earthen floor. The rest of the room was too dark to make out anything. The place smelt as if rats had died in there.

"Our hidden room," Kane announced as Dylan joined them. "Told you, didn't I? And there you were, about to give up and go home. We'll have you back in your own body in no time flat." He felt around inside, but couldn't find a light switch or dangling chain. "Is there a torch around here?"

"Yep," said Arika, hurrying back to the shelves. "Over here."

She returned with a small flashlight and a battery-powered lamp.

Taking the lamp, Kane reached out and dangled it in the darkness. The room was smaller than the basement, largely unfinished, with a dirt floor and walls formed from rough-hewn stone blocks, mossy and discoloured, irregularly patched with concrete. The walls of the room were lined with furniture, most of it busted and dust-covered – but what had immediately captured the attention of everyone was the enormous bronze plate in the centre of the earthen floor.

"Whoa!" cried Arika, gripping Kane's arm. "That looks like … It's …"

"A trapdoor," said Kane.

"It's a trapdoor."

Stepping into the room, Kane found the light switch and turned it on. Yellow light flooded the room from a lone bulb that dangled from a thick black cord. Turning off the lamp, he placed it next to the wall, went down the steps, and knelt beside the bronze plate. It was definitely a trapdoor, more than a metre in diameter. The top of the plate was moulded into the shape of an octopus, an archaic creature with a bulbous head and a single, half-closed eye in its centre. Its tentacles divided the plate into five sections, each featuring an underwater theme. One section showed submerged mountains; a second was of rocky plains teeming with fish; the other three depicted underwater cities built of stone and coral: buildings clinging to a cliff face, a long avenue of irregular pillars planted with rows of seaweed, and an amphitheatre with a statue of a crab-like monster at its centre.

"Stinks down there," commented Dylan from the steps.

Kane placed his hand on the cold metal. "I hate to think what's underneath this thing," he said to Arika.

She traced the line of a tentacle with her finger. "I don't recognise the artwork. It looks ancient. Atlantis theme, maybe. It might have come from a temple to Poseidon or Dagon." She tried to get her fingers under the edge of the plate.

"You'll need a crowbar," suggested Dylan, leaning over them.

"There must be a catch somewhere."

Kane took the torch from Arika and bent close to the dirt so he could examine the plate from the side.

"Look at the end of that tentacle," he said, pointing. "It's not flush with the rest of the plate."

Following the line of his finger, Arika reached out and pressed the raised tentacle. As it made contact with the plate, there was a metallic click, then a whirring noise. The trapdoor trembled, then started to rise.

They all drew back and stared in amazement as the plate rose on a metal lever and locked with a shudder in a vertical position.

Its opening released a horrendous stench. Kane and Dylan backed away, but Arika wasn't to be deterred. Picking up the flashlight, she turned it on and aimed it down the well.

"Definitely smells like something climbed down there and died," she observed.

The smell, strong as it was, soon dissipated, and Kane returned with the lamp and held it over the well.

"This is unbelievable," he said, his voice echoing in the darkness. "It just gets weirder."

Inside the well, a series of metal rungs led down the brick wall to what looked like a dirt floor a few metres down.

"Can you see anything?" Kane asked, leaning further into the well with his lamp.

Arika nodded at him. "Are you thinking what I'm thinking?"

Before Kane could answer, a muted ringing sounded above their heads. It was Wilfred's phone, in the parlour above the laboratory. As they waited for the ringing to stop, Kane pondered his options if someone answered it. Whoever it was would soon discover Arlene was dead, Dylan missing, so there was really only one option, and that was to take the offensive and face the person head on.

After ringing for what sounded like five minutes, the phone suddenly cut off.

Kane stared at Arika, then turned to Dylan, who was standing close, sneering at him. It took him a second to remember the sneer was Wilfred's natural expression and had nothing to do with how his brother was feeling. "You okay?" he asked, just to be sure.

Dylan's expression didn't change. "Do I look okay to you?"

Kane winced. "Sorry, man. You know what I mean. I hope." Patting his shoulder, he tried to look confident. "We'll find that book, Dylan. Whatever it takes. I won't rest till that bastard is back in his stinking corpse … No offence, little brother."

His words confirmed in his mind his next actions. Despite the danger of Wilfred and others returning and cornering them in this subterranean cell, finding the Necronomicon had to be their number one concern.

He glanced around. It was clear the book wasn't hidden amongst the fragments of furniture that lined the walls. The well was the logical place to search next.

Placing the lamp on the ground, he said, "Okay, I'm going in."

"I'll be right behind you," said Arika.

Kane stared at the wall. He should have known that was coming.

"You two better stay here."

He glanced at her and saw her face harden.

"It only takes one to find the book."

"I'm not a helpless damsel, like you seem to think," she said, her eyes boring into him. "I'm not sitting here like a spare tyre not knowing what's going on down there."

Kane shook his head. "I don't think you're helpless. You've proven you can handle yourself … more than once. But …" But there was no way he'd let a woman he only just met climb down into God knows what, no matter how many secret agent skills her father had taught her. "I just need to scoot down and grab the book and come back soon as I can. Fast in, fast out. The job doesn't need two."

"Who's to say some of Waite's henchmen aren't down there? You should have back-up."

"I don't need somebody around I need to rescue if there's thugs waiting down there."

That shut her up, though not in a good way.

After glaring at him a few seconds, she said with eyes narrowed, "Firstly, Mr Gates, I don't need to prove anything to you or anybody else. And secondly, I'll do what I damn well please."

Don't I know that! thought Kane, though he was canny enough not to say it out loud.

"You're not leaving me here all by myself," chipped in Dylan.

Kane sighed in frustration. "How you gonna climb down that ladder, bro? You can hardly walk."

Dylan puffed out his puny chest. "If Wilfred can do it, so can I."

"We're wasting time, standing around arguing," Arika pointed out. "Waite could come back any minute."

"Fine," huffed Kane. "I'm only the professional emergency services worker here. What would I know? Let's all go and get massacred together."

Dylan rubbed his liver-spotted hands together. "Sounds like a plan!"

24

Below

THE RUNGS WERE worn smooth with age, crusty with rust at the places they were joined to the bricks. After testing the stability of the first rung, Kane slung the rifle over his shoulder, gave his two companions a taut smile, and began his descent. It was awkward carrying the lamp, but he wasn't about to descend into a foul-smelling abyss beneath a house of horrors without being able to see what might be waiting for him at the bottom.

Twenty rungs down, the well ended, and Kane stepped onto bare earth. Lifting the lamp, he saw he was standing at the top of a flight of stairs. The first two steps were broken, the slabs of stone cracked and crumbling, but after that they seemed largely intact. They were smooth and shiny from years of traffic, and it occurred to Kane that at some point in history the stairs may have led all the way to the surface, perhaps to a house that pre-dated this one.

"Anything down there?" Arika called from above.

"More stairs!" he yelled over his shoulder.

"Shall I come down?"

Raising his head, Kane used his arm to shield his eyes from the glare of her torch beam. "Sure!" he returned, barely able to conceal his reluctance.

But it wasn't Arika who came down; it was Dylan. His thin arms strained as they fought to hold onto the rungs. His legs wobbled and he grunted softly with each step. As he neared the last rung, Kane reached up and helped him down.

"You should start working out. Them arms is like spaghetti."

Dylan stood catching his breath, sneering at him. "It's such a crock being old."

Arika came next, a heavy-duty flashlight hanging around her neck.

The strap of her bag was slung over one shoulder, the bag rubbing against her hip (no doubt with the gun and wrench inside), and if that wasn't enough, she was holding an axe awkwardly under one arm.

"Where'd you get that from?" laughed Kane, stepping into the stairwell to make room for her in the well.

"Dylan found them."

"In a box of tools," said Dylan. "And I got this," he added, pulling a cattle prod from the waistband of his pants.

"Be careful with that, bro. You don't want it zapping your you-know-whats."

"They're not my you-know-whats." He jabbed his crotch with the end of the cattle prod. "It'd serve Wilfred right if I burnt them off."

Arika, swinging the axe by her side, smiled at him.

"Look at us," said Kane: "all armed and ready to meet the zombies."

Arika froze. "Zombies?"

"Just a figure of speech."

"I hate zombies."

Kane was surprised by the vehemence in her voice. "You're okay with mad wizards and killer housekeepers, but not zombies?"

"It's something about eating brains. I like my brain."

"I doubt there'll be zombies all the way down here. I guess we'll find out soon enough, though, won't we?" Turning to the darkness, he said, "Let's go find the book."

"Jesus," said Arika, shining her light on the stairs. "Where do you think this leads to? We'll end up in China at this rate."

"Wine cellar?" suggested Dylan.

"A long way to go for a bottle of red."

"Only one way to find out," said Kane.

He started down the stairs. After the first few steps, the brick-lined corridor turned abruptly to the right and then resumed at a right angle. They descended in silence, their clothes rustling, their footsteps echoing up and down the dark corridor. The further they went, the colder it seemed to get.

After a time, Kane began to discern a distant wailing. He stopped and held up a hand.

They looked at each other. As they listened, the wailing, which seemed to be coming from deep underground, increased in intensity until it became a long howl. It was a stark, lonely sound – something you might expect from an animal caught in a trap. A chill like he'd never felt before travelled up and down Kane's spine.

"More dogs?" suggested Arika.

There was a human quality about the howl, which made Kane doubt it came from a dog.

"Maybe it heard us," whispered Dylan.

"It's probably the wind," Kane said to comfort them.

"Yeah, sure," said Arika. "A right storm happening down there."

"If it's anything more, we'll deal with it. Like we have with everything else."

"I don't know about this," piped Dylan, his voice cracking. "Maybe we should go back and get help."

"And how do you suggest we do that?" snapped Kane. "You wanna call in the cops and wait around till they send some rookie to see if there's probable cause for a search warrant? We could tell them there's a ghost in trouble in the wine cellar. That might hurry them up."

"I just thought –"

"Maybe if we tell them you're a teenager trapped in an old man's body, that'll push them along. We better suggest they bring along their wands in case there's a magical fight with the sorcerer and his horde of reanimated zombie friends."

"Easy there," warned Arika, striking his shoulder with the palm of her hand. "Your brother's allowed to be scared. He isn't in the best physical shape if something happens down there."

"Why do you think I said he should stay upstairs? Why does no one ever listen to me?"

"The he-man has spoken."

"It was only a suggestion," grumbled Dylan. "Why do you have to have a conniption fit over everything?"

Kane took a deep breath. He was gripping the lamp handle with such force his hand hurt, and he realised he was more anxious than he'd let himself admit. He was scared that if they didn't find the book soon,

Dylan would have a coronary or die of old age. He also worried that the longer Wilfred had possession of his brother's body, the greater would be his ownership of it, and the more difficult their job of evicting him.

"Let's keep going," he said. "The sooner we're out of this madhouse the better."

He held up the lamp and Arika played her flashlight on the stairs as they went deeper and deeper underground. The air was cold and damp, though the stink of rot and mould had largely dissipated – or maybe they'd gotten used to it. Kane could hear Dylan wheezing, and behind him, the tap of Arika's boots on stone. In his mind, her footsteps seemed to rise in volume until they drowned out every other sound.

His heart began booming in his ears at the thought of what he was doing: leading a woman he barely knew into an unknown danger that didn't really concern her. It was different with Dylan – his mission here was life or death – but Arika was a hanger-on, an unnecessary distraction. The fireman in him berated him for even letting her get as far as the farmhouse gate.

She cleared her throat, and the noise pushed a new thought into his head. Is she looking at me? – staring at the back of my head? He wondered what Arika was making of this situation, whether she was impressed by the depth of his loyalty to his brother, the steps he was taking to save him. It would be a complete turnaround from their first encounter, when he'd acted like an oaf and she'd hardly given him the time of day.

He chuckled to himself at the absurd thoughts. What a time for his testosterone to be acting up! As if Arika would be thinking about anything outside of what might be awaiting them at the end of these stairs!

Yet here in the bowels of the earth, entombed in suffocating darkness, with the threat of bodily harm or death around every corner, Kane was experiencing something he'd longed for his entire life: the courage and determination of a hero. Not a hero who's paid to put out fires and rescue cats from trees; a hero who puts his safety and other selfish concerns aside and risks his own life to protect the lives of others. Today he came here of his own volition to rescue his brother, someone he'd hardly spoken with in the past five years and felt little real connection to. And now he had two people to protect, two lives that depended on him.

During their descent, the wailing had receded to a whine. Like the foul smell, it became part of the background. With his thoughts now firmly on the protection of his brother and Arika, the remnants of Kane's fear dissipated and his anxiety gave way to an adrenaline-fuelled thrill of anticipation at the thought of what wonders or horrors were awaiting them at the end of their quest. He was here to fight a battle for his brother's future, for his very existence, and anything that tried to stand in his way was up for the fight of its life.

"Oliver would be proud of me."

Kane frowned at the voice in his head. Usually when a thought of Oliver popped into his mind, he booted it out before it could take root. His role in his brother's death, the role of self-centred negligence, was something he still felt acutely, something that had threatened to send him the way of his mother and his brother if he dwelt too closely on it. In the year following Oliver's death, his therapist had advised him to do the opposite, encouraging him to work through his thoughts and feelings and face them head on. She said that excising the bad stuff would be the starting point of his recovery, and for a while he tried to follow her advice. But he was only fifteen at the time, and all this did was keep him in a state of despair and anxiety that seemed to overwhelm him and have no end. His father was the first in the family to recover from the tragedy, and his advice to Kane was the advice he took on board. "Live your life as a hero," Mike told his son. "Make Oliver's death mean something by being the best man you can be." They were great words, and Kane recalled them now and gained strength and confidence from them.

Engrossed in these thoughts, he almost didn't see the end of the stairs. They'd come to a blank wall.

"That doesn't look good," commented Arika, playing the torch up and down the bricks.

"It's okay," Kane assured them over his shoulder. "There's an exit here."

To his left was an opening in the wall, an archway that led into inky blackness. Dangling the lamp in the opening, he bent forward and peered around the corner.

"Holy shit!"

"What is it?" came Dylan's voice, thin and trembling in the rarefied air.

Kane stepped through the archway. "Come and see for yourself."

The lamp light illuminated the walls and ceiling of an enormous passage built from thousands of bricks. Wide enough for a dozen people to walk through side by side, and almost as high, it comprised a series of barrel-vaulted arches that melted into the darkness. Between the arches were square openings, some with wooden doors, some just yawning black spaces.

"Far out," breathed Dylan.

"Simon will die," was Arika's contribution.

The whining stopped.

Kane was reminded of how crickets stop chirping when someone gets close. The silence was deafening.

"I think I preferred it when it was howling," he whispered, moving to the first of the openings.

The room had no door, though Kane could see that hinges had been ripped out sometime in the past. The room was square and featureless, the brick walls at the back and to the left bulging inwards, buckled by the pressure of the earth behind them. The bare floor was thick with dust.

"Ever seen anything like this before?" he asked Arika.

She played her flashlight around the room. "No freaking way. These types of places belong in ancient Rome, not under some old farmhouse in the middle of nowhere."

"How could anyone have built such a thing all the way down here?" Dylan asked.

"Tunnels like this were sometimes built as tombs," said Arika. "But this is so far underground, I'm not sure. Unless it started off closer to the surface and something happened to bury it."

"Then someone found it and built the well," suggested Dylan. "And turned it into this bunker."

"Maybe that's what it is," suggested Kane: "a fallout shelter." He couldn't think of anything even remotely more likely than that. "They did some weird things in the 'fifties and 'sixties."

He crossed to the other side of the passage, where a rotting oak door with horizontal belts of iron bolted along its width led to the first of the rooms on that side.

"What's the bet this one's filled with cans of soup and tuna?" he joked.

Pressing the iron handle, he leaned his body weight against the door. It creaked open a little and then jammed, instigating an avalanche of clatters. Placing the lamp and rifle on the ground, he braced his feet, applied his shoulder and pushed harder, but still the door only opened enough for him to get his head inside.

"Torch," he said to Arika.

She handed it to him, and he returned to the room and moved the light around.

"What's in there?" Dylan asked as Kane stood frozen in the doorway.

The room was similar to the one on the other side, except this one wasn't empty. Stacked from the back of the room to the door were thousands of bones. Some looked like the bones of large animals, such as sheep or cows, whereas others were obviously from smaller animals, like rats and rabbits. He guessed the pile had become so high and unstable that at some point an earthquake or gravity had caused it to collapse. It was the bones that were stopping the door from opening any further.

"A bunch of animal bones," he reported over his shoulder, then caught his breath. The torch beam had come to rest on a human skull. The skull had no jawbone and part of the right cheekbone was missing, but there was no denying it had once been a living, breathing person. Its black eye sockets stared at him as if challenging him to pretend it was something less sinister.

"Lemme see," urged Dylan, touching his arm with his cold, leathery hand.

Kane withdrew and handed Dylan the torch. Dylan leaned into the room.

"Gross," he said, coming out and making room for Arika.

She had a quick look. "That's years' worth of meat," she observed. "Looks like someone was living down here for a long time."

Kane recalled the howling they heard earlier. If it was human, it didn't sound like it came from someone who was here voluntarily. Had Wilfred been keeping prisoners in these rooms? It was unlikely he had friends or family living down here in the pitch-black cells, not when there was a house and a small village above them. Kane had been repulsed by the thought of the old man reanimating dead things and creating monsters from stolen corpses, but kidnapping and murder were next-level evil.

"Let's keep going," he said, retrieving his rifle and the lamp and moving down the passage to the next door.

This room was lined with wooden shelves, which held stacks of grey trousers and matching shirts – the kind that might be sold in an army surplus store. Beneath the shelves were dozens of boots of different sizes and colours, some modern, some dust-caked and looking like they were decades or even centuries old.

"Freaky," said Dylan. "What would he need with all those clothes?"

"Maybe this was an army bunker," suggested Arika. "That might explain it. Soldiers could have been living here … during the war …"

Kane smiled as her words petered out. Like him, she was probably thinking by now: What would an army barracks be doing out here in the middle of sheep, cow and goat country? – built beneath an old farmhouse? – abandoned and forgotten? His idea of a fallout shelter was more likely – though not a shelter from nuclear war. When the plague came to Jacob's End early last century, perhaps the residents banded together and built this place to escape the creeping death they feared was ending the world.

He recalled an old movie he'd seen as a boy: *The Time Machine*. The monsters in that movie – the Morlocks – started off human and then moved underground, where they mutated and fed on the compliant humans living above them. The horrors from that movie welled up in Kane's mind and he imagined things sinister and cannibalistic lurking in the black rooms of this nighted tunnel, waiting to pounce on them and rip the meat from their bones with their claws and fangs.

Pulling the rifle from his shoulder, he held it at the ready. Though it was only a tranquilliser gun, it gave him comfort to know they also had an axe, a cattle prod, a wrench and Arika's pistol if anything came at them. And with any luck, there would be a weapons storage room down here to complement the army surplus store.

Moving across the dark passage to the next room, they found something different again: a large black coffin, displayed almost ceremonially on a wooden trestle table.

"Shit," said Dylan, going up to it. "Do you think there's a body in it?"

"I'm not that curious," Arika replied from the door.

But Kane *was* that curious. He wasn't taking the risk the Necronomicon was hidden in one of these rooms, and a coffin seemed to him a logical place to keep a book of the dead. Handing his lamp to Dylan, he stepped up to the coffin and with an effort pulled up the lid. As it rose, it slipped off the coffin and fell with a clatter to the floor. At the same time, Kane heard a quiet yelp from somewhere outside the room.

Dylan said, "Is it –?"

"Sh!" interrupted Kane, staring out the door.

The sound wasn't repeated.

"Did you hear that?"

"It's probably the thing that was howling," said Arika, who was standing in a defensive position, half in and half out of the room, axe at the ready.

"The casket's empty," Kane announced, staring at the white satin material that still held the shape of a body.

"This is hopeless," moaned Dylan. "The stupid Necronomicon could be anywhere."

"Exactly," returned Kane, taking the lamp back. "Which is why we're looking in every damn coffin in every damn room."

"Did you need to rest?" Arika asked Dylan.

"No time for rest," answered Kane, annoyed all over again his brother hadn't taken his advice to stay upstairs. "Waite and his goons will turn up soon enough, and they'll know we're here. Unless we speed this up."

But when he turned back to Dylan and saw his drawn face and bloodshot eyes, his mood softened. "Maybe you should wait here while I go on."

"No," replied Dylan, straightening his back. "I'm not sitting here in the dark while you two go off and have all the fun."

"You're in no shape to be exerting yourself, man. I can't let you die of exhaustion before we find that damn book."

"I'll stay with you if you like," offered Arika.

"I said no. Wilfred told me he was immortal; he can't die."

"Dylan –"

"He's two hundred years old. His body can surely last another two hours."

Kane frowned at him. "You shout out if you're in any pain or – if you need a rest. We'll all rest together. But for now, we gotta keep moving before that body snatcher comes back and finds out what happened to his housekeeper."

When Dylan nodded, Kane turned and crossed to the next room on the other side of the passage. This one had an oak door like the earlier one, reinforced with belts of iron, though this door was in a much better shape. He pressed the handle. The door was locked.

"That's interesting –" he began to say, when he was checked by a small noise coming from inside the room. It sounded like a rattle of metal against metal.

"Hello," he called softly, his mouth against the door. "Is somebody in there?"

His question was greeted with silence.

"What is it?" asked Arika.

"I thought I heard something."

"Look at the floor." She used the axe to outline an area where the dirt had been disturbed, where there'd been recent traffic. "Do you think the book might be in there?"

He pressed his ear against the door. "I dunno." He tried the handle again, pressing his shoulder against the wood. "This is one mother of a door. Let's keep going. If we don't find the book, we'll come back and use the axe on it."

On they went. The next room had no door and contained more coffins, about two dozen of them, stacked against the walls. Most of the caskets were broken, and Kane could see they were empty. He did a quick search of the ones on top, then led Dylan and Arika back into the passage. He knew without looking that the Necronomicon wouldn't be in there. What would be the sense in puny old Wilfred Waite hiding his precious book under a pile of heavy coffins?

The next room, however, revealed something new and exciting. Wilfred had set it up as a study. There was a table in the centre, four wooden chairs, shelves lining the brick walls. The shelves were bending under the weight of row upon row of old books, along with stacks of notebooks and loose papers.

"Jackpot!" cried Kane, placing the lamp and rifle on the table. He turned excitedly to Dylan. "Can you see it? It's gotta be here." Warm relief flooded his body. He felt his shoulders relax. He hadn't realised till now how wound-up he was. "It's about time," he commented to Arika, who was already going through the books and papers. "I was beginning to think we'd never find it."

Arika was too engrossed in her search to respond.

Dylan moved about the study in the opposite direction, checking out each of the shelves.

Kane lit an oil lamp that was standing on the table and warm yellow light filled the room. He turned off the other lamp to preserve the battery.

"It's not here," Dylan announced from the other side of the room.

Kane spun around. "You didn't look very hard."

His brother glared at him.

"What I meant was, your eyes aren't what they used to be. Did you look over there?"

"I looked everywhere."

"On the top shelves? How can you see that high up?"

"I said it's not here!"

"Okay, bro, no need to shout. I just wanna make sure you've looked properly."

Dylan glowered at the floor.

Arika came to his defence. "He's exhausted, Kane. Don't forget he's older than my grandfather."

Dylan turned his glare on her. "I don't need you to speak for me."

"I'm sorry, I was just –"

"Okay, okay, let's cool it," interjected Kane.

He peered worriedly at Dylan. Was his brother starting to take on Wilfred's crusty personality? Was the old man's warped brain poisoning him? Right now, he seemed indistinguishable from the evil wizard.

"If you say it's not here," he said, aiming for conciliation, "it's not here."

"It's impossible to miss," explained Dylan, also making an effort to control his temper. "It's half the size of this table. And when you're near it, there's a kind of static electricity that pulls you towards it."

"What do you mean?"

His brother looked exasperated. "Don't you ever listen to me? It's full of black magic, like I told you a thousand times, and it wants people to read it and release all that power. Or else, what's the use? It'd be just another stupid spell book."

"I've got to get my hands on that thing," muttered Arika.

Kane gave her a dirty look.

"For – purely academic reasons. It's a classic."

"Winnie-the-Pooh is a classic," corrected Kane, picking up the oil lamp. "C'mon, let's keep going."

25

The chamber

THE NEXT FEW rooms were empty, though they appeared to have had recent inhabitants. There was straw on the floor, a chair in each room, a tin bucket, a few bones. They also had metal rings and chains attached to the walls. There was an awful smell about the rooms, the smell you might find in a pigpen or filthy outhouse.

"This must be what that room back there is like," Kane said as the wailing recommenced behind them. "Only there's somebody in it."

"You think he's scared of us?" asked Dylan.

"Not us," suggested Arika, lifting one of the chains and letting it drop.

Kane rested his hand on the door frame and stared into the dark cell. He was thinking: What will Wilfred do if his goons catch us down here? Chain us up in these cells, starve us, leave us here to go mad in the dark? It confirmed in his mind that if Wilfred and his henchmen turned up with guns or knives or machetes, they would have no choice but to fight for their lives, fight to the death. The alternative was worse than death. He glanced at Arika's bag and wondered how many bullets she had in her Glock.

Meanwhile, Dylan had wandered up the passage and was standing with his back to them, holding up the battery-powered lamp. "There's no more rooms," he said, his voice thin and hollow in the darkness.

Kane went to look. Dylan was right. The passage continued, but there were no more doorways, only the repeating pattern of bricks and vaulted arches, extending unbroken into the blackness.

"There's plenty of places we didn't check yet," he said, though he knew they'd searched all the logical hiding places. The only places left were the places the book was unlikely to be.

"No, there's not," countered Dylan. Dropping his head, he turned and began trudging back the way they'd come. "The book's not here. If it was, it'd be in the study. This is a waste of time."

Dylan's negativity – his propensity to give up at the smallest obstacle – infuriated Kane. It reminded him of everything he'd disliked in his brother all these years, all the things he hoped would be swept away now they had a common enemy.

"It has to be here," he asserted, looking around. He truly believed it. There wasn't any other outcome that made sense, certainly not the outcome where his brother lived out the rest of his life as an old-age pensioner.

"He must have took it with him."

"We've already been through this, Dylan. It wasn't there."

"Maybe it was in the car."

"Why? – when he was doing a spell at the altar?"

"He might have taken notes, like he always does."

"Then why leave the book in the car, where somebody could come along and steal it?"

"I don't know!"

"The book is buzzing with energy; you said that yourself. If he had it, it would have been at the altar. And it wasn't."

"It isn't here, Kane! Let's just go!"

"Go where?"

"Home."

Kane shook with frustration. "May as well take you straight to a nursing home. Give up. Die of old age at seventeen."

Instantly regretting his words, he went up to his brother and placed a hand on his shoulder. Dylan was trembling, and Kane's temper melted away as he gazed into Wilfred Waite's wet eyes and saw his brother staring out of them. Dylan was terrified. They were both terrified.

"I'm not gonna stand here and let that bastard win. I'm staying here till the job's done, even if that means waiting for Waite to get back and ripping the book from his – from your – hands. Now, how about we get you out of here, and I'll come back and finish looking myself?"

Dylan squeezed his eyes shut. When he opened them again, they were shiny with determination. "I'm sorry to be a crybaby, Kane. This damn body is getting to me."

"I know, bro. It's getting to me too. You're so bloody ugly."

They both smiled.

Dylan stared back up the dark passage. "We may as well go all the way to the end, hey? Now we're here."

"Okay. Come on, we'll try go faster."

Up ahead, the passage curved to the left. They followed the curve and soon spied the final arch. As they approached it, they could see that beyond the arch was blackness, a blackness the light from the two lamps was unable to penetrate. There were no more arches, no more brick walls; only the start of stone slabs on the floor. Emerging from the darkness, barely discernible, was a sound – or rather a multitude of sounds: howls and wails that continued at a steady level, as if they were made by the darkness itself.

"Jesus," breathed Arika. "More of those things."

"As long as they're locked up, we'll be fine," Kane assured them.

At the sound of his voice, something above them took off with a heavy flapping of wings.

"Was that a bat?" asked Dylan in a low voice.

"Sounded too big for a bat," said Arika.

"I hope it's not another Messenger."

"You know how to kill a Messenger," Kane reminded him.

Dylan was looking spooked. "If I had the spell and the powder I could."

Kane glanced at Arika's axe and Dylan's cattle prod and knew they would be of little use against the types of creatures Wilfred was able to summon. Even Arika's gun would be like a pea shooter to them.

"Not to worry," he said, trying to sound unconcerned. "It was flying away from us, so I doubt it's a soul-sucking demon from another dimension."

Stepping into the blackness, he turned and raised his lamp to examine the walls of the chamber, which were comprised of gigantic stone blocks, each one a head taller than him. He ran a hand over the stone. The blocks were cold and smooth, and fitted together with such precision there was barely a crack between them.

"Impressive workmanship," commented Arika. "Someone took real pride in building this."

Stepping back, she ran the torch beam all the way up the wall to the domed ceiling, which towered at least six storeys above their heads. As she moved the beam around, they could see the ceiling comprised a complex system of intersecting domes, strangely beautiful in its alien, irregular design. The chamber was like a cathedral made for giants.

"This is no fallout shelter," she said.

They were interrupted by a groan from Dylan. Rushing back to the brick passage, they found him on the ground, back against the wall, a hand pressed against his eyes.

"Hey, bro, what's wrong?"

"Just … a dizzy spell."

Kane knelt beside him. "Let's rest awhile. Then we'll go and see what else Waite has hidden down here."

Arika glanced from brother to brother. "I'm tired too, Kane. We're not super-fit fire officers like you."

"Trainee," interjected Dylan, unable to help himself.

"Trainee?" repeated Arika, raising her eyebrows.

"Didn't I say I was a trainee? I must have." Kane put on his most angelic face, though he knew very well he hadn't mentioned he was still in the training program.

"Anyhow," continued Arika, "the point is: you're a super-fit machine and we're not. So if you want to keep searching, I can stay with your brother while you have a look around."

Kane felt a burst of happiness at the prospect of breaking away from his two companions. He could pick up the pace and finish the search in half the time.

"If you're sure," he said.

"We're sure, aren't we, old man?"

Dylan nodded.

"Okay," said Kane, getting up. "I'll try and hurry." He glanced at Arika's axe, which was leaning against the wall next to his brother's lamp. "Let's swap weapons. If Waite comes back, you're better off with the rifle. It's Dylan's body, so the sedative should work on him. If not, use the cattle prod and keep him cornered till I get back."

"And I've got my real gun if his goons turn up," she reminded him.

He handed her the rifle and picked up the axe. "Just don't shoot my brother."

With a final smile at them, he entered the chamber carrying the axe and the oil lamp.

As the darkness enveloped him, he heard Arika say to Dylan, "Come on, grandpa, let's get you back to the study."

26

The altar

INSIDE THE CHAMBER, Kane walked to the left, staying close to the wall. It was his guide rope, so to speak, his way back should there come a need to escape at speed.

He soon discerned that the wall curved inwards, indicating the chamber was circular, and based on the low degree of curvature, it was clear to him the chamber was gargantuan. His plan at this early stage was to follow the wall all the way around until he returned to Dylan and Arika, at which time, if he hadn't found the Necronomicon, he would criss-cross the chamber in case it was somewhere in the middle.

Here in the chamber, the noise and stench intensified. Kane also noticed a slight breeze, or rather a gentle stirring of the air that he felt like a caress against his face. He figured the breeze was caused by an exhaust system (the source of the droning noise he'd heard earlier?) though it could also point to the chamber being open to the surface at some point. At first he breathed shallowly, hating the thought of the putrid air settling in his lungs, but he soon gave up and did his best to turn his mind to other things.

It wasn't long before he came to the first distinguishing feature since entering the chamber: a shallow indentation in the wall. A metal gate barred the opening, though the cell was only home to piles of clothing: uniforms, similar to the ones in the earlier room, but much older, and mostly dusty and worm-eaten.

Further along were two more cells, and these clearly had a sinister use. Shackles were attached to the wall, two at shoulder height and two resting on the ground, and the walls were smooth and shiny. The rotting straw on the floor stank like urine and faeces and decay.

Kane felt light-headed. It was becoming clearer to him with each revelation what this place was all about.

What he saw next, though, blasted away this preconception.

Just beyond the three cells, the wall was scored with high-relief carvings: dense patterns etched in the stone. The carvings represented no earthly objects, as far as Kane could tell. They were recurring fractals: spirals, twirls and curls that exploded along the wall or flew up the stone face before plunging down to the floor. Not only were the shapes impressive in their detail, they were enormous.

Moving the lamp along the wall, following the lines of the fractals with his eyes, Kane felt a growing dizziness. Shapes began to appear, three-dimensional shapes suspended in the air: irregular pyramids, multi-limbed starfish, and other objects, which later, with Arika's help, he would identify as antiprisms and rhombic polyhedra. They twisted out of nothing, ballooned into kaleidoscopic colours, then folded in amongst themselves, to be replaced by new shapes and colours. And in the background, mixing with the ever-present sound of wailing, he thought he heard a beat of faraway drums and the piping of flutes playing something frenzied and atonal.

With an effort of will, he pulled his eyes away from the wall. For a time, the fantastic shapes continued twisting, ballooning and folding in his mind, and then the sounds receded, the colours melted away, and all Kane saw was the dull brown stones of the chamber floor.

This was when he noticed that, further along, the high-relief fractals on the wall joined with the floor and became a bas-relief version that led away from the wall and towards the centre of the chamber. He raised the lamp. The light didn't travel far, so it was impossible to see where the path led, but he was certain there must be something of importance there, something that would justify all the work put into the etchings. Could this be where Wilfred was hiding the Necronomicon?

Following the path, holding the lamp low, Kane examined the bas-relief carvings. He could see now that the pattern was more than simple fractals. The shapes were formed from dendritic worm-like creatures that writhed together in a vaguely erotic way. The shapes held a remarkable amount of detail – they looked more like fossils than carvings – but if he examined them too closely, or for too long, the forms and sounds he experienced earlier would reappear, and he would have to stop and look away.

Half-blinded by the visions, Kane was startled, on looking up, to discover blocks of stone emerging from the darkness. At first, all he could discern was a series of thick, black, rectangular pillars of varying heights – from a metre or so to over five metres tall – but as he went past the first pillar, he spied something massive in the midst of them: a stone cube, more than three metres square.

When he approached it, he saw that, unlike the chamber walls, the stone had been roughly hewn and sheared irregularly at the edges. Sitting atop the cube was a thick black plate, comprised of some kind of metal. The fractals ascended the nearest side of the cube until they reached the top, at which point they disappeared under the plate. The block was covered in a greenish-black resin, which had run unevenly down the sides of the stone and felt spongy to the touch. Holding the lamp close, Kane discerned, locked within the resin, string-like fibres and what looked like fragments of bone or teeth.

Hardly able to process what he was seeing, he walked around the cube to the other side. Attached to the tallest of the stone pillars here, at least four metres from the ground, were thick iron rings, around a metre in diameter. Rust had eaten away much of the metal, which, to his relief, suggested great age – though it also came to him that perhaps the damp air and proximity to the ocean had caused the corrosion, and the rings weren't as old as they appeared.

As Kane was worrying about this, he continued circumnavigating the cube, and discovered something more recognisable: a second cube, this one much smaller: about the size of a kitchen table. There was no mistaking what this one was. Etched into the surface was a pentagram, along with a repeating pattern of hieroglyphs and geometric shapes.

"An altar," he said.

His words echoed amongst the pillars and sparked a muffled sound from the floor at his feet.

Lowering the lamp, he could see there was a row of holes in the flagstones at the base of the altar. The first thing he thought of was breathing holes.

Placing the lamp and axe on the floor, he got down on his hands and knees and tried to see through the holes. The light from the lamp wasn't strong enough to penetrate them, but he could tell that whatever had made the noise was still moving around. A scrambling noise; a grunt; the occasional whine: it was obviously some kind of animal.

"A rat," he pronounced in disgust, getting to his feet. "Just another bloody rat."

Then he heard what sounded like a voice.

Dropping again to the floor, he moved his mouth close to the holes. "Hello," he called softly. "Is somebody down there?"

Whatever was beneath him scratched at the stone with talons or nails. Then came silence. A few seconds later, he heard a guttural whisper.

"What?" he cried. "What was that?"

He listened again, his ear to the floor.

"Hep … may," he now heard, from a throat that sounded swollen and thick with phlegm.

"I'm here!" he cried, getting excited. "Name's Kane! Hold on, I'll find a way to get you out!"

He listened again, and heard the voice say, "Huuuryyyy."

Despite everything he'd seen and heard so far in this hellish place, it was almost impossible to conceive of evil on this scale. But here at last was confirmation that Wilfred had prisoners locked away here in the cold, black bowels of the earth.

Placing his fingers in the holes, Kane tugged at the flagstone. The stone was heavy and hurt his fingers, and at first it seemed immovable; but after pulling at it until it felt like his arms were separating from their sockets, the square of stone made a sudden grating noise, and with that, he was able to lift it enough to drag it to one side.

The noise spurred a flurry of activity below. "Come … down … hep … may," urged the voice.

Grabbing the oil lamp, Kane got down on his stomach and dangled it into the opening. A shaft descended a couple of metres before the space opened into a larger cell. The shaft was too narrow to crawl down, but Kane surmised there must be stairs somewhere that led to another level below the chamber floor.

"You still there?" he called out.

"Hurry," growled the voice, louder now, more insistent. "Come now."

"Where are you?"

There was no response.

"You still there?"

"Come now. Bing food. Bing. Bing meat."

"How do I get down there?"

"Hungry."

"Where's the stairs?"

"Sooo hungry."

"I don't …"

Uncertain what to do next, Kane lifted the lamp out of the shaft and glanced over his shoulder. On the other side of that sea of blackness, Dylan and Arika were waiting for him, depending on him to find the book and deliver them safe and well to the surface. His purpose here – his sole purpose – was to rescue his brother. If Wilfred came back and found Dylan and Arika in the study, who knows what the evil bastard might do to them? This whole mission might be lost.

He turned back to the shaft. He couldn't risk spending valuable time saving someone else, no matter how dire their circumstances. This rescue would have to wait.

"Look," he called down to the prisoner, "I'll get help … I'll get the police. Just hold on a while longer. I'll send somebody, I promise."

He clambered to his feet, and heard a frantic scrambling down below.

The voice shouted hoarsely, "We-baaahh! We-baaahh! Come down! Come now!"

"I'll send the police. Just hold on."

There was the sound of fast, raspy breathing. Then, at a low volume: "I kill you."

Kane froze. "What the hell?" he cried into the abyss.

The voice began screaming insanely. "I kill you! I eat your lungs! I drink your marrow! I chop you into pieces and feed on your flesh! Your meat, your blood. Aahh-aaahh! I feed! I feed! We-baaahh! We-li-baaahh! We-li-baaahh!"

The voice dissolved into a string of obscenities and threats that pierced the darkness of the chamber like a knife.

Kane backed away, glancing about in panic. If any of Wilfred's cronies were holed up down here, the yelling would be sure to lead them straight to him.

Grabbing the axe, cursing the invisible fiend under his breath, he left the cube and fled down the path.

27

The Necronomicon

A T THE WALL, Kane turned and stared into the darkness. The mad cannibal had quietened down, uttering only the occasional yelp of anger or despair, and he couldn't hear any other noises of concern – no shoes slapping on the stone floor or shouts from a mob of pursuers. Wilfred's gorillas appeared to be elsewhere (probably robbing a bank or beating up old ladies, or doing whatever else it was that sociopaths did when they weren't helping a sorcerer lock up prisoners in underground dungeons or torture reanimated corpses).

"No more distractions," he muttered to himself, and with his mind firmly on his mission, picked up the pace of his circumnavigation of the chamber.

There were no more cells after the fractals, only the gigantic stone blocks rising unbroken to the domed ceiling. Despite himself, Kane was unnerved by his encounter with the prisoner in the floor. All around him, outside the miniscule circle of light thrown by his lamp, was darkness absolute, filled with the ever-present background noise of what he now knew were starving creatures wailing and howling, while beneath his feet were hidden cells populated by cannibals. Who knows how many of the horrors were wandering about unfettered in the dark? Fortunately, the breeze against his cheeks felt stronger now, and the stench had reduced to almost nothing, a small mercy in this ghastly, never-ending nightmare.

After continuing for some time, he saw the stone blocks were coming to an end. Breaking into a run, he approached the wall's end, and staggered with shock when his lamp revealed what lay beyond the wall of the cyclopean chamber. It was an immense cave, even larger than the chamber he was standing in. The cave appeared naturally formed, in contrast to the perfect construction of the chamber, and extended from the wall of the chamber into an inky blackness that devoured the cave and all light and anything else that might have been out there.

But it wasn't just the vastness of the space that took Kane's breath away. Leading down into the abyss was a gargantuan flight of stairs.

Each step was more than half Kane's height and twice as deep. The steps were hewn from the rock, and they continued in a broad semi-circle until they disappeared into the unending night.

Standing at the mouth of the abyss, a stale breeze sweeping up from unknown depths, Kane tried to imagine the nightmare beings that would use stairs of that size, the horrors that had crawled out of the gulf of blackness and swarmed towards the central altar. All he could conjure were the mindless monsters he'd seen in movies and comics, but something told him that these monsters – spawned deep in the bowels of the earth, intelligent enough to conceive of and worship a deity greater than themselves, savage enough to chain their brethren or other unfortunate creatures to the stone pillars before sacrificing them on the giant, resin-stained cube – would be worse.

He leaned further into the abyss, hoping for the sake of his sanity that he wouldn't see or hear anything, that whatever monstrosities had clambered up and down these giant steps were long dead. He could make out a distant whooshing noise, which he guessed was running water, probably an underground stream, but apart from that, the only sounds were coming from the wailing creatures in the chamber behind him.

A sudden clatter rattled up the stairs.

Kane's body spasmed in fright. The noise sounded hollow, like a bone dropping to the rocky floor of the cave, a bone dropped by something alive, something that right now might be peering at the glow at the top of the stairs, licking its lips, commencing its ascent towards him.

A second clatter sounded, followed by a succession of scraping sounds.

A long chill ran up and down Kane's spine. Standing there with axe raised, for all intents and purposes defenceless, he felt a suffocating paralysis akin to being trapped in a coffin.

For a long time, there was silence.

"To hell with you," Kane muttered at last, to give himself strength.

Lowering the axe, he listened carefully into the black emptiness. The noises weren't repeated. After waiting a few more seconds, just to be sure, he took a deep breath, released the air from his lungs, and continued his journey along the top of the steps.

Soon enough, the lamp light revealed the point the chamber wall began again. Kane was dismayed when he realised he must now be midway through his search, judging by the curvature of the wall. Tired, rattled, worried, nowhere nearer to finding the Necronomicon, he muttered encouragements to give himself hope, and continued on.

The wall stretched a long distance, following the same gentle curve as before. There were no more cells, but after a while, Kane discerned what he believed was a faint glow. Getting closer, he could see it was coming from a stone arch: the opening to a brick-lined passage. He slowed his step. As he approached the passage, he began to hear the tinny strains of ragtime, a grotesquely cheerful sound in this stygian, stench-filled netherworld.

Turning down his lamp, getting a better grip on the axe, he crept silently up the dim-lit passage, breathing through his mouth. After all this time of searching, all the disappointments and dead ends, he was trembling with excitement at the prospect of confronting Wilfred or one of his accomplices. The music hinted at a living, breathing person, not some mindless zombie or cannibal, and that meant it was someone he could interrogate about the whereabouts of the Necronomicon.

The music was coming from the second room on the left. Placing his lamp on the floor, holding the axe in both hands, Kane approached the doorway and readied himself to face whoever or whatever was around the corner.

He peeked into the room.

Sitting with his back to the door, hunched over a large desk, was a skinny, dirty man with a speckled bald spot and long, brown, tangled hair that fell to his shoulders. He was dressed in green and brown rags, his arms wrapped in loose grey bandages, his hands encased in black woollen gloves with the fingers cut out. He appeared to be copying something from a large book into a smaller notebook. On a raised table next to the desk sat an old-fashioned gramophone with a flared brass horn, the arm bouncing as it played a jaunty piano riff.

"Put down the pen," Kane ordered, stepping into the room.

The man stiffened. He glanced over his shoulder. On seeing Kane at the door with axe at the ready, his slitted eyes opened wide, and with a squeal of excitement, he slid off the chair and stood wringing his hands, looking Kane up and down as if he'd never before seen anything quite like him.

"Who are you?" demanded Kane, feeling himself sweating from the clammy heat in the room.

Placing his hands against his mouth, the man hopped from foot to foot. He had a thin face, long ears, hooked nose and close-set eyes behind round, wire-rimmed reading glasses. His lips were loose and black, his neck hanging in a series of folds, though the skin across his cheekbones was stretched so tight it shone in the yellow light of a dozen candles.

"Oh! Oh! Oh!" he piped, shuffling closer. "A man! You alive?" He extended his neck and sniffed the air. "Indeed! Gilles know! Warm breathe. Gilles know warm!"

Kane raised the axe, recalling what the thing under the altar had threatened to do to him. Who knew what these freaks were capable of? This one, though slight of build, had sharp yellow fingernails that Kane knew could do real damage if he wasn't careful.

"I said: Who are you?"

"Excusee," said the strange man, nodding obsequiously. "Gilles. Pleasing meet. Very pleasing." Stepping closer, he thrust out a hand.

Kane stared at the filthy woollen glove. "What are you doing down here?"

The man frowned at his hand, pulled it away and stuck it inside his jacket. He seemed confused by the question. "Gilles live."

It took a moment for Kane to understand what he was getting at. "You live down here? Is that what you mean?"

He nodded excitedly.

"Why?"

"Assist to Mr Waite."

"Ah," said Kane, glancing at the narrow metal bed pushed against the wall, the yellow-stained pillow, the thin mattress piled with ratty blankets. "You're one of those."

Gilles nodded. "One those."

"Are there any more around?"

"Please?"

"Any more Waite's assistants?"

Gilles shook his head. "Oh no. Gilles special."

"Oh yeah, I can see that. What do you assist him with?"

"Study. Necronomicon. Book no easy reveal. Secrets must learn."

Kane stared past him at the book that lay open on the desk. The realisation of what it was hit him like a jolt of electricity.

"That's the Necronomicon!" he cried, pushing past him. "It's the damn book! I don't believe it!"

Gilles glanced at it. "Damn book. Yes. Necronomicon you know?"

"I've heard of it."

The yellowed pages were scrawled with text and symbols, none of them familiar to Kane. Next to the Necronomicon was the notebook the man had been writing in. He'd made almost perfect copies of the text from the open page.

He closed the book. As Dylan had described, it was bound in brown leather (human skin, according to legend), the leather warped and cracked with age. The head of a hideous horned devil leered at him.

It was hard for Kane to get his head around the fact that this book was central to the awful things that had happened to them in the past few weeks. And now that he had it in his hands, it would be the source of Dylan's liberation. He felt a confusing set of emotions, ranging from hatred and anger to exhilaration and joy, but his overriding feeling was relief. No matter what happened next, Wilfred had lost the source of his greatest power. With the book in his possession, and with Arika to help interpret it, they could figure out how to reverse the body-swap spell, and Dylan would be saved.

He glanced about the room, in case there was anything else that might assist in their battle with the wizard. The room was large and square, lit by candles, some in candelabras, some standing on wax-covered books. A bench at the far end was covered with flasks and test tubes, the shelves above it stacked with different kinds of laboratory equipment. Next to the bench was a long wooden table with straps attached at the top and bottom. The room wasn't dissimilar to the basement laboratory.

"What is all this crap for?" he asked Gilles. "What do you do down here?"

Gilles had moved uncomfortably close and was staring up at Kane with what looked like adoration. He smelt fusty – the type of smell you'd expect from a fungus that grows on dead animals. He was breathing fast, like a bird.

"Necronomicon not easy reveal secrets," he said, and began stroking Kane's hand with a dirty finger.

Kane moved away. "Yeah, I get that. But what specifically are you doing?"

Gilles followed him, trying to take hold of his sleeve. He reminded Kane of their former neighbour's dog, Buddy: an annoying mutt that would come bounding over every time the brothers played in the front yard. It would chase their ball and jump on them and get tangled in their feet and nudge their hands so they'd pat it. This was a million times worse.

"Learn. Know."

"Learn and know what? What's Waite planning? Did he build this place? How did he get all this stuff down here?"

"No Mr Waite. Own Master Dark."

"Muster Duck? What's that?"

"No what," cackled the man. "Who."

Kane suddenly remembered the paintings in the house, the ones Arika said were of the wizard, Jonathon Dark. "Ah, right, Master Dark."

"Master Dark bring all. All." Gilles waved his hands around the room, then clapped them against his chest. "Bring Gilles. Bring all."

Kane was confused. According to Arika, Dark disappeared decades ago. Surely this Gilles character wasn't that old.

"Is he a friend of Waite's?" he asked.

"Friend no. Enemy."

"Enemy, hey?" Kane smirked. "Very interesting."

So Wilfred had enemies. The enemy of your enemy is your friend – isn't that what they say? It was a shame Jonathon Dark was no longer around. He might have been useful. "What happened to Master Dark?"

"Vanish. Pouf! Here now … gone now."

"When was that?"

Gilles shrugged. "Here now … gone now," he said, lifting first one hand, then the other.

"Did Wilfred Waite have something to do with it?"

"Mr Waite long time Master Dark gone. Looong time. Gilles wait, wait, wait … One day … Mr Waite!" At this, he bent over and cackled till he choked.

By this time, they'd done almost a complete circuit of the room, Kane moving away every time the repellent man nuzzled up against him.

"Do you know what Waite did to my brother?"

"Did brother?" Gilles frowned. A black tongue darted out the side of his mouth. "Ahhh!" he cried, bouncing on his toes. "Fit jigsaw! Rescue young!"

"Yes! The young kid! That's my brother! Dylan! Do you know what happened to him?"

"Gilles know. Gilles fit."

"Fit what?"

"Fit two two together!"

"Two two together? What does that mean?"

"Mr Waite steal spell. Master Dark learn spell Gilles." He threw out his arms. "Two two … Gilles fit!"

Kane thought hard. "Are you saying Jonathon Dark taught you the spell?"

Gilles shook his head. "Learn spell Gilles."

He thought again. "You taught Jonathon Dark the spell?"

Gilles nodded till his glasses fell off.

Kane eyed him warily as he retrieved them from the floor. After blowing on each lens, he placed the glasses back on his nose, then stood squinting at him. He didn't look clever enough to *say* a spell, never mind create one.

"Do you know how undo spell?"

Gilles flicked a hand at him. "Easy. Take body hard. Keep body hard. Take back … easy!"

Kane's heart raced. He grabbed the man's bony shoulders. "How do you do it?"

"Gilles show spell."

"Tell me how to break it."

"Gilles show make."

"Look, man, I'm in a hurry. I don't need to know how to make the spell … just how to break it."

Gilles stuck out his lower lip like a spoilt child. "Show spell."

"Tell me how to break it … I don't have all night."

"Gilles have all night and day and night and day and night and day and –"

"All right, all right. Show spell, then show break."

He danced a little jig. "Gilles tell. Master stroke. Two two fit."

"Yes, tell me how two and two fit."

He moved his thin face closer. "All know Borellus, true? See self other eyes? Borellus spell."

Kane shrugged.

"Borellus trick. Stare eyes, take body, see self."

"Yeah," agreed Kane, to hurry him on. "Everyone knows that."

"Everyone know see. Everyone not know keep. Gilles read Necronomicon, read demon possess. Fit two two together. Make forever see self other eyes."

Despite his fractured words, Kane understood his meaning instantly. "Make forever?"

"Forever."

"But … Waite can't have a permanent hold on Dylan's body. He comes and goes. It can't be forever."

"Long time make forever. Many sacrifice, spell stick."

"How long?"

"Master Dark three year take."

"Three years?" He let out a sigh of relief. "So all I have to do is get

Dylan away from Waite, and he won't be able to make the swap permanent? Is that what you're saying?"

Gilles shook his head, a wide grin on his black lips. "Gilles learn speed. Covens together, open gate, summon Yog-Sothoth. Make forever. Young man no young more. Old man young. Young man old."

Kane gaped at him. So here it was at last: the reason Wilfred Waite had summoned the Messenger. He'd tried to trick his brother into helping him steal his body.

"Mr Waite win."

"Not if I've got anything to do with it."

"Yog-Sothoth come."

"I'll stop him."

"Gilles stop."

"What do you mean?"

"Gilles help."

Kane narrowed his eyes. "Why would you do that?"

Gilles narrowed his eyes too. His mouth pulled down at the corners. "Mr Waite strong grow. Mean grow. Master Dark back, make dust Mr Waite."

Kane couldn't help but smile at Gilles' loathing for the old wizard. It was good to know Wilfred's accomplices weren't all brainless acolytes, mindlessly doing his bidding. It meant they had potential allies in bringing him down.

"What makes you think Dark will come back?"

"Master Dark open gate, commune gods. Gilles wait. Master Dark come. Gilles here."

Kane turned back to the book. "Okay, tell me how to break the spell."

"Easy!" Gilles dragged the Necronomicon towards them. He flipped over a few pages and stopped at a picture of an eye inside a circle of symbols inside a seven-pointed star, all drawn in rust-coloured ink. Slamming his hand down on the page, he said, "Necronomicon power here. Hand page, stare eye, think self. Necronomicon break spell."

Kane pulled the book closer. "Let me get this straight: Dylan puts his hand on the page, concentrates on the eye, and wills his body back?"

"Hand, stare, think self."

"It's that easy?"

"Hard steal, harder keep."

"Thank you," breathed Kane, grabbing Gilles' hand and pumping it enthusiastically.

Letting go, he wiped his hand down his trousers. He felt suddenly invincible. He'd not only found the book, he'd received a lesson in how to use it to save his brother. The nightmare would soon be over.

"Listen, man: I'll get you out of here. You don't need to stay here one minute longer. You can leave with us."

Gilles raised his skinny arms as if Kane had threatened to attack him. "No!" he cried. "Master Dark come! Gilles stay!"

"You can wait anywhere. Up in the farmhouse, maybe. Better than down here in the dark."

Gilles wasn't listening. "Master Dark come! Gilles stay!" he cried, anguish twisting his face.

"Okay, okay," Kane assured him. "Calm down. It was just a suggestion."

"Mr Waite come! Gilles no leave!"

Kane glanced at the door. "He's coming back?"

"After spell."

"Not yet?"

"After spell."

"What spell is he doing?"

Gilles quickly regained his composure. "Want know?"

Kane glanced at the door again. "If you can tell me in thirty seconds or less."

"Want know?" Gilles asked again, sidling up to him.

"Yes! Tell me what Waite is up to – besides stealing my brother's body."

"Master Dark bring. Mr Waite filthy steal." He grabbed hold of Kane's sleeve. "Gilles show."

"No, no, I don't have time … we've been here too long already."

"End world."

Kane stared at him. "Come again."

"Come new world order."

"What does that mean?"

"Mr Waite summon gods."

"Yeah, I heard that."

"Summon gods, open gate. Thousand year chaos. Rivers turn blood. Cities burn. Oceans boil. New world order. Mr Waite stand foot of gods. Secrets universe learn. Come god."

"That's insane."

Gilles cackled. "Insane … hehehe. Mr Waite call god, come god."

"How can a weak old man think he can bring about the end of the world?"

"Raise army."

"Raise an army? He must be mad if he thinks he can do that."

"Mad," nodded Gilles.

"Is he mad?"

Gilles nodded.

"Is he raising an army?"

Gilles nodded. "Show," he said, tugging at Kane's sleeve. "Follow. Lamp! Lamp!"

Kane hesitated, torn between getting back to Dylan and Arika and learning more about what Wilfred was up to. It didn't take long to decide. If this freak was correct, and Wilfred was able to make good on his plan, saving Dylan would be the least of his worries – a short-term solution at best. He had to stop Wilfred from summoning his gods, otherwise they were doomed. They were all doomed.

He followed Gilles out of the room, picking up his oil lamp on the way. Gilles turned left, scooted off, came back, took hold of his sleeve and pulled him down the passage.

"Find Master Dark. Bring back. Dust Mr Waite. Find Master Dark. Bring back. Dust Mr Waite," he kept saying, growing more excited with each step.

After passing a number of closed doors, they reached the end of the passage. Before them was a heavy iron door, with thick iron hinges and a large, diamond-shaped locking plate, reinforced with hexagonal bolts. Letting go of Kane's sleeve, Gilles pulled from his pants a bunch of rusted jailer's keys, selected one, inserted it into the lock and with both hands twisted it until the lock clicked. Then he held the door handle with both hands and pulled with all his might.

The door creaked slowly open, releasing a stench that was worse than any Kane had encountered so far in this hellish place. There also arose a shuffling and murmuring in response to the noise and the light. Gilles waved Kane through.

"You first," Kane said, keeping a keen eye on his shifty companion.

Bowing at him, Gilles stepped into the darkness. Kane followed with the oil lamp.

They were now in a large room with a low ceiling. Kane glanced around. The room seemed empty, though the light didn't penetrate all the way to the end.

He shook his head. "What is all this?" he demanded, annoyed at whatever game the man was playing.

His voice caused the murmuring to rise in volume and intensity. It seemed to be coming from the floor at the far end of the room.

"Seeeee," hissed Gilles, pulling at Kane's sleeve. "Heeere. Heeere."

Kane moved cautiously forward, making sure Gilles remained in front of him. After a few steps, his guide stopped and turned to smile at him. Kane stepped closer.

They'd come to the edge of a precipice. A metal railing and five metal steps led down into the blackness, ending in mid-air.

Kane raised the lamp and gasped. The light illuminated a scene from a nightmare. The floor of the chamber dropped about a storey, and standing and sitting and lying there staring up at them were dozens of men.

But when Kane leaned on the railing for a closer look, he realised they weren't men. Some appeared to be half formed, melted, incomplete. Others didn't seem human at all. They were all wearing the grey pants he saw earlier stacked in piles in the cells.

"Dark army," announced Gilles, throwing out his arms.

Some of them, realising Kane wasn't their master, began yelling at them and leaping up the wall of their dungeon. At this commotion, more appeared from the outer edges of the darkness, and before long more than a hundred of them had gathered, an awful, seething, stinking horde of mutants.

"What in God's name –" he began, turning to Gilles – and then he saw with a shot of alarm that Gilles had ducked behind him. He felt two hands on his back, a shove, and suddenly he was falling forward.

With lightning reflexes, he reached back and grabbed Gilles' shirt. Gilles yelped and dug his fingernails into Kane's arm, but Kane held on, and together they tumbled down the steps.

The lamp followed them and crashed to the floor of the chamber, where it exploded in flames. Some of the things screamed, but if any of them caught fire they were quick to douse the flames. The fire burnt brightly for a few seconds, before dying and plunging the chamber into darkness.

Kane had managed to save himself by grabbing onto the railing at the bottom step. The chamber now erupted into bellows and shouts as, below him, the prisoners leapt up and clambered over each other to get at him.

His body hurt all over. It felt like his right arm had been pulled from its socket, and though he was holding onto the railing with both hands, his legs were dangling in the abyss. And his grip was getting weaker.

Gilles was moaning on the step above him, invisible in the darkness. After a while, he began murmuring, "Mr Waite, Mr Waite," and with each refrain his voice grew stronger.

Kane tried to haul himself up. Though his muscles burned, he managed to grab the next rail up; and then the stairs squealed and shifted under his weight, sending him into a panic that the whole structure was about to break away and fall to the floor below.

Changing tactic, he tried lifting his leg up to the step. He didn't have the strength to make it that far, so for a time he lay there with legs dangling, hoping that by resting, he would gather enough energy to pull or push himself up.

Then something happened that drove him deeper into panic.

Gilles was crawling up the stairs. Kane could hear his laboured breathing and the scrape of clothes and shoes against metal as his body moved further and further away.

He knew that if Gilles made it to the door, he'd lock him in this hellhole, and that would be the end. It was impossible to conceive of anyone coming to rescue him, even if Arika and Dylan were able to make it to the surface alive. They'd have to convince the authorities to take action, and a search warrant would be needed – but who would believe the failing old man with his story of a body swap, or the out-of-towner with her claims of wizardry and cosmic gods? And if, by some miracle, the police did come, how would they find him in this labyrinthine structure, with its network of corridors and rooms, and with him locked away behind an impenetrable iron door? How many days could he survive in this dank dungeon, even assuming Wilfred left him alone and didn't release some supernatural horror into the room to eat him alive?

With a superhuman effort, he pulled himself up, swung his leg, missed the step, pulled up and swung his leg again.

He could hear Gilles dragging himself along the stone floor, grunting with the effort, getting closer to the door.

He tried again. He pulled his body up; felt his arms screaming in pain; swung his leg up; felt a sharp pain as his shin connected with the step. As his legs dropped back, something touched his foot, and he yelped and kicked it away. Cold sweat ran down his body. He wasn't going to make it. The horrors below were climbing on top of each other, starvation driving them towards him, and any minute now a hand would grab his ankle and pull him down, and that would be it.

With a curious sense of indifference, he tried again, and suddenly, almost without knowing how, he was on his knees at the top of the steps, dripping with sweat and panting like a dog.

In the distance was a dim grey rectangle he knew must be the doorway. Getting up, limping towards it, he got there at the same moment that Gilles, pushing with his shoulder, shrieked in triumph and swung the door shut.

Kane threw his back against it. He heard a yell of complaint from the other side of the door, braced his legs and shoved with all his might.

The door creaked open. Gilles was leaning against it, but his skinny body was no match for Kane. As soon as there was enough of a gap, he slipped through and jumped away as the iron door slammed shut.

"Pain, hurt, ow," Gilles moaned, massaging his leg, sneaking furtive glances at him. "Hurt."

"What was all that about?" yelled Kane. "You tried to off me!"

"Gilles hurt. Ow, ow."

"I thought you were helping me!"

"Gilles help. Man fall."

"I didn't fall! You pushed me!"

"Gilles trip. Man fall."

"You liar. You tried to push me into that pit."

"Gilles fall."

"Don't lie! You tried to kill me! Why would you do that?"

He stood for a while regarding the repellent man, wondering what to do. Chain him to a wall? Lock him in a cell until he could send in the police? Both were tempting ideas, but Kane had the feeling Gilles was as much a victim of Wilfred as those poor souls in the pit. The fireman in him couldn't stomach being the cause of further distress or harm, and he had no real urge for vengeance and no real fear that Gilles could do anything more to hurt him. Now the Necronomicon was in his possession, now Gilles had revealed Wilfred's plans, he didn't need to stick around. It was time to get out of here, collect Dylan and Arika, and leave it to the police or the army to come down and deal with Wilfred and his band of cronies.

Shoving Gilles against the door with his forearm on his chest, he pulled the keys from the lock.

"Mine! Thief! Swine!" Gilles yelled, trying to grab them off him.

Kane pulled away from him. "I tried to help you," he said with real emotion, "and you tried to kill me. I thought we were friends."

"Gilles friend."

"You need help."

"Help friend."

"Maybe the police will have better luck."

"No police!" screamed Gilles, throwing himself at Kane's feet. He grabbed hold of his leg and hugged it hard. "Bad big! No police, no!"

"Listen, man," said Kane, extricating his leg from Gilles' grip: "you need to get out of here, away from that madman. You'll thank me for this."

Turning, he limped away, Gilles' screams chasing him down the passage.

Back in the room, Kane collected the Necronomicon, the notebook and the axe and shoved them into a black leather bag. Slinging the bag over his shoulder, he grabbed another lamp and hurried back to the chamber.

28

Where there's a will ...

"ARE YOU SURE it was a baby?"

Arika was standing at a pile of books, waving a parchment in the air. She'd been rifling through a stack of papers, but hadn't found anything of interest. Most of the papers were detailed records of conversations, presumably between Wilfred and whoever he brought down here to interrogate, written verbatim, regardless of substance or interest. Most documented day-to-day chores, interactions with friends and neighbours, trips to the city, records of livestock purchases and the like.

"Dylan?"

Dylan didn't look up. This was the third time she'd asked the question, and she'd probably keep on asking it until he said, "No, it was a cat." He shouldn't have told her about the baby. It was just that Kane had been gone for so long, and he was getting frustrated they hadn't found anything. He turned over the page. He was browsing through a green cloth-bound book that had pages crammed with long strings of text that looked like spells.

"Pretty sure," he said at last, though in reality he wasn't. He was dazed after popping back into his body, up there on the hill. The squirming thing wrapped in a dirty jacket might have been an animal, the hand he thought he saw, a paw.

"It couldn't have been a baby. Really."

Dylan shrugged as he thumbed through the book. The text was small and crabbed, written in a foreign language, so it was impossible to tell whether these were spells or just the attempts of a wannabe poet. He clapped the book shut. Probably the Necronomicon was just as indecipherable, and this whole expedition would end up being a complete waste of time. A tear of frustration rolled in a line down his cheek and dropped with a splat on the book.

"We'd have heard something if babies were going missing," Arika said.

"Suppose so," shrugged Dylan.

She had a point there. People tended to make a big thing of it when their kids went missing. It was probably a cat. But what type of divine being did Wilfred expect to conjure through sacrificing a boring old housecat? He changed his mind again. It must have been a baby.

Arika dropped the parchment and lifted a bulldog-clipped set of papers from the shelf. "Can you imagine the things Waite gets up to down here, all alone?" she asked, her eyes roaming the room.

Dylan shrugged again. He laid the book on the table and picked up another.

"The thought of … well, you – here – doing God knows what … makes my stomach churn."

"Aw, thanks. Just the thing a red-blooded teenager wants to hear from a girl."

"Sorry," smiled Arika. "You know what I mean."

"Don't worry about it. My stomach churns whenever I look at me too."

Replacing the papers on the shelf, she stepped towards him and pulled out a chair. "How does it feel? Being in that body?"

Dylan glanced down at his rumpled clothes, at the squat, shrunken, wrinkled body inside them that didn't make any sense. "Just … weird."

"It would be a researcher's dream to study this."

"I'll donate my body to science after I kick the bucket."

Arika didn't react; just kept staring in fascination at his body. "Does it feel different to your own body?"

"Course. It feels … smaller. Everything's bigger."

"Does it hurt?"

"All the time. He's got arthritis something chronic. And wind. You've never felt wind till you've felt old man wind."

"Do you feel old, or is it more like your brain's working normally but your body isn't?"

Dylan was starting to resent all the questions. They were here to get his body back, not while away time discussing the physiology of ageing.

"It feels like I'm in a rubber chicken suit," he answered, opening the book.

"Like you're yourself, but in a costume?"

He ignored her.

She ignored the snub. "Maybe over time you'll get used to it. The body is pretty adaptable."

Her remark sent a stab of anger through him. Arika seemed to be assuming he was in this rotting bag of meat to stay.

"I'll get out," he shot back, glaring at her. "Kane will make sure of it."

She patted his scabby hand. "I know he will. He won't stop for anything."

"I wonder how he's going."

Arika took out her phone. "Still no signal."

"We should've made a plan for how long he was gonna take. We could be waiting here forever, not knowing when he's coming back." An icy dread rolled over him. "He could be lost … or something worse."

"If he's not back in fifteen, we'll go look for him."

With a terse smile, Arika got up and went back to the bookshelf.

"Do you think Waite is still trying to raise Yog-Sothoth?" she asked, picking up the wad of papers again.

"That was the plan."

"What will that be like?"

"We never got to that part."

"He didn't say?"

"He made it sound like it would be this booming voice from the sky … like God."

"He wasn't expecting any physical manifestation?"

"I think he was expecting to see it. The Messenger was supposed to clear the way, so it could appear in person."

"I wouldn't mind being a fly on the wall for that."

"Apparently the spell has to be done in a place called Mlal'orla. It's a charmed place that pulls in mystical energy from all over the planet. Yog-Sothoth isn't an easy god to summon."

"That makes sense. Did he say where this charmed place was?"

"Nup. It could be in another country, for all I know."

"That's not likely, seeing as he raised the Messenger here. Must be somewhere close. It could even be the altar you saw. Mlal'orla might be Big Martha."

"I did think of that. But it could be anywhere. Those spells in the Necronomicon are pretty specific. Get one thing wrong and nothing happens."

Arika's face turned pensive. "He seems bent on gaining immortality, doesn't he?"

"Wilfred? He thinks he already is."

"After two hundred years, I suppose you've either had enough of life or you've tasted eternity and want more. I'm not sure where I'd sit." She thought for a moment. "I suppose if I was offered immortality, I'd have to take it, just to see what it was like. But if I didn't like it, the only way out would be suicide, I guess, which isn't a nice thought. Unless life is just stretched out, like Waite did before he stole your body. You'd have more time, but there'd still be an end."

Dylan was trying to read his book, a treatise on demonic possession.

"I wouldn't mind being around for space travel – going to Mars and beyond. That'd be worth waiting around for. Not so keen on seeing how global warming or cyber-terrorism or the next pandemic play out, though. How about you, Dylan?"

"Yeah," he grunted, not really paying attention.

"Don't you think immortality is the ultimate form of greed? If you make the most of the life you have, you should have plenty of time to do everything. I guess. It's hard to tell. I know a lot of people work hard all their life and don't have time to enjoy it till they retire, so being immortal would at least stretch out your retirement. As long as you're healthy enough to enjoy it. Which is Waite's thing, isn't it? – why he had to steal your body. Now he has another three decades of youth to enjoy."

He heard that bit.

"I mean – that's his aim. Not that we'll let that happen."

Looking sheepish, she turned her attention to the papers in her hand. As she read, her eyes opened in shock.

"Oh. My. God."

Dylan raised his head. "What is it?"

At first she appeared not to have heard him. With an effort, she pulled her eyes away from the papers and waved them at him.

"Dylan, old man, you will never guess what this is."

29

Back

"**I**'M HEIR TO his fortune?"

Arika was frowning down at the wad of papers. She ran her fingers through her hair. "Two centuries of savings and investments."

"Two centuries? What is that worth?"

"It doesn't say. Oh wait. Here's a list. The farm. The shop. A castle in Hungary. Gold bullion in a Norwegian bank …"

"Oh my God."

"… more bank accounts. Another castle …"

"Two castles? What am I gonna do with two castles?"

"What would you do with one castle?"

Pushing himself out of the chair, Dylan went to see the list for himself.

"Why would he do that? He wants me dead."

He wondered whether Wilfred really meant it when he said he was in his debt and would look after him. But leaving him gold and two castles …? Then it hit him what the crafty old necromancer was up to. "No. Of course. He wants Waite dead."

Arika's eyes widened. "He's leaving his fortune to himself."

Dylan felt a surge of nausea. The walls and ceiling closed in on him, his legs buckled, and he swayed and grabbed onto the table for support.

"Oh shit, I'm gonna puke."

"Don't worry, Dylan," Arika reassured him. "We won't let anything happen to you."

"I feel sick. Oh shit! No, no! Not now!"

"Here," said Arika, taking his arm and helping him to the door. "Do it out there."

"He's coming back!"

Her eyes flew up the passage.

"It's Waite!" cried Dylan, tearing his arm away. "He's in my head! Y'ai'ng'ngah Yog-Sothoth! The Tseg of Kra! They've breached the gulf! The gulf … The gate … Ia! Ia! The Goat with a Thousand Young!" He grabbed Arika's wrist. "We've got to get out of here!"

His face froze. He gaped at her, terror-struck, not moving. Then, slowly, his rheumy eyes glazed over, his grip relaxed, and his mouth stretched into a brown, derisive grin.

"Well, well, well," Wilfred declared in a throaty voice, "I see there are benefits in not having full tenancy over my new vessel."

"What?" piped Arika, confused.

"I find out what my young benefactor has been getting up to. Naughty Dylan. Down in the dark with a dolly bird."

Arika pulled her arm away. It was clear from the evil shining from those black-rimmed eyes that this was no longer Dylan.

"A lady should not stand gawping with her mouth open," Wilfred sneered, sinking into a seat. "Ah, that's better. Damn these old bones. They do crack like kindling wood these days."

Arika grabbed the rifle from the table and pointed it at him.

He glanced at her. "And a lady should not hold a rifle like a common infantryman."

She looked him up and down. Dylan had always seemed weighed down by the burden of Wilfred's frail and failing body, but with the return of its owner, it had taken on a rigidity born of contempt and conceit.

"Come now, dear, would you really shoot an unarmed man?"

She raised the rifle. She needed him to believe it was full of bullets, not darts, but so far he was acting as if he didn't think the rifle was loaded at all.

"What did you do to my father?"

"Put down that weapon, you silly girl. You'll put someone's eye out."

"Where is my father?"

"I'm sure I have no idea what you're bluthering about."

"My father was looking for this farm, and now he's missing. What did you do to him?"

Wilfred raised his eyebrows. "Your father? Are you sure about that?

I can't see any family resemblance. You surely didn't inherit his good looks, did you dear?"

Arika ignored his pathetic attempt at an insult. "So you did know him."

"Did I say that? No, dear, you're confused. I'm young Dylan Gates, your beau's brother. What would Master Dylan know about your precious papa?"

"I'm not afraid to use this thing."

Wilfred raised his hands in mock surrender. "What do you think my brother would do if you shot his only remaining sibling; what with our dear parents fresh in the ground? I dare say he would tear you limb from limb and leave you rotting down here with the rest of the dead things." He bent forward. "You can't trust the boy, you know. He would turn on you in an instant if he thought you had the nerve to cross him."

"Shut up."

"Does he know you're only sniffing around him for your own selfish reasons?"

"Where is my father?"

"No doubt he doesn't. He probably feels … how do you say it? … you have the hots for him. He's not thinking with his brain, I can vouch for that. He *is* an impressive specimen, don't you think? A shame it was his brother who responded to my call. But never mind. Youth is youth. I have a lifetime to bend that young body to my needs. And then I will find another … and on and on until I evolve to my next glorious incarnation. I certainly have a debt to pay to that old curmudgeon, Jonathon."

"Shut your mouth or I'll shut it for you."

"Nice way to talk to a defenceless old man."

Arika lowered the rifle. "That's right. You're a defenceless old man. I don't need to shoot you. I can hurt you in a hundred different ways."

"Now you're starting to impress me. I could use someone like you by my side. Not in this old throwaway, of course," he added, gesturing down at his body. He squirmed to the edge of the seat. "But think about me in my lithe new body. I'll harden it up, so it's just like its brother's. You'd like that, wouldn't you? I'll have you panting after me. You must find me tempting: a young body with a mind that's travelled down through the ages. I've had eons of practice in the erotic arts, you know. Though I must admit to having slowed down a tad in recent times. But I've acquired a powerful new engine, and you can be the first to road test it."

"Will you shut up? You're making me sick."

Wilfred seemed to find her disgust amusing. "You won't say that when I'm back in my fresh new skin. You'll be begging me for it."

"Just answer my damn question!"

"What question was that, dear?"

"Where is my father?"

"Who is your father again?"

"Corbin Livingston. A private detective. He came looking for this farm."

"If he found it, surely you would have heard?" He glanced around the room. "I can't see him bound and gagged in a corner. Can you? So I'd venture he failed."

"You did something to him; I know it."

"Maybe he grew sick of you and your whingeing harridan of a mother. Maybe the old fishwife was dry and he went in search of sweet new fruit. Did you think of that?"

"You're a disgusting old man. And you can't be more wrong about my family."

"The truth can sometimes be dirty."

"You know what happened to him. I can see it in your eyes. You've seen him. If you don't tell me what happened, I'll …"

"You'll what, dear? Pull out my fingernails? Choke the truth out of me?"

Arika scowled at him.

"I love a good throttling as much as the next man," sighed Wilfred, pushing his old body to its feet, "but regrettably there'll be no time for that. Something knows you are here, and it's been loosed from its pen." He moved towards her. "Can you hear it, dear? It hears you: your fast-beating heart, your pathetic whining. And it smells you; smells the flesh cooking inside from the heat of your tender young body. My pet has a special appetite for hot sweet marrow like yours. It will have such a feast when it arrives."

Arika backed away, felt for the door jamb, glanced nervously down the passage.

Wilfred stood watching her. "Can you hear it yet? It slithers like a slug and crushes like a snake. It will pull you in and suffocate you as it digests you alive. The end is closer than you imagine."

"Kane!" yelled Arika, leaning into the passage. "Kane!"

30

Sebastian

O N HIS WAY back to the study, Kane passed two more arch-fronted corridors. Their yawning mouths were dark and silent, though he doubted they were empty. The authorities will have a field day exploring this place, he thought as he hurried past them. On his part, he was just thankful the nasties and creepy-crawlies would soon be far behind him, someone else's problem, never to be seen, heard of or hinted at again.

As he was completing this thought, out of the darkness came something unexpected. He stopped, slipped the bag off his shoulder and blinked in disbelief. It was a square, red-brick cottage, standing in a random spot a few metres out from the chamber wall. With its thatched roof, panelled door and two casement windows, it resembled one of the huts in the farmyard above.

Despite his eagerness to get back to Dylan and Arika, curiosity got the better of him, and he limped over to check it out.

Holding his lamp near the window, he was surprised to see a skinny old man slumped on the straw-covered floor. His back was resting against the wall, his head turned away, his feet sticking out in front of him. The man's face was square and skeletal, his eyes closed, his white hair so long it dangled all the way to the straw.

As the light entered the room, the man's eyes flew open, he convulsed, threw himself on his hands and knees and scrambled away. His leg was chained to the wall, and the links bounced and jangled as he scurried across the straw. When the chain pulled taut, he fell flat on his face, pulled his knees into a fetal position and covered his face with his arms, whimpering like a child.

This man, unlike the others Kane had encountered, was naked. Also unlike the others, he was not deformed, apart from being impossibly skinny. His skin was stretched so tight across his bones, he looked more like a skeleton than a person. His buttocks showed no sign of muscle, and Kane could count every bone in his spine. He was filthy and covered from head to toe in ugly boils, welts, bruises and scars.

"Hey," he called out. "Who are you?"

The man was rocking and whimpering and showed no signs of hearing him.

Reassured by the chain attached to his leg, Kane went to the door and pushed against it. Surprisingly, it swung open. He stepped inside.

"What are you doing here?" he asked, knowing this was something different to the freaks he'd encountered so far. This man looked human – pathetic, starved and terrified, but unmistakably alive. "Hey there, you okay?"

The man whimpered a little more, but the sympathy in Kane's tone appeared to penetrate his terror. He peered under his arm, squinting against the light.

"Why has Waite got you chained up down here?"

Tears fell from the man's eyes, and then his eyelids closed and his head dropped to the straw.

Rushing over, placing the lamp and bag on the floor, Kane knelt beside him. "Hey, man. Hey. You alright?"

He glanced around and saw in a corner of the room a bucket of water with a metal cup hooked over the edge. Crawling to it, he dipped the cup in the water, had a quick sniff, then took it back, lifted the man's head, and placed the rim of the cup against his mouth.

The man, groggy but awake, held Kane's hand in a cold grip as he drank, all the while staring at him in fear and wonder.

After finishing with the water, Kane dropped the cup and helped the man lean up against the wall, where he sat staring into his face with round, bloodshot eyes, his look of rapture suggesting he was beholding an angel or a god.

"What's your name?"

The man opened his mouth to speak, but before a word could come out, he froze, grey tongue resting against grey, toothless gums.

"What's your name?"

He appeared confused by the question.

"I'm Kane. Kane Gates."

The man mouthed something, then jutted out his chin and said with an effort, "Se-bas-jun."

"Sebastian? Is that it?" Kane nodded. "I'm Kane. I'm a fireman," he added to reassure the man about his intentions. "What are you doing down here?"

The man looked confused again. Shaking the confusion from his mind, he swallowed heavily and said, "The sorcerer."

"Yes, Wilfred Waite. Did that bastard imprison you down here?"

Sebastian moved his head up and down.

Kane looked at his emaciated body. "How long ago?"

His breathing grew faster. "Don't know. Was in cellar … for long time. Brought here …" He frowned at the floor. "Don't know when." Tears streamed down his face. "I don't know," he wailed. "Who … are you?"

"Kane. I'm Kane."

"What are you? Are you –?" His eyes opened wide, and he drew back in terror.

Kane waved his hands at him, before realising the gesture was probably more alarming than reassuring. "Don't worry, Sebastian, I'm not here to hurt you. I'm here to help. I'm a fireman. Waite did something bad to my brother, and I'm here to save him."

Sebastian stared at the open door as if expecting some horror to come creeping through.

Kane checked the door too, just in case, then glanced around the room, trying to figure out why this man was chained up in a cottage instead of in one of the many cells he'd passed. More to the point, why was this place here at all? Who would build a house in the middle of an underground dungeon?

"Why does he have you locked up in this hut, Sebastian? It makes no sense. As much as anything down here makes any sense."

Sebastian's eyes were searching Kane's face, tracing a line along his mouth, to his ear, his hair, his eyes, his nose, back to his mouth. He had that confused look again.

"Do you know why? Did he ever give you an explanation?"

"I applied for job." Reaching out, he touched Kane's arm, mesmerised by the curve of his biceps. Kane's arms were almost the size of Sebastian's legs. "Woke up … chained up."

To Kane, it sounded similar to what happened with his brother. "Was it a job as his assistant?"

"Yes."

"I –"

"Shop assistant."

"Oh," said Kane. Then this must have something to do with Wilfred's store. He'd used coercion on Dylan, but Kane wasn't surprised Wilfred would resort to plain kidnapping if it suited his needs.

Placing his hands between his legs, Sebastian rocked from side to side. He didn't appear embarrassed by his nakedness, and didn't seem to feel the cold. "Summer job," he added.

"Summer job? What does that mean?"

"University summer job." Shutting his eyes, he dropped his head back against the brick wall. "Six weeks shop assistant."

Kane stared at him, at his long white hair, deep wrinkles, pasty skin and scarred, bruised body. His initial thought had been that this was another body swap – an earlier attempt. But then, why were both he and Wilfred old? And if Wilfred had already swapped bodies with a young Sebastian, why did he need Dylan's body? It didn't make sense.

"How old were you when you were kidnapped?"

"Young. Nineteen, twenty."

"Did Waite swap bodies with you?"

Sebastian frowned at him. "Kidnapped," he insisted.

"No magic?"

"He drugged me and kept me in his cellar. Then here."

Kane scratched his chin. "That sounds like something a garden-variety psychopath would do. Not Waite's style. What could he –"

Suddenly the awful truth hit him and sent him bounding to his feet. "You've been Waite's prisoner since you were nineteen years old?"

Sebastian cowered against the wall, frightened by Kane's violent movement and raised voice.

"That must be at least … forty years." Forty years of being locked in a cellar, and now this awful dungeon. Forty years of living in darkness, chained to a wall, starved and beaten. "Why would he do that?" he asked himself, getting faint with anger.

Sebastian stared up at him. "He comes in and watches me."

"That's creepy, even for Waite."

"And he brings things: a whip or a knife or …"

Kane held his breath. "And he –?"

Sebastian traced the bruises and scars on his abdomen with his forefinger. "He hurts me."

Kane felt the blood drain from his head, saw black spots before his eyes.

"He says I need to understand he has no choice. But he never explains why."

"He tortures you?"

"Hurts me, then leaves me in the dark till the next time. His assistants too … bring food: bones in water and old meat with maggots and mouldy bread. They're worse than the sorcerer. Enjoy hurting me."

Kane couldn't believe what he was hearing. Stealing bodies was bad enough, interrogating resurrected dead people the work of a psychopath; but torturing this pathetic human being for forty long years for no apparent reason was evil on a level he couldn't begin to comprehend.

"Waite has kept you alive all these years just to hurt you?" he asked, hoping that by saying the words out loud it would help him make sense of the situation.

Sebastian nodded.

"Did you know him before he kidnapped you?"

"No."

"You didn't upset him somehow? Or your family? … they did something to him?"

"I wasn't from anywhere near Arbroath. I went to see about a job. That was the first time I met him."

Surely there's more to it than that, Kane was thinking. But he didn't have any more time for questions. Glancing at the door, he said, "Look, Sebastian, we need to get going, before that bastard gets back. I'll get you to safety, then we'll deal with Waite and those freak assistants of his."

Pulling out the keys he'd stolen from Gilles, he tried one after the other in the shackles. Eventually one worked and the chain fell away from Sebastian's bony ankle.

"Come on, mate," Kane said, helping him to his feet.

It wasn't easy supporting Sebastian while carrying the oil lamp and the heavy leather bag, but fortunately Sebastian didn't weigh much and the cottage was close to the passage that led to the study.

As they reached the opening, Kane was halted by a sound behind them.

"Can you hear that?" he whispered. But Sebastian was unresponsive, almost comatose, and didn't respond.

Kane listened again. Something was approaching them in the darkness. He raised the lamp, squinted, and listened hard as something flopped and sloshed across the floor of the chamber.

"Jesus," he muttered, thinking: It's that sadistic, murderous freak, Gilles. He's sent something after me.

That was when he heard Arika calling his name.

Hoisting the bag higher on his shoulder, he took off down the passage, dragging Sebastian behind him.

At the door to the study he stopped, panting and staring. Arika was holding onto a chair, looking in his direction, the terror in her eyes suggesting she'd feared it wouldn't be him at the door. Dylan was seated next to her, slumped over the table, his forehead resting on one arm. His old body was struggling to breathe.

"Arika, what's wrong with him?"

"Thank Christ you're back, Kane. It's Waite. He was here."

Kane glanced at the old man's back. "You mean …?"

"It's Dylan again. But Waite … came back. He said something was coming for us."

"Yeah, I heard."

Dragging Sebastian into the room, he deposited him in a chair, placed the lamp and bag on the table, went to his brother and lifted him off the table.

"Who's this?" Arika asked, staring at the naked white-haired skeleton.

"We need to go. Whatever it is, it's close."

He nodded at the bag. "Take that, will you? I found the book. It's in there, with the axe. I'll help Dylan."

"The book? Did you say 'the book'? You found it?"

His brother raised his head. "Kane," he groaned, "it's Waite: he's –"

"Yeah, I know. But we need to move."

He helped Dylan to the door, while Arika darted about the room shoving papers and books into the black leather bag, along with the rifle, cattle prod and her own bag.

"Kane," said Dylan, "Waite is –"

"Oh shit!" cried Kane.

Down the passage, at the place where the bricks curved towards the chamber, a brown, slug-like thing had taken hold of the wall and was dragging itself towards them.

"What is that?" murmured Dylan, stiffening.

More of the thing oozed into the passage, its slimy skin shining with phosphorescence, illuminating the bricks with a sickly brown glow.

Arika peered under his arm. "It's Waite's pet. He said it was like a snake. That doesn't look like a snake."

Kane wasn't about to hang around to see the rest of it. But they still had Sebastian to consider. Leaving Dylan with Arika, he went back to the old man, who'd slipped off the chair and was curled up on the floor.

"Sebastian," he urged, shaking his shoulder. "Sebastian, you need to get up."

But the man was unresponsive. His body was limp, his breathing barely discernible. Kane's heart sank at the realisation they would have to leave him behind.

Pulling a cushion off one of the chairs, he placed it under Sebastian's head, took off his jacket, draped it over him like a blanket, then rejoined Dylan and Arika.

"Come on," he said, ushering them out, closing the door behind them. "We need to get to the stairs."

The snake-slug thing was closer now, though thankfully it moved more like a slug than a snake.

With a final glance at it, Kane hurried Dylan and Arika along.

31

Out of darkness

I T WAS MUCH harder going up the stairs than going down. Arika had the black leather bag slung over one shoulder, and despite its great weight, was handling it as well as most of the fully geared-up fire officers Kane worked with. Dylan, on the other hand, was finding the going tough, his energy sapped from the long day in an old man's body. Kane had to carry him most of the way, and with his own scrapes and bruises, it was a long and painful climb. If Wilfred's body hadn't been so small and light, he doubted he would have made it.

They didn't see the snake-slug thing again. The sound of its pursuit had stopped, and as they ascended, the only sound they heard was the whining of the thing locked in the cell near the study, which grew steadily fainter the closer they got to the surface.

At last they came to the bend in the staircase, and a few steps later emerged into the well. After a brief rest, they began their climb. Arika was first, followed by Dylan, then Kane.

Once they were safe in the sub-basement, Kane handed Dylan the lamp, grabbed hold of the metal plate with both hands, shoved it down with a grunt, and watched with satisfaction as it slammed shut. Not content with it self-closing, he jumped on it, and kept jumping until he was sure the thing was locked.

Free at last from the noxious underworld and its relentless horrors, they stood smiling at each other, taking a few moments to catch their breath and savour their success. All that was left now was to open the Necronomicon and have Dylan wish his body back. Then get the hell out of here.

"Perhaps I'm feeding my pet too much. He doesn't fit up the stairs."

Kane whirled around to find his brother standing at the top of the steps, leaning on a brass, ball-topped sceptre. But of course, it wasn't his brother. Anger surged in him like an explosion at the memory of everything he'd discovered in the dungeons below their feet, every nasty, depraved, disgusting thing Wilfred Waite had done to the living and to the dead.

Wilfred nodded at the leather bag on the floor at Arika's feet. "I believe that belongs to me," he said.

Kane pointed at his brother's chest. "And that belongs to my brother. Wanna swap?"

Wilfred chuckled. "I like you, boy. Shame I didn't take *your* body."

"You're not taking anyone's body."

Stepping off the trapdoor, Kane knelt by the bag and pulled out the Necronomicon. He slammed it down on the dirt floor and opened it to the page featuring the seven-pointed star with the piercing eye in its centre.

"Dylan," he ordered, snapping his fingers. "Here."

Dylan fell to his knees.

"See that picture?" said Kane, jabbing at it with his finger. "Put your hand on the page and stare at the eyeball and think of being back in your own body."

Wilfred started down the steps. "Give that to me!" he demanded, wielding the sceptre like a club.

Leaping to his feet, Kane approached him with fists raised. "Just because you have Dylan's body, doesn't mean I won't kick your bony arse across the room."

Arika went to help Dylan, who was kneeling over the book. "What else does he need to do?"

"I … d-don't understand," stuttered Dylan, who was looking every one of his two hundred years.

"The book is the secret to undoing the spell," explained Kane without turning around. "Focus your attention on the page, and the book will do the rest." He remembered Gilles' words and said them to Wilfred: "Steal easy; keep hard."

That was enough for Arika. "Here," she said, taking Dylan's thick brown hand and placing it on the page. "Wish your body back."

Dylan frowned down at the book, concentrating hard, his body trembling with the effort.

Wilfred's legs faltered. After a few moments of trying to maintain his balance, he dropped the sceptre and sat hard on the step. Grabbing handfuls of hair, he screamed, "Get out! This body is mine! You're not taking it!"

"You're losing," Kane taunted, hoping to distract him and aid in breaking his hold on Dylan's body. "You're going back into your stinking carcass where you belong, and you will die a pathetic loser."

"Ia! Ia!" cried Wilfred – but if that was the start of a spell, it ended in a gasp of horror.

With a groan, Dylan fell face down on the Necronomicon.

Kane swung around and rushed to help him.

"Dylan," he cried, pulling him off the book, hugging his frail body against his chest.

Behind him, his brother said, "Kane …"

Kane peered over his shoulder. Dylan was sitting on the step, staring at him with scared eyes. His face looked like he was seventeen again. "I can see you," he said.

Kane glanced down at the old man in his arms, cried, "Gah!" and pushed him away.

Wiping his hands on his shirt, he snatched up the Necronomicon, threw the leather bag over his shoulder, and went to join his brother.

"You okay?"

Dylan, nodding, took hold of his arm and pulled himself to his feet.

"Where were you born?"

His brother frowned at him. "Salters Point."

Kane hugged him hard with his free arm, then dug his hand in his hair and pressed their foreheads together. "Welcome back, youngster. It's great to see you."

Turning to Arika, he said, "We got what we came for. Let's go."

Arika didn't respond. She was standing over Wilfred with arms crossed, and had that look in her eye, the one she got when she was hellbent on getting her own way. It was a look Kane had seen a lot in their short acquaintance.

"Not till he answers my question."

Kane pulled a face at Dylan. What's she going on about? the look said. What could possibly be worth staying in this madhouse one minute longer than was absolutely necessary? Then he remembered that an eon ago, they'd uncovered Wilfred's potential involvement in her father's disappearance.

"Arika!" he barked. "We can do that later. We need to go."

"Where is he?" she demanded.

Wilfred smirked up at Kane. "You dust mites have no idea who you're dealing with."

"Arika! … Arika!"

Kane stared daggers at her, but she refused to take her eyes off Wilfred. He, in turn, acted as if she didn't exist.

"Come on, Dylan," Kane said, turning away. "Let's go. She won't stay here by herself."

Placing a hand on his brother's back, he shepherded him up the steps.

"That meat sack is mine."

Kane felt a hot burst of anger. He swung around. "Say that again and you're dead."

"Kane," urged Dylan, grabbing his arm, "forget it. He's trying to get a rise."

"Where is he?" Arika asked again, kicking Wilfred's leg.

Wilfred turned his gaze to Dylan. "Don't fight me, boy. You're a scared little insect flapping its wings at a near god."

"I said shut up."

"There's no sense resisting. I always win. The immortals are destined to inherit the Earth and all that walk and slither and crawl across its face. What hope do you clots have against the likes of me?"

"I'll stop you," said Kane.

Wilfred closed his eyes. "How many times have I heard that from a mealybug with pretensions of grandeur?"

"Kane!" cried Arika.

Kane stared at her. Her eyes were fixed on something at the top of the steps.

He spun around. A huge white hand with dirty brown fingernails was grasping the edge of the wall.

Behind him, Wilfred said, "I have an army of the dead at my disposal, and you have … a schoolgirl and a child barely out of nappies."

He crawled out from Arika's shadow, got to his feet and hobbled to the steps. "Hugo," he called, "you may enter."

The hand flexed and a bald head entered the room, followed by a shoulder, a leg, and then the rest of Hugo.

Kane grabbed Dylan and pulled him down the stairs.

Hugo was a tall, heavyset, hairless man, quite obviously dead, wearing the same grey pants they'd seen in the underground cells. His eyes were milky, his barrel chest chalky and bare. His ribs and arms were pinned with metal bands and studs; his face too: a band extended from his lower jaw to his cheek and up to his bald head, where it was affixed by a large bolt. He was no longer a human being, dead or alive. Wilfred had turned him into a weapon, a mindless thing that would obey his every command.

Standing ape-like at the top of the steps, he regarded the room with dead white eyes.

"Hugo," said Wilfred, "please get me my book."

When Hugo's face fixed on them, Kane pulled Dylan towards Arika and dropped the bag at his feet. Standing in front of them, he pressed the Necronomicon against his chest and watched as the hulk lumbered down the steps and stumbled towards them. He felt like a small boy about to pee his pants. And like a child, part of him hoped the book's energy would spiral out and protect him, like the Genie in Aladdin's lamp. He clutched the Necronomicon tighter and thought he sensed vibration and a growing heat from it, but as Hugo neared and the book grew heavy in his arms, he realised it wasn't about to offer any protection.

"Brave boy," Wilfred chuckled at him. "Most cockroaches will skedaddle when faced with such danger. The ones that stand in defiance get squashed, unfortunately for them."

Throwing open his arms, the hulk lunged at Kane and took him in a bear hug. Kane lost his grip on the Necronomicon and it slipped between them and dropped to the floor.

Arika ducked in, pulled it from between their legs and stepped away.

Wilfred turned to her. "If you value your friend's life, young lady, you will give me my book."

"Don't!" yelled Kane as he struggled to free himself from the hulk's embrace.

"Hugo was a championship boxer," Wilfred explained, "before his untimely death. When I resurrected him, I took the liberty of making him stronger. At my command, he will snap the boy's back like a twig."

Dylan, springing into action, grabbed a wooden dining chair, raised it in the air, and swung it down with as much force as his skinny arms would allow. It collided with the hulk's back, bounced off, and fell with a clatter to the floor.

"I can make Hugo stop," continued Wilfred, retrieving the sceptre. "With a word I can spare the boy's life, and then you two lovebirds can run off and live happily ever after, somewhere far away from here. And play house and make babies together to your little hearts' content. Or you can choose to defy me, and die down here like rats. The choice is yours. The book is mine regardless."

Diving into the black leather bag, Dylan retrieved the cattle prod, raced back to Hugo and stabbed him in the side. Grunting in pain, the hulk pushed Kane to the floor and turned on Dylan.

"Hugo!" cried Wilfred, waving the sceptre at him. "Stop playing games with those boys and bring me my book!"

Like an automaton, the hulk swerved away from Dylan and advanced on Arika.

Springing to his feet, Kane ran at Hugo and hurled himself at his back, propelling him to the ground. Without really exerting himself, the dead boxer rolled over, and suddenly Kane found himself underneath what felt like a ton of flesh. A gargantuan hand clamped around his throat.

"Now," continued Wilfred, "one more time, missy: give me my book, or I will order Hugo to squeeze until the boy's eyes pop from their sockets."

Dylan, staring at Wilfred, poked Arika's arm. "The sceptre," he hissed, close to her ear. "It's not a weapon. I think he's using it to control the thing."

Arika's eyes flew to the brass staff, and a smile flitted across her face. Without a word, she raised the Necronomicon and stepped towards Wilfred, presenting the book like an offering.

"The slattern shows sense at last. Leave it at my feet and back away to the stairs. Both of you."

As Wilfred watched smugly, Arika approached him and placed the book on the floor. Once her hands were free, she grabbed the sceptre, tore it from his grasp, and kicked the Necronomicon towards Dylan.

"Smash it!" yelled Dylan. "Smash it!"

But once again, Arika was staring angrily at Wilfred. "Tell me what happened to my father."

"Give me that!" he demanded, swiping unsuccessfully at the sceptre.

"Smash it!"

When Dylan realised Arika's agenda didn't include saving his brother, he abandoned her, ran back to Hugo and stabbed him hard in the back with the cattle prod. This time, Hugo swiped at it like he'd been stung by a mosquito. His huge hand remained clamped on Kane's throat, immune to Kane's efforts to pull it away.

"Answer my damn question!"

"Smash it!" yelled Dylan as he jabbed Hugo in the face over and over again with the cattle prod. "Arika! What are you doing?"

Wilfred sneered at her. "Destroy the sceptre and I guarantee the outcome will not be a pleasant one. The walls of this residence will come tumbling down on all of us. You would not want that to happen."

Arika glanced worriedly at Kane, who was tugging at Hugo's wrist, struggling to draw breath. Dylan had wrapped his arm around the hulk's throat, and was pulling back with all his might.

"If that's true, you may as well tell me what happened to my father. If I'm about to die anyway, what's the point in playing games?"

"Playing games is my specialty," returned Wilfred.

"Was he here?"

"Was who here, dear?"

"My father. Corbin Livingston. Was he here?"

"Perhaps if you would kindly return my sceptre, I may have an answer for you."

Her face ablaze with frustration and rage, Arika glanced again at Kane, glared at Wilfred, then with a groan, swung the sceptre and smashed it hard against the step. Something inside it broke, and purple liquid bubbled out and dripped onto the floor.

"You stupid bint!" yelled Wilfred, backing away.

Stamping on the ball until it was flat, Arika stepped away and watched as the purple bubbles popped, turned clear, and faded away.

"Do you realise what you've done?"

Hugo did. Whining like a puppy, he released his hold on Kane's neck, brushed off Dylan, and hauled himself to his feet. For a few seconds he stood with shoulders slumped and arms hanging, peering around the room, as if he'd awoken from a nightmare and forgotten where he was. Then he turned his head to Wilfred and opened his mouth in recognition. Raising his arms, making guttural noises that seemed to vibrate from his barrel chest, he staggered towards him.

Arika retrieved the Necronomicon and rushed to Kane's side.

"Thanks … I think," he said from the corner of his mouth.

She didn't look at him or say anything. She seemed guilty and angry at the same time.

Behind them, Hugo cornered Wilfred, placed his hands around his scrawny throat and lifted him off the floor. While Wilfred gurgled, flapped his arms and kicked his legs, Hugo stared into his face and grunted incomprehensibly, like he was trying to tell him something.

"Hey!" yelled Kane.

When Hugo ignored him, he leapt up, ran at him, jumped on his back and hooked his arm in a stranglehold around his neck. He squeezed with all his strength, jerking his arm back to force a reaction, but Hugo's only interest was in watching Wilfred as the final breaths gurgled from his throat.

Releasing his hold, Kane slid off the hulk's back and scanned the room for a weapon. The first thing he spotted was the axe handle poking from the bag, and he realised with a sinking feeling that if wanted to save Wilfred's life, he had no other choice.

Racing to the bag, he pulled out the axe, took a deep breath, returned to Hugo, raised the axe above his head, and brought it down, burying the blade deep in the dead man's back.

Hugo jerked his head around in surprise. Tossing Wilfred aside, he arched his back and tried to reach the axe with both hands. When this proved impossible, he flew into a rage, spinning in a circle, smashing furniture and raising clouds of dust.

"Out!" yelled Kane, grabbing the bag, pushing the others before him.

They ran up the steps. At the door to the basement, Kane stopped and turned for one last look at the destruction below.

Though Hugo had managed to dislodge the axe from his back, he was still spinning around, trying to grab at the wound in his back, destroying everything he fell against.

Wilfred was lying where Hugo had thrown him, his black-rimmed eyes open wide, staring lifelessly at the ceiling. As Kane watched in horror, the ancient body began turning a nauseous shade of green.

32

Call Simon

"DO YOU THINK it's dead?"

Arika and Dylan were leaning against the grill of Kane's truck, arms folded against the cold, debating what to do next. Their attention was fixed on the farmhouse, on the front door, which they'd left open in their haste to escape. The evening was dark, the house even darker, but they knew if Hugo came stumbling out, they'd know it from his pasty white skin.

"Course it's dead," Dylan replied. "It's a zombie."

Arika didn't seem to get the joke. "I can't see an axe in the back doing much to something already dead."

She looked at Kane, who was pacing in the mud, unable to stand still. He was worried the sceptre controlled more than just Hugo, which meant all hell might break loose now the thing was destroyed. He reached the gate, turned, and started walking back to them. The wrench was in his hand, swinging by his side. When he neared the truck, he turned and walked back to the gate.

"If it's still running around, we can't just leave it there," she said, staring at the wrench in Kane's hand. "What if it escapes and hurts someone?" She rubbed her arms. "I think we should go back and barricade the basement, pile up furniture against the door. That might buy us some time, if it's still alive … or animated … reanimated … whatever." She looked at him. "The powder of Vraith … do you think it could work on zombies?"

Dylan shrugged. "Like an all-purpose poison? – or acid?" He shook his head. "I doubt it. The Messenger came from another dimension. The powder didn't kill it; just sent it back."

"Do you know where he kept it? … the powder? In the lab?"

Dylan grunted a laugh. "If you wanna go back down there, be my guest. That thing is a monster, and I think we pissed it off."

"Was it in the lab?"

"Dunno. He only gave me one flask. I don't know if he had more."

"What did it look like?"

"Red. Powder. In a glass flask."

She screwed up her nose. "I don't remember seeing any red powder down there. Brick-red or fire-engine-red?" When Dylan didn't answer, she went back to staring at Kane. "I thought breaking the sceptre would kill it."

"No, just controlled it."

She glanced at him in annoyance for stating the bleeding obvious. "He super-charged that thing; all that rigging. I'm sure it wasn't just for cosmetic appeal. I wonder how many more of those things he's built." She nodded to herself. "Simon will know what to do."

"Bullet in the head usually works with zombies. Not sure your pea-shooter will do the trick, though," he added. "Not for something that size. We need a real gun, one that'll blow its big fat head off." He yelled at Kane, "Hey Kane, can you get a real gun? – one with exploding bullets? We need to shoot ourselves some zombies!"

Kane turned to him. "Is that something you learnt from that bastard Waite?" he shot back.

Dylan cringed. "Movies," he piped.

Kane went back to them, swinging the wrench like a baton. His pain and worry had manifested as anger, and he was trying hard to control it so he could stay focused on what to do about the mess they'd left in and under the farmhouse. He reminded himself his brother's ordeal had hardened him – toughened him up – which wasn't a bad thing. Better a Dylan making crude comments about zombies than one depressed and susceptible to nutjobs like Wilfred Waite.

"I can't get a real gun," he said, his voice steady. "And even if I could, I don't know if I could blast a guy's head off." He waved the wrench in the air. "Even if he *is* already dead."

"I don't think the axe in the back stopped it."

He winced. "It was the only thing I could think of."

"I'd lay bets it's still walking around," said Arika.

"Yeah," agreed Dylan. "You have to destroy a zombie's brain to stop it."

"In the movies, at least."

"Hey, if we can find another axe, we could chop its legs off. That'll slow it down."

"May as well chop its head off and be done with it," Arika said.

"Oh yeah." He glanced at Kane. "I'm thinking we'd need a chainsaw for that – that thing had a neck like a tree trunk. Hey Kane, what should we do? We can't hang around here all night. I'm freezing my arse off."

When Kane didn't reply, he asked, "Do you think Wilfred is still alive?"

"No."

"I saw that thing throw him against a wall. He might be hurt."

"He's not hurt. He's dead."

"But –"

"He was rotting. Like an apple."

At the memory of Wilfred's skin turning a fungal green, Kane tasted vomit in his mouth. No matter what awful things the man had done – and threatened to do – it was traumatising to see a person die and rot in front of his eyes.

"The centuries caught up with him, and good riddance, I say. Now shut up and let me think."

"What will the police make of all this? Do you think they'll believe us? We might need evidence – like pictures. We should have taken pictures."

Kane glared at his brother. Why was it the one time he wanted him to stay quiet was the time he refused to shut up?

"A supernatural problem needs a supernatural solution," said Arika. "Should I call Simon?"

Dylan reached for the Necronomicon and opened it on the truck bonnet. He began turning over pages. "Maybe there's a zombie annihilation spell to fix this. Like the star-eye thing that makes all the dead things drop dead."

"Shut that damn book!" yelled Kane.

Dylan stared at him.

"No more magic. Now shut the book before it starts … sending out mystical energy and … turning us all into toads."

"You need magic to fight magic," Dylan muttered.

"Close it. Now."

"Okay, okay."

"Kane," said Arika, "we can't risk those things getting loose. We should call Simon. He'll know what to do."

"There might be more of those slug things around," added Dylan. "We need to warn the police before they go in."

"Don't forget that freaky housekeeper thing," said Arika. "She was like the Terminator. With a bad wig and knives."

Kane fixed his eyes on the farmhouse. They didn't know the half of it. He hadn't told them yet about the army of the dead, and what happened to him in the pitch black of the dungeon. His pulse quickened at the thought of his legs dangling like worms on a hook after that psycho Gilles pushed him into the pit.

"Do you think the skinny old guy is okay?" asked Dylan.

"Probably safer in the study than in his little cottage of hell," said Arika.

Sebastian. He survived being held captive for forty long years, tortured and starved, and then along comes Kane and feeds him to a giant slug. Unless the door held.

"Call Simon," he said to Arika.

"Are you sure?"

He wasn't. But he wasn't keen on calling the police either. They would be totally unprepared for what was waiting for them, no matter how much he described the horrors he'd seen. And with his brother's involvement in Wilfred Waite's affairs, there was no telling how much of the blame might attach itself to him once all the evidence was put on the table. It wasn't worth taking the risk. Not when they had an alternative.

"Call Simon."

They all stared at the farmhouse. The evening was still and cold, a light mist resting on the damp ground. The farmhouse door stood open like it was inviting someone or something to enter.

Suddenly a dog howled, making them jump. Probably one of the dogs shaking off the effects of the tranquilliser dart.

"Who's Simon?" asked Dylan.

33

Hugo

T HE MAN WAS lying face down in the mud, naked from the waist up, a
yellowish-pink opening in the back of his head.

Police Chief Ames knelt beside him and shone his torch on the deep
gash in his back. The flesh was grey; there was almost no blood. And
what was the deal with all the metal? It looked like he was rigged up after
a terrible accident and they forgot to take the belts and screws out.

"Somebody really went to town on this joker," he muttered to himself.

"Hey, Chief, move your worthless carcass out of the road," said
Officer Len Pederson, a thin, silver-haired man with skin like crispy
chicken. "I'm tryin' to get some clean ones."

Pushing himself to his feet, Ames rejoined Sam Morgan, who was
just getting off the phone.

"What do you think?"

Morgan shook his head. "Not your run-of-the-mill prowler, I'll give
you that."

"Shirtless? In this weather? He must have been some tough-skinned
mother."

Morgan nodded to himself. This one was nothing like the monsters
they found in the Six Hills. If you ignored the metal banding, it looked
almost human. A strange, chalky consistency to its skin, yes – not to
mention the curious lack of blood – but all the limbs and muscles
seemed to be of the right size and proportion.

"Is he one of them chaps you're looking for?"

Morgan glanced sideways at him. "I'm pretty sure, yeah. We'll take
him back to base, check him against the files."

"Hey, Len," Ames called out, scratching his beer belly, "when you're
finished with the pictures and shit, turn him over so's we can take a
good look at him."

"Oh yeah," muttered Pederson, "let the old guy break his back the month before his retirement."

He struggled to turn the body over. "Sheesh!" he cried. "This fella weighs a bloody ton."

Morgan went to help.

"On three," said Pederson as they took hold of the dead man's shoulder and hip. "One, two … three!"

They heaved together, and the huge body rose and fell on its back. Pederson gasped. The cause of death was now clear: a bullet had entered the man's left eye and exploded in the back of his skull.

"What's with all the metalwork?" asked Ames, coming in for another look. He leaned closer and screwed up his nose. "Some type of body art? Looks like it's bolted into the bone. Not seen nothin' like that before. Maybe it's next gen S&M."

Pederson said nothing, which was unlike him. The chief glanced up and saw the blood had drained from his face.

"What's up, Lennard?" he asked. "Looks like you're about to puke your guts out. Don't go messing up my crime scene again."

"Lordy heaven," breathed Pederson. "It can't be."

Morgan, who was inspecting the bolt in the thing's head, looked up. "You know this man?"

Pederson was staring wide-eyed at the thing.

Ames answered for him. "No one from around here," he said. "At least no one with a record."

Morgan got to his feet. "Len?"

Pederson blinked a few times. "It can't be … But it looks just like him."

"Who?" asked the chief.

Pederson shook his head.

"Who?"

He opened his mouth, but no words came out.

"Come on, Len," prompted Morgan. "Just say it."

"It's Hugo Petrusch," Pederson blurted out at last. "Hugo 'The Block' Petrusch. I swear it's him. But … it's not possible. He was a local thug. He …"

The police chief raised his hands in exasperation. "Come on, Len, spit it out."

"… died in a fight. In the lockup. Almost … fifteen years ago."

34

Simon to the rescue

AT GEORGE UNIVERSITY life floated on, oblivious to anything outside the institution's hallowed walls. The sun was out and the campus was busy, with groups of students sitting on the grassy slopes or wandering along the paths. Some were engaged in lively conversation or debate, but many were silent, engrossed in their laptop, tablet or phone. No one seemed to be in a hurry or have much of a purpose – unless being a student counted as a purpose. As Kane watched them, he felt invisible, like an earthling come to study a strange and pointless alternate reality.

"Here he is," announced Arika, brightening.

Kane turned. Coming down the steps was an elderly man, very tall and stooped, with a long, thin nose and short white beard. His black suit, rumpled and dusty, just as Kane had imagined it would be, was a size too small for him. His hairy wrists poked from the sleeves; green plaid socks peeked from the cuffs of his trousers. He was wearing a cream silk scarf, looped around his neck and tucked into his coat.

"Professor Orwell," said Arika, herding Kane towards him, "this is Kane Gates."

The professor approached them with a smile and arms outstretched in welcome.

"Pleased to meet you, son," he said, fixing him with a steely blue gaze. His eyelashes were white, as were the hairs sticking out of his nose and growing crookedly from his ears. "Arika told me about your ordeal. Abominable. Fascinating. Unlike anything I've heard in all my long years of study. I was hoping you might give me a first-hand description of everything you saw."

"Fascinating is hardly a word I would use, Professor."

"You would be amazed by the things that fascinate me."

He was staring at Kane like Kane was one of those things.

"Did you find out anything about the … assailant?"

"Indeed, I did." The professor smiled down at Arika, who looked like a schoolgirl beside him. "I just got off the phone to my friend in the sheriff's office."

Kane's heart skipped a beat. "It didn't hurt anyone, did it?"

"No, Mr Gates. Nothing to worry about on that account. You will be pleased to hear it has been put down."

Kane felt a vague distaste at the professor's choice of words. "What do you mean 'put down'?"

The professor nodded. "Apologies. A rather blunt way of describing it. The creature was, in fact, shot in the face."

Kane's eyes opened wide. "What? How did that happen?"

"Apparently it was peeping through a kitchen window and the homeowner shot it. In the face, as I just said."

"My God," breathed Arika, turning to Kane. "Is everyone in Quorn that trigger happy? Straight for the head. Lucky it wasn't just a regular peeping tom."

He opened his mouth to remind her that she and Dylan had discussed doing exactly that to the zombie, but thought better of it.

"Interestingly," continued the professor, "it ran down the road for some distance with a hole in its head, before expiring in the mud a few minutes later."

"That'd be right," Arika said. "Waite made out it was invincible, yet in the end, all it takes is a bullet in the brain."

"So, nothing else happened?"

"No, son. All good on that account."

"Did they say anything about … like, it's modifications? How it didn't look human?"

"I felt it best not to ask. All I said was my research assistant had been in Quorn doing some work for me, and I'd heard there was a madman on the rampage. They assumed I read it on Facebook."

"Well, I think we did well to contain it," said Arika. "Kane probably weakened it during the fight."

"Yeah, it must have taken a lot out of it to strangle me like that."

Arika didn't seem to pick up on his sarcasm.

The professor waggled a finger at her. "You're lucky it didn't bite you, Arika. Or you, Mr Gates. The magic that raised it is almost certainly contagious."

"How's that?" asked Kane.

The professor peered down at him. "In the case of the reanimation spell," he said, adopting the lecturing tone he no doubt used with his students, "the magic injects the cells with a form of mystical energy, which spreads like a virus through the body. Once the brain is affected, it controls the energy throughout the rest of the entity. And then, when affected cells enter another body, they spread in much the same way, replacing life as we know it with this … I suppose you'd call it 'interdimensional energy'."

"And it's irreversible?" asked Arika.

"Dead is dead," said the professor.

"But a shot to the head still kills it," Kane pointed out. "Dylan was right: it's just like in the movies."

"Popular culture usually has its roots in some kind of truth," commented the professor.

"Well it's dead now, so that takes care of the immediate problem. What do we do about everything else at the farmhouse?"

The professor stroked his beard. "I've been thinking long and hard about that, and I know just the people to bring in. Best to place this kind of mess in the hands of the experts. They'll sort through the details, clean out the farm and everything beneath it, and take care of whomever is responsible."

Kane felt a blanket of dread fall on him. He'd known all along it would be necessary to call in the police at some point, but a part of him had hoped the professor could simply wave a magic wand and make everything bad disappear.

"Professor," he said, "I need to make sure my brother isn't implicated in this. He isn't responsible for anything – apart from being young and stupid – but he was around when some of the weird stuff happened. If you go to the police, is there any way you can leave us out of it?"

"Oh, it's not the police, son. It's specialists in this kind of thing."

"There's specialists in this kind of thing?"

"Oh yes. There have been wizards and the like down through the ages."

"And witches," added Arika.

"Witches?"

"Yes, witches too."

Kane shook his head. Since his discussion with Arika in the coffee shop, he hadn't given a thought to whether this kind of thing had happened before – but it made sense that Wilfred couldn't be the only sorcerer who ever succeeded in creating a zombie or raising a Messenger. There must be wizards and witches casting spells all over the place. He glanced around at the students going about their business, worried about their student loans, assignment deadlines and test results, and in that moment longed to join them in the land of the normal and boring, where he wouldn't have to worry about mystical forces coming after him and Dylan to finish what Wilfred Waite had started.

"So you'll leave us out of it?"

"Of course. You have my solemn word. I will say the university received an anonymous tip. We don't need them scratching about for innocent scapegoats when the real perpetrators of this evil are still out there, do we?"

"They are; you can be sure of it," asserted Kane, thinking about Kenny Snyder and Gilles and the damage they might yet cause if left unchecked. "Now, Sebastian: he's not in a good way. Somebody needs to get him out first."

"My thoughts exactly. I will make sure he is the absolute priority."

"I've drawn up a map. He's in the study."

"Excellent. That will come in useful."

"Or he might be in the cottage in the main chamber. Snyder or Gilles might have found him in the study and taken him back."

"I will direct the unit to both places."

"If he's not there, he might be in Gilles' room. They treat him like some kind of pet."

"I will make sure they look everywhere."

"Thank you, Simon," said Arika.

"Yes, Professor," added Kane, feeling the tension melting from his shoulders. The professor seemed to know what he was doing, and importantly, knew the right people to talk to. He was relieved to hear there were experts in this kind of thing: people who'd dealt with wizards, zombies and monsters before. It meant they likely wouldn't need his, or Dylan's, further involvement. "Will you let us know how it goes?"

"Of course, son. Now, shall we go inside? I'd like to hear a complete description of your grand adventure, so I can start preparing my brief."

"I'll fill you in on everything Waite told me when he returned," said Arika. "There were a few hairy moments there for a while."

Her words brought back to Kane the memory of how she'd stopped to interrogate Wilfred while the zombie hulk was strangling him at her feet. Arika was preoccupied with finding her missing father, obsessed almost, and he wondered whether there was more to his disappearance than she was saying.

He also reminded himself that she saved his face from being bitten off by a rabid dog and a homicidal housekeeper, and now she was handing him a solution to the mess they left at the farm. So, on balance, he figured she was more a force for good than for evil.

It suited him to think that way. As he followed Arika and the professor up the steps, he stared at her lustrous brown hair and inhaled the fresh scent of her dress. Although he'd known her for only a day, she was already like an old friend; he felt closer to her than he'd ever been to January. He'd never met anyone like her, someone so strong and smart, and he was determined to find an excuse to see her again after the Dark farm was contained. Perhaps he and Dylan should move close to George University – that was as good a reason for choosing a new home as any, wasn't it? And it wouldn't be considered stalking, would it?

Smiling to himself, he wondered how hard she would hit him if he dared to reach out and touch her.

35

Going in

T HE BLACK-OVER-SILVER BENTLEY chugged into the yard and pulled up outside the farmhouse gate. The engine died, a shadow moved inside, the door swung open, and out climbed Simon Orwell. After taking a quick look around, he stepped to the rear passenger door, opened it, reached inside and took out a brown leather satchel.

That's when he heard the sound of running feet. It was two huge, ugly Rottweilers, just as the Gates boy had warned him. On catching sight of Simon, they barked out a warning before slamming headlong into the gate, almost knocking it off its hinges.

"Nice doggies," he cooed, approaching the gate. "Aren't you protective?"

The dogs sprang and growled and barked, their red eyes locked on him in murderous rage.

Reaching into the satchel, Simon pulled out a handful of bluish-grey powder. "Somnus quies Koth," he quoted, and threw the powder over them.

The dogs dropped to the ground.

"Pleasant dreams, fellows," he said, then returned to the car for his bolt cutters.

"WHAT DID HE say?" asked Kane, once he was safely out of earshot.

He'd left the gang in the rec room, playing cards. They were ribbing him about January Bell, and Arika's call had come as a welcome interruption. Since January's surprise visit to the station on Monday, she'd been a hot topic of conversation amongst the guys. The basket of fruit on her arm; her platinum-blonde hair; the sunshine-yellow figure-hugging dress; the way she flirted with all and sundry while raving about Kane's finer qualities: they were all rich fodder for gossip and jokes.

A wind sprang up and shook the trees, dislodging leaves and dropping them on Kane's head. High above, a strong wind was driving the clouds at speed across the sky. They were rain clouds, and would soon dump their watery load on the town.

"They found Sebastian safe," came Arika's voice on the other end of the line. "Waite was dead, as you know."

Turning the corner, Kane headed for his truck. "Was he in the study?"

"Where we left him."

"Where did they take them?"

"I don't know. It's all top secret. I assume to hospital."

"But Sebastian is alright?"

"Simon said he was definitely alive."

"That's a relief. What about Gilles and the other monsters down there?"

"They didn't get that far."

He stopped. "What do you mean?"

The phone went quiet.

"Arika?"

"They only did a search and rescue to the study and back."

"Why the hell would they just do that?"

"They –"

"There's other dangerous things down there. Wasn't I clear enough about that? What else did he say?"

"After they got Sebastian out, they secured the well. They haven't gone any further yet. There's too many unknowns. They're bringing in experts from New England before they go down again."

"New England? Where the hell is that?"

He imagined Arika smiling at his ignorance. The thought irritated him. Didn't she know Wilfred's acolytes still posed a threat to his brother? She sounded too relaxed and unconcerned.

"All they need is assault rifles and hand grenades." He started off again. "I'm heading out there."

"Kane … no. What will you do when you get there?"

"Just look around, see if I can find out what's happening."

"That's a bad idea. The farm is under surveillance."

He stopped and placed a hand on his truck. "What do you mean?"

"They're watching to see who turns up. They're out to catch them all, not go in half-cocked and scare the worst of the worst away. If they catch you, they might think you're –"

"They should be tearing up the floor, killing all those – dead things. Didn't you tell him that?"

"Simon knows –"

"He's an old schoolteacher; what would he know about military operations?"

"He doesn't. He was only telling me what the NSO told him."

"What's this NSO? Are they army?"

"I don't know. I didn't ask."

"Why? Aren't you interested?"

"Of course I'm interested … in what's at the farm, not the structure of our armed forces."

"Well, I am."

"Well, go and ask Simon yourself, then. Don't expect me to be … some kind of … brainiac about everything. I'm just relaying what Simon told me."

Pulling the phone from his ear, Kane took a series of short, sharp breaths. Arika was right: his frustration was getting the better of him, making him demanding and unreasonable.

"I'm sorry," he said into the phone. "You're right. I'm just –"

"Simon said their priority is to catch the people Waite was working with. That's the end game. They don't want those crazies going underground."

"Underground," smirked Kane. "Very funny."

"You know what I mean."

"They don't care if Gilles starves or something? He's a homicidal maniac, but he's still a human being. At least, I think he is."

"I'm sure they factored that into their plan. It's not our business anymore."

Kane felt the plash of water on his head. He peered up at the clouds, which looked to him like dark ghosts stealing across the roof of the sky.

This was the side of Arika he didn't like: the self-involvement that drove her to disregard anyone who got in her way, or people she no longer had any use for.

"Is that what you really think?" he asked at last.

His heart was thumping as he waited for her reply. He wanted Arika to say she cared about the fate of the stranger who was kept underground for so long he went insane; that whatever happened from here on in might have serious ramifications for his brother; that they uncovered all this, so it *was* their business.

But all she said was, "You don't want them connecting you with the stuff they find there, Kane."

He ran his hand over his hair. "I've got nothing to hide."

"No … but Dylan does. Let's wait a couple more days and see what goes down. I'll let you know when I hear more from Simon."

She hung up quickly, and Kane wasn't sure, after the conversation they just had, whether that was a good or a bad thing.

36

Simon wants the book

DYLAN WAS AWOKEN by voices. He turned his head to the curtain and saw it was still light outside, though he guessed from the texture of the light that the day must be winding down.

Rubbing his eyes, he tried to clear the fog from his mind. Since the long spell in Wilfred Waite's body, all he wanted to do was sleep. Thankfully the nightmares had stopped, and he had nothing much to do until Wilfred's death was confirmed and they could start the ball rolling with the will, so he was spending most of his time lazing in bed.

When the voices rose, he pushed himself off the bed and shuffled to the top of the stairs.

"… said they have to tread carefully," said an unfamiliar voice. It was a man's voice, cultured and slightly gruff.

"Was that it?" Kane asked.

"It's unlikely we'll hear more. National security being what it is."

"Jesus. I don't know about this. They need to put an end to it. Now."

"They do know what they're doing, young man."

"I know … I just can't help thinking they should be doing more."

"That's only natural, given the circumstances. You're worried about your brother; I can understand that. But please, trust the process. No nasties are coming after you; that's one thing I can guarantee."

There was a pause. "How can you guarantee that if they don't know about Dylan and me? You haven't told them about us, have you?"

"No, no. Don't worry on that account. I simply meant the NSO have the suspects under surveillance. They would let me know if they were up to anything suspicious."

"Suspects? Who are they? I only know about Snyder and Gilles. Unless they mean Waite's henchmen."

"They haven't gone into any detail, naturally. But they assured me they are following up all leads, including those they garnered from the search of the farmhouse and study."

"I suppose that's a start."

Intrigued by the conversation, Dylan went downstairs. Entering the kitchen, he found Kane sitting at the table with an elderly man, dressed like a wedding guest in a black suit, off-white shirt and red-striped bow tie. The man was drinking from a sky-blue teacup embossed with gold: his mother's favourite china. His brother was fingering the handle of a similar cup, this one full of milky tea.

Kane noticed him first. "Hey, bro," he piped. "Did we wake you? Sorry about that."

He frowned at the old man. "Who's that?"

Kane got to his feet. "Dylan, this is Simon – Professor Orwell. He's come to pick up the book."

The professor pushed out his chair and stood too. He was tall and angular, with hair and beard as white as snow. His heavy-lidded eyes were too blue for a man of his age.

"Pleasure to meet you, son. I've been updating your brother on events at the farm. An eye-popping situation, to say the least. I doubt in all my years I've come across anything so incredible."

Dylan looked at him. "Why do you want the Necronomicon?"

"NSO wants it," answered Kane. "National Security Office."

"So why aren't they here asking for it?"

"I haven't told them about you boys," said Simon. "At your brothers' request. But they do need the Necronomicon to purge the farm of its terrors."

"The NSO has people trained to take care of it," said Kane.

"The book is dangerous," added Simon. "It needs to be kept under lock and key."

"Which is what we've done."

The professor sputtered a laugh. "Son, that book can destroy lives. It's a ticking time bomb. The government can't be confident with a boy hiding it under his bed."

Dylan ignored the jibe.

"It needs to be in protective custody."

Dylan yawned, stretching his arms out to the side.

Simon glared at him. "Are you listening to me? The book is dangerous."

"I get that."

"I'm not convinced you do. You've no idea what you've gotten yourself involved in. We're not playing games here, young man."

Stepping past them to the fridge, Dylan pulled open the door, glanced around inside, took out a carton of iced coffee. "I've been living inside an old man's body," he said as he opened the carton; "casting spells; fighting a Messenger from another dimension. Don't tell me what I don't know."

Simon bowed his head. "My apologies, Dylan. That came out all wrong. I only meant there is an historical context that few people would understand, or can even imagine. The Necronomicon holds the key to dark magics that could end the world as we know it. That's the stakes we're dealing with."

Dylan leaned his back against the kitchen counter. The man was pompous and hadn't told him anything he didn't already know.

"The book is dangerous. I get it."

"Then you can release it to me, and I will assure its security."

He drank from the carton. The milk was ice cold, and he grimaced as he felt a brain freeze coming on. Bunching up his face until the feeling subsided, he grunted, "How will you do that?"

"What do you mean?"

"You heard me."

"I'm afraid I don't –"

"How can we be sure someone else won't get corrupted by it?"

"That, Mr Gates, is none of your concern."

"It is, as long as I've got the book."

"It's none of your concern full stop. The NSO and I have a wealth of experience and resources at our disposal, and we are well aware of how to handle artefacts of this nature."

"Artefacts? It's not an artefact. You don't know the half of it."

"I know everything about the Necronomicon."

"I doubt that."

"I've studied it for decades. You've had it for five minutes, and you have the nerve to lecture me on its power. Do you know how offensive that is?"

"I'm asking a simple question. How can you guarantee you – or anybody else – won't get corrupted by it?"

"I repeat: I've studied the Necronomicon for decades –"

"Then why are you here? If you already have a copy, what do you need ours for?"

Simon's face went red. "The book is dangerous. If you were hiding a nuclear bomb, I would be here for the same reason."

"No, the NSO would be here. Sounds to me like you're here to get your hands on what's *in* the Necronomicon, not bury it. If you've studied it for so many decades, I don't see why you need my copy." Feeling he was gaining the upper hand, he added, "Unless you don't have your own. Have you ever seen the Necronomicon? Outside of pictures in a text book?"

Simon approached him. "The book does not belong to you. I suggest you hand it over right now."

Dylan glanced at his brother, who was sitting at the table with a bemused smile on his face. He took another drink of iced coffee, deliberately slowly to frustrate their visitor and show he wasn't afraid of him.

"How do we know you won't pick up where Wilfred left off?" he asked as Simon moved uncomfortably close.

"Dylan!" cried Kane, trying hard to frown. He raised his palms. "Sorry, Professor. Our mother always said Dylan is too honest for his own good."

Simon released a tight smile. "Don't mention it, Kane," he said without turning around. "I understand completely. Your brother has had a series of terrible scares. Traumatising for one so young and impressionable. Now, I really must be getting back to the office." He held out his hands. "If you don't mind, Dylan … the book?"

Kane got up, crossed to the dishwasher, opened the door, reached out a hand, and froze. The dishwasher was empty.

"Dylan," he said over his shoulder. "Where –?" At Dylan's smirk, he asked, "What have you done with it?"

Dylan took the opportunity to slip away from Simon's shadow. "It's in a safe place."

"I said I would take care of it."

"By giving it away?"

"The professor is working with the National Security Office. They need the book."

"How do we know any of that's true?"

"Professor Orwell is a world-renowned academic. I've been to his office. At the university. I've seen his students. Of course you can trust him."

Dylan was reading the ingredients on the side of the carton of iced coffee, trying to find out how much caffeine was in it. Maybe if he drank enough, it would help him stay awake. The carton didn't say, and he felt like going back to bed, so he guessed it wasn't much.

Kane asked again: "Where's the book, Dylan?"

"Son," interjected Simon, "this is a state affair now. You could get into a world of trouble for impeding a lawful request."

"Why haven't you asked me about all the things Wilfred Waite did to me?"

"I beg your pardon?"

"And all the things we did before he stole my body." He placed the carton on the table. "You seem to be more interested in the book than me."

"Your brother told me about what happened with you."

"You're happy hearing about it second hand? Do you think I told Kane everything? … and that he remembered every little detail? That sounds strange for a world-renowned academic."

"Dylan," said Kane, "Professor Orwell is in a hurry. He knows enough to work with the authorities and make sure nothing else gets loose. This isn't all about you."

Dylan felt a stab of anger at his brother's dismissive attitude. It *was* all about him. He was there at the start; he'd assisted in all kinds of incantations; he was Wilfred's chosen one – the chosen one of the gods, if Wilfred was to be believed. It was everyone else who were the bit players.

"Thank you, Kane," said Simon. Then to Dylan: "I'm not a novice in these matters, son. I was researching cults and the occult well before you were born. What seems fresh and new to you is my bread and butter. When all this is over, we can re-group and discuss your experiences. I would be very interested in adding your stories to my body of research." His face brightened. "And Arika, my research assistant; she has a special interest in the Dark farm. You like Arika, don't you? She talks about you boys all the time. In fact, I will arrange an appointment with her as soon as I get back."

"What will you do with it?"

"Pardon?"

"The Necronomicon. What will you do with it?"

"Oh, the book. That, my boy, is for the government to decide."

"The government? The same government that spends a trillion dollars a year finding new ways to kill people?"

Simon clenched his fists. "Don't be a child!" he sputtered. "Give me the book! Right this moment!"

Dylan fell into the closest chair, stretched out his legs, placed his hands palms down on the table top.

"Professor," said Kane, "Dylan is the most stubborn person I know. He won't give you the book."

Simon jabbed a finger in Dylan's face. "I could have you arrested for this, boy."

Picking up the carton, Dylan drank the rest of the iced coffee, then aimed the empty carton at the sink, which was filled to the brim with dishes and rubbish.

"Hey, man," he said, throwing it, wincing when it hit a plate and bounced to the floor; "knock yourself out."

TWENTY MINUTES LATER, Kane approached Dylan's bedroom door. Rapping on it, he pushed into the room without waiting for an answer.

The room was empty. Going to the bed, he spied Dylan sitting on the roof of the porch. It was a habit he'd had since giving up nappies, a habit that used to drive their mother mad. Dylan was staring at a pile of papers in his hands, which Kane recognised as Wilfred Waite's will.

"You're not getting the book," he said without looking up.

"I don't want the book."

"Good. Because you're not getting it."

"I think you were right."

Dylan glanced over his shoulder. "I saw him leave. He seemed pretty pissed."

"To put it mildly."

"Do you think he'll dob us in to the cops?"

Kane leaned both hands on the window sill. "I don't think so. He wants to keep this quiet as much as we do."

"What about the NSO?"

"If the NSO comes, we'll deal with it then. No point worrying about something before it happens."

"They could storm the house when we're asleep and make us disappear."

"You've been watching too much TV."

"Maybe."

"I kinda told him you'd left packages with five of your closest friends, to be sent to reporters if any weird shit happened to you."

Dylan laughed. "Who's the one been watching too much TV?"

"Obviously not the professor. He went white when I told him that."

"I don't like him."

"You don't like anyone."

"I like Arika."

"Really? You like the domineering femme fatale type?"

Dylan smiled.

"Okay," said Kane, straightening, "do I got a fight on my hands?"

"A fight?"

"For Arika's affections."

"Nah. Wouldn't be fair: cool computer whiz-kid versus brainless jock." Dylan glanced at him. "And you're welcome."

"For what?"

"For being the reason you and Arika met."

"You mean when you raised a demon from hell and almost killed everyone in Quorn?"

"Yep."

"You're jumping the gun, mate. I can't see a smart girl like that falling for a village hick like me."

When Dylan returned his attention to the will, Kane asked, "You think she likes me?"

"Can't keep her eyes off you."

"Stop it. You're jerking me."

"Going into the catacombs like that, to rescue me. Never giving up. Getting us all out alive. She thinks you're a hero."

Kane felt his face go red.

Dylan lowered the will. His face was turning red too. He was breathing heavily, staring out at the McLeods' house across the road.

"What you did for me, Kane: I'll never forget it. I just wanted you to know that."

Stepping over the window sill, Kane pretended to look in both Dylan's eyes. "Are you sure that's my little brother in there?"

"It's me."

He sat next to him. "You seem more … grounded."

"Being inside an old man can do that."

Kane grimaced. "You probably shouldn't say that too loud, bro."

When Dylan didn't react to his joke, he said, "Hey Dylan, are you gonna be alright?"

His brother looked down at the will. "You know," he said, smiling at the papers in his hands; "I think I probably am."

37

NSO is watching

THE OLD TRUCK was parked on the side of Big Martha, the last of the Six Hills, at a low stone wall that marked the boundary of an ancient, forgotten estate. The words 'Sunny Morning Eggs' were painted in an arc on the truck's side, below a bright yellow sun rising over puffy white clouds. It was the only trace of sun evident, the dome of the sky being blanketed with thick grey cloud that hadn't moved all day.

Inside the truck, Sam Morgan watched the distant farmhouse in a monitor. He was slumped in the driver's seat, wearing brown overalls and a blue baseball cap with the initials FSC embroidered on the front in white. Stretching his bad leg, he shook out the pins-and-needles, then reached over and wiped a speck of dirt off the screen. The day's light was fading and it was getting harder to see anything; he'd soon have to turn on the night vision.

When he heard footsteps approaching the truck, he pushed himself up in the seat.

"Took your time," he said as the passenger door opened. "You and your Chinese bladder."

Cleo Grieves climbed in and pulled the door shut. She was dressed the same as Morgan, in brown overalls and a blue baseball cap.

"Jamaican bladder," she corrected as she finished keying a message into her phone. Job done, she dropped the phone in her lap, punched his shoulder, and said, "Cheeky so-and-so. I went for a wander, stretched me legs, did a few push-ups, then made a few calls is all."

"Getting back into training?"

"Trying. Wife said the hips are gettin' fatter than hers. Them's fightin' words."

Morgan laughed. "Truth hurts much?"

"Hey, I still fit in the same pants I had when I was twenty-five!"

"Whatever gets you through the day." Turning back to the monitor, he adjusted the brightness. "Nothing happening here."

"He's on his way."

"Orwell?"

"Yep"

"How far?"

"Bout ten mins."

"Was it Jana?"

Grieves nodded.

"Did she say anything about the Gates boys?"

"Report just came in. Parents assaulted and killed four weeks ago by assailants unknown. Knife attack. There's –"

"Is that right?" interrupted Morgan. "Coincidence?"

"I don't believe in coincidences."

"Well I must say, your gut instinct's never been wrong."

"Presiding theory is a robbery gone wrong, but sounds like over-kill to me. And since when do ice-heads try and hide the bodies?"

"Anything else?"

"Elder boy a firefighter – trainee. Younger one unemployed. A third boy, first grader, died five years ago."

"How?"

"Fall from a tree. Broken neck."

"Fair share of tragedy there. Any family connections to the supernatural?"

"Not that we can find. Family moved to Quorn after inheriting the house from the paternal grandfather of the boys. Father, Michael Gates, was a draughtsman. Set up his own business operating from Quorn. Mother, Lauren, worked for Sotheby's in London; seems to have tried to set up an online auction house from Quorn, but the youngest boy's accident put an end to that. Grandparents on both sides were in trade: butcher, carpenter – after some time in the army – seamstress, house-wife."

"Sounds pretty pedestrian. That all?"

"For now."

"Any priors anywhere?"

"Totally clean."

"What's the connection to Orwell?"

"Appears the elder boy, Kane, is involved with Arika Livingston. We're still not sure why they met up with Orwell, or what they were doing together all that time."

"So, Arika. What have you got on her?"

"Twenty-two. Orwell's research assistant for almost a year. Studied under him before that. Grew up in London with a relative on her father's side, Beatrice Carlyle, since age eight, after her mother took off. Mother, Gabriela, whereabouts currently unknown. Father, Corbin, ex-Royal Navy, now a private detective. Interestingly he seems to have disappeared as well."

"Disappeared?"

"Hold on, there's more. He was implicated in the death of two men in London. No one's sure what happened. They were Japanese businessmen, in the arts business, and he was caught on CCTV leaving the hotel the night they were shot."

"That all?"

"Whoever did it cleaned up the scene like a pro. CCTV is all they got."

"He a serious suspect, you think?"

"Ooh yeah."

"What's your gut say?"

She patted her stomach. "Guilty."

Morgan blew out his cheeks. "Both parents gone, huh? And now she's seeing a man with two dead parents. And affiliated with a man with no past. There's definitely something fishy in all that." He stared into space for a while, then turned his vacant eyes to Grieves. "Anything more on the good professor prior to his appointment to George University?"

"He was curator at a museum in Prague for six years. Erm, what's the name? ... Have? Have-it? No, gone. Before that, he seems to have been in Bulgaria – at least that's the story he told around town, according to our Czech contacts – but the trail there is cold."

"So there's unlikely any prior connection to the Gates." Morgan pulled at his lower lip, trying to connect the dots: three bizarre humanoid mutants found in the Six Hills; a dragon monster terrorising people around the corner from where those things had been found; the younger Gates boy witnessed it; the professor with the dodgy past was visiting an isolated farm near where a dead hoodlum had turned zombie and was shot in the face; the older Gates boy, whose parents were both murdered, dating the professor's assistant, whose parents have disappeared. Most of the action seemed to revolve in or around the farmhouse, but that didn't explain the relationship between the professor, his assistant and the Gates boys.

"Cleo, explain to me: Why would Orwell pay the boys a visit? By himself. So soon after Kane Gates spent all that time with him at the uni. That's the connection I can't figure."

Grieves shrugged. "Bizarre love triangle?"

"Perhaps it's innocent. The younger Gates boy witnessed the Messenger thing; Arika Livingston went to find out more and fell for the older Gates boy. Love at first sight – he's a strapping young fellow and she's a definite looker. Professor goes to visit as a substitute parent to ascertain the boy's intentions with his substitute daughter." He pulled a face at her. "Stranger things have happened."

"Not so sure about that last bit, boss."

"What?"

"The guy's five seconds away from death. A long way to drive to protect a young girl's honour."

Morgan raised an eyebrow. "There goes that gut instinct again."

"I'm starting to wonder whether there's something behind your continual references to my gut."

Morgan laughed. "I'm sure Liv thinks the more of you there is, the better."

"Ha, ha. The correct response was: 'Cleo, you're not fat'."

He thought it best not to respond to that one. Instead, he scratched his chin and stared at the monitor. He wished the professor would hurry up and arrive. He always hated these long, boring stake-outs. Adrenaline was more his thing.

"Hey, Cleo, I've got some news of my own."

"Hit me."

"The DNA typing has come back on the mutants."

"Don't tell me: Russian."

"One of them is."

She punched him again. "Bingo!"

"The other two are local."

"I was only putting money on the woman. You don't find too many giant Russian bodies going missing not long before a giant female monster turns up."

"The DNA of all three is really degraded. Might explain their abnormalities."

"Being resurrected after you've been buried for years might explain that too."

"It's good knowing there might be some kind of scientific explanation to all this mumbo-jumbo. Dealing with magic is doing my head in."

"Whereas I'm perfectly at home with it. Must be all that *Bewitched* I watched as a nipper. I always wanted to be Endora."

He laughed. "The evil one?"

"She's not evil. Just protective and a strong woman."

"She scared the hell out of me. I think I identified with Darrin –"

"Derwood."

"See: even that sends a shiver down my poor old spine. I did think she was evil. I was scared one day she'd turn Darrin into a pile of ashes, rather than a goat or a dog. Gone for good. Dead."

"You were a serious youngun, weren't you? Interesting how you're hunting the Endoras and her brood now."

He smiled at her. "I never thought of it like that."

"Subliminal it was. I went into weight training and you turned witch hunter."

"I really hope there's no witches involved in all this. Zombies and dragons I can handle, but the thought of going up against Endora does my head in."

Grieves glanced at her watch. "He's due any minute."

Morgan's eyes went back to the monitor. Besides Orwell, they hadn't seen any activity at the farm; no comings or goings; no lights, movement or noises. The farm was owned by a holding company, its owners nameless and faceless (for now). Morgan had a suspicion it was acquired for some kind of illegal activity. Yesterday, under cover of darkness, he led a covert search of the property. The caged dogs (the ugliest brutes he'd ever encountered), the smell of bleach in the kitchen, the remnants of what looked like a laboratory in the basement – they all pointed towards a meth lab or something worse.

Grieves' phone started vibrating. It was Liv, asking if she'd be home for dinner. Grieves put her on hold.

"Sam, I can see what's bouncing around in that over-sized head of yours. But we're stretched too thin to put a tag on the Gates boys and Miss Livingston too."

He screwed up his face. "Fine. But if anything turns up in the surveillance record, you call me straight away."

38

The return

WHEN KANE ARRIVED home from the supermarket, he was startled to find his brother in the living room, watching TV.

"Hey, Dylan, what you up to?"

Dylan glanced at the shopping bags. "Just needed out of that room."

"You *have* been up there a lot."

Kane nodded at him. Since Monday's events at the farm, Dylan had been mostly sleeping and gaming – things that required little or no effort and enabled him to stay wrapped in a warm and familiar cocoon. He seemed to believe that venturing out of the house would expose him to harm, and it was easiest to just stay in bed and let Kane do everything for him.

This worried Kane, and he'd been urging Dylan to get back to normality as soon as possible, the way he'd done. Kane was back at work, going out on his bike, driving around in his truck, catching up with friends. Dylan had never done any of those things before Wilfred, and he had no urge to do them afterwards.

He stretched his arms and legs. "What did you get for me?"

"Fruit, vegetables, chicken, steak, bread. Thought we should get back to a healthy routine. Don't wanna get sick after all that dust and shit we breathed in at the farm."

Raising his eyebrows, Dylan went back to watching TV. It looked like a program about Egypt, judging by the hieroglyphs the host was pointing at.

"What's that?" asked Kane, nodding at an artist's pad on the coffee table.

He dropped the shopping bags on the floor and went to join his brother on the sofa. "You been drawing?"

Dylan picked up the pad. "Sorta. Been thinking about doing a graphic novel."

"Hey, that's great. Can I see?"

"It's just sketches for now." He opened the pad to a pencil drawing of a blue-faced man in green tights, hovering above a rudimentary city. "It's about benevolent aliens who come here with the solution to war and poverty, and about how superheroes fight them to keep the status quo."

"That's cool. Is that one of the aliens?"

"Just an initial design."

"Looks really good."

Dylan turned the page, to a picture of a young woman (human this time) in red tights, a black cape and black boots. This one wasn't so good; she looked like someone Dylan might hang out with, more so than a superhero.

"Cool."

Sensing his lack of enthusiasm, Dylan closed the pad. "I figured I should do something creative, you know, while I'm living between my two castles."

"Good idea. Keep busy, that's my motto." He bounced up. "Better get that stuff in the fridge."

Collecting the shopping bags, Kane went to the kitchen. As usual, Dylan had left the cereal box, empty milk carton and coffee jar on the counter – he seemed incapable of putting anything away. In the sink were a bowl, cup and glass, all dirty and filled with water. The other thing Dylan seemed incapable of was rinsing or washing dishes; he just filled everything with water and left stuff in the sink for Kane to deal with.

Placing the shopping bags on the counter, he went about emptying them and putting away things in the fridge and cupboards. That done, he stood back and considered what to prepare for dinner – some kind of meat and some kind of salad was his plan.

He went back to the living room, calling out, "Hey, Dylan, what do you want for –" and stopped at the door. The TV was still on, but both Dylan and his pad were gone.

Kane glanced at the ceiling. Dylan was no doubt back in bed.

Oh well, he thought, he's made the first step. Now we just need to make it to step two.

Bounding up the stairs, he called out, "Hey, Dylan! Grilled chicken salad – whaddaya think?"

DYLAN FELT HIS stomach gurgle. The girl in the next line elbowed her friend, who smothered a smile, so he guessed they must have heard it too. It was the smell of grilling meat that did it.

"Hope the burgers taste as good as they smell," he remarked, pulling off his headphones. But he wasn't banking on it.

The customer service operator held out a paper bag.

"Thanks," he said, taking it from her.

The girl, dressed in a powder-blue uniform, hair pulled back in a tight ponytail, gave him the perfect smile of an android. "Enjoy your meal," she piped in a fourteen-year-old's voice.

Walking off, Dylan opened the bag, pulled back the wrapper and lifted the bun to make sure they hadn't put pickles in it.

"What the hell?" he muttered on seeing the pale green discs. Pickles!

He was starting to turn around when nausea rippled through his body. The bag slipped from his hands and plopped to the floor. The room went brown.

"Hey," he heard a girl say from far away. "The food isn't that bad, is it?"

Then everything went black.

Dylan returned to the room to find himself sitting in a white plastic chair. The lights seemed dimmer than before, he felt dizzy, and there was an awful smell in his nose. Everyone was staring at him.

"What happened?" he asked the faces around him.

"I think you barfed in your bag," a girl in a school uniform said.

Pushing himself to his feet, he felt sickness trickle through his body again. He stared at the girl in horror. Her skin darkened and the people and the booths and the wall behind her faded away, until all he could see was the whites of her eyes.

"What's happening to the lights?"

She glanced at the ceiling. "Nothing. They're … on."

Dylan backed towards the exit, as people stared and moved out of his way, mumbling to each other. A child began to cry.

When he reached the door, a bearded man in a grey jacket and tie came up with his bag and handed it to him. He heard the operator shout, "Have a nice day!" – and then he was outside, and everything went back to being normal and boring.

"Do you really think I'd tell you creeps?" laughed Kane, leaning back in his chair.

He was in the rec room with Ricky, Zach and Thanh, playing Texas hold 'em. When they were bored, they played cards incessantly, betting with small change. Today Kane was winning, which meant he was in a good mood, and so he was going along with them as they teased him over the latest visit from January. This time she turned up with dessert for everyone: a lemon tart, home-made. She stayed long enough to watch them gorge on its lemony goodness, and then she took the empty plate, placed it in her tote bag, and sailed out of the station on a ray of sunshine.

When they kept on staring at him, their animal faces plastered with smiles, Kane bent over the table. "Just deal, why don't you?"

"Spill it, man," urged Ricky. "Hot girl like that. We all know what you're like."

He tried to grab the deck, but Ricky was too fast for him.

"I told you there's nothing going on."

"That's not the impression *she* gave ... nod, nod, wink, wink."

"Ding, ding, ding goes the Bell when Kane's around," quipped Zach.

"More like dong, dong, dong," threw in Ricky, always one to take a joke too far.

"Come on guys, settle down. We're just friends."

"With benefits?"

"With lemon tart."

"I'd like mine with whipped cream."

"Hey, dumbhead, don't be sexist. She's a human being, not a dessert."

"Sure looks sweet to me."

"Cut it out, you idiots."

"You were eager to get out of here," observed Thanh. "Both of you."

"I walked her to her car."

"And got in the back seat?"

"You guys need to get a life … or a room."

"Kane," interrupted Zach, nodding at something behind him.

Kane turned his head. Dylan was standing in the doorway, squeezing his hands together, rocking from side to side, looking like he just saw a ghost.

"Dylan? What are you doing here? What's wrong?"

In place of an answer, Dylan turned and walked away.

Kane got up and followed him to the street.

At the kerb, Dylan stopped, turned, and said in a gravelly voice, "He's trying to get back in."

He was so upset he was struggling to breathe. As Kane stared at him, unsure how to respond, he coughed, choked, dry heaved, bent over and spat white spittle onto the road. "I think I'm gonna faint," he murmured, swaying over the gutter.

"Calm down, Dylan," Kane said, patting his brother's back. "Just focus on breathing. Deep breaths. Concentrate on the air going in and out of your lungs. Don't think about anything else." He watched him. "You're having a panic attack. That's all. I've had them, and they feel worse than they really are. It'll pass."

He waited until his brother was breathing normally, and then said, "Now try to stay calm and tell me what this is all about."

Dylan gripped his arm, hard, digging in his fingernails. "I felt it, Kane. It was him!"

Kane drew back his head. His brother was making no sense. He couldn't be talking about Wilfred Waite, could he? The old wizard was dead and gone; surely mush by now. The army, NSO, or whatever they were, had taken his body away. Simon said so. But if it wasn't Wilfred, could someone else be casting the body swap spell? Gilles maybe? Or Kenny Snyder? Didn't they need the Necronomicon to do that? Or at least Wilfred's notebook? Dylan had hidden both of them, so it couldn't be that.

"Wilfred!" screamed Dylan, seeing the doubt clouding his eyes. "Wilfred Waite! He's trying to get back in!"

Kane smiled incredulously. "No, Dylan. That's impossible. Waite's dead. You know that."

Dylan's face went red. "I know the feeling! I'm not making this up! It was him!"

"Dylan, that creep is worm food. I saw him die with my own two eyes. The professor confirmed it."

Dylan scowled at him.

"Okay," said Kane, taking him by the shoulders. "Tell me exactly what you felt."

Dylan drew a ragged breath. He closed his eyes. "There was a sick feeling. In my guts. Then in my head. Then everything went dark."

"It's gotta be a side effect. You had a rough time."

He shook Kane's hands away. "I'm not crazy. Don't say that. I know what I felt."

"I'm not saying you're crazy. I'm just saying you've been through some really awful shit. You need to give it some time. Take it easy, Dylan. Don't stress about anything." When Dylan turned away, he said, "It really does sound like a panic attack. If it happens again, we'll get you checked out."

Dylan was staring across the road, at a corner shop, where two old men sat on milk crates smoking, chatting, watching the world go by. "Kane … remember our secret hiding place when we were kids?"

Kane watched his brother's back. He never really noticed before how narrow his shoulders were, how weak his brother was. It was hardly surprising he was still feeling the fallout from his ordeal.

"Sure," he said. "Yeah, I remember."

"That's where it is. In case anything happens to me."

Kane reached out and ruffled his brother's hair. "Nothing's gonna happen to you, kid. Except someday, real soon, you are going to be the proud owner of a magical farmyard and a truckload of money."

Dylan spun back to him, pleading with his eyes. "Are you sure he's dead? I mean, really sure?"

Kane was certain. No one could have survived what that murderous

Goliath did, definitely not a frail old man who was already at death's door.

"One hundred percent certain," he declared. "I would bet my life on it."

PRESSING HIS FOOT on the brake, Dylan pushed the ignition button and smiled as the car burst into life. He made himself comfortable, switched on the radio, turned up the volume, and nodded like a headbanger as AC/DC blasted from the speakers.

"Maybe we should turn that down," suggested the salesman. He was an older man, weedy and nervy, wearing black-rimmed specs and an impeccable blue suit and gold tie. The dome of his head was almost the same shade of red as the sports car.

"It helps me concentrate," Dylan said, brushing hair out of his eyes.

It also helped keep thoughts of Wilfred Waite away. Since his talk with Kane, he'd figured maybe one of Wilfred's cronies was trying to take up where Wilfred left off, and the best way to resist was to stop thinking about his nemesis. Thinking about magic might be part of letting it in. Get some new interests, was his plan. Ditch all thoughts of the past few weeks, spend some money (Wilfred's money) and, once the will was settled, get the hell out of Quorn.

"Okay, sir," said the salesman, "let's go. Careful on the pedal ... she's very sensitive."

With a glance over his shoulder, Dylan stomped on the accelerator. The car shot off down the road.

"Maybe ease your foot off the pedal?" implored the salesman.

"I'm only going the speed limit."

"I don't think so."

"Chill, man. I've all but bought the thing. If you don't let me enjoy it, I'll take my business down the road."

Pulling on the steering wheel, he sped around a corner. Two tyres lifted from the road; the other two tyres whined; his heart leapt into his mouth.

"Oh my God!" he breathed as he regained control of the vehicle. He laughed at the road ahead, at the people watching him fly by in a shiny new sports car. It felt incredible to let go of the fears that had pinned him down for the past few days – to redirect his adrenaline from panic to exhilaration. This must be how Kane felt when he was competing, or doing fireman stuff. Dylan nodded to himself. Today was his rebirth, the start of a reinvention of himself, an undertaking to get as far away as possible from the stodgy old-man body Wilfred had forced him into.

The salesman slid down in his seat. "She's a six litre V-12, twin turbo, with five-speed automatic transmission and overdrive. Zero to one hundred in less than fifteen seconds – Sheeiiiiiit!"

Dylan swerved to avoid a plastic bag, and the car went skidding across the road. It screeched to a stop a few inches from a garbage truck.

The salesman clutched his chest.

Dylan stared wide-eyed at him. "That was amazing!" he cried. "When my inheritance comes through, this is the first thing I'm gonna buy!"

39

Crazy, man

DYLAN COULDN'T STOP thinking about the car. As he made his way from the dealership to Killer Gamez, the shiny redness of it sat behind his eyes, like the impression remaining in your retina after you stare at a light. He could still feel the leather steering wheel and smell that intoxicating new car smell, and his loins buzzed with the memory of the vehicle's quiet power as it carried him down the road. It beat Kane's fat, ugly, orange man-truck and his father's boring, white, old-spinster Honda Civic hands down. They weren't even in the same competition.

Elation surged inside him, lifting his heels from the pavement. Kane was right: Wilfred was dead and gone. The lanky old professor had confirmed it, and if one of Wilfred's cronies wanted to step in and steal his body, well then, first of all he'd need the Necronomicon. Dylan also suspected the body swap spell needed some kind of genetic or emotional connection between the usurper and his host to work. Of course, this meant the Gates had to be related somehow to the Waites, but Wilfred hadn't given any indication he had living relatives, so Dylan was fairly sure a distant cousin wasn't waiting in the wings to take his place.

It was now only a matter of time before Wilfred's death certificate was signed, and then they could cash in on the will. Then, the car.

He walked for a few paces on tiptoes, singing, "Thunder – ahhhhh. Thunder – ahhhhh," imagining Bert's reaction when he saw the red convertible. His grandfather, a car enthusiast all his life, had taught him to drive, and Dylan couldn't wait to return the favour by taking him for a spin. Once the car was his, he'd make the long drive to Briarwood and turn up in his grandparents' driveway unannounced, blasting the horn and waiting for Bert and Elizabeth to come outside to see who was sitting in their driveway in a shiny red sports car. Maybe a shock like that was all it would take to bust Bert out of the fog of confusion he was floundering in, and bring that smile of affection back to his face.

As he nodded in agreement with himself, a long-haired, middle-aged man, dressed in pink trousers and a blue floral shirt, wearing open-toed sandals and white socks, came striding towards him. A small green bag, hanging from one shoulder, banged against his hip as he walked. Behind him was a short, middle-aged woman with frizzy red hair and too much mascara, wearing a flowing caftan printed with large purple hibiscus flowers. She was weighed down with two recycled hessian shopping bags, and appeared to be having trouble keeping up.

"Excuse me," the man said, barring Dylan's way. "Sorry to trouble you. How are you? If it's not too much bother, would you happen to know where I can find the nearest police station?" He shook his phone at him. "I can't seem to get a signal."

Dylan looked at him. Looked at the woman. Their faces were blank. Police station? What would these ageing hippie characters want the police for? They looked out of place in Handleford – like colourful cartoon people a child might scrawl in crayon over a photo of a dreary town scene. A fear shot through his mind that this was a trap, that the NSO had uncovered his involvement in Wilfred's affairs and they were here to kidnap him, bundle him into the back of a black van and make him disappear.

"That way," he replied, jerking a thumb over his shoulder, then ducked around the man and walked quickly away.

With each step, he wondered what the couple were doing behind his back. (Creeping up on him? Calling for back-up? Waving a black van towards him?) They reminded him of the people he saved from the Messenger, and this alarmed him even more. The NSO were sure to have seen his interview on the news by now; this would connect him to the attack, and to Wilfred. They might even assume he was a sorcerer himself. That being so, once he was in custody and locked and bound in a concrete room in some isolated bunker, why would they believe him when he said he had no idea what Wilfred was up to when he stole a corpse, drew all over it in black marker pen, cast a spell from the book of the dead and released a deadly demon on the world? In fact, what was to stop them shooting him in the head right here and now, before he had time to conjure another Messenger to send after *them*?

Safe around the corner, he came to a halt. Bubbles of panic rose in his chest as he realised he was thinking about Wilfred again – more than that, he was recalling their spell-making, letting him in. "Red sports car … Thunder – ahhhhh. Thunder – ahhhhh," he sang, pressing on. But it was too late. The panic swelled into nausea and an awful pressure grew inside his head. Day became night, his legs gave way, he felt himself fall. Though his eyes were open, everything was black. He had no feeling in his body, no sensations at all, apart from the horrendous smell of something rotten.

Dimly, he heard voices:

"Are you okay?"

"Are you hurt?"

"Larry, do something!"

When he raised his head, light flooded into his eyes, hurting him. Getting into a sitting position, he pressed his palms against his face.

"Let's get him to a hospital," he heard the colourful man say.

Then someone touched his shoulder, and he removed his hands and opened his eyes in a squint.

Around him were the tree-lined street, the huddle of shops, the blue sky, a small crowd of onlookers – everything still so bright.

Then it all went black again.

"Uht-ah-ell," he murmured.

His mouth felt strangely wet and slimy, his lips loose. The stink was back: like the smell in the dungeons below the Dark farm magnified a thousand times.

He felt a hand patting his back, and with that, the light returned.

Dylan looked up in horror. There was no doubt now what was happening. Leaping to his feet, he grabbed the strap of the man's bag, screaming, "The Crypt! It was the Crypt of Gemnemnon! It's Dhagdar! He wants to kill you! He's trying to end the world!"

The man pulled away, slipping the bag off his shoulder and shoving it into Dylan's chest. "Take it!" he screeched. "There's nothing in it! Muesli bars and water! Don't hurt me! I've got kids!"

Caftan flapping, his wife ran up and kicked Dylan in the groin.

"Yiaargghhhh!" he screamed, and swung the man's bag at her. "Get away!" he cried. "He's coming! Get out of here! You're all as good as dead!"

When the woman stepped in for another kick, he stumbled backwards onto the road. A slow-moving car swerved to miss him, its horn blaring, and almost collided with a van coming from the opposite direction. Confused and afraid, the world bending and dimming in waves, Dylan staggered across the road, tripped over the kerb, fell. He threw out an arm to cushion the fall and everything went black. The last thing he felt was his shoulder hitting the ground.

"YOUR BROTHER IS physically fine," said the doctor from the corner of his mouth.

"What do you mean 'physically fine'?" asked Kane, walking fast to keep up.

The doctor stopped so suddenly Kane almost ran into him. They were now in the middle of the corridor, blocking the way, people sweeping past them like leaves floating around submerged rocks.

Kane waited for an answer, while the doctor, a youngish man with colourless hair and frameless glasses, frowned at something going on behind him. He didn't have the best people skills, and seemed always in a rush to be somewhere else.

"He was hysterical," he answered at last, looking at him. "Like a madman. We had to sedate him."

Kane placed his hands on his hips. "That's ... really weird. Dylan isn't the hysterical type."

The doctor crossed his arms and moved his weight from one hip to the other. Clearly, he wasn't used to being challenged. "Has he been taking drugs?"

"No."

Kane glanced down at his feet. He re-thought his answer. "I don't know. Our parents ... were murdered. He's been through hell. I don't know what he's been up to. But drugs ... I'd say no."

The doctor nodded, as if his diagnosis was now confirmed. "When erratic behaviour is out of character, drugs are usually the reason.

Particularly for someone your brother's age."

"What about magic?"

The doctor straightened his back. "How do you mean?"

Kane laughed. "Sorry, doc, I was … making a joke."

The doctor began walking again. "We'll know more after the tests."

Leading Kane to a room, he motioned him in.

Dylan was sleeping in the bed closest to the door, his head turned away from them. Someone had brushed his hair behind his ear. He looked like a young boy, his skin so clear it was almost translucent. There was a curtain drawn across the centre of the room, and someone on the other side was reading aloud from a book.

They stood at the bottom of the bed.

"He's not mad," said Kane. "Stupid, but not mad."

"He was threatening to kill people."

"That's the way Dylan makes friends."

The doctor glanced sideways at him. Having no sense of humour, he left.

Kane stepped closer and stared down at his brother. He was scared and frustrated and angry – in fact, he couldn't think of a bad emotion he wasn't feeling.

"What's happening, Dylan? Why did you go crazy like that?" He ran his hands over his hair. "What will it take to get things back to normal?"

He sucked in air through his nose, exhaled it slowly through his mouth, tried to steady his nerves. It didn't work.

Dragging over a chair, he sat down and held his brother's hand. "We'll be right," he said, though now he was talking to himself.

IT WAS JUST after six, and Kane was sitting in the hospital waiting room, his head resting in his hands. He was focusing on the sounds around him, trying to empty his mind of all negative thoughts. The murmur of voices, the ringing phones, the tap of footsteps, the sounds of trolleys and machines: they were strangely calming – but his brain wouldn't stop panicking about Dylan. What if the doctor was right and he was on drugs? Even worse, what if Wilfred's body swap had caused long-term mental health problems? Would there ever be an end to this?

"Here," said a voice.

He glanced up. Arika was holding out a chocolate protein bar.

"Dinner," she said.

He held out his hand. As she took a seat next to him, he read the writing on the side of the packet. Sugar, carbs, kilojoules; not a lot of protein. He didn't eat chocolate, but not wanting to appear rude, tore open the packet.

Arika's presence brought a sense of normalcy to the room. And comfort. After he rang to tell her about Dylan, she drove all the way here without a second thought. It made Kane realise he was wrong about her. She wasn't one-eyed and selfish. If she cared about someone, she'd be there to support them, no matter what. He now viewed his encounter with the dead boxer through a different lens. Yes, Arika stood there arguing with Wilfred while the zombie was strangling him, but very quickly she smashed the sceptre and gave up any hope Wilfred would reveal what happened to her father. That was the opposite of selfish in his mind.

"Kane, do you know an Oliver?"

He looked at her.

"Dylan," she continued: "he was mumbling it in his sleep. When you were talking to the nurse."

He tapped the chocolate bar against his lips. "Oliver was our brother. He died," he clarified, "when we were kids."

"I'm sorry." Arika smoothed a crease out of her pants. "I … thought it might have had something to do with –"

"Funny he'd be thinking about Oliver." Kane placed the chocolate bar on the seat next to him. "He hasn't mentioned him since he came back from Gramps' place."

Biting his thumb, he stared straight ahead. This didn't make any sense. Or perhaps it did. Oliver's death had defined their family relationships for over five years, so it wasn't beyond the realms of possibility that thoughts of their brother would surface at this stressful time.

"Oliver fell out of the treehouse," he explained, "when Dylan was looking after him. Well, technically I was looking after them both. I was babysitting."

A nurse came towards them as if she had something to say, then pointed a finger in the air and veered away.

"He hasn't been the same since," he said to her back. "He got so angry and depressed, for such a long time." He glanced at Arika. "They were being stupid up there. Shoving each other. Play-fighting. Hanging off the tree like idiots. Dylan blamed me – for not being there." Arika seemed about to say something, so he said quickly, "It *was* my fault. I was the oldest. They were in my care and I left them alone while I was – well, that doesn't matter anymore."

"Kane –"

"I know," he interrupted. "It was no one's fault. Of course it wasn't: it was an accident. But that's … ah, it's pointless dredging this up. It's ancient history." He placed his hands between his knees.

Arika was staring straight ahead. Whatever she was about to say, she seemed to have decided to keep it to herself.

"After it happened, I went kinda crazy for a while. Funny thing was, my mind kept imagining I wasn't there that day – that somebody else was the guilty party. Even now, I can hardly even recall being there; but I know I was. Such a weird feeling …" Shrugging, he said, "I'm sure that's why Dylan is the way he is: a bit of a weirdo. He probably thinks the same as me."

Shaking off the self-indulgence, he looked around for the nurse, but she was nowhere in sight.

"I had a younger sister once," Arika said suddenly.

The way she said it raised Kane's eyebrows. "What happened to her?"

"She died. In a car accident. They both died: my mother and my sister. I was eight; my father was still in the navy. He wasn't always around, so I went to live with my aunt in London."

"I'm so sorry. Here's me going on about my own tragedies …"

"It was a long time ago. I kinda remember them, but not really."

"How old was she?"

"My sister? Four."

"Cor, that's tough."

"How old was Oliver?"

"Six."

She nodded in sympathy.

"How long did you live with your aunt for?"

"Until I was seventeen. Even after my dad left the navy, his work took him all over the country – all over the world – so he thought it best I stayed at Aunt Beatrice's flat until I was old enough to look after myself." She smiled. "Or, as things turned out, until I was so loud and unruly I drove my poor suffering aunt up the wall. That's when I moved back to his place. To give poor Aunt Bea a rest."

"You? – loud and unruly?"

"More rude and pushy, is it now?" She bumped his shoulder. "Look at us: two young guns weighed down by family tragedy. We should be out enjoying ourselves, partying and drinking ourselves stupid, not reminiscing on lives lost like the grannies in my aunt's bridge club."

"I doubt that's either of our styles – the drinking, I mean, not the bridge."

"I don't really see you as a bridge buff either."

"Ahh, you'd be surprised: I'm a whizz at solitaire – and Texas hold 'em. I could probably teach your Aunt Bea a thing or two."

"I think you two would get on like a house on fire – no pun intended." Standing, she looked down at him. "It's getting late. I should be getting home."

Kane stood too. Arika didn't move, and he found himself standing so close he could feel the warmth coming off her body. She appeared slightly flustered, and he considered for a moment whether to lean in for a hug … it seemed the natural thing to do after sharing their stories of loss. And wasn't hugging the thing you did when someone close to you was sick in hospital? But he thought about it for a second too long, and Arika took the opportunity to back away. She rummaged in her bag for her car keys.

"You don't really have to go, do you?"

"I have to get home some time."

"I want you to stay," he blurted out, so loudly a man sitting opposite jerked up his head in surprise.

A look of embarrassment flitted across Arika's face. She smiled into her bag and said, "Well … I do hate driving at night. Especially all that way."

"You could stay here," he offered, lowering his voice, ignoring the man, who was staring at them like they were performing an impromptu play. "At, um, our place. There's plenty of room. A spare room, we have. Like a hotel. A sleepover."

Arika seemed amused by his little-boy way of suggesting it. "I don't have a change of clothes."

"I'm sure we've got something that'll fit."

Before she could answer, the nurse who walked past a few minutes ago returned. "Mr Gates," she said, "your brother is awake."

"Oh, great. Is he … okay?"

"As much as can be expected. A little dazed, but he recognises who he is and why he's here."

"Thank Christ. I suppose you still don't know what happened to him?"

The nurse shook her head.

"And you don't know if he's back to normal?"

"You're probably the best person to answer that. Let's go see him."

"He'll get through this, Kane," Arika reassured him, placing her keys back in her bag.

"He has to. The rest of my family is dead. He's all I've got left."

40

Interloper

THROWING OPEN THE door, Kane stood aside and waited for his brother to go in. The house looked the way it had when their mother was alive, thanks to an army of cleaners he'd marshalled first thing that morning.

"Like the house?"

He stared blankly at him.

"It's clean!"

"Yes. Very."

He walked around peering into each room, as if seeing them for the first time. "Nice," was his only reaction.

Kane followed him, concerned his brother might have sustained a head injury in addition to the concussion. The doctor had warned him to keep an eye out for short-term memory loss, slurred speech, dizziness, fatigue and confusion, and so far it was three out of five.

"Arika stayed last night," he said, trying to make conversation. "She was worried about you too. She had to go back to work this morning, or else she would have been here. Nothing happened," he rushed to add. "I don't think she likes me that way."

His brother was frowning at something in the dining room.

"Not to worry. There's always Janny!" He laughed awkwardly. "Or not. Can I get you anything, Dylan?"

"No … nothing." He went to the stairs. "Would you help me to my room?"

"Huh? Oh. Right. You wanna rest?"

"My head is killing me."

Headache – that was another sign. Four out of six.

"Did you want another pill?"

"A rest is all I need right now."

Kane placed a hand on his brother's back, and together they made their way up the stairs. At the top, he turned to go the wrong way. "No, this way," said Kane, and steered him towards his room. He watched at the door as his brother walked to the bed, sat down, and then, with a soft sigh, fell back.

Kane went up, lifted his legs onto the bed, dragged him towards the bedhead, placed the pillow under his head.

"Listen, Dylan, I need to get back to work. Will you be okay for a few hours?"

He opened his eyes. "Eh?"

"I need to –"

"– work. Yes, of course. Go. I'm not a baby."

Kane watched him, thinking about yesterday, when Dylan was at the station claiming Wilfred Waite was trying to get back inside his head. But that was impossible. Not when Wilfred was dead. His brother was acting weird, but it was the kind of weirdness the nurse said should be expected after a concussion. Still, he determined to keep a close eye on him over the next few days, stock up on fresh fruit and vegetables, keep his mind occupied, make sure he was strong enough to recover from whatever was happening to him.

"Is there something more?"

"No." He stepped back. "I'll leave your medicines in the bathroom."

He closed his eyes.

"By the way, I moved the Necronomicon to a new hiding place."

His eyes sprang open. "What?" He got up on his elbows. "Why?"

"I thought –"

"Where is it?"

"Don't you worry about that."

"Why did you move it?"

"When you told me about Waite coming back, it got me thinking about his cronies and how they might come after you. Thought it safer if you didn't know where it was. There's only me … until we can decide what to do with it."

He sat up. "You need to tell me where it is."

"What did I just tell you? It's safest if I'm the only one who knows."

"Don't you trust me?"

"It's for your own protection."

"I don't need your protection. Can you please tell me where it is?"

"We'll talk about it tonight. I'm thinking of just giving it to the NSO, and to hell with it."

"No, no. Don't trust anyone. We're the only ones we can trust." He leaned forward. "You haven't spoken with them, have you?"

"Course not."

"Have you spoken with anyone?"

"No … just Arika."

"You can't give the Necronomicon away, not to anyone."

"We'll talk about it tonight." He pointed his finger. "Get some rest."

Kane turned and went downstairs. The cleaners did a great job, he thought as he looked around. He could almost imagine his mother coming out of the kitchen, having heard his footsteps, a packet of her favourite Monte Carlo biscuits in hand – her sweet reward after finishing a spring clean. It was a shame, in a way, they wouldn't be here long enough to enjoy it. The minute Dylan was able to travel, they'd be leaving Quorn for good.

Pulling his phone from his pants pocket, he rang Arika. The call went to voicemail. "Hey," he said, "it's me: Kane. Kane Gates. I … just wanted to talk to you about concussion. It's Dylan … of course. Just wanted to run a few things past you. Anyhow … call me. Or I'll call you. I, um … I … ah … Speak soon!"

Hanging up, he frowned at the ceiling, frowned at his phone, shoved it back in his pocket, then went to collect his keys.

THE KITCHEN LOOKED like a hurricane had swept through it. All the cupboard doors were open. Pots and pans and cleaning products were strewn across the floor.

Dylan's head appeared from under the sink. He swore under his breath and glanced around for somewhere he might have neglected to look.

"Where would that worm hide it?" he asked himself. "Where, where, where?"

Standing, he moved to the living room, which was in a similar state.

Frustration spewed up inside him. "You stupid, interfering, useless maggot!" he growled, clenching his fists. "Looks like we'll have to do this the hard way."

He pictured his array of torture equipment, and a thrill passed through him. It had been a long time since he practised his art of interrogation on a living person, a long time since the blood flowing from the cuts he made had run rich and hot. It would be like spending years eating margarine and then tasting real butter again. His mouth watered at the thought.

"I warned you not to cross me," Wilfred muttered, a smile twisting Dylan's lips. "Don't say I didn't warn you."

Going back to the kitchen, he began replacing pots and pans in the cupboards.

APPROACHING THE END of the drive, he spied an unfamiliar car parked by the farmhouse gate. It was an early sixties' Bentley, if he wasn't mistaken. Well maintained, recently polished; it looked like a collector's car.

Parking the Honda beside it, he tapped his fingers against the steering wheel. Clearly it wasn't the car of a police officer or soldier, he thought with relief. It was an old man's car. It was empty, so whoever owned it must be inside the house. He could hear the dogs barking from behind the house, so the car's owner must have found a way to overpower them and lock them up.

"Cockroaches," he muttered. "Dirty, disgusting, filthy cockroaches."

He pulled out Dylan's phone to ring Kenny Snyder, then thought better of it. Kenny was getting too big for his boots. He'd come to his rescue after the encounter with the Gates boys, squirrelling him away at the shop, cleaning up Arlene's mess (or rather, the mess that was Arlene), locking up everything – and since then, he'd begun getting airs, as if Wilfred owed him something. During the time Wilfred was making preparations to regain possession of his young body, he forbade Kenny from going anywhere near the farm (a precautionary measure to stop him nicking anything) and it wouldn't look good to ask for his help now, at the first sign of trouble.

Replacing the phone in his pocket, he pushed open the door. He had a stash of rifles, pistols and swords in the chapel, hidden in one of the coffins near the trapdoor. He'd get rid of his visitor the old-fashioned way.

Creeping up to the house like a commando, shotgun at the ready, Wilfred wondered who the Gates boys had revealed its secrets to. There were no signs of the police or armed forces, so he figured Kane Gates was telling the truth when he said he'd stayed mum – except, of course, for the owner of this car. It was no doubt some relative or friend, out here looting the place while the oaf was busy at work. It was exactly as he predicted: the young upstarts were acquiring his many treasures, intent on taking his place. They had the Necronomicon, they'd rummaged around in his hidden chambers, and the power would soon be in their grasp to control everything he'd resurrected, tamed and built. He seethed with rage at the thought of all the things he'd gained being purloined by imbeciles.

He went inside, shotgun raised, expecting to find a stranger going through his things. Instead, Simon Orwell was there, lounging in his favourite armchair with the grimoire of Theodosius in one hand and a cup of tea in the other.

"Wilfred, you naughty boy!" he cried, looking Dylan's body up and down. "You found Jonathon Dark's farmhouse and didn't tell me!"

Wilfred felt a wave of revulsion pass through him. "Simon," he groaned, lowering the gun. He glanced around to see if anything was missing. "It's been … forever."

"Not quite forever. Just a lifetime."

"And now you're back."

"Yes, Wilfred old man. You too … back from the grave, so to speak. I heard you were dead and buried."

"Unfortunately, you don't always get what you hope for."

"On the contrary, my dear man. I very much hoped young Gates was mistaken. I've missed you."

"Missed thieving from me, you mean."

"You always did hold a grudge. But I forgive you."

Wilfred's body tensed. "It was *you* who crossed *me*!"

"Let's not squibble over old wrongs –"

"You stole my Borellus."

"Borrowed, dear Wilfred."

"You've had it for sixty years."

"What's sixty years between friends? Anyway, if I understand correctly, you don't need the Borellus anymore. You have the Necronomicon."

Wilfred stared contemptuously at him.

"Or maybe you don't," smiled Simon. He stroked his beard. "I heard the tome has been whisked away by some young rascals, who somehow managed to outwit you. Tsk, tsk, old man. You're losing your touch. Beaten by babies. Who would have thought?"

Wilfred squeezed his fists. "They had a bastardly run of luck! No one outsmarts me!"

"The fact remains, old cock: they have it and you don't. You should hear them gloat about it. They're positively gleeful." Tactfully, he decided to change the subject. Running his eyes over the young body, he said, "Tell me, Wilfred: how did you survive the attack of the killer zombie? Kane Gates was certain you were a goner. I was expecting to come here and find you squashed in a pool of guts on the floor."

"Hoping, you mean."

"But no, you managed not only to survive against all the odds, you also regained that delectable body. I'm impressed. Bravo, old man."

Despite himself, Wilfred felt his face warm at the praise. The competition between them was as strong as ever after all these years, and it was clear, just by looking at the two of them, who was winning.

"It pays to have friends," he remarked, raising his chin. "Loyal friends," he added with a sneer, "not the back-stabbing type."

"It pays to pay protectors. Was it that Snyder creature I heard about? He sounds like an unpleasant character."

"They're the most trustworthy kind."

"I wouldn't be too sure about that. But I don't know him."

"He worships the ground I walk on. That's the most precious kind of friend to have."

Simon had a little laugh. "We have very different interpretations of the word 'friend', old man."

"That we do."

Simon stared at him with a Mona Lisa smile. He shook his head, dislodging some private thought. "We were such good friends for such a long time, dear Wilfred. I miss those days of gallivanting around, creating mischief."

"The good times ended a long time ago."

"More's the pity."

"I told you to return my things, and you decided to leave the country instead."

"I had urgent business to take care of."

"For sixty years?"

"What's sixty years to an immortal?"

"You stole some of my most precious possessions! It took me years to recover!"

"And look at us now: reunited after all this time. The deadly duo is back in business."

"What are you doing here, Simon?"

He raised his palms. "I was hoping to find you here and join you in your little excesses."

"You just said you thought I was dead."

Simon was nonplussed. "I knew it would take more than a mindless zombie and a rag-tag band of adolescents to end you. I know your talents too well, old man. But … if by some miracle they *had* achieved the impossible, then in that case I would have continued your work; delivered on your legacy, so to speak. No point letting all your remarkable work go to waste, not with the riches of the Dark farm exposed at long last. And who better to pick it up than little old moi?"

"You're like a scab in the middle of my back, an itch I can't seem to get rid of."

"You found the farm and you found the book. Good for you."

"I found the book and it's mine. You won't get your thieving hands on it."

"Of course not. Because, alack and alas, you lost it. And now we're back to wishing and hoping."

"I'm getting it back. Sooner than you think."

"Wishing and hoping."

"It's only a temporary setback."

"Wishing and – Oh goody, a plan! I knew you'd have something in the works." He leaned forward, hands clasped. "What is it?"

Wilfred smirked at him. Typical Simon, trying to pump him for information. It was patently obvious he was here to steal the Necronomicon – and whatever else he could get his hands on. The thought raised a small panic in him that Simon had already appropriated half his things. There was nothing much of value here, but downstairs was a different matter.

"Let me guess … a little torture in the afternoon?"

Wilfred gave him a tight-lipped smile.

"I'm sorry to thwart your little excitement, but that would be the worst thing you can do."

The smile disappeared. "What do you mean? When is torture not the shortest line between two points?"

"When it would bring the whole security force down on your head." Simon inspected his fingernails, which he still kept long, no doubt with the sole aim of irritating Wilfred: he knew how much it irked him. "So far I've kept them from your door by telling the youngsters I am handling it. If Kane Gates were to go missing, I don't think I will be able to hold my assistant back from going straight to them."

"I'll do both of them then."

Simon stiffened. "No, no, no. No, you won't. I've already had a visit from the National Security Office, thanks to that errant Messenger of yours. How will it look if my assistant goes missing, along with the brother of the boy who witnessed the murderous creature? No, Wilfred, we can't risk that."

"We? There is no 'we'."

"Of course there's a 'we'. There's been a 'we' for … what is it? – one hundred and sixty – no, seventy years. Since ever since you were my apprentice."

"Your slave, you mean."

"Everyone has to start somewhere, old cock. We quickly became friends back then, if you recall. I shared my magics with you, including the magics that have allowed you to stand here today. We had a mutual enemy; we raised some of the most famous and infamous men who have ever lived; the world was at our feet."

"Strange how things turn around."

"We had a mix-up. An unfortunate misunderstanding. Let's let bygones be bygones. There's so much we can achieve together."

When Wilfred didn't respond, Simon picked up a hand mirror from the side table. "Have you been staring at yourself much, Wilfred? I certainly would, if I looked like you do now."

"How did you know it was me? When I walked in?"

"Whereas look at poor old Simon. Ghastly. Time may have slowed, but three hundred and thirty years does pile up eventually."

Wilfred folded his arms. "What do you want, Simon? I have more important things to do than stand around chinwagging with you."

He laid aside the mirror. "I'm not here because I want something. On the contrary, I can be of assistance to you."

Wilfred sat on the arm of the chair opposite. "*You?*" he snorted. "Help *me*? Don't be an ass."

"I've been working on the Gates boy. Gaining his trust. I could re-cover your book."

Wilfred stopped breathing. He placed his hands on his knees. "And why would you do that?"

Simon raised his bushy eyebrows. "As a goodwill gesture. To earn your forgiveness." He picked up the mirror again, lifted his chin. "And perhaps there may be some mutual benefits to be had." He waggled his turkey neck. "What's it like being young again, old man?"

Simon's question made it clear what he was after. Not surprising, really: he was looking awful. Wilfred glanced down at his own slender young body. He made the muscles in his legs move, filled his lungs with air, let them deflate until his smooth belly was concave. His body was the perfect vessel in which to deliver on the next stage of his plan. His shot in the dark, the calling spell, had succeeded beyond his wildest dreams. It was more than magic … it was a miracle.

"Does it feel like being reborn?"

Wilfred looked at him. "Rejuvenated is the word I would use."

"More energy?"

"Definitely. In every part of me," he added with a leer.

Simon poked out his white-coated tongue in disgust. "Surely it can't be like being a teenager again. You've been alive for more than two hundred years. You've seen and learnt and experienced everything there is. No teenager has ever experienced that. You've been everywhere, tasted everything; nothing is new anymore. Aren't you still bored by it? – by the sameness, the monotony, of everything? Surely a new, lithe body doesn't change that."

"You'd be surprised how a change of curtains brightens up the room."

Simon leaned his head back. "It all sounds so tremendously exhausting. Starting all over again? I don't know, Wilfred. Maybe I prefer to be the traveller who's looking forward to the rest at the end of a very long journey. Not searching for more adventures, just reflecting on the adventures he's had. And there are plenty of those. Ah, the men I've raised: the famous, the angelic, the demonic; the secrets I've prised from them. My head is filled like a balloon about to burst with the knowledge gleaned from a thousand lives. I'm one with the Sphinx, replete with the mystery and wisdom of the ages. Nestled in the warm bosom of my hoary university, I am revered by the young and all those who seek to learn, from the master, that which they will never experience for themselves. I'm not so sure being a boy all over again stands up against that."

Wilfred stared at him with Dylan's keen eyes. Maybe he was wrong about Simon's intentions: he didn't seem envious of his newly-acquired youth at all. Rather than put his mind at ease, his former associate's disdainful attitude towards immortality antagonised him. That wasn't the reaction he was after. Simon was supposed to burn with envy.

"You're a balloon that's about to deflate and shrivel into a flaccid piece of rubber," he corrected with a wave of his hand.

Simon laughed. "Ah, Wilfred, old friend, you do have a peculiar view of the world. Then again, you're more than a century younger than I am. A child of a different age, so to speak."

"Whatever our differences, I'm not a lousy quitter, sitting here waiting to crumble to dust, like you seem to be. I'm disappointed in you, Simon. I thought you were better than that."

Simon lifted and dropped his shoulders. "Each to his own. I'm winding down gracefully, accepting my fate, not fighting against it with a vain attempt to steal a boy's life, just so I can keep doing the same old same old for another three hundred years."

Here Wilfred laughed like a real teenager. He pushed himself off the chair and strode to the window. Though it was filthy and almost impossible to see anything through, he pretended he was studying the landscape.

"What makes you think I'm doing the same old same old?"

"What exactly *are* you doing?"

He turned. "Learning the secrets of the Necronomicon."

"Don't we already know those? From the Latvian copy?"

"You know it was only a copy. Nothing in it worked."

"Some things worked. And I'm not so certain an original version is as powerful as they claim it is. There can't have been *that* many copying errors."

"I beg to differ."

"Really? Tell me more. What kinds of marvellous things can the real tome do?"

Rocked by a burst of anger, Wilfred grabbed his hair in his fists. He was sick of talking about the book when he should be pulling out fingernails to retrieve it.

"No more words! I need my book! This – intercourse – is getting us nowhere!"

"Which brings us back to my offer."

Wilfred glanced at his shotgun, which he'd left leaning against the chair. He should have shot the interloper on sight, like he planned from the start.

"I don't need a thieving sewer rat like you to get me my book."

"Perhaps," mused Simon, going back to checking his fingernails; "perhaps not." He looked up. "But you do need me if you want it by Magacanta." He pushed himself out of the armchair. "You see, Wilfred,

I've done a little research and, as I understand it, if you don't retrieve the Necronomicon by the Feast of Sidusater, you stand to lose your tenancy over that sweet young body. Pouf! Back into that rotting corpse of yours. And then who'll be the one sitting around waiting to crumble to dust? – or melt into sludge, in your case."

Simon's words made the shadows in the room darken and swell. Wilfred squeezed his eyes shut. Something was wrong. He could smell something rotten, and he knew exactly what it was. Holding onto the window sill, muttering the binding spell, he struggled to stay in control of his body.

When the crisis passed, he opened his eyes to find Simon smiling at him. Fear turning to rage, he leapt at him and pushed him against the wall, his forearm held hard against his neck.

"I will not lose this body! I've worked too hard and too long to let that no-good runt steal it back!"

Simon regarded him placidly, patting his shoulders like a father reassuring his child. "Calm down, dear friend. Obviously stress is not good for you. I'm saying I'm here to help."

Wilfred breathed furiously. He was livid, mostly because Simon was right. He was in a race against the clock to recover the Necronomicon and use it to finalise the body swap at the Feast of Sidusater. It's the one time of the year when the stars and planets come into alignment and the collective power of hundreds of minds converges in a blaze of magical energy. He needed the Necronomicon to pull in all that energy and make the change permanent; otherwise … the alternative was to return to that disgusting decomposing body and melt by slow, painful degrees into a pool of slime.

Releasing his hold on Simon, he stalked to the other side of the room. "What makes you think the Gates boy will hand the book over to you?"

Simon adjusted his collar. "He wants all this nasty occult business to go away. If you could only hear the dreadful things he says about you and this place. Positively blood curling. His dear mother would turn in her grave. She *is* still in her grave, isn't she?"

"Unfortunately his elders were cremated. Otherwise I would teach that bastard a lesson he would carry to his own early grave."

"He's a strong-minded one, that boy. He won't crack by force, I can promise you that."

"Damn that meddling cur! I should have gutted him when I had the chance! As soon as I get my book back …"

He hugged his body, fighting to control the emotions this new body seemed to amplify. He hadn't realised the boy's hormones would make him feel as young as he looked. It was as if Dylan Gates was getting his revenge for the possession spell by turning things around and possessing *him*.

"Very well, Simon," he conceded as his rage settled. "Go get me my book." He jabbed a finger at him. "But mark my words: in the past sixty years I have learnt a thousand and one new ways to make a man suffer. Cross me again and I will make you burn from the inside."

Simon gave him a pained look. "Dear Wilfred, it cuts me to the bone how you don't trust me."

He walked to the door, paused, and turned back. "By the way, we spent the better part of a century searching for the Dark farm. How on earth did you find it?"

Wilfred smiled at him. "Google."

41

Arika receives a visitor

ARIKA YAWNED, STRETCHED, and let her head fall back against the wall. Since escaping the farmhouse almost a week ago, she'd hardly slept. Whenever she closed her eyes she saw dead things: dead fields, dead trees, dead dogs, dead people coming back to life. She knew with time the images would fade and lose their potency, but that wouldn't come until she had a few nights of solid sleep. And that meant not waking at four every morning and staring at the ceiling until the sun rose.

A car with a noisy exhaust sped past the apartments, the roar receding until it faded to a dull rumble. The sound stroked the inside of her head, as if the car were driving over the surface of her brain rather than the street below. The feeling was hypnotic. As the background hum of traffic returned, she felt herself slipping into sleep.

A knock sounded at the door.

Arika raised her head, momentarily confused. Blinking away the light, she pushed herself off the couch, stumbled to the door and peered through the peephole.

It was Simon.

"Hey there, Professor," she yawned, leaning on the door.

Simon looked tired too. The bags under his eyes, his mouth, his jowls: they all sagged like melted cheese. He didn't look happy. She guessed the events at the Dark farm were taking their toll on his health, and then wondered what would bring him all the way out to her apartment on a Sunday.

"Everything okay?"

He shook his head a little.

"Come in."

Pulling the door open wider, she stepped aside and let him pass. Her heart was racing at the thought that something had gone wrong at the farm. It had to be big. The only thing she could think that would bring Simon to her door was something involving Kane or Dylan.

"Apologies for disturbing you at home, Arika," he said at last, glancing around the apartment. "I didn't feel comfortable discussing this at the university – national security and all."

"Of course."

She breathed a little easier on hearing it was national security he was here to discuss, not some disaster involving the Gates boys. Simon hadn't been updating her on events at the Dark farm, and her heart leapt at the hope he was here to bring her back into the fold.

She motioned him to a chair, and then saw the dirty laundry she dropped there last night. As he moved towards it, she rushed over and gathered the clothes in her arms. Just her luck the professor would visit in a week when everything had gone to hell – including her housework.

"The job at the farmhouse is not going well, I'm afraid," Simon began, taking a seat, conveniently looking the other way as she threw her clothes into the bedroom and closed the door. "Not well at all."

Arika came back and fell into the couch. She pulled her legs up.

"The magics are extremely complex, and I'm worried that without the Necronomicon we'll be unable to put the horrors to rest."

"The copy isn't working?"

"It's a poor transcript. And incomplete. Useless in a situation like this."

"You think the one Kane has is an original?"

"I'm certain of it."

His confidence surprised her, considering he'd never set eyes on it.

"What makes you so sure?"

He smiled at her, though only with his mouth. His blue eyes were veiled, and in that moment she hardly recognised him.

"Only that Mr Waite used it to conjure up all those evil things you and the brothers saw. A cornucopia of horrors like we've never before encountered. It's not something one can do with any other text I know of, and as we've learnt, a copy is next to useless. Like a copy of a key that only works if you know exactly how to manipulate it. And we don't. We have no frame of reference. We need that book. The one Mr Gates has. It's the only one."

Arika pressed her hands between her knees. "I can't see how I can help you, Simon. If you want Kane's book, you'll need to ask him."

"I was hoping you might do that, Arika. Use your feminine wiles? Tempt the red-blooded beast, so to speak?"

She shook her head at him. Same old chauvinistic Simon: thinking he was complimenting her when he was doing the opposite.

His mouth turned down at the corners. "As you will recall, the first time I asked I was told in no uncertain terms I couldn't have it. I hoped with time the elder boy would be able to convince the younger to change his mind, but the reverse happened. Now they've both dug their feet in."

Arika felt a jab of betrayal. Simon wasn't here for advice or to offer her a role in the security or study of the farm; he was here to use her. Was it because she was so tired she felt so annoyed?

With an effort, she said, "They both saw what the book can do, and they don't think they can trust anyone else. In a way, I think they're right."

"What on earth could you mean by that?"

"Kane is strong and decent, and if anyone can hide the Necronomicon and not be corrupted by it, it's him."

"I trust you have the same faith in me?"

His question was juvenile and only annoyed her more. "Of course, Simon. But as you said, Kane has it and he doesn't want to hand it over."

"That boy is in above his head. If he's not careful, the NSO will go in and take it from him."

"You told them about Dylan?"

"I felt I had to."

"What was their response?"

"They have no interest in small fry. Unless, of course, those small fry get in the way of their operation."

"So if it's that important, why doesn't NSO get a warrant?"

Simon tapped his forefinger on the arm of the chair. It seemed like all his frustration was concentrated in that one small action. "This is a highly secretive affair. The Home Secretary wants to keep it that way."

"I'm sure there's more to it than that."

Simon sighed. "I wasn't going to tell you this, Arika, because I know you're feeling rather … protective of the boys; but they've done something very stupid. They've left notes with their friends that will be released to the media if anything happens to them. We can't afford to let that happen. It would cause widespread panic and all kinds of crazies to descend on the farm. So we're left with polite cajoling. For the time being, at least."

Arika suppressed a smile. What Simon was telling her sounded like something from a B-grade movie. Were Kane and Dylan really that tactical, or were they bluffing? She didn't know them well enough to know, but either way it was a smart move.

"Kane is as stubborn as a mule," she said. "I doubt he'll give you the book."

"Which is why you, my dear, are our only hope."

Arika scanned his face. A forced smile was stretching his mouth; beads of sweat were standing out on his brow; his finger was still tapping on the arm of the chair. Something didn't feel right. Why would NSO send an ageing professor on such an important mission, when it had trained officers who could put real pressure on Kane? It was hard to believe the NSO would be scared off by the old I've-left-notes-with-four-of-my-closest-friends trick.

"I'll ask him," she conceded. "But I can't promise anything. Maybe the Home Secretary would have more luck."

Simon frowned, the sarcasm going over his head. "It's best left with us. The Gates boy was right in one respect: the government can't be trusted. Who knows what they might do if they got their hands on that much power? Militarising magic would make the atomic age seem like the bronze age." His face adopted a smug expression. "I let the NSO know the book is like a highly sensitive explosive and needs to be handled by an expert. A.k.a. me. I suspect they're scared stiff of it – as well they should be." He fixed her with a stern gaze. "You should be aware, Arika, that in time the book *will* corrupt that boy."

"I'll be sure to mention that to him."

She stifled a yawn, but by this time she was energised by the thought of her new mission. It gave her an active role in events at the farm – not as active as she would have preferred, but it was like opening a door a crack before pushing her whole body into the room. And as an added bonus, perhaps this time she could get a real look inside the Necronomicon.

"I might go out there tomorrow, if you can spare me."

"No time like the present," countered the professor, pushing himself to his feet.

"You mean today?"

"Time is of the essence."

Arika wondered whether it was sensible going back so soon. She left Quorn only yesterday morning. Kane might get suspicious. Even worse, he might think she was interested in him for more than just the book.

"When you gain possession of the Necronomicon, be sure to bring it straight to me, Arika." He pointed a finger at her. "Don't be tempted to read it yourself."

Simon knew her too well. He also knew she had a stubborn streak and would do whatever she felt like doing, regardless of his warning. But what choice did he have? Arika smiled at him, not bothering to lie and tell him she wouldn't read it.

"I'll ring you one way or the other," she promised as she led him to the door.

"Thank you so much for doing this, Arika." Simon gazed warmly at her. "I realise it's an imposition."

"Not at all, Professor. It's a lovely day for a drive."

She opened the door. "We'll talk later."

"That we will."

The professor left. Closing the door, Arika went to the bathroom and splashed water on her face. After drying herself on a towel, she applied concealer to a couple of spots on her cheek, brushed her hair, applied lip balm, checked herself in the mirror. Arika had never thought of herself as attractive. Her face was too wide, her ears too large, and her eyes bulged a little. She was the product of too many genes – from Norway, Morocco, the South Seas and a few countries in-between. The mixture was too crazy to make sense; at least in her eyes. Her best asset was her brain, though she guessed men like Kane were hardly likely to have that at the top of their list of desirable attributes in a woman.

Kane. It was funny how he kept popping into her head. She'd known him less than a week, and in that time she'd thought about him more than she'd thought about any other man in her lifetime (besides, of course, her father). Frowning, she reminded herself their shared experiences had forged a bond between them, a connection shaped by family, history, danger, death and magic – a potent combination. It was hardly surprising he was always on her mind.

Still, she didn't think of Dylan that way.

Shrugging at herself in the mirror, she said, "It is what it is," and turned and left the apartment.

42

Arika receives another visitor

A S ARIKA APPROACHED her car, she heard footsteps.

"Excuse me," a voice said behind her.

Spinning around, she came face to face with a man who looked vaguely familiar. Dark hair going grey, five-o'clock shadow, wearing a navy-blue suit, black shirt and charcoal-grey tie.

"Ms Livingston," the man said, placing a hand inside his jacket, "have you got a moment?"

Arika pulled her bag closer, preparing to reach in and grab the gun. Her first thought was that he was here to bring news about her father, but he could just as easily have come for nefarious reasons.

"Don't be afraid," the man said, reading her mind. "My name is Sam Morgan. I'm with the National Security Office."

Pulling out an identification badge, he held it in front of her face. It did little to ease her fears.

"O-kay," she said, assuming this had something to do with Simon's visit. Perhaps it was a good-cop, bad-cop kind of thing. "I don't –"

"Can we go back inside?"

Her mind went momentarily blank. "Inside?"

"Your apartment."

"My –" She closed her mouth. Simon's unannounced visit, and now the NSO. Were they really that desperate for her help?

"What's this about?"

"I'd like to have a word about Professor Orwell."

"Of course. He was just here."

"Yes, we know."

"We?" She glanced around. He seemed to be alone. "Simon said you were leaving it to him to fix. The book."

"He said that, did he?"

"National security and everything."

He smiled. "That's exactly why I'm here."

Arika was confused. Morgan was speaking in riddles, something that frustrated the hell out of her. She suddenly remembered where she'd seen him: at George University, the day the story about the Messenger appeared in the paper. That day, he was waiting in Simon's office with a heavy-set, serious-looking woman.

"Shall we go inside?"

She followed Morgan as he led the way up the steps to her apartment. It worried her he knew which apartment was hers, but there was so much cloak and dagger happening lately it wasn't entirely a surprise. She tried to anticipate his motive. Was he here to put additional pressure on her to get the Necronomicon from Kane? If so, it was hardly necessary. And why had Simon said the NSO were leaving it to him to retrieve the book, and yet the next minute they were here?

It didn't take long to find out.

"Do you know anything about the White Horse Farm on the old beach road out of Quorn?" asked Morgan as he took stock of the apartment.

She was still standing at the open door.

"Would you close that please?" he added in a pleasant voice.

Arika did as she was told, slowly, using the time to think about how much she should reveal of what she knew. As little as possible, was her conclusion.

"Simon – that's Professor Orwell – said he's been out there," she said, starting off with something they already knew.

"We're aware of that."

A strange choice of words. "Aware? Isn't he working with you?"

Morgan's smile was like ice. "I take it that's what he's been telling you?"

She stepped closer. "He isn't working with you?"

He squinted at her as if deciding how much he should reveal.

"Is he working with you? You need to tell me."

Morgan turned away. "Not by any stretch of the imagination." He picked up a wooden carving of an African tribal warrior, a souvenir

Arika picked up in Nigeria, and weighed it in his hands. "He's been frequenting the old farmhouse, and we believe he might be involved in something nefarious with one Wilfred Waite and Dylan Gates."

Arika's breathing grew rapid. Her heart raced. This didn't make any sense. Why would Simon lie about the farmhouse? And make up stories about conversations he had with the NSO? And what would possess him to go out there alone after everything they told him? Did he intend on keeping its terrible secrets for himself? All she could think was perhaps he was preparing a research paper and would reveal his findings about the Dark farm to a shocked academic world at some upcoming confer-ence. Keeping secrets about world-beating research – it's what professors do.

But that's not what Morgan was thinking.

"What do you mean by nefarious?"

"We're yet to find that out."

"You're not suggesting he has anything to do with those – things that happened out there?"

"We don't know at this stage. We do know the farmhouse belongs to a company owned by Wilfred Waite, who no one has seen for over a week. He runs an antiques store in Quorn and has missed several appointments. Do you know Mr Waite?"

She stared at him. "I wouldn't have any reason to know him."

By the look on his face, he recognised her reply as an evasion. Per-haps he already knew the answer to his question.

"The other thing we don't understand just now," he went on, "is the connection between Dylan Gates and Simon Orwell."

"There is no connection," she rushed to assure him. "Not really. Simon sent me down to interview Dylan about that dragon thing in the paper."

Morgan squinted at her. "The Messenger."

"That's right."

"They appear to be working together," he announced in an official-sounding voice.

"Who? Simon and Dylan? That's impossible. They don't get on at all."

"So they do know each other."

"They only met the other night … Thursday. I heard it didn't go well."

"At the Gates boys' house."

"How did you know –?"

"I knew Simon had visited. Care to tell me what that was about?"

Arika had already decided not to say anything about the Necronomicon. She still didn't know who to trust in this affair – except, of course, Kane.

"It was personal," she answered.

"In what way?"

"Well, not really personal. He had more questions about the Messenger."

"What's wrong with the phone?"

"You're asking the wrong person."

He stared at her.

"Quorn has a history of supernatural happenings. It was the scene of mass panic in the eighteenth century, when witches were hanged left, right and centre; and then there was that thing about fairies in the late eighteen-nineties. There's been records alleging sorcery and devil worship since records began. Professor Orwell has all sorts of reasons to visit Quorn. In his official duty. Any more, you'll have to ask him yourself."

Morgan seemed to accept her explanation. "Tell me about your father," he said, his eye on a framed photo on the bookshelf.

"Why do I get the feeling you already know all about him?"

"I wouldn't be doing my job if I didn't. He disappeared recently, didn't he? You put in a missing persons."

"That's right. He was doing some investigative work for Simon. He said he had a lead, and that was the last we heard from him."

"Do you feel the fact he's a wanted man has anything to do with his disappearance?"

Annoyed by the flippant nature of his question, Arika replied, "He's not a wanted man. He's a person of interest. I know my father. He's not capable of murder. If he was around, he would have come forward to clear all that up. Something's happened to him."

He was silent again.

"Do you know something about those murders I don't?"

"I've looked into the investigation and your father's disappearance. They're both cold."

Her heart sank. "Do you think my father's dead?"

"I have no way of knowing that. I only know there was no evidence at all at the murder scene, apart from the vision of him leaving the hotel; so if he was alive, I would have thought he'd have come forward to clear things up. It looks more guilty to run away than give a simple explanation as to why you were at a hotel. There's no other connection to the two murdered men; no DNA or evidence left at the scene. He'd know that."

"Which is why I said he's only a person of interest. I think Wilfred Waite had something to do with his disappearance."

"Why do you think that?"

"He was looking for the farm that Waite now owns."

"Is that so?"

"It's too much of a coincidence."

"How much do you know about Waite?"

"He's creepy, and probably a psychopath."

"Sounds like you know him well."

"I've only had the displeasure a couple of times. Doesn't take long to take the measure of him."

"Anything more you can tell me about Waite?"

She shook her head.

"Okay, let's go back to your father's disappearance. That was about the time you started working for Professor Orwell, wasn't it?"

"Simon was sympathetic and offered me a job. He was amazingly supportive. I think he was feeling guilty for what happened to Dad."

"Why would you think that?"

"Simon may have been one of the last people my dad spoke to."

Morgan squinted at her again. "You realise the professor might have had some part in your father's disappearance?"

The thought had never entered her mind. Instinctively, she leapt to

Simon's defence. "That makes no sense. Dad was working for Simon, and I can tell you without a doubt, Simon wants to know what happened to him almost as much as I do."

Morgan started walking around the apartment, checking for anything that might be out of place or useful to his investigation.

"The professor has been acting highly suspiciously lately. And his past shows all signs of a cover-up. He's impossible to trace. He's hiding something and we need to know what it is."

Arika pondered again how much she should tell Morgan. She needed to speak with Kane first: it was his brother's future that was at stake if everything was brought out into the open. This man, though professing to be in control of the situation, seemed to know very little. It was time to turn the tables and find out exactly how much he knew or suspected.

"Do you know what's been happening out at the farmhouse?" she asked.

"It's obviously connected to the recent troubles at Quorn."

"What recent troubles might they be?"

"The Messenger. A rather … strange death."

"Any more?"

He half-smiled, probably thinking: Aren't I the one who's supposed to be asking the questions?

"Have you actually been into the farmhouse yet?"

He turned to her. "Miss Livingston, what I am about to say to you is subject to the utmost confidentiality. If you mention it to anyone – even hint at it – you could be subject to a term of imprisonment for a period of up to fifteen years. Do you understand what I'm saying?"

Arika nodded. "Yes," she added impatiently when he continued staring at her.

"Repeat it to me."

She sighed. "If I spill the beans to anyone, I could go to the slammer for fifteen big ones."

Morgan seemed to relax after that. "We have the farmhouse under surveillance," he said, "as well as Professor Orwell. And, as of yesterday, Dylan Gates."

"Why as of yesterday?"

"He was out at the farmhouse."

"Oh. Really?"

"With Orwell."

"With Simon? Why? What were they doing there?" She glanced about the room as if the answer lay within its four walls.

"We don't know that yet. But it's classified information as well. You can't tell Orwell or Kane Gates about Dylan – nothing. You understand?"

She nodded.

"Repeat it to me please."

With a heavy sigh, she said, "I can't tell Simon or Kane that I know Dylan might be in cahoots with Simon."

"Or else …"

"Or else I could be sent to prison for up to fifteen years."

"Precisely. We can't afford to have any leaks or tip-offs at this stage in the investigation. Now, Arika, I need you to tell me everything you know about what's been happening out there, and then I need your help in notifying me of anything the professor does or says."

"You want me to spy on him?"

"If he's doing nothing wrong, there can be no harm."

"What if he *is* doing something wrong?"

"Then whatever it is could be extremely dangerous."

She sat on the arm of a chair. "Mr Morgan, it sounds to me you have no idea what's happening beneath the farmhouse."

"Beneath?"

She slid down into the chair. "Take a seat. We may be here for a while."

43

Simon's grand plan

"WHO THE DEUCE is it?" asked Simon, annoyingly close to his ear.

Wilfred was bent over a pile of grey dust on the stone floor, holding a brown amphora urn, emptying more dust onto the pile. The room was small and dark, the only light coming from an adjoining chamber lit with candles and lamps. At the far end of the room was an arched aperture that led to a narrow alcove. A symbol in the shape of a ram's horns was carved into the stone above the arch.

He shook the urn to empty the last of the dust, relishing the ease with which his young muscles handled the heavy pot. As an old man he struggled with even the simplest of spells, but now his muscles felt like springs: well-oiled springs that pushed and pulled and lifted and twisted with ease.

"He knows how to control the Messenger of Yog-Sothoth," he muttered, straightening and pushing Simon out of the way.

Replacing the urn on a long shelf, he turned to watch the fruits of his labour. There were four such shelves, each holding a dozen or so urns labelled with a code: two digits and what appeared to be a date. Arranged on the floor were six more urns, these ones labelled with the names of animals: bull, lion, hyena, eagle, wolf and ox.

The stone of the floor was etched deeply from wall to wall with a pentagram. At each of the five points was a hieroglyph; between the hieroglyphs were concentric circles that swirled with fractals. The grooves in the floor were filled with a purple liquid that glistened in the dim light.

Lifting a heavy bucket, Wilfred carried it with both hands to the pile of dust. He removed the lid, dropped it with a clatter to the floor, and began tipping the contents onto the dust. Blood and entrails slopped out and splashed on the floor and on his black boots. The room quickly filled with a sweet, sickly scent.

As the bucket emptied, he mumbled a chant. The mixture began bubbling.

"Yog-Sothoth," scoffed Simon, who was standing in the doorway reading from Wilfred's notebook. "What a bore!" He turned the page. "Bore, bore, bore."

Dropping the book on a table, he went back to Wilfred. "Why not go straight for the great Kragn? Nothing like a little pandemonium to preface the end of the world."

Wilfred shot him an angry glance. "Impatience will be the end of you, Simon. Things must be done in the correct order."

"We're talking about chaos here, old man."

Wilfred squinted at the bubbling mass of blood and entrails on the stone floor. "Creating chaos is like building a house of cards. You have to build it high to truly appreciate its destruction."

"Spoken like a true pedant. Well, Wilfred, forget that for a while. I have news for you. I went back to my old Borellus – sorry, your old Borellus – and remember that spell that allows the dead to sense the whereabouts of the Necronomicon?"

"What about it? We tried that a hundred times. It doesn't work."

"Apparently we were missing a vital ingredient."

"Which was?"

"The Necronomicon."

Wilfred turned to him. "What are you talking about?"

"You need a mouse to catch a mouse."

"Don't play games with me, Simon. I don't have the patience for it."

"I'm not playing games, old cock. Borellus transcribed the text from memory, and he made a few mistakes."

"And how did you suddenly come upon this little gem?"

"I took your advice and googled it."

Wilfred shook his head. Everything Simon did annoyed him. "So … cough it up. Impress me."

"Think of a dog being sent off to search for a lost child. It needs to have a whiff of something the child has touched. How else would it know what it was looking for?"

"So we needed to have the book and then lose it in order to find it again?"

"Precisely."

"And you just happened to find this on Google?"

"Well, perhaps I shouldn't take all the credit. I set it as an assignment. Two of my students found it. It's a brand new world, Wilfred, and the young are set to inherit it."

"I couldn't agree more. So, what do you suggest we do?"

Simon smiled at him. "Cast some spells. Raise the dead. Find your book."

Wilfred turned back to the entrails and watched the form starting to take shape. He always loved this part of the ritual. It was the time when life re-entered the dust of the dead, the time when he felt closest to becoming the god he knew he was destined to be.

But right now he was too distracted by Simon's news to concentrate on the resurrection. Still, he'd be damned if he'd show it. Simon was already too cocky for his own good.

"I'm not drawing any more attention to myself," he said without looking away. "You know what happened to Jonathon when he grew rash and stupid."

Simon took the empty bucket away. "What exactly do you think happened to Jonathon? Have you found any clues since you've been here?"

"Either he succeeded spectacularly or failed miserably. I suspect the latter. The price on the head of a master wizard is extreme, and I'm betting some hell demon conquered him, ground him to paste, and used his essence in whatever vile ritual it was performing."

"I suppose you're right. He was so fixated on summoning Kragn, we would certainly know if he succeeded."

"That we would."

"Jonathon was always shooting for the impossible. But he did teach me everything I know … at least, everything he knew back then." Simon sighed. "A shame we became enemies. We may have learnt so much more if we worked together."

"He almost cost you your neck."

Simon had grown wistful. "True. The closest I ever got to the hangman's noose. If ever there was a pathological narcissist, Jonathon was it. After Joseph's death, he got even worse. It wouldn't have cost him tuppence to break me out, but no, he left me there to have my neck stretched. And so commenceth the wizard wars."

The misty look in his eyes turned into that mischievous look he got when a nasty thought slithered into his mind. One thing hadn't changed over the years: Simon could never keep his fool mouth shut.

"Just think what would have happened if he hadn't betrayed me and almost caused my demise. You and I wouldn't have met. He wouldn't have seduced your wife, and then she wouldn't have run away with Ephraim to America, and we wouldn't have found out about this farm. All things lead to the present. And so here we are, you and I: friends again, close to having everything Jonathon built, without having the psychotic control-freak around to kowtow to and threaten us with annihilation if we don't do precisely what he orders."

Wilfred was staring at the bloody mess on the floor and hardly took in any of Simon's monologue. He held out a hand. "Pass me another bucket."

"A what?"

"Bucket! A bucket!"

Simon dragged over another bucket filled with blood and entrails. "So, Wilfred," he began, taking off the lid, "shall we cast the search spell?"

Wilfred was thinking of a way to cast the spell himself, without Simon's interference. Trouble is, Simon had his Borellus, and there wasn't time to go out and find another before Magacanta.

"How else will you get the book?" Simon persisted. "A couple of living dead, late at night, no one about. What could go wrong?"

Wilfred mumbled the chant as he poured the contents of the second bucket over the bloody mess on the floor. The mess was moving, spreading out. The arms, legs, torso and head were now clearly discernible.

"A couple?" he said.

"Pardon?"

"You said a couple of living dead. Borellus said three."

Simon was staring at the body forming on the floor. He knelt close to the face, which was slowly revealing a forehead, chin, cheeks, nose and ears. "I think I might know him. Can you give me a clue? … Where did you dig him up?" He glanced at Wilfred with a smile. "You're right: three. They have to be recently dead, and related. If you remember, they triangulate the whereabouts of the Necronomicon, and together retrieve it."

"Three recent carcasses?"

"And related. Can you manage that?"

"Of course. A breeze." Wilfred wracked his brain. Always keen to kill three birds with one stone, his mind soon landed on the ideal candidates.

"Any ideas, old man?"

"I know a family. Local layabouts. An annoying waste of space. High time they did something useful with their pathetic lives."

"Excellent. I knew you'd come through." Simon pushed himself to his feet. "Now you *are* going to let me have a play with this fellow, aren't you?"

"Gilles!" yelled Wilfred.

When Gilles appeared in the doorway, Wilfred said to Simon, "Our friend here will have to wait. I need to ring Snyder and put the wheels of my plan in motion."

To Gilles: "Call Rudi and get this to the holding cell." His face relaxed into a smile. "You will be pleased to learn, dear Gilles, that your master is about to retrieve his book and end this ridiculous farce once and for all."

44

Hospital disorderly

THE PHOTOS ON the mantelpiece showed three boys playing cricket in a tree-lined park; a bride and groom in a sun-lit tropical garden; two faded children in blue school uniforms; a large-nosed woman with a blonde perm in a glamour pose; a man with a camera bag on his shoulder pretending to hold up the Leaning Tower of Pisa. More frames clung to the walls like beetles. The wallpaper, peeling at the edges in places, was patterned in green and blue stripes, colour-matched to the pencil pleat curtains and wall-to-wall shag carpet.

A Barry Manilow record sleeve (*Manilow Magic*, its cover scuffed with use) was leaning against the brick fireplace, Barry gazing wistfully at the lounge furniture, which had been pushed to the back of the room to allow space for four large white folding tables, on which were spread computers, monitors, files, folders, binoculars and various-sized black, white and stainless-steel boxes. Cameras in each of the windows pointed down the hill towards a distant farmhouse, which from here appeared no bigger than a grain of rice. It was just after nine and the sun had set long ago, but the clouds were lit bright by the moon, which made it possible to see, in addition to the farmhouse, a barn and what appeared to be a small village of huts. All perfectly normal – if this was a productive farm with labourers and animals to house. But none of those were evident, or expected.

Henri picked up the wedding photo. She guessed the picture was thirty or forty years old, but the joy of the bride and groom was frozen in time and oozed through the glass. Henrietta Appleby was a fifty-nine-year-old classical librarian, divorced eighteen years ago after her husband ran off with one of her junior assistants, and the sight of a happy couple always made her nostalgic and a little bit mad. The picture made her wonder where Norman was now. What was he doing? – and was he doing it with her twenty-three-year-old former assistant?

"Where did you send them?" she asked, waving the frame at Cleo Grieves.

Grieves was at the window, where she'd been for most of the past hour, staring at the tiny farmhouse. Every so often she would cross to a monitor and stare at a green night-vision version of the house, and then return moments later to the window. She didn't seem to hear Henri, or was too preoccupied to respond.

Henri returned her gaze to the photo. She could see her image reflected in the glass: long grey hair, twisted into a side braid; red-framed glasses with rectangular lenses; an average nose, thin maroon lips (her favourite shade), nice eyes (if you discount the crinkly crow's feet). Everyone always said how nice her eyes were: small and hazel and kind. Shame they hadn't seen what her husband was up to in the six months before he ran off with that man-thief Jenny Borutski!

Placing the frame face down, she turned to Sam Morgan, who was sitting at one of the folding tables listening into black, sound-blocking earphones. He was so intent on listening, it was like the rest of the room didn't exist. The table was laden with sound equipment, two laptops and scattered hand-written notes of what he'd heard to date.

"Appleby!" he yelled, leaping up so fast his chair fell back.

"Ooh!" Henri cried, rushing over. "Movement at the station!"

She righted his chair, then pulled up another close to a speaker. Morgan turned up the sound, Grieves joined them, and together they cocked their heads and listened. It sounded like two or more guttural voices were chanting in unison.

"If I'm not mistaken, it's a spell," murmured Henri, stroking her braid. "A summoning spell. They're calling something."

Morgan squinted at her. "What?"

She listened some more. "Something … dead."

Leaning close to Grieves, he whispered something in her ear. She nodded, grabbed her bag and left the room.

Henri raised her head. "Where's Cleo going?"

"Find out what it means," he replied, pointing to one of the laptops. "I need to know what those two are up to."

She frowned at his impudence. He seemed to think she was one of his lackeys. "I need to listen some more. It's a dialect I can't pin down."

"Well, hurry the hell up."

They listened. Before long a low rumble arose, and it quickly became evident it wasn't coming from the speakers. As the chanting continued, the rumble grew to a roar that shook the house for what felt like a minute, before receding to a dull murmur. The noise seemed to originate from above them, from the moonlit sky, but it sounded nothing like thunder. Meanwhile, the chanting went on, a monotonous drone that was almost soothing.

A yell sounded outside.

"What's that?" Morgan asked, getting up.

They went to the window and immediately spied a sickly green glow seeping from the farmhouse windows. Grieves was beneath them, on the driveway, staring in the same direction. She glanced at them, looked back at the farmhouse, then continued on to her Jeep.

Morgan collected two pairs of binoculars, handed one to Henri, and together they stared hard at the distant farm.

Henri was the first to discern what was happening. "It's leaving the building," she said. She was referring to the green glow, which appeared to be creeping up the side of the farmhouse.

"What in hell?" breathed Morgan, craning his neck forward. "What in hell are they up to?"

The glow advanced like a liquid dripping upwards. When it reached the roof, it continued rising into the night air.

Henri pulled the binoculars away from her eyes. "My guess," she said, "is they're up to no good."

THE MORGUE SMELT awful. The walls were the colour of old urine, and they were gouged and scuffed from countless encounters with trolleys, shoes and body parts. As expected in a regional hospital, the equipment was dated, the grey-and-white floor tiles scratched and broken.

The morgue often lay empty, but today there were three bodies on the trolleys. The three – an older man and woman, along with a middle-aged man with the face of a boy – were dressed in grey uniforms. They wore bands on their ankles that stated their names: Claude Barry; Lila Barry; Ormond Barry. The bodies arrived two hours ago, the police report recording the probable cause of death as double-murder-suicide: each had a single gunshot wound to the chest. The presiding theory was that the older man had gunned down his wife and son before turning the weapon on himself. There was a history of mental illness in the Barry family – everyone knew about it: social isolation; random threats of violence; the son's inappropriate staring at young girls whenever he was in Quorn. It appeared the father and husband had snapped following some never-to-be-known incident, and just like that, a longstanding local family had been erased from existence.

The morgue attendant gazed down at them, his straggly ginger hair falling in his eyes. He stroked the bloody moon symbol on Lila Barry's forehead, the same symbol that was etched into the forehead of the two men. In life, Mrs Barry had been an attractive woman in her early sixties, with a trim build and shoulder-length blonde hair, streaked with grey. Her son and husband, on the other hand, both had large, doughy bodies and receding hairlines.

"A shame we didn't meet in better circumstances," Kenny Snyder crooned, stroking her hair. "I do love me some tasty boiler every now and then, eh?" He glared at her dead husband. "You wouldn't have needed to stay with that old geezer if I was in your bed. No, missus. We'd have had ourselves a right old time, eh? Maybe I should have waited awhile before shooting you."

He was moving his caress down her cool cheek when the chanting began. It was almost a non-sound, coming from inside his head if anywhere – but he knew straight away what it was.

Stepping away from the table, he wrung his hands together, trembling with expectation as the chanting grew in volume until it filled the room.

"Come on, come on," he urged, leaning forward.

As if responding to his urging, the youngest of the three bodies twitched.

"Yee-aah!" yelled Kenny. "Done deal! Done deal!"

Standing with rounded shoulders, he watched in triumph as the corpses shook with life: his creations; the living proof of his burgeoning talents. One by one the Barrys turned their heads and stared at him with glazed, half-closed eyes, waiting for his command.

Tripping to the door, he propped it open with a metal chair, then returned to the bodies.

"This way," he ordered, waving them along.

The three Barrys moved with difficulty, flapping their arms and jerking their legs and bodies with increasing violence as they tried to respond. They weren't able to sit up, but eventually they rolled off their trolleys and fell to the floor in a succession of heavy thumps.

With no apparent pain or panic, they pushed themselves to their feet.

"Ooh yeah! Ooh yeah! Who's da bomb? Who's da bomb?" Kenny chanted, punching the air.

The Barrys stared dully at him, awaiting instructions.

He stopped his song. "Alright then, this way," he said, and led them towards the open door.

The corridor was deserted. Kenny was the only one on duty tonight and visitors to the morgue were rare. All he had to do was get them to the exit where his truck waited, and then it was up to the three born-again bloodhounds to do their work and find Wilfred's book.

But as he waved the bodies along, a bell dinged, and Kenny turned to see the lift opening. Frozen, he watched in horror as a trolley emerged, then a body under a sheet, then a hospital orderly pushing the trolley into the corridor.

"Oh shit," he swore, and reached into his pocket for his garrotte.

As the trolley turned towards them, the three Barrys became animated, grunting and jerking their bodies, excited by the sound or smell of the new arrivals.

"No, no, no!" Kenny screeched as they spun around and staggered after the orderly. "Stop! I command you to stop!"

But the dead Barrys were now operating by instinct. Ignoring Kenny's shouts, they mobbed the terrified young man, pulling him to the ground and tearing the flesh from his face and arms with their teeth and fingernails. He screamed and grunted and flopped about on the tiled floor, while Kenny yelled and the family of zombies bit and tore and chewed and swallowed and sucked up the blood which now seemed to be everywhere.

Kenny banged his fist on the wall. "No! No!" he yelled. "Get off him!" He shook his fists at them. "Obey me, you poxy minions! Obey! Obey! You need to obey!"

They were too busy eating to take any notice – if indeed they even understood English anymore.

Kenny pulled his phone from his pocket and with shaky hands dialled Wilfred.

"Mr Waite!" he cried as soon as the voicemail message kicked in. "Flamin' 'eck, you gotta help me! The zoms are running amok! They won't –"

At this point, he glanced up to see the last of the family entering the lift. It dinged as it closed.

"Oh shit!"

The mutilated orderly sat up and stared at him.

"Oh – shit!"

MORGAN HUNG UP and turned to Henri. His face was white.

"Get your things. We gotta go. Something's happening at the hospital."

45

Attack of the zombies

A T LAST KENNY regained control over the three blood-covered Barrys and herded them down the back stairs and into his truck. He'd also attracted two hangers-on: a doctor and a nurse, who appeared to have been caught up in the power of the spell. They followed him down the stairs and climbed into the truck behind the others.

"What the heck," shrugged Kenny, smiling at the muscle-bound doctor and thirty-something nurse milling around with the Barrys. "Let's go have ourselves a knees-up."

Shutting and locking the doors, he went around, climbed into the truck, drove out of the hospital parking lot, turned right, and started towards the Gates' house. Wilfred believed the boys would be stupid to hide the Necronomicon there – the most obvious place imaginable – which made it the logical place to start. It soon became clear he was right. The closer the truck got to the Gates' place, the more furiously the Barrys threw themselves against the grate behind Kenny's seat, pushing him to go faster.

"Hold your horses!" he called out, thumping the grate. "We don't wanna draw any attention, do we?"

KANE CLIMBED THE ladder and jumped into the treehouse. Kneeling, he placed his flashlight on the floor and pulled open the door of the secret compartment.

"I moved it here when Dylan was in the hospital," he explained as Arika came up behind him. "He didn't know anything about this place. I made it when he was away, to hide my stash of …"

Grinning awkwardly, he picked up the flashlight and pointed it at the compartment. There lay Wilfred's black leather bag from the farmhouse.

"See? If Dylan was working with Simon, he would have taken it before I moved it. I mean, he was the one who hid it. From Simon. What that NSO guy said is madness."

Arika was stumped too. "He definitely said Dylan and Simon were working together."

"Maybe they were seen somewhere and it was misinterpreted. Maybe … the professor ambushed him to try and get him to hand over the book."

"Agent Morgan said they were both at the farmhouse."

Kane refused to believe that. After their stand-off last week, it would be a turnaround of epic proportions if Dylan and the professor were now best buddies. Then again, Dylan had steadfastly refused to stop working with Wilfred in the beginning, so who's to say the professor hadn't simply convinced him they could pick up where Wilfred left off? How much did he really know about his brother? Until recently, they were little more than strangers – they hadn't even liked each other.

"Why would Dylan hide the book, refuse to give it to Simon, then work with him two days later?" No matter how many times he said it out loud, it still didn't make sense.

"The NSO might have Dylan mixed up with someone else," Arika suggested, though he could see she didn't believe that. "When did you last see him?"

"This morning."

"How was he?"

Kane shrugged. "Fine. I suppose. I didn't really notice."

She gave him a look that reminded him of the looks his father used to give him. "You haven't asked him about Simon?"

"I thought I'd wait till you got here. He'd just deny it if I asked out of the blue. You haven't said anything to Simon?"

"I haven't heard from him since I told him you wouldn't give me the book. If what Agent Morgan said is true, he's probably at the farmhouse right now."

"With Dylan, you think?"

It was her turn to shrug. "Has he been home much?"

Kane screwed up his face. "Kind of. He's taken up his art work again.

Sounded like a healthy thing to do, considering. I've been at work the past two days, so I don't really know about his comings and goings. Hey, you don't think him and Simon are just doing artsy stuff?" He dismissed the thought as soon as the words had finished leaving his mouth. Which put them back at square one. "You're probably right: they've mixed him up with somebody else. Let's ask him when he gets home."

"Do you know when that'll be?"

He didn't. Dylan had gone back to being his quiet, reclusive self, and Kane had moved on with his own life. They were reverting to their pre-Waite relationship, where they went about their lives in parallel dimensions.

He glanced at his watch. "What time is it? – twenty past nine. He mightn't be home for hours." He looked at her. "What do you feel like doing? A movie or something? There's not much else to do on a Tuesday night in Quorn."

"Here, let's have a look at the book." Arika lifted out the bag. Removing the Necronomicon, she opened it on the wooden floorboards.

"I'm not sure this is a good idea," said Kane. But he wasn't about to issue any more directives. If Arika thought looking through the book could help settle whatever was happening with Dylan, he was prepared to go with her judgement.

They both stared at an illustration of a splayed man, his skin peeled away from his body and pegged to the dirt with wooden stakes. Slug-like creatures were feasting on his torso, and a Punch-looking man with a long nose and big chin appeared to be collecting them and placing them in a wicker basket. The way the torchlight played on the parchment made it appear like the slugs were moving.

Arika turned the page. The left side was crammed with ancient text, curves, lines and dots, all written in brown ink. The right side had a detailed illustration of five corpses hanging upside down, their flesh being sliced away by an ogre wearing a butcher's apron.

Closing the book, Arika stared down at the horned devil on the cover. In the reflected light of the torch, her face looked a little grey.

"I think I've seen enough for now."

Kane couldn't help himself. "Still say it's a classic?"

"I don't know what to do about all this," she admitted, sitting back. "My answers were about Simon. And now … I've got no idea. I don't know who to trust."

Kane wanted to say, "You can trust me," but he knew that was the kind of thing an untrustworthy person might say. It was more important to let his actions speak for him.

"Let's put it back," he suggested. "This is as good a hiding place as any. While Dylan's safe and no maniac has this book, we don't have to make a decision. Let's play it by ear."

She climbed to her feet. "You got anything to drink in the house?"

"Should be cola in the fridge."

"I was thinking of something a bit stronger."

He raised his eyebrows. "Beer? I think … if Dylan hasn't drunk it all."

"Stronger?"

He laughed. "There's Scotch in the sideboard in the dining room. Why don't you go pour? I'll be right down."

CLEO GRIEVES RAN down the corridor, gun raised, past rooms and doorways where patients, nurses, doctors, hospital workers and family members stood in shock or paced the floor in silent panic.

The male nurse running with her pointed at a closed door opposite the lift. He looked like the living dead himself, his face ashen, eyes glazed, lips grey. "They're in there," he hissed, gripping her arm.

Edging up to the door, Grieves peered through the window and spied a young woman wearing a bloodied hospital gown hunched over a man in a bed. The back of her gown had been torn, revealing a gash in her back through which Grieves could see part of her spine and several rib bones. She was chewing on the man's shoulder. The sheets were wet with blood, droplets splashing to the floor, joining a growing red puddle around her feet.

As Grieves stared in horror, a half-eaten face slammed against the window. Leaping away in fright, she lifted her gun and in the same motion kicked open the door. The impact threw the body off balance, and it fell back with arms in the air and dropped heavily to the floor.

Grieves could see now it was an elderly woman. As she rolled over and scrambled to get up, Grieves trained the gun on her head. The woman was wearing a turquoise flowered frock with a ruffled collar – bloodied and torn, but quite clearly the type of dress a grandmother would wear. She had on only one shoe; the other was lying under the bed, next to a small gold wristwatch with a broken band.

Grieves stood watching as the woman struggled to get up, slamming her hands against the floor, slipping and sliding in the smeared blood. She was having trouble getting to her feet, mostly because chunks of muscle in her arms had been eaten away.

"Don't be fooled," Henri Appleby had told her. "No matter how much it appears human, once it's been bitten, it's dead. There's no pitying it and there's no bringing it back. Shoot it in the head. Or chop it off. Most importantly, don't let it bite you, and don't let it escape to bite someone else." It was weird hearing the words coming from the mouth of a mousy, maternal-looking librarian – almost laughable at the time, but now it told Grieves the awful truth about what she needed to do next.

Stepping closer, she placed the muzzle against the woman's temple.

"She's dead; she's dead," she reminded herself, frowning at the denuded arms, trying hard to screen out the curly grey hair and turquoise frock. "She's never coming back."

With one last look at the hole in the old woman's face, she turned her head away, grimaced, and pulled the trigger.

The noise was deafening, the impact spinning the woman's body along the floor. Blood and brain matter spattered across the room.

"Holy crap," muttered Grieves, going over and kneeling beside her. She made the sign of the cross, even though she wasn't religious. Up close, the woman looked like Liv's grandmother, with the obvious difference that Liv's grandmother didn't have half her head missing. Still, she was someone's grandmother – possibly that someone was the young woman gnawing on the patient in the bed.

"Oi!" she cried, getting to her feet.

The woman ignored her.

Picking up an overturned chair, Grieves threw it at her, then quickly raised her gun. The woman growled like an animal warning off scavengers, but was too intent on her meal to turn around.

"Bloody heck," swore Grieves, and went up and poked her in the back of the head with her gun.

This time she spun around, lips pulled back from her bloodied teeth. Grieves backed away. Sensing fresh meat, the dead woman lifted her arms and staggered towards her like a lover eager for a hug.

Lifting the gun, Grieves shot her in the middle of the forehead.

A scream echoed down the hall, sparking other screams and yelps of horror.

The bloodied man in the bed jerked, sat up, and swung his legs off the bed.

"C'mon Sam," murmured Grieves, aiming the gun at a point between his eyebrows; "drive faster."

KENNY PARKED THE truck close to the Gates' house, jumped out, went round to the back, unlocked and pulled open the doors. The three Barrys were waiting eagerly and emerged together, walking into air and tumbling to the road face-first.

Pushing themselves up, they clambered to their feet and stumbled forward, blood dripping from their mashed faces. The two hangers-on followed suit, but it was clear they didn't have the same radar for the Gates' house. For a time they walked around in circles, until Kenny steered them towards the Barrys, and they hurried on after them.

Kenny stayed close, phone at the ready in case anything else went wrong. Back in the wards, the Barrys had created havoc, running around biting people like hungry kids at a smorgasbord. Eventually Kenny managed to get through to Wilfred, who reminded him of the right way to pronounce the subservience sub-spell, and he was at last able to herd the trio towards the back stairs and get back on track with his mission. Fortunately, hospital security was busy dealing with the mayhem upstairs, so the unplanned detour had, in a lucky twist of fate, aided their escape.

At first all five zombies kept to the roadside trail, walking single file, but as they neared the Gates' house, a curious thing happened. The three

Barrys separated. Ormond went towards the front door, Claude veered to the left, Lila went off to the right. The doctor and nurse followed Ormond, the slowest and biggest of the targets.

"Triangulation," Kenny smiled, recalling Simon's description of how the spell worked. "They find it like a mobile phone." Waving his own phone in the air, he cried, "Minted! Kenny S, you're a certified genius!"

OPENING THE FRIDGE, Arika bent to inspect the contents. It contained a surprising amount of fruit and vegetables – she expected to see it filled with pizza boxes and beer. Good on you, Kane, she thought with a smile of respect. A lot of guys Kane's age would have gone to pieces after losing both parents so tragically, but Kane continued to impress her with his strength of mind and character.

Taking out the half-empty bottle of Coke, she carried it across the kitchen, past a leering face in the corner of the window. It was Kenny Snyder, hidden in the darkness.

In the dining room, Arika opened the doors of the sideboard and located the bottle of Scotch, alongside six glass tumblers. The sideboard was also home to empty bottles of vodka and gin. It seemed Dylan wasn't averse to spirits; he just wasn't a fan of Scotch.

Collecting the bottle and two glasses, she went back through the kitchen. Halfway across the floor, a scuffling noise outside the window made her stop in her tracks. Placing the glasses and bottle on the table next to the Coke, she crossed to the window, put her hand against the glass and peered into the night. The window opened to the side of the house – it was the same window she peered through the first time she visited. There was no one there.

She stared a few more seconds while her eyes adjusted to the darkness, then shrugged, turned, and left the kitchen carrying the Scotch and two glasses, the bottle of Coke wedged under her arm.

"Kane!" she called out. "I thought you were –" and then her eyes took in the alarming scene at the treehouse. Everything dropped to the grass.

Standing around the tree were a nurse, a doctor and a stocky old man in a grey uniform. Near the top of the ladder was a thin woman with blonde hair, and not far behind her, a plump younger man, both also decked out in grey uniforms. Arika recognised the uniforms straight away – they were the ones they saw stacked in a room in the catacombs, the ones Kane said Wilfred's army of the dead were wearing. She also knew as soon as she saw their blood-stained clothes and hands and faces that these were no ordinary visitors.

"Kane!"

Up in the treehouse, Kane was turning the pages of the Necronomicon. Despite his earlier disgust, he'd decided to take another look at the seven-pointed star with the eye. He had a sudden notion that perhaps it was more than just a means for reversing the body swap spell; perhaps it was a general wish-fulfilment spell, a funnel for all the Necronomicon's power. With nothing to lose, he was intending to place his hand on the page and wish away all the mad wizards, resurrected dead things and steam-punk zombies, and return his and Dylan's life to normal.

Before he got there, he passed page after page of scary monsters and nauseating gore. Some of the illustrations were so detailed and bizarre, he began to think the monsters must have sat and posed for the artist, or at least been viewed in real life. The more he saw, the greater became his fascination. Disgust receded and was replaced by a burning need to see what the next page would bring. He was starting to appreciate there was a world out there he'd never suspected existed, with dimensions that excited him and energised him and made his mind boggle. This world – this universe – was bigger than himself and Dylan and Arika – bigger than the family he'd lost – bigger than the sum total of his life to date – his life to come – of all their lives. With each turn of the page, the feeling grew that he was missing out on something, that a power beyond comprehension was within his grasp, the opportunity to be greater than he was, to realise his potential in ways he could never before have imagined. Arika was right: they needed to mine the Necronomicon for its spells and secrets. They needed to release its power on an unworthy world and surf that power to greatness and –

Her voice broke the book's spell.

Kane glanced up, feeling a nausea akin to motion sickness. As his head cleared, he raised his flashlight and saw what appeared to be a thin woman with greying blonde hair and a blood-smeared face staring at him from the top of the ladder. Her skin was pale, her eyes red, and there appeared to be the symbol of a half moon inscribed in her forehead.

"Kane!" he heard Arika yell. "Zombies! They're climbing the ladder!"

He gaped at the woman, trying to process her image, and his paralysis lasted long enough for her to finish her climb to the top rung and launch herself at him.

Scuttling away like a crab, he watched her fly towards him, watched as she fell flat on her face, her head landing in the secret compartment. Before she could recover, he scrambled back and slammed the trapdoor hard, wincing at the sickening crunch.

Picking up the flashlight, he pointed it at the ladder. A bloodied man had taken the woman's place, a soft, chinless man, with the same pallor as the woman, the same red eyes, the same half moon carved into his forehead.

Dropping the flashlight, Kane ran towards him, swung on a tree branch, and booted him in the face.

The man threw out his arms and fell backwards. Two seconds later, Kane heard an ugly crack.

He peered over the wall of the treehouse to find him lying across the back of the wrought-iron park bench, his body bent at an impossible angle. Despite the fact the man's spine was clearly snapped, his arms and legs thrashed as he tried to get up.

Behind Kane, the dead woman shuffled to her knees, threw off the trapdoor, climbed to her feet.

He spun around in time to catch sight of her grabbing the Necronomicon. She tucked it under her arm, and with surprising energy, leapt over the wall and dropped like a lead weight to the ground.

He ran over and looked down to find her pushing herself up from the grass. Then he saw Arika running from the house with her gun. She spotted the zombie and stopped. The dead woman's skull was crushed, her right shoulder dislocated from the fall, but none of that was stopping her. As she stooped to pick up the Necronomicon with her one working arm, Arika lifted her pistol and shot, blowing the side of her face away.

That didn't stop her either. Holding the Necronomicon against her body, she stumbled towards the house, jerkily, like a broken marionette.

Arika lifted the gun again, but the stocky bald man had her in his sights and was barrelling towards her.

Holding the gun with both hands, she shot the dead man in the half moon, a perfect shot, and watched as he crumpled to the ground. When she was sure he wasn't getting up again, she turned back to the woman. But she'd escaped down the side of the house and was nowhere in sight.

Kane was leaning over the wall of the treehouse. "Are you okay?" he called down.

"There's more!" she yelled. "At least three!" Then she took off after the woman.

Kane whirled around. The first thing he noticed about the man jumping into the treehouse was his blue scrubs; the next thing was his huge muscles. The doctor was taller than Kane and had broad, gym-built shoulders and thick legs. He didn't have any obvious injuries slowing him down, and Kane realised with a sinking feeling that this one wouldn't be as easy to deal with as the old woman and her flabby accomplice.

When the doctor lunged at him, he made a spot decision to retreat. Springing into the air, he grabbed a tree branch and swung his legs up, just in time to avoid the dead man's grab for his ankles.

That's when a brown-haired woman in a nurse's uniform appeared at the top of the ladder.

"How many of you buggers are there?" Kane yelled at them.

Arika was now at the bottom of the ladder. She'd arrived in the front yard in time to see the dead woman being dragged into the cab of a parked truck. As the truck pulled away, she was torn between giving chase and going back to help Kane, but when she remembered her keys were inside the house, the decision was taken from her. The truck would be long gone by the time she managed to retrieve the keys and get back to her car. Recovering the Necronomicon would have to wait.

She peered up at the dead nurse, who was struggling to finish her climb into the treehouse.

"Hey!'

Hearing her voice, the woman glanced around in confusion, looked down, saw her, snarled like a tiger, then started to descend.

Arika stepped back for a clearer shot. Raising her gun, aiming carefully, she squeezed the trigger, and once again her aim was spot on. Blood exploded from the zombie's head, she released the ladder and dropped with a thud to the ground.

Racing around the tree, Arika craned her neck to see how Kane was doing.

Up in the tree, he was watching the muscle-bound doctor climb towards him. He knew dead men had no fear, and it was clear this one would keep on climbing until there was no more tree to climb. Then there would be nothing to stop him sinking his teeth into Kane's ankle. He bit his lip. There was only one thing to do: go down and face the zombie head on.

He started moving down, his fear escalating as each step brought him closer to the man's snapping mouth.

When he was just out of reach, he braced his back against the trunk, raised both legs, and booted the man in the face with all his strength.

The doctor's head snapped back, but miraculously he held on. The kick only seemed to make him hungrier for Kane's leg. He resumed his climb, faster now, bloodied lips pulled away from his broken teeth.

Backing up to the next branch, Kane braced himself again. He waited until the doctor released his grip, then kicked hard. This time his boots hit the mark; the man lost his hold, fell backwards and crashed through branches, landing with a ground-shaking thud next to Arika.

He grabbed her ankle.

Arika yelped in surprise and tried to pull away, but the dead man's grip was too strong, and she fell to the ground, reaching out in vain as her pistol bounced away.

The dead doctor started pulling himself towards her, his broken mouth chomping in anticipation.

Arika stretched a hand towards her weapon, but it was out of reach. Digging her fingers in the grass, she dragged herself closer. With each pull, the zombie advanced too, his grip like a vice on her ankle. Just as her fingertips touched the gun barrel, the terror-filled thought came to her that she might be out of bullets. How many shots had she fired? The count paralysed her for a moment, but as the doctor's snapping teeth made contact with her shoe, she lunged at the gun, grabbed the grip, swung it around, and shot the rest of his teeth out.

His brains splattered over Kane's legs.

"Oh shit! Sorry! What a mess!" She looked behind him. "Hey, another one!"

Kane turned to find that the zombie with the broken back had succeeded in pushing himself off the park bench and was now dragging his body across the grass towards them. The dragging action had pulled his pants down and they were tangled around his ankles.

It was such a weird sight, Kane couldn't help but laugh. He stepped closer and bent over the man, staying well out of reach of his groping hands.

"You want a piece of me, do you? A nice juicy calf to chew on, maybe? Mmm, yum; you'd like that, wouldn't you?" He turned to Arika, who was sitting on the grass with legs crossed. "What is it with these things?"

She pointed her gun at it and pulled the trigger. The barrel clicked. She was out of bullets.

"Maybe we should save this joker for that agent friend of yours," Kane suggested. "He might wanna dissect it or something."

Getting to her feet, Arika reached into her pocket, and with a trembling hand pulled out a new magazine. "I'm not taking any chances," she said, and reloaded her pistol.

Kane glanced around. "Where's the book?"

46

Battle zone

B Y THE TIME Sam Morgan and Henri Appleby arrived at the hospital, the local police had cordoned off the building and secured all the exits. The building and car park were lit up with floodlights that turned night to day, the heat from the lights making it feel like a balmy summer evening.

They had a few short words with Chief Ames before being escorted to the emergency department doors, where Officer Pederson was waiting.

"What you two planning to do in there?" Len asked as he handed them all-area security passes.

Henri held up a plastic shopping bag.

"Bag of magic tricks," Morgan explained.

"Well I hope that includes a magic pop gun and magic hand grenades."

Morgan patted the assault rifle slung over his shoulder.

"We don't need weapons," remarked Henri, "or even to get close; just within earshot so the infected hear the spell."

"A spell?" Len looked dubious. "Like a hocus-pocus, toil-and-trouble kinda spell?"

"More like a kick-arse Gandalf spell," Morgan said.

"Not that kind of spell at all," lectured Henri, who was clearly taking this more seriously than the two men.

"Well, um, good luck," said Len, unlocking the door. "I hope there's no more big buggers like Hugo Petrusch in there. I'd venture it takes more than a spell to stop one of those. More like a bazooka. Remember, he went halfway down the road after copping a bullet in the face."

"Thanks for the pep talk, Len," said Morgan.

"Don't mention it. Part of the friendly service."

"Will you be here to let us out if anything goes wrong?" Henri asked him.

Len looked to Morgan.

"Come on, Henri," he replied. "Nothing will go wrong," and he turned and led Henri through the hospital doors.

The doors closed quietly behind them. Inside the waiting room were three rows of blue chairs in the centre of the room and lime green chairs around the perimeter. There was no one there. After checking out the reception and triage station, they crossed to the doors to the emergency room and peered through the narrow windows. There didn't seem to be anyone there either, but the emergency room opened into other rooms and corridors, which presented the threat of hidden dangers, dangers that might come flying from any and all directions.

Swiping his card, Morgan leaned his body against the right-hand door, poked his head inside and peered around.

"Can't see anything from here," he whispered to Henri.

Pulling the rifle off his shoulder, he entered the room. Henri followed close behind.

One by one, they looked in each of the cubicles. Nothing. Next, they went down the branching corridors and checked out the treatment rooms. Morgan had been briefed that this side of the hospital had been quarantined and evacuated before the epidemic spread, but after Henri's warning about the repercussions of a single scratch from a dead person, he wasn't prepared to take any chances. Despite the assurances provided by Ames, every time he opened a door or pulled back a curtain, he braced for the surprise of a dead-eyed freak bursting out and sinking its teeth in him.

Fortunately, none of this happened. Once the emergency department was secured, they paused at the door to the wards to go one last time over their plan. Morgan was confident he had the reflexes and firepower to put down any physical threat, but Henri was a weak spot, an ageing librarian whose only merit in this situation – her ability to cast a spell – wouldn't save them from an ambush. They needed to be clear and tight on their next steps.

"We find a room within earshot of those things, barricade ourselves in, and cast the spell," he said. "Got it?"

"Got it."

"What are you going to do?"

"What do you mean?"

"Repeat the plan."

She smiled. "Do you think it's that complex a plan? It seems quite straightforward to me."

"Repeat the plan."

Her smile grew wider. "Is that really how it's done in your world? Fascinating."

"Repeat the damn plan."

She pulled a face. "We find a room; you barricade; I get started on the spell."

Without another word, he unlocked and opened the door to the wards.

Entering the corridor, tiptoeing along the tiles, they approached a T-junction. To the left, a few doors down, was a small band of blood-spattered zombies huddled over a mass of red and white on the floor.

Morgan held Henri back with one arm. He pointed to the right, towards a nurses' station, the door of which was open, and nodded a question. She nodded back, and they started towards it.

Before they got there, one of the zombies raised its head, saw them, and immediately started scrambling on all fours towards them. Its pursuit was noticed by the others, and one by one they leapt up and took off after them. Running and slipping and crawling, they came hurtling down the corridor.

Morgan pushed Henri into the nurses' station and slammed the door shut. As the first zombie arrived, he upended a bookcase, pushed it against the door, then dragged a table in front of that.

"Why are there so many of them?" he asked Henri as the pack descended on the nurses' station. "I thought you said the spread would be slow."

"That was our modelling," she said, eyes agog as they banged on the glass with their hands and heads and shoulders. "The magic was supposed to have diluted itself out, but it seems to have kept on going and going."

"That doesn't sound good."

"They must have amped up the power in the spell. What in heaven's name could they be playing at?"

As they watched, more blood-soaked bodies appeared from the wards, attracted by the commotion.

"Remember the plan?"

"Oh!" piped Henri, lifting the shopping bag. "Plan. Yes." Crouching, she upended the bag on the floor. "I'm not sure how long this thing takes."

"How long does it usually take?"

She shrugged.

The gesture concerned him. His people never shrugged. "How many times have you done this?"

"About a dozen." She lined up on the floor a notebook, four small paper bags, three black candles, a mirror, a bunch of chicken feet wrapped with twine and a large dead rabbit. "At our annual retreat. Last year and the year before that."

"With live zombies?"

"In … role play games."

"Role play? Like Dungeons and Dragons?"

"No. Not like Dungeons and Dragons. Like an ancient order practising its rituals."

"But not practising them on live zombies?"

She looked at him, said, "How easy do you think it is to find live zombies?" then went back to her spell-making. "Do *you* remember the plan?"

"I thought you were a world expert on the supernatural?"

"I work in a library. With books and the internet. This kind of thing doesn't tend to happen in libraries."

"It doesn't tend to happen in hospitals either, but here we are: stuck in a fishbowl with the living dead about to eat our brains for supper. Sheesh, we should've paid more and gone for an expert."

Henri's back straightened. "How rude! Do you talk to all your underlings like this? I'll have you know, there hasn't been a zombie outbreak in living memory. I'm as much an expert as you'll find."

"So tell me, Ms Expert, what happens if they get in here before your damn spell works?"

"They won't, because that's *your* part of the plan."

"You didn't say there would be this many."

"What difference does that make? I told you what to do. You shoot them. In the head. Surely you brought more than twenty-five rounds?"

"Okay, okay." Despite himself, Morgan was impressed by Henri's bravado. It wasn't often people spoke back to him, and she was pretty good at it. "Let's get on with it." He checked out the paraphernalia on the floor. "What happens with all that?"

"First I light the candles." She lit the first one.

"Then?"

She glanced up in annoyance. "Then I stuff the rabbit."

"Don't tell me: then it goes in the oven for forty-five minutes?"

He watched her light the second candle, then glanced up at the window. It was cracked in several places. Though he guessed the glass was tempered, he knew it wouldn't stand up to much more of a beating from the horde of dead things that were hellbent on smashing it and getting in.

"Can't you cast another spell … a faster one to, like, make them disappear?"

"You sound like Officer Pederson. I'm not a witch."

"How about something to incapacitate them? – slow them down. A slumber spell."

She looked up at the window and her face froze – not with fear; it was more like intense fascination. "Not that I know of. Let me check." She took out her phone.

"Is that what we're paying you for? To google the answer?"

"It's what librarians do. We can't be expected to know everything off the top of our heads."

Going up to the window, Morgan took out his own phone. He rang Chief Ames.

"Anything happening out there?"

Ames reported everything was quiet. The cordon remained intact and nothing had tried to escape the hospital – yet. "But some kind of SWAT team just arrived. I'm on my way to see what they got planned."

"That's great. Look: there's dozens of those deadheads in here. We haven't managed to start the spell yet, so for the time being the only way to stop them is to shoot them in the brain … No, it's irreversible according to Ms Expert here. Shot in the head … Right. I gotta go. Let me know when you find out who those guys are. Mine won't have made it yet. They're en route; ETA" – he glanced at his watch – "ten minutes. And look, Chief, whatever you do, don't let a single one of those things escape or bite anyone, or this town is doomed!"

He hung up and watched as a dead biker with an orange beard and multicoloured tattoos on his neck lifted his bowling-ball-sized head and rammed it against the window. This time the glass fractured and bent inwards. The others around him appeared to recognise this was their opportunity, and they began grabbing feverishly at the glass, poking their fingers into the cracks and tearing it away. Blood poured from their hands and rolled down the window in streamlets.

"Get under the desk!" yelled Morgan.

Grabbing a chair, he used it to push the zombies back from the hole in the window.

"Don't let them bite you!" cried Henri as she opened one of the paper bags. She poured the dirt into a cavity in the dead rabbit's chest. "If they bite you, I'm done for!"

Morgan's phone vibrated in his pocket. "Henri, can you get that? I can't reach."

"I need to finish the spell."

"It might be important."

"If it's important they'll leave a message. I need to finish the spell."

The phone fell silent. Morgan leaned all his weight on the chair, feeling the mass of the zombies pushing him back. They were making a weird clicking noise, more like a bunch of insects than former humans.

His phone buzzed again. The next moment, he was taken aback by the sight of five armed officers in helmets and dark blue uniforms bursting into the corridor. The leader raced towards them, aimed his assault rifle at the biker zombie and shot it in the side of the head. The other soldiers quickly followed and went after the others.

Henri was crouched under the desk, holding a pen in her fist like it was an attack knife. With her other hand, she was emptying a reddish herb from a paper bag into the rabbit's chest. Most of it was going on the floor. "Is that the cavalry, Sam? Are we saved?"

Above Henri, Morgan was using his body weight to push the chair against a middle-aged zombie in a brown suit, whose head and torso were inside the nurses' station, his pot belly jammed in the hole the others had torn in the glass.

Leaning down, Morgan watched Henri unwrap the twine from the chicken feet and use it to wrap them around the rabbit.

"Okay, we slowed 'em down for you. Now how's that spell coming?"

Minutes later, Morgan was standing in a lake of blood surveying a pile of dead zombies.

"Round up every last person in this hospital," he told the commanding officer, "and get them to intensive care. Shoot anyone who tries to leave. That's an order."

He went back to Henri. "Put those things in the bag and we'll do the spell in ICU, when everyone's in the same room. I'm not taking any chances with this. No one's leaving here without hearing the spell. And no one's going without a full body check and a pulse."

He glanced around. "Has anyone seen Grieves?"

"Who's Grieves?" asked the commanding officer.

"Cleo Grieves. My senior investigator. She was first on scene."

"Don't know her, sorry mate."

Morgan pulled out his phone and dialled her number. She didn't pick up, but he heard a phone ringing down the corridor to his right. Phone to his ear, he started walking towards it.

The ring was coming from the very last room. Pushing open the door, Morgan entered and found Grieves with her back to him, standing beside a bed. The man on the bed was dead, the skin torn away from his face, a dark cave where his eyes and nose used to be. A pool of blood, mixed with grey matter, had collected on the floor on and around Grieves' boots.

"Cleo, there you are. Why didn't you answer?" He glanced again at the dead man. "Who's that? Oh no, don't tell me it's someone you know?"

At the sound of his voice, Grieves turned her head and growled from the back of her throat. She was holding onto something pinkish-grey and red, and as Morgan watched, she pressed it against her mouth and chewed noisily. He could see now that the front of her suit was soaked with blood.

"Cleo … Oh no … Oh, Jesus Christ, no."

As tears filled his eyes, a wild thought entered his mind. He could save her. A doctor – a witch doctor maybe – could find a cure, and she'd be alright. He couldn't see any injuries. Grieves was extremely resourceful; what if she only suffered an incidental bite? – a scratch? She could be saved. Maybe even cured by Henri's rabbit-and-chicken-feet spell.

But Henri's words rang in his ears: a bite was fatal; the magic took over; there was no coming back from it.

Meanwhile, Grieves was happily eating the brains. She didn't appear threatened by him. Turning away, she dipped her fingers into the dead man's skull and brought them to her mouth.

Morgan stepped closer. He lifted his gun, put the barrel close to the back of her head, steeled himself to do what needed to be done.

"Don't you worry, Cleo. Your hips are not fat."

His finger tightened on the trigger. He held it there. Pressed some more. Stood with arm trembling. Felt like he was about to throw up. Inched the gun closer.

Grieves kept chewing.

He lowered the gun.

"Damn you, Henri," he swore under his breath. "Damn you to hell."

He raised the gun again, but by this time he knew he wasn't going to shoot. He'd let hope slip through a crack in his common sense, and if he went ahead now – if he did the unspeakable and shot his best friend – he would forever feel like a murderer.

Putting the gun away, Morgan took out his handcuffs and fixed one end to a rail on the wall. Then, in a single motion, he pulled down Grieves' wrist and snapped on the other. The brains slipped through her fingers and fell with a plop to the bloody floor, and she turned on him in a rage, snapping and snarling and pulling savagely at the cuffs.

Morgan leapt out of reach. As voices approached behind him, voices that might as well have been speaking in a foreign language, he stood watching her, watching the alien thing that resembled his friend, waiting for his reason to return and tell him what the hell to do next.

47

Homecoming

KANE TURNED HIS gaze from the road to Arika. She was sitting on the edge of the sofa, cleaning her gun with one of his father's beige chequered handkerchiefs. Now the danger had passed, she was uncharacteristically quiet. Perhaps she was reflecting how she shot several people in the head tonight. Zombies or not, they still bled.

"Doesn't look like any more are coming." He took another peek outside. "Funny no police have come. Surely the neighbours must have heard the gun shots."

She rubbed the barrel hard, not looking at him.

"Maybe I should go talk to them; blame it on the TV or rabbit hunters or something."

"We should lock up and leave. Before they get here. Denial is the best policy, at least till we get the NSO out here."

He watched her cleaning the gun. "Where did you get that thing anyway?"

She laid it aside. "Simon."

Kane raised his eyebrows.

"He was worried about me – living alone in Northside with all the dealers and hookers."

"And now he's sending zombies after you. That guy is seriously stuffed."

"That wasn't Simon."

"It wasn't Waite,' he huffed. "You think it was Dylan?"

"No." She picked up the gun and began cleaning it again. "I think – Waite had friends … acolytes. They're taking up where he left off."

Kane was having trouble believing there were crazies out there as reckless and homicidal as Wilfred. You don't send a bunch of zombies to someone's house without expecting murder and mayhem, and you need a special kind of sociopathy – the Waite kind – to do something as rash and dangerous as that. But who knows how many creeps it took to keep those dungeons going? It wasn't beyond the realms of possibility that Wilfred's mania would rub off on some of them.

"I need to find Dylan," he said, "before this gets any worse. And we need to get away from Quorn, like, tomorrow. We –"

A thud sounded at the back door.

Arika rocketed off the sofa. Kane grabbed the baseball bat he'd left leaning against the wall.

The thud sounded again. There was silence for two seconds, and then began a dull knock that continued at a slow, regular pace. Boom – boom – boom – boom. Though it wasn't particularly loud, it felt like the whole house was shaking.

Kane crept towards the kitchen, long chills running down his spine with every thud. He was convinced it was more zombies sent to finish them off, but it could also be a crazy like that Snyder dude playing mind games with them, trying to unnerve them.

Boom – boom – boom – boom.

Arika touched his arm, startling him. "Kane, be careful. There could be a whole army of them out there."

He kept walking. Whatever was on the other side of the door needed dealing with – now – by whatever means necessary. Like with the muscle-bound doctor following him up the tree, there was no alternative but to tackle this head on.

Arika followed him into the kitchen, holding her gun in both hands. At least there was a fresh clip in there, which meant – what was it? – ten bullets? He glanced at the gun and she nodded, as if she'd read his mind.

He approached the door, hand outstretched, bat raised.

The knocking stopped.

He turned to Arika and their eyes locked.

Silence. The only sound was the ticking of the clock on the wall. It was almost worse than the knocking.

Stepping closer to the door, Kane took a firm grip on the handle. Part of him hoped that whatever it was, it had given up and gone away, but that would only mean it could come back later, maybe when they weren't as prepared, when they were asleep or too exhausted from lack of sleep to put up much of a fight. It was best to face whatever was out there, and get this over and done with.

"Ready?" he mouthed, nodding at Arika.

She blinked her reply and raised her gun to head height.

Kane put his foot against the door and opened it a crack. It was dark outside, but there was enough light to see that no one was there.

Heart pounding, he opened the door a little wider and squinted into the garden. As his eyes grew accustomed to the dark, a dread built inside him – almost a premonition – that monsters were preparing to race out of the shadows, descend from the sky and crawl out of the earth. He stood for a moment in two minds: should he take the offensive and go out in search of them, or shut the door and barricade the house until dawn, when hopefully the monsters would give up and return to their black pit of hell?

A gust of wind blew a foul odour into the kitchen, making Kane choke and clamp a hand over his mouth and nose. He glanced down. A brown lump was lying on the doorstep, leaning against the jamb; clearly the source of the stink. Opening the door wider, he leaned out and bent closer. The thing looked like a ventriloquist's dummy, small and shrunken, wearing an over-sized brown trench coat, woollen scarf and burgundy fedora hat.

As he watched, the shape moved, and one of the coat's arms stretched out. It was holding a page torn from a notepad.

He reached out and took the note. It was smudged and dirty, and it said in large, scrawly writing: 'Kane. Help me. Wilfred Waite has stolen my body.'

The world went black. Kane backed away, feeling dizziness fluttering in his head, acid churning in his stomach, vomit rising in his throat. He bumped into the kitchen table and kept backing away as it screeched across the floor.

"What is it?" Arika asked, lowering the gun.

The tiny figure waddled into the room, leaving a brown smudge on the lino in its wake. After a few paces, it collapsed. Its hat fell away, revealing the decaying face of Wilfred Waite.

AFTER MAKING DYLAN comfortable, Arika sat on the bed and watched as he drank iced coffee through a straw. He sucked it up greedily, and she realised he probably hadn't eaten in a while. When the sucking went on and on, she wondered: Can dead people die of starvation? Then: Is he dead or alive? After getting tangled up in these thoughts, she realised this was something they hadn't seen before: a living person in a dead body – a dead body that stank to high heaven.

When Dylan was finished, she took the glass off him, put it on the bedside table, and turned worriedly to the door.

After a while, she said, "I'll be back soon," and smiling at him, got up from the bed.

Downstairs, Kane was staring through a crack in the curtains. His head was down, his back bent, and he was standing at an uncomfortable angle. Sighing, he moved his weight from one hip to the other.

"Hey there," Arika called softly from the other side of the room.

He turned to her. "He okay?"

"As much as anyone can be in that situation. He drank some milk, so he's still functioning … still alive."

"How did he get like that?"

"It seems the immortality spell can transcend death." When Kane looked confused, she explained: "Waite did die that night, but his soul – or consciousness or whatever – survived. And somehow he was able to keep living inside the dead body."

"That's insane. It doesn't make logical sense."

"My guess is one of his henchmen found him in the basement and cast a spell to keep his body animated. Like a zombie, but with his consciousness intact."

"You're saying Dylan is a living zombie?"

"That's one way of looking at it." She shook her head. "I could understand a bit of what he said, Kane. He was locked in a dark room most of the time. He doesn't know how long he was there."

"That was – what? – three, four days ago."

"They kept him alive. They must have known if he died, it might pull Waite back and he'd die in that body."

His face lit up. "And Dylan would get his body back?"

She sat on the arm of the sofa. "I don't know. Possibly. But it's just as likely Dylan would be the one to die. Or maybe they'd both die. We just don't know."

"So we're in the same boat as Waite. We need to keep the dead body alive until we're sure."

"Until we can get Dylan back in his own body."

Kane turned back to the window. "So Waite has Dylan's body, and he's been conspiring with Orwell at the farm. Damnit! We should have known!" He wiped away the fog his breath had made on the glass. "How did Dylan get here? He's in no shape to walk."

"That's the interesting part. Snyder brought him here."

He spun around.

"He took him to the hospital, picked up those zombies, then drove them all here."

"I can't even … What was all that about?"

"Getting the book back."

"Or murdering us."

"Then why leave Dylan here?"

"Is that what he said?"

"Snyder left him on the kerb. Like some kind of special delivery."

"On the kerb?" He joined Arika on the sofa. "Is he playing some kind of game?'

"Mind game? Could be. Trying to distract us, keep us occupied with an invalid while him and Waite do God knows what."

"Probably finish the body swap spell."

Arika rubbed her eyes. "But giving us Dylan runs the risk we could do something to reverse the spell. He must have known we'd try even harder to get his body back when we saw him like this. We wouldn't sit here watching him wither away and die. We'd go after him. Whereas if they kept Dylan hidden, we wouldn't know what to do. Even if we went to the farm and kidnapped Waite and brought him back, what would we do with him if we didn't have Dylan as well? If I was them, I'd keep both Dylan and the book. They'd have everything; we'd have nothing."

Lost in thought, she didn't notice Kane had gone quiet. She glanced down at him and saw he had his face in his hands. He was breathing heavily, as if each breath required a herculean effort.

She laid a hand on his back. "Are you okay, Kane?"

He took a while to answer. "I've never felt so … helpless. So frustrated. And scared."

"It's a shock, I know."

He looked at her with wet eyes. "What can we do, Arika?"

She moved her hand to the back of his neck and gripped it tight. "Switch them back, of course."

He made a strange gurgling noise in his throat, then coughed and said, "He won't last much longer."

"So we better get started."

"He came to see me. He said this was happening. I told him he was imagining things."

"How could you have known Waite was still alive inside his dead body? That's crazy town."

"We're too late. He won. The evil bastard won."

She took her hand away. "We are not too late."

"We don't know where he is. We don't have the book. Dylan is falling to pieces before our eyes."

"We need to stop the decomposition. He could probably last a year or more, as long as that body stays in one piece."

"What if it doesn't? How long can he live inside a rotting corpse?"

Leaping up in a burst of violence, he returned to the window.

Arika watched his back as he strove to control his emotions. At the thought of the pain he was feeling – the awful realisation that the last of his family was about to die, in possibly the worst manner yet – her anger rose to boiling point.

"We will not let that runt win!" she announced, loud enough for Dylan to hear through the ceiling.

Getting up, she pulled Morgan's card from her pocket and tapped it on her palm. "Time for reinforcements."

MORGAN STORMED INTO the office, flicking on the light switch on the way past.

"No more waiting!" he bellowed at the empty room.

Henri was close behind, stepping into the office with arms raised. "Act in haste, Sam, repent at leisure."

Stopping at a bookcase, Morgan squeezed his forefinger and thumb hard against his chin, then swept his hand across the books on the middle shelf. They made a surprising amount of noise as they crashed to the floor.

"Whatever those mental cases are doing, I want it stopped … now!"

"Sam, we need more time."

He went up close to her, so close their shoes were almost touching. "Time for what? To see more of my friends die?"

Stepping away, Henri returned to the door. She turned and stared at him from across the room. "Is this about Cleo?"

He threw out his arms. "What –? What do you –?"

His phone rang, and he glared at her as he pulled it from his pocket. The caller was Arika Livingston.

"Not now!" he barked at the screen, and threw the phone on the desk. He glared at his watch, then said to Henri, "You've got twelve hours. That's how long it'll take to get mobilised."

"Sam –"

"Twelve hours. And then we're going out there with the biggest arsenal I can muster, and we will erase Waite's farm and everything in it from the face of the earth."

48

Toasting success

W ILFRED RAISED HIS champagne flute and with a flourish brought it to his young lips. "To me!" he toasted, and took a sip. Champagne had never tasted better, or gone to his head so fast. "To brilliance and ingenuity, and having a vigorous body in which to enjoy its fruits and favours!"

He took another sip, then slid down in his chair in rapture. "Ah Moët, what a friend and comfort you have been to me over these past many years." He raised his glass again. "To life; to me; to … the next stage in the evolution of mankind!"

He glanced at Simon, who was hunched over the Necronomicon, reading intently, his face wolfish as his eyes ran along the lines of text.

"Drink up, Simon."

At first it looked like Simon wasn't going to reply. Then, his eyes not leaving the book, he said, "My poor old body doesn't stomach fizzy wine the way it used to."

Wilfred smiled smugly. "Find a new one then. All you need is a blood relative or someone emotionally close – a friend or a lover. Surely you have plenty of those types around."

Simon glanced at him, curling his lip at the sarcasm.

"If only we knew of this spell earlier, we could have created our own livestock," Wilfred mused. "Hosts – a host of them – lined up in a row, waiting for us to choose the tallest and strongest. The best the world has to offer. Each one, ours for the taking, until the time comes to select the next one. 'Sustainable resources' they call it these days." He sighed theatrically. "Now, I'm sorry to say, it may be too late for you, old man. Too, too late." He ran his finger up and down the stem of the glass, enjoying this little tease. "You're welcome to try the calling spell, Simon. You may be lucky; you never know. A shot in the dark is better than a fizzling balloon, don't you think?"

Simon's face darkened, which brought another smile to Wilfred's lips.

"Then again, you prefer to be the Sphinx, if I recall correctly. Slowly decaying to dust, and all your knowledge with you."

Simon folded his arms on the book. "That reminds me. I've been wondering: do you still need your Vicarial now you're young again?"

Wilfred took another sip of champagne. He cocked his head at the ceiling, intrigued by Simon's question. "I'm not entirely certain. I gather it depends if I want to extend my years in this body or switch to a new one in a couple of decades. I can't see why I would need a Vicarial if I wasn't stealing years."

"Stealing bodies would be the more efficient path."

"True."

"Ronald can be such a burden on my time."

"Snyder and Gilles come in handy that way. They don't mind helping out with Sebastian." He grinned like a proud father. "Not at all."

"I'd venture to say I've gotten a few more years doing it myself. I'm sure it helps if the puppy knows it's you doing the punishing." He pushed himself up. "I don't mind, really. It's like shaving: a necessary evil."

"I'll miss Sebastian. He's become like a brother to me. I won't know what to do with myself when he's no longer around."

"You've decided to do away with him then?"

Wilfred rubbed his fingers over his smooth cheeks. He was recalling some of his favourite torments over the years. They say the more you hurt your Vicarial, the more years you earn, and he'd been sure to visit Sebastian regularly. The visits by Gilles and Kenny were just icing on the cake.

"You'll find some new distractions, I'm sure."

"In this virile body, yes indeed." He raised his glass and stared at the room through the bubbles. "How's yours going? What's his name again?"

"Ronald. Ronnie." Simon heaved a long sigh. "I'm not sure he'll last the year, to be honest. It's such a bother having to find a new one. The kidnapping, the spell, the taming of the spirit. Such a bother."

"I can help, if you like. You being so decrepit and everything. Snyder loves that kind of thing."

Ignoring the insult, Simon turned the page. After a few moments, he said, "I may well take you up on your offer of the calling spell. Why wear glasses when you can have laser surgery? There must be some distant relative out there who'll respond. He wouldn't have to be a baby, like yours."

Wilfred bent forward in delight. "Aha! I knew it! Not so much the Sphinx now?"

"Let's say your good fortune has inspired me."

He raised his glass high. "To me! To my inspiration and good fortune!"

Simon was eyeing him closely. "So tell me how you did it. How did you switch bodies with the boy?"

Twisting in his seat, Wilfred threw a leg over the arm. He wasn't in the mood to discuss history when there were so many new plans to make ... and their present victory to savour.

"We'll discuss that some other time. Tonight is for celebration."

"No, Wilfred, tell me. You know me: need to know now."

"It was a highly elaborate ritual."

"One you promised to share with me."

"One minute you don't want eternal life; the next, you need to know right this moment. You do frustrate me, Simon."

"I've been thinking about what I could do with a body like yours. All the beauties I could attract."

Wilfred's face warmed. Lately, he'd been having a recurring daydream about walking into an exclusive men's club, one that had Moët on tap and the most beautiful young women in the world: mobbing him, desiring him, eager to do any sexy, depraved, painful thing he demanded of them. The fantasy would come to him night and day, distracting him from his long-held plans to open the gate between the dimensions and command a new world order. He wondered whether the distraction was caused by his new body's rampant hormones or the simple fact that he'd never before in his life been attractive. Now, suddenly, he had the world at his feet. He could have his pick of what *this* world had to offer. Suddenly he had choices.

Simon was looking petulant. "Forgive me if the thought of woman-kind makes me impatient. I'm only human."

"I suppose you haven't had much in the way of feminine company lately, looking like that."

"As with you in your gnome's body, before you acquired the young Gates boy."

"Touché," said Wilfred, tipping his glass.

Simon's continual staring was making him angry, so he said, "First summon a responsive soul, one who shares your blood."

"I know that part."

Now he was really getting on his nerves. "Simon, find yourself a host and then ask. Now, raise your glass and drink a toast to our success in retrieving the Necronomicon."

"I'm really not that thirsty."

"If you don't drink, I'll take it as a personal insult. I don't like drinking by myself. We're supposed to be celebrating, not mooning about like two old men."

"If I drink with you, you'll tell me about the spell?"

A nerve twitched beneath his eye. "Very well."

He watched as Simon raised his glass and drank.

"There now, isn't that better? Now drink up, so I can begin the summoning of Yog-Sothoth."

"The Messenger, you mean?"

"No. Yog-Sothoth."

When Simon looked perplexed, he said, "While you were out, I had a little play with my new friend, and I extracted a shortcut from him. No more messy Messenger to get in the way."

"That's handy. How?"

Wilfred motioned for him to drink up. Simon tossed back the champagne like someone drinking a shot.

"Excellent. Top up?"

He waved no. "So, Wilfred, tell me about this shortcut."

"All in good time."

"You keep saying that."

Wilfred made a gesture with his hand that implied Simon's words were as meaningless as the air.

"If you won't tell me about Yog-Sothoth, the least you can do is tell me how to transfer into a more suitable host. I find a subject, and then what?"

Wilfred huffed angrily. Simon's nagging never failed to raise his hackles. "I will ask Gilles to write it down for you. Suffice to say, it's no simple task to dislodge a boy from his body."

"No doubt." Simon returned his attention to the Necronomicon. "But an old man squatting in a young boy's body is another thing altogether."

Placing both hands on the page, he began mouthing something.

Wilfred felt the room rock. It wasn't the champagne; it was something he'd never felt before: a disconnection of reality, like the room was jerking away from him.

Meanwhile, Simon went on whispering, oblivious to Wilfred's discomfort, ignoring his boyish cry when champagne spilt in his lap.

"What –" he sputtered, "are you – doing – Simon?"

Simon glanced up, his face a picture of innocence. "Oh, I forgot to tell you: I already had a little chit-chat with Gilles. And he told me all about the tri-spell. And how I might adapt it, so to speak. To our current situation."

With a little shrug, he returned to the book and began whispering again.

Now Wilfred was feeling a growing heat in his head, a pressure in his skull, like his brain was pushing his eyeballs from their sockets. Thoughts that weren't his were crowding in on his own: Simon's whispers; they were inside his head.

"Get out, you fiend!" he cried, leaping to his feet, sending the glass flying off his lap. "Find your own damn body!"

"But this one is so handsome. And so young and convenient."

Wilfred pressed his palms against his temples, trying to trap his thoughts inside his head. Drawing long breaths, blowing out air through his nose, he strained with all his might to eject the intruder. With desperation on his side, he soon felt himself regaining control of his young brain.

Simon began chanting louder, unfazed by Wilfred's temporary victory.

Once more, Wilfred felt his mind getting squeezed out of his head. He knew Simon's spell was too strong to resist. Simon had double-crossed him again, and this time he was planning to play the game all the way to the end, to Wilfred's end. This was no body swap; this was Simon obliterating Wilfred's thoughts until there was nothing of Wilfred left.

Through gritted teeth, he said, "Do you remember – what I said – would happen – if you crossed me?"

"Oh, Wilfred, it's a pity your talents have never measured up to the scale of your threats."

"A greater pity for you – I don't – need you anymore."

A look of horror struck Simon. His face went bright red; the whites of his eyes turned black. Howling, he scratched at his clothes, pulling them away from his throat, tearing buttons as he tore his shirt open. Smoke trailed from the corners of his mouth, from his nostrils, from his eyes and ears. Throwing himself off the chair, dropping to the floor, he scrambled back until he hit the wall.

"Professor Orwell," said Wilfred, bending over the table, pulling the Necronomicon towards him, "say hello to Varafti, Sultan God of Fire."

Simon opened his mouth to scream, and out flew a spear of flame. As hoarse yelps coughed from his seared throat, the flame rose into the room like a burning snake, then twisted down and wrapped itself around his body. Suddenly his clothes were alight, then his skin and beard and hair. Rolling around on the floor, he bucked and jerked in agony, as the stench of burnt flesh filled the chamber.

Finally, with a shudder, his body went limp, a scream gurgled out of his lungs, and then his throat closed up, and all that could be heard in the room was the cackle of fire.

Wilfred, pouring champagne into Simon's glass, said, "I suppose I owe you an explanation. You see, Varafti agreed to help me summon Yog-Sothoth in return for the soul of a powerful wizard. Fortunately, I convinced him to take you instead."

As Simon burned from the inside, the ropes of flame squeezed him tighter and tighter, until the fire collapsed into itself and only smouldering embers were left on the floor.

Wilfred raised his glass. "Farewell, dear friend. You've no idea how helpful you've been to me."

He sank into his chair, took a long sip of champagne, smiled into the air. With Dylan Gates' body reclaimed, with the Necronomicon in his hands, with two-faced Simon out of the way, with Magacanta just around the corner, his carefully-laid plans were back on track. The world would soon be his.

Suddenly he shot forward. "Hell and damnation!" he cried, glaring at the ashes on the floor. "I forgot to ask what you did with my Borellus!"

49

Going in

"WHAT ARE YOU freaks up to in there?" Morgan muttered, pulling the binoculars away from his face.

Stifling a yawn, he glanced over at the two-toned Bentley and white Honda parked side-by-side near the gate. They looked strange together, like Orwell and Gates themselves, the odd couple shacked up in Wilfred Waite's farmhouse raising zombies and monsters to unleash on the world. The cars had been disabled, but Morgan was under no illusion about the wizards' power. Staring up at the hole in the roof, he half expected them to come barrelling out astride broomsticks, wands primed to zap the whole attack force into oblivion.

Tapping his phone against his leg, he stepped through the plan once more in his mind. Early that morning, during a series of tactical meetings with senior officials across the NSO, it had been determined that the odds the wizards would surrender under any scenario were close to zero. This led to agreement on two primary tactics. First, the attack would be dynamic entry, so the wizards would have little or no chance to cast a spell or release any zombies or other nasties from whatever restraints they were presently held under. Second, it would happen in daylight, so the zombies would be at a disadvantage if they emerged into the light after so long spent in darkness.

He smiled at Henri, who was standing next to the military truck scrolling through her phone. She'd dressed sensibly, if a little unfashionably, in a mustard-coloured long-sleeved blouse, burgundy slacks and black schoolgirl shoes. Uncharacteristically, she'd overdone her make-up – he guessed to hide her drawn complexion and the bags under her eyes. Not only that: just before dawn, after lying awake worrying for most of the night, Henri had taken her scissors and cut off her braid. When Morgan first saw her, he gave her a queer look and asked, "Are those new glasses?" and she reminded him of the braid and told him about her wake-dream of dead people grabbing hold of it and taking bites out of her neck. Even now, five hours later, she couldn't stop rubbing the spot her phantom attackers had sunk their teeth into her.

Morgan's phone rang. Spinning back to the farmhouse, he pressed the phone against his ear. "Morgan. Talk."

He frowned. He'd expected it to be Posniak, ringing with further orders about the attack, but it was Arika Livingston. She'd been calling his office all morning, to the point where he went from ignoring her because he had so much to organise, to ignoring her in retaliation for her pestering. And now someone had stupidly patched her through.

"Arika," he puffed. "Look, I'm sorry: I can't talk. You'll have to speak to my assistant. I'm in the –" He held the phone away from his ear. "Okay, okay, calm down. What's this about?"

As Morgan listened, his mouth fell open. His eyes moved back to Henri.

"You've got to be kidding," he said. Then: "Are you sure?" He listened a few seconds more. "Hey, wait. Hold on."

He put the phone on speaker, whistled at Henri, waited as she toddled towards him through the mud, and then said into the phone, "Now, Arika, repeat what you just told me. I've got someone here who needs to explain to me how this is in any way possible in a sane world."

KANE WAS FIXING the bandage on Dylan's arm when Arika appeared at the bedroom door.

He glanced up, forced a half smile, then let his eyes fall back to the greenish forearm he was wrapping in a white dressing.

"This should keep the flesh on those old bones a bit longer," he said, raising his brow, trying to make it sound like a perfectly normal thing to say to his seventeen-year-old brother. Despite his flippancy, he was having trouble keeping his voice steady, and when he wasn't busy wrapping, he had to hold his hands under his thighs so Dylan wouldn't see them trembling.

"Kane, can we talk?"

When he looked again at Arika, his heart rate doubled in an instant.

There was something unnatural in the tone of her voice, a quaver he hadn't heard before. A few minutes ago she was energised by righteous anger. All he could think was, What now?

"In private," she added.

He went back to winding the bandage around his brother's rotting arm. "Anything you can say to me, you can say to Dylan."

She seemed ready to argue with him, but then entered the room and sat on the bed. Staring at Dylan, she said in a flat voice, "NSO – or whoever they are … Something's happening."

Kane scrunched his face. "What's that supposed to mean?"

"I told Morgan about last night, and all he said was leave it to him and don't worry."

"Isn't that same as what he said last time?"

"It was the way he said it."

He shook his head in annoyance. Arika's words reminded him of January, who was always finding hidden meanings in phrases or tones or glances. It was a weapon she used to try to control him, and though Kane knew it wasn't Arika's style, it was still a trait that irked him.

"Did you tell him about Dylan?"

"He definitely reacted to that."

"And?"

"And what?"

"Did he say he knew anything about where Dylan's body is?"

"I asked him, but he wouldn't say either way. But Kane, he said there was an incident at the hospital last night, something involving out-of-control dead people; and when he had to go, he apologised and said something like, 'We all have to make sacrifices', like he was talking about *us*."

Kane looked at her. "Out-of-control zombies?"

"That was the gist of it."

He stared into the air. "Did he say anything else?"

"Just that they contained it – whatever that means."

"Hmm, Snyder must have left some of his zombie horde behind. I wonder why. Did you tell him about the book?"

"I figured I had to. He needs to know what we're up against."

"And he's still not inclined to help us? Doesn't he know we can help each other?"

"It was after I told him about the Necronomicon, he was suddenly in a hurry to get off the phone."

"Hardly surprising, I suppose."

Collecting the bandages and scissors, Kane got up from the bed.

"I think they're planning to attack the farm, Kane – and I think they've decided Dylan is expendable."

Kane stared down at his brother's corpse. His arms and legs were fully bandaged, as well as most of his head, and fortunately this had reduced the stench of decomposition to an almost bearable level. Perhaps Arika was right: with the right care, they may have months, even years, up their sleeve.

"Nah," he countered, shaking her words out of his head. "That's a big leap in logic from a quick phone call."

"It's not just the call, Kane. They've had the farmhouse under surveillance, and plenty of time to prepare for a raid. Now there's been two zombie attacks in one night, not to mention Hugo. If I was them, I wouldn't be waiting around for the next disaster to happen. I wouldn't. I'd go in. It's what Dad taught me, and if anyone knows how the armed forces think, it's him."

Kane went to the window and gazed down at the empty street. He was mentally exhausted and only half-comprehending what Arika was saying. He didn't want to believe that everything was about to go south, but if she was right, Dylan's body – his real, seventeen-year-old body – might be blown to smithereens before the end of the day, and then all he would have left would be this rotting, stinking carcass. This would be his life – *their* life – for God knows how long.

He turned back to her, alarm escalating inside him.

"You sure he understood what you were saying about Dylan?"

"Definite. I had to repeat it to someone else who was with him. A woman."

"You told him it was Waite in Dylan's body?"

Now it was Arika who looked annoyed. "Twice."

"And what did he say to that?"

"He said, 'Leave it to me. And don't worry.' And when I asked what he was planning to do about it, he said he couldn't tell me, but it was under control. Then he said he had to get off the line, and said that thing about us all having to make sacrifices."

"Ring him back."

She pulled out her phone and rang Morgan's office number. It went straight to voicemail.

Kane walked in a tight circle. A mixture of fear, anger and panic was whirling in him, threatening to explode into the room. He breathed shallowly, trying to hold it down.

"They can't kill him," he murmured. "They can't. That's murder. It would be his death warrant. He'd have to – We wouldn't –" Stopping, he gaped at the bandaged figure on the bed.

Arika got up and took him by both arms. "They can do whatever they like, Kane. They don't care about one casualty if it saves other lives."

Pulling away from her, he headed for the door. "That's not gonna happen. They are not gonna kill my brother."

Dylan picked up his notepad and began scribbling.

"Wait, wait," cried Arika. "Dylan …"

Kane turned as Dylan held up the smudged note.

"Take me," it said.

HENRI WAS CLEANING her glasses with a tissue when Morgan yelled, "Go!" Piping out a shriek, she dropped the glasses in the mud.

Morgan bent down, picked them up, returned them to her, then raised his binoculars and trained them on the farmhouse.

Lieutenant Darryl Sparks, the troop commander, was kneeling on the portico, trying the door. It was locked. He motioned to another soldier, who bent down and cracked the lock.

Sparks gently pushed open the door with one arm as he waved the rest of the soldiers over with the other.

The soldiers were all in black: black helmets, black gloves, black boots, carrying black assault rifles. They massed on the portico like pudding, then, close on each other's heels, filed into the farmhouse.

Morgan waited, the binoculars glued to his face. Henri was standing next to him, her anxiety palpable. She was wise enough to stay quiet, a departure from her usual tendency to vocalise whatever was on her mind, and he wondered how much the events of last night had scarred her. Cutting off her hair after having nightmares of flesh-eating zombies: it didn't bode well for her mental health.

Very quickly, black shapes began moving in the downstairs windows. Morgan guessed the soldiers were also upstairs by now, though the boarded-up windows hid the second-storey activity from view. He saw the soldiers in his mind's eye: entering the rooms two by two, fanning out to each corner, rapidly detecting any threats. They would be swift and noiseless – unless of course there was something or someone that needed putting down by deadly force. Then all hell would break loose.

Sparks re-appeared on the portico, raising his hand. He put his phone to his ear, and at the same moment Morgan's phone buzzed.

"It's clear," came Sparks' voice.

"Got it." Morgan lowered the phone and shook his head at Henri. "They must be down below."

Taking the strap of her binoculars, she slipped them off her neck and hung them on a fence post. Frowning at the house, she said, "I'd be willing to bet my grandma's frilly knickers on it."

Morgan almost laughed out loud. He was still trying to figure out whether Henri was courageous, chicken or plain cuckoo. Just when he thought he'd pigeon-holed her, she turned around and surprised him again.

"We ready then, Henri?"

Rubbing her neck, she replied, "As ready as we'll ever be."

Her reluctance was obvious, and suddenly Morgan found himself with an aversion to dragging her through the mud and into the farmhouse, where an army of horrors crept and crawled beneath their feet. She's a librarian, he reminded himself, not a soldier. He was surprised she even turned up today after all she went through at the hospital. Courageous, chicken or cuckoo? Whichever it was, the NSO needed her; that much was clear. She had special training in this kind of thing – she proved that with the success of her anti-zombie spell – and for this reason was likely their most valuable asset. It made his job of protecting her even more important.

"It can't be any worse than what we went through at the hospital," he reassured her. "And this time we have back-up."

"I'm not sure I agree it can't be worse."

"Our guys are the best in class."

"Still not convincing me, I'm afraid, Sam."

"We'll keep you behind all the guns."

"In a rock/paper/scissors-type scenario, I'd say monsters beat guns. And magic beats monsters."

"Well then, just think about all those delicious books you'll get your hands on. Maybe even some lovely magic wands and … flying broomsticks."

"Oh, Samuel Morgan," Henri purred coquettishly, "you really know how to talk sexy to the ladies, doncha?"

He dropped back his head and laughed. An image had popped into his mind of Henri lurking in the human biology section of the library, secretly checking out pictures of naked men. When in his vision her clothes morphed from frumpish burgundy slacks and orange shirt to sexy librarian dress and fishnet stockings, he laughed even harder.

"Come on then, Henri," he said, pulling himself together. "You're right: we're nowhere near ready. But then again, neither are they."

AT FIRST WHEN the bell clanged, Wilfred ignored it, but after a few clangs he jerked up his head in annoyance. On the table, the man he'd resurrected earlier lay panting, his mouth filled with bubbles of blood.

Laying down the knife, brushing his hair away from his face, Wilfred crossed to a computer. The screen was showing video from hidden webcams in each of the farmhouse rooms, and as he watched, black shapes floated past the cameras. There was the glint of light on a gun barrel.

Intruders. Soldiers this time, not a bunch of bumbling kids or an impotent old man with his greedy, thieving eyes on everything in sight. This was worse. These intruders were bent on eradicating him and his history and everything he'd ever achieved.

Trembling with rage, Wilfred took the monitor in both hands and shook it violently. "Infidels!" he screamed at the screen. "Insects! Vermin! Pond scum!"

He stopped and blinked hard, willing the images away. With the Necronomicon in his possession and Varafti on his side, he half believed he could make the trespassers vanish or burn from the inside with the force of his mind, but the reality was, he didn't have anywhere near that much power. Not yet. And Varafti, his new ally, was gone, taking Simon's essence with him to use in whatever foul rites he was planning in his own fiery, home dimension.

The black shapes continued to move about. The soldiers were searching through the cupboards and drawers and in any nook and cranny they could find, determined to confiscate or destroy anything of interest or value.

One of them stopped, and a woman's face peered into the camera.

Squeezing the monitor hard, as if he were squeezing her head, Wilfred shouted, "Get out! Get out! Get out!"

Her hand rose and the camera went black.

He couldn't believe their timing. Just yesterday, the Necronomicon had chosen to return to him, to favour him as the instrument of its dark powers; Varafti had sealed a pact to help him summon Yog-Sothoth and open the way for the return of the Great Old Ones; everything was in place for the Feast of Sidusater and the final confirmation of his consciousness in this perfect young body. All was ready to set in motion his long-awaited ascension to the throne of the world.

Releasing his grip on the monitor, Wilfred went back to his project. Staring down at the silent corpse, he settled his nerves with the thought that the universe was actively plotting against him, trying its darnedest to sabotage anything he did that might aid Kragn in his grand plan to return to the Before. It wasn't a personal failure. Quite the opposite: Wilfred's powers were so immense, so extraordinary, the universe had been forced to take notice of him.

He collected the knife from the table. In reality, this intrusion was a temporary setback at most: a few more ants to crush on his way to his throne.

"I tried to do this the civilised way," he smirked, running a finger down the bloody blade. "In my benevolence, I may even have spared some of you to kneel at my feet and open your pigs' eyes to the dawn of the new world. But with your arrogance and interference, you have forced me to take the path of chaos. The gods will not be pleased. They will insist on retribution. And it will be these youthful hands that wield the flaming sword of vengeance and strew your steaming innards across the blood-soaked wasteland."

Picking up a rag, Wilfred wiped the blood off the knife. He tossed the rag aside and held the blade close to a light, turning it over, watching it glint sharply. Smiling with satisfaction, he replaced the knife on the table, pulled his shirt over his head and stared down at his slender body – at Dylan Gates' slender body. He ran his hand down his smooth chest and over his hairless belly. It was a shame to deface its milky perfection, but he had no choice. The time had come to cast open the gate and unleash the leviathan. There was no other way.

Tossing his shirt across the room, he swiped up the knife and held its point close to his nose. "Lord Azathoth!" he screeched in the voice of a teenager. "In your righteous service, I affirm my name! Pain is my call! Blood is my promise! Chaos is my gift! I beg you: release your agent and unfold on these worthless maggots your power and your majesty!"

Bending forward, he placed the knife blade against his side and slowly sliced it down to the line of his trousers. Grimacing and grunting in agony, he went on cutting the knife into his skin, slicing bloody lines and curves, gritting his teeth and squirming in pain, until at last he'd carved the word Dhagdar across his belly. By the time he was finished, blood was streaming into his trousers, dripping down his legs, soaking his socks, filling his boots.

"Azathoth!" he screamed through the white-hot pain. "I writ my name in your infinite majesty! Your sacrifices are begun! I beseech you: ready the gate! Accept my unworthy tributes! I beseech you twice: ready the gate! I beseech you thrice: ready the gate! Your sacrifices are begun! Ready the gate! I beseech you in the name of all this miserable rock and its stinking vermin have to offer!"

The floor rumbled; the lights flickered; a chill wind flew around the room, arising from nowhere, carrying with it the smell of sulphur and rot and death. The dead man sprang up shrieking, and as if in response, the wailing in the dark corridors rose to an unholy cacophony of howls and screams.

Wilfred, cackling like a maniac, raised his face to the ceiling, flung open his arms and spun madly in an ecstatic dance. Blood from his wounds flew across the floor and spattered against the walls and furniture. He bumped into a chair, knocked it over, collided with a table, fell dizzy and laughing across the corpse's legs. Pushing himself up, he spied Gilles' anxious face at the door, but he was feeling too drunk with power and anticipation to care about any of it.

As Gilles' face withdrew, a booming voice shook the room, stopping him in his tracks. Cowering under the dust and dirt falling from the ceiling, he muttered, "Yes, Master, bloodbath first, dance later."

KANE LEANED OVER the steering wheel, egging the truck to go faster. Arika, in the back seat, was hanging onto Dylan, making sure he didn't roll over and fall on the floor.

A terrific boom shook the air, and for an instant Kane lost control of the truck. It swerved and ran off the road; he spun the wheel and came to a stop in a ditch.

"They've started!" he cried, twisting in his seat. "They're bombing the place!"

In the back seat, Dylan gurgled. He was trying to say something.

"Write it down," prompted Arika, pushing the notepad and pen into his hands.

He scribbled something and held it up.

"It wasn't an explosion," read Arika.

Kane looked at his brother. "What does that mean?"

He scribbled something else. This time he gave the pad to Kane.

"It was a voice. Of a god."

Arika gaped at him. "They're fighting back."

Kane frowned at Dylan, not knowing whether this was good news or bad news. At least if Wilfred and Simon were taking the offensive,

Dylan's body was safe for the time being. It would give them some breathing space, a chance to intervene and hopefully convince the NSO not to destroy the farm and everything in it.

Handing the pad back to Dylan, he lifted his foot off the brake and slammed it on the accelerator. The wheels spun in the dirt and they took off in a surge of power.

Around the next curve, Kane screeched to a stop at a roadblock.

Two soldiers in black approached the truck. They were holding rifles at the ready, but they were sauntering up as if they had all the time in the world. Behind them, a third officer stood guard at the barrier, his stance making it clear that no one would be getting past him.

Arika leaned forward. "Should I keep going?" Kane asked her, hardly moving his lips.

The soldiers stopped at his window. One of them motioned him to lower it.

"Can't go any further, mate."

"We've gotta see Sam Morgan."

The soldier gave him a glacial stare. "Don't know any such person by that name."

"Sam Morgan. NSO."

The soldier blinked.

"He knows us. It's a matter of life or death."

The soldier blinked again.

"Come on, man. How would I know his name if he didn't know me?"

The second soldier wrinkled his nose. "What is that awful stink?"

He stepped towards the back passenger window and placed his hand against the glass.

"Kane –" began Arika, trying to block the man's view of Dylan's shrunken, bandaged-wrapped corpse.

Kane was thinking the same thing. Adjusting the gear shift, he reversed and turned the truck around. As they sped away, he watched the two soldiers in the rear-view mirror. They were strolling back to the roadblock, sharing a laugh, probably over a fart joke.

Around the curve, he parked the truck and wracked his brain for a

Plan B. Perhaps they could approach the farm from the flank by driving over the fields. Surely the NSO wouldn't be expecting anything like that. It was worth a try.

"Can you ring Morgan again? They might have let him know we were there."

Arika's face showed she considered his suggestion pointless, but with a sigh she dialled the number.

Dylan was scribbling again. He handed the pad over the console to Kane.

He took it from his brother's hands. "Are you sure about this?"

Dylan gurgled.

"What is it?" asked Arika, the ringing phone pressed against her ear.

Kane was so keyed up he could hardly breathe. Here was hope at last, their Plan B, a chance to complete the battle he'd believed they won a week ago.

"Dylan's figured it out," he said in a hoarse voice. "He knows where Waite is."

50

The descent

ORGAN AND HENRI watched as Sparks pressed the raised tentacle and stepped back. The bronze plate whirred, shook, and lifted to an upright position, revealing the well.

"There's that stink," commented Henri, waving her hand under her nose.

Morgan held his torch over the edge. As Arika had described, metal rungs were attached to the brick wall, extending down several metres to bare earth. It was the perfect point of defence for whoever or whatever was down there – and the perfect place for a trap.

He waved his hand, and two soldiers approached carrying halogen lamps. They erected them on tripods on opposite sides of the well, switched them on and stepped back. The lamps flooded the well with cold white light, exposing the ancient brickwork, dirt floor and the beginnings of the subterranean stairs.

Next, a soldier approached with a large black case, to which was attached a reel of blue cable that ended in a small stainless-steel camera and light. She opened the case, revealing a monitor and keyboard, and then took the camera and began feeding the cable down the well. Morgan and Sparks watched through the monitor as the camera descended towards the dark stairs.

"Looks clear," said Morgan as the light illuminated the empty tunnel and stairs. "What do you think, Henri?"

She was peering at the monitor. "Do we have a choice?"

He blew out his cheeks. "I'd like nothing better than to seal this up and blow the whole place to kingdom come. We'd have one big bad bonfire and then go home knowing it was a job well done. But that's not my orders."

She regarded him warmly. "Sam, you're a good man. And I would guess an even better soldier. I'm ready when you are."

He nodded at her, then turned his nod to the lieutenant.

"Taylor," ordered Sparks, motioning a waiting soldier towards the well. Taylor obeyed mechanically, hoisting his rifle on his shoulder, backing over the edge, beginning his climb down the metal rungs.

Krastev was next. Sparks motioned her after Taylor, and she followed with face taut, focussing hard on the task ahead.

Standing around the well, Sparks and Morgan watched with guns ready as the two soldiers descended. When they reached the earthen floor, the lead officer raised a hand to signify the all clear, and then they entered the stairwell.

Morgan cocked his ear. He thought he could hear the soft tread of their boots on stone, which quickly faded to silence.

"Approaching the bend," came Taylor's voice through Sparks' radio.

Then something began happening down there: a shuffling sound and animal noises like you might hear at an agricultural show.

Sparks lifted his radio. "Taylor, Krastev, can you hear me?"

The only response was the crackle of static.

"Do you read me?"

Gunshots rang out, echoing up the well, followed by screaming. More shots. More screaming.

"Taylor! Krastev!" Dropping his radio, Sparks leaned over the well. "Taylor! Krastev!"

In response came an animal whimpering. Then something sounded on the stairs: clomp – clomp – clomp, accompanied by a scraping noise.

"Something's coming up," breathed Henri.

An arm appeared on the wall of the staircase, and as they watched, Krastev's face materialised from the darkness, bloodied and terrified.

Grabbing the bottom rung, she began her ascent. Each step was agonisingly slow, and it was clear from her torn and bloody uniform that she'd sustained an injury to her right shoulder and leg.

Spinning around, Sparks descended the rungs at speed. Halfway down, he met Krastev and reached a hand towards her, but as their fingers met, something else emerged from the darkness of the stairwell: a bear – or jackal – or gorilla; a lumbering beast with brown, shaggy hair, long arms and a fat, toothy snout. Sparks gaped. Following the line of his stare, Krastev looked down and began whimpering.

The monster took hold of the first rung.

"Quick!" yelled Sparks, gripping her wrist.

But she only made one more rung before a hairy paw reached up and grabbed hold of her ankle.

Krastev stared at Sparks in terror. The monster jerked her down a few times, gently, like it was toying with her, allowing her the hope she had a chance of breaking free, but although she managed to reach up and grab the next rung, her captor was not about to let her escape.

"Out of the way!" Morgan yelled, aiming his rifle past Sparks and Krastev at the huge hairy body.

Sparks flattened himself against the wall at the same time Morgan shot at the mass of hair. The bullets went in with no discernible reaction from the beast. He shot again, this time aiming at the monster's arm, but still it refused to let go – refused even to acknowledge it had been shot.

Sparks resumed his desperate struggle to haul Krastev to the next rung, but the thing was not letting her budge an inch. Tiring of the game, it began pulling her down with a series of jerks that loosened her hold on the metal rung and strained Sparks' grip on her wrist.

Krastev gazed up at him with resignation, almost a look of apology, and then, with a final tug from the monster, dropped to the floor.

The mass of hair, claws and teeth fell on her, clamped its jaws around her head and dragged her backwards down the stairs.

Sparks scrambled up the rungs.

"Behind you!" cried Morgan.

Sparks didn't waste time looking down. He made the last few rungs in a matter of seconds.

As he leapt out of the well, Morgan and Henri stared in horror at the shaggy beast rising towards them. It was breathing fast, making a staccato noise in its throat that sounded like a snigger. Its black eyes shone like onyx; its snout dripped with snot; its blood-stained fangs were fixed in a macabre smile. Curved nails clinked on the rungs and a foul animal smell rose into the room as it ascended.

"Close it!" yelled Morgan, dragging Henri back. "Now!"

The lieutenant was already onto it. Leaning his body weight on the trapdoor, he rode it down, assisted by two other soldiers. Once it was locked in place, they lay gaping at each other, while the foul thing that had been crawling towards them howled and thumped in frustration at the underside of the bronze plate.

IN ANOTHER HOUSE, another trapdoor flew up. The black-haired boy who pushed it open disappeared briefly, before reappearing carrying a lantern, shoulder pack and backpack. He climbed the steps into the basement, and then stood surveying the room, puffing noisily as he paused to catch his breath.

"Hmm," Wilfred said, placing the lamp and bags on the cracked concrete floor. He crossed to the stairs and switched on the light. "Well, well, Snyder, what hi-jinks have you been up to?"

The basement was fitted out as a laboratory, a mirror version of his own. There was even a torture table in the middle of the room – though unlike his, this one was filthy. In fact, the whole room was filthy. There was a row of cages along the back wall, with disgusting brown straw on the floor, chains on the walls, and slop buckets Wilfred didn't dare look in. The stench was almost unbearable.

The basement was in disarray – it looked like a fight had taken place. The doors to the cages were hanging off their hinges; chairs and tables were overturned; shelves had been pulled down; glass flasks lay smashed on the floor. In one corner, at the end of a bench, a Bunsen burner lay upended and there were smoke stains all the way up the wall.

When Wilfred spotted a familiar book on a bookshelf, he went to investigate.

"That's my Lexicon Antigua," he gasped in disbelief. "And Johnson's Theologorum. I've been looking all over for that! You thieving snipe! I bet half that equipment is mine too!"

He stood huffing in anger, the feeling of betrayal dizzying. Simon he could understand – he'd always been a sticky-fingered piece of slime – but who would have thought snivelling Snyder would be so brazen? And stupid.

He pressed the bandages on his stomach to bring his mind back to his mission. "I will deal with you later," he warned, and collecting his things, went upstairs.

The house wasn't in a much better state than the basement. It was a small cottage, with small rooms and a low ceiling. The dark wooden beams were so low in places, Wilfred had to stoop to avoid hitting his head (a problem he'd never experienced in his old body). Boxes, electrical equipment, clothes and general rubbish were scattered all over the furniture and floor. A broken window had been fixed with a large piece of tin.

"Slob," he spat; "disgusting, thieving slob," and left the house by the front door.

The most noticeable thing about the yard was the number of vehicles there: cars, motorcycles, vans, a butcher's truck. Most were rusted and in pieces, their gutted shells and parts strewn about the yard, but some looked like fairly recent models. Wilfred glanced around, figuring Kenny had a side job selling vehicles and spare parts. He wondered where he found the time, what with his job as morgue attendant and grave robber, before realising Kenny didn't need to find time. It appeared that as well as stealing bodies and selling them to the highest bidder, he had a sideline appropriating and selling his victims' possessions.

"Stinking thief," said Wilfred, though this time there was a note of admiration in his voice.

For a time he stood in the desolate garden, the wind blowing his hair in his face, staring in the direction of the farmhouse. It wasn't visible from here, but he could see in his mind's eye the tanks and attack vehicles in the yard, the soldiers swarming in every room, including the second basement. That Gates fool and his whore had no doubt told the authorities everything.

Except they didn't know everything. Smirking, Wilfred wondered whether the army had found his little surprises yet. He couldn't hear any gunshots or explosions, so it seemed not.

"Only a matter of time," he declared, his words carried into the sky by the wind. A shame he wouldn't be around to see it, but he had more important things to do while the idiot soldiers were screaming and dying.

Hoisting his bags higher on his shoulder, Wilfred began trudging up the hill.

51

Pandemonium

Giving up on the basement, Morgan and Henri went up the hall to the front door, past the staircase and the portraits of Jonathon and James Dark. The rest of the squad went the other way, to the back door, where they could hear Sparks yelling orders to secure the perimeter.

Morgan re-checked the dining room, while Henri slipped into the parlour to see if there were any books worth collecting.

"Anything?" he asked, joining her at the mantel.

"A few mildly interesting books, but nothing magical or supernatural. Sam," she ventured, replacing a tattered brown tome on the shelf, "there must be another way down. It can't only be the well. They need a way to carry furniture down. And coffins, and prisoners."

Morgan nodded. "We're onto it. There's a search in progress: the barn and village."

"Maybe we should have waited for that before going down the well."

With a last glance around, Morgan moved off.

"It must be close by," Henri went on. "Somewhere with stairs. Maybe even an elevator, or one of those electric chairs that go up and down the bannister – for Wilfred. I can't see him walking up and down a hundred steps in his condition. What's your guess? – the barn or the village?"

Morgan stopped at the door. Henri hadn't done too bad a job with her scenario assessment. Nowhere near as good as Cleo, but then, Cleo was one-of-a-kind.

"My gut instinct says the village. They look to have been vacant for a while, but the ground has been disturbed."

"Can we go and help with the search?"

"That's the plan," said Morgan.

"Sam, what happens if we can't find another entry?"

"We'll blast our way through. Or drill. Depends on the situation assessment."

"How long will the situation assessment take?"

He glanced at his phone. "Another twenty-three minutes."

"And then … boom?"

He was scrolling through his messages.

"So now we've lost the element of surprise, what's the rush for blowing things up and macho shootouts? Slow and steady wins the race."

He looked up. "Haven't we already had this conversation?"

"If you stick with your containment strategy for a few days, you could set up communication with the wizards, maybe convince them to surrender."

Morgan's mind went to Arika's description of the underground rooms. Whoever was down there probably had provisions to survive for weeks, even months … enough time to cause untold mayhem. Just look at the damage they achieved in a few days. And there might be other avenues of escape – the giant steps on the other side of the chamber, for example. Who knows how far the catacombs went, how many exits there were? Within a couple of hours, Wilfred and Simon could slip through their fingers and disappear completely. They couldn't take that chance.

"We're doing whatever it takes. No delays. End of story."

"But, Sam –"

"Henri, why don't you stick to advice about ghosties and leave the tactics to –"

Morgan was interrupted by an eruption of shouting and gunshots from the farmyard.

"Stay back," he warned, standing in front of her.

Slipping the rifle off his shoulder, he opened the door a crack.

Outside was pandemonium. Living nightmares, some barely recognisable as human, were running and crawling and slithering out of the barn. Many were misshapen or had missing limbs, and some were enhanced with metal bands, same as Hugo Petrusch. They were all wearing grey pants. Some ran at top speed at the soldiers; some limped on deformed limbs; the stragglers dragged themselves along the ground.

As Morgan watched in horror, a huge shaggy paw shot up from the stone well and landed on the edge of the wall; another paw followed; then one of the hideous, hairy, jackal-like ghouls they'd seen in the sub-basement dragged its bloated body out of the well and into the light.

Resting for a moment on the wall, its white fangs curved in a grotesque smile, it glanced around for its first victim. When it spotted a soldier running towards the farmyard gate, it uttered a wolfish howl, leapt to the ground and loped after him.

Throwing open the door, Morgan rushed to the portico step, took aim with his rifle and shot. The bullet hit the ghoul's shoulder, but with barely a flinch, it continued its pursuit. Leaping into the air, landing on the soldier's back, it clamped its jaws on his neck while its momentum propelled him to the ground.

Morgan shot again, this time aiming for the ghoul's ear. The bullet hit its mark, but again there was little reaction. Its jaws went on tearing at the soldier's head, tossing flesh, bone and blood left and right until there was nothing left to tear.

Licking its bloody snout with its long black tongue, it looked around for more prey. A soldier was backing away from the barn, shooting at the dead things emerging from the open door, yelling instructions to others around him, oblivious to the bear-sized monster sizing him up for its next meal. The ghoul's jaws opened in a wide smile.

"Hey there!" yelled Morgan, waving his arm at the soldier. "Behind you!"

But the soldier was distracted by the gunfire and pandemonium and didn't hear him. The ghoul crept closer, sat on its haunches as the man backed towards it, then raised an enormous paw and swatted him, almost decapitating him with one fell swoop. After completing the separation of his body and his head with another mighty swing of its paw, it looked around for its next victim.

Motioning Henri to stay put, Morgan jumped off the portico, and abandoning his attempt to kill the ghoul, began shooting at the dead things emerging from the barn. Shots to the head felled them, but still more came, until they outnumbered the soldiers by five to one. In the meantime, more ghouls were emerging from the well.

Then, cutting through the sounds of shots and screams, Morgan heard the creak of timbers. It was coming from the barn, which was swaying like something gargantuan was moving around inside, bumping against the walls, trying to find a way out. He stopped shooting and watched in wonder as the wooden structure shuddered, settled, shuddered again. What kind of monstrosity could shake a whole building? he asked himself with mouth hanging.

It didn't take long to find out. The barn shook violently one last time, and then a wall exploded and the roof collapsed, bringing down the whole building, and out of the debris and devastation crawled two huge, brownish blobs. Gelatinous and semi-transparent, each one the size of a small truck, they resembled gigantic, deformed lice, though unlike lice, they crawled on protoplasmic legs, shooting out ropes of jelly and pulling themselves along the ground. Like heat-seeking missiles, they zeroed in on living bodies, flinging out protoplasmic tentacles, dragging their victims towards them, pulling them into their gelatinous bulk. As the blobs crawled away, the dim outlines of the soldiers could be seen inside them, dissolving into red slush, which was piped through their bodies until it became indistinguishable from the general reddish-brown hue of the things. Clothes and rifles and other indigestible materials sank, to be excreted in black heaps in the monsters' wake.

Realising his firepower was no match for the ghouls or these new monstrosities, Morgan returned to the farmhouse, where Henri was standing on the portico, watching the battle as if in a trance. He ushered her back over the doorstep, and together they stood at the open door and stared out at the mayhem and death.

"What the hell are the blobs?" Morgan demanded.

Henri couldn't take her eyes off them. "Tseg," she breathed, as a third one emerged from the destroyed barn. "I don't believe it. They're real."

"What's a Tseg?"

"They're supposed to be white or grey. The redness must be from their diet. What has Waite been feeding them?"

"What's a Tseg?"

Henri shook her head. "A Tsug. Tseg is plural. They're livestock of the Great Old Ones."

"The things that were supposed to have lived here two-hundred-and-fifty million years ago?"

"Or more."

"I've never heard of carnivorous livestock."

"The Great Old Ones are further up the food chain than we are."

"I hope you mean 'were'."

She glanced at him. Her look told him she wasn't intending on correcting herself.

"How do we kill them?"

"We … don't."

Suddenly, a skinny dead man in grey pants spied them, and with a high-pitched shriek came racing towards the house. Slamming the door shut, Morgan twisted the lock and rushed into the dining room, returning a moment later with two chairs. He propped one under the handle as the man slammed against the door. Going back and grabbing two more chairs, he stacked them on top of the others. Henri followed his example, dragging out a mahogany cabinet that looked like it weighed more than she did.

The dead man, intent on getting at them, threw his body at the door again and again. Morgan and Henri stood back and watched as the door bowed inwards and creaked on its ancient hinges.

Suddenly, the assault stopped. As they watched in horror, the handle slowly descended. Something banged against the wood. The handle rattled furiously; there was another bang; then silence.

Pulling out his phone, Morgan rang Sparks. No answer. He tried Jurgens' phone. It went straight to voicemail.

Crossing to the parlour, he pulled aside the ratty curtain and looked towards the door for their attacker. There was no one there – the man must have given up and gone in search of someone more available.

Spying movement, he leaned his forehead against the glass and saw below the window a legless, semi-human corpse dragging itself towards a dead soldier. It pulled itself over the woman's face, tore open her uniform and dug its fingernails into her stomach.

Grimacing, Morgan looked beyond the gruesome scene to the battlefield. The soldiers appeared to be winning against Wilfred's army of the dead. Many of them were slow and stupid, and the soldiers were trained to bring them down with a single shot to the head. Their major challenge was the sheer volume of them. But the jackal-like ghouls were another matter. They seemed to revel in killing for the sake of killing, bounding from one kill to the next, not bothering to eat what they slayed. And they were almost invincible. Even after being burnt with a flame-thrower, they continued hunting, having no apparent sense of pain or peril. It was only when their muscles or joints were damaged to the point of failure that they finally fell, jaws snapping, to the blood-soaked ground.

The Tseg had separated, and Morgan could only see one from where he was standing. It was headed towards the farmyard gate, where the combat vehicles, armoured personnel carrier and a small squad were stationed, taking a circuitous route as it honed in on any warm body in range.

New horrors had also appeared: brown, cylindrical, fungus-looking things, covered in black scabs and grey-green lichen, resembling plants more than animals. They moved jerkily on woody legs, and their sole interest appeared to be dead bodies. Ignoring anything alive, they moved from corpse to corpse, lifting limbs with woody, arm-like appendages and chewing on them like a stick of candy.

Henri was behind him, keying into her phone.

"What are you doing?" he asked her, trying to see the screen.

"Researching Tseg."

"You seem to know plenty enough already. Like how they can't be killed."

She ignored him, either intentionally or because she was so busy reading she hadn't heard him.

"Henri, what did you mean by 'they can't be killed'?"

"That's what I'm looking for."

Morgan was getting annoyed by her lack of answers. She seemed to know a little about a lot, but not much that could be deployed in a live situation.

"What about them?" he asked, nodding at the fungus creatures.

"What are they?"

Henri glanced out the window, glanced down at her phone, jerked up her head in surprise.

Grinning like a child, she moved closer to the glass. "OMG. They're incredible, aren't they?" She pushed her glasses up. "They look vegetative. A subterranean life form, I'd say. Alien? Hmm, probably," she answered herself.

"So you don't know what they are."

She went back to her phone. "Can you take a few pics? I really need to find out more about Tseg."

As Morgan was taking photos of the fungus-things, he noticed the Tsug to his right had locked on the heat of the soldiers stationed outside the gate. A second Tsug now came into view on the other side of the barn, headed towards the house. The third was nowhere to be seen. Morgan estimated the Tseg were fifty percent larger than when they broke out of the barn. The one near the gate had four shapes inside its protoplasmic body, and its general colouring had turned from light brown to a dull shade of red. How many soldiers had died to supply that much colour? he wondered, feeling sick at the thought.

As the Tsug approached the gate, machine gun fire on the light attack vehicles strafed it. The bullets shot into its body, slowed to a halt, then descended through the jelly, following the clothes and weapons and other indigestible materials that were sinking to the ground before being excreted in the blob's wake.

"Blow it up," murmured Morgan, raising his phone. He rang the section commander.

"Sir!" came Lowry's voice.

Morgan was about to say, "Blow it up" when he saw a man with a light anti-tank weapon on his shoulder stepping forward. "Good work," he said instead. "Destroy that thing, and then go after the other two. One's this side of the barn, heading towards us in the house. The other went behind the house, I think. I can't get hold of Sparks or Jurgens. They may be holding it back there."

He hung up and watched nervously as the Tsug rolled over the gate, flattening it.

The soldier with the anti-tank weapon dropped to his knee, aimed and released a missile. The rocket shot forward, flew through the air and hit the Tsug dead centre, exploding in a flash of fire, sending gobs of reddish protoplasm flying everywhere.

Morgan whooped in triumph, while Henri stood quietly at his side, taking pictures with her phone. As the jelly-like pieces splattered to the ground, he shook her shoulder, trying to get her enthused over their win.

The soldiers were also cheering, raising fists in the air, some patting others on the back. The Tseg were the largest of their adversaries, so far displaying immunity to both bullets and flame-throwers, and this victory suggested the battle had turned in their favour.

But as their cheers went on, some noticed something strange happening. Henri had seen it too and was nodding to herself, as if she'd been waiting for this all along.

Throwing a frown at her, Morgan moved his face closer to the window. He could see shock on a growing number of faces, and eventually all the soldiers went quiet. At first Morgan couldn't make out what they were staring at, but then he saw movement on the ground. The reddish blobs were creeping towards each other, joining up, melding into larger masses. More disturbingly, they seemed to be forming two separate, smaller Tseg. Within less than a minute, the two Tseg were complete and moving towards the vehicles.

As Morgan gaped, there came a crash of glass in the dining room.

He grabbed Henri's arm and they rushed to the hallway in time to see a bloodied man pulling himself through the dining room window. His red teeth clicked together as he stared at them with eyes popping with hunger.

Morgan raised his rifle and shot him in the forehead. Another mutated thing dragged him out of the way and took his place. He shot that one too. Two more hungry faces appeared in the window.

There was a crash of glass behind them in the parlour.

"Basement!"

Pulling out his phone, Morgan pushed Henri towards the door under the staircase. "Sparks! Are you there? Sparks? Sparks?"

He wasn't.

Following Henri into the basement, Morgan slammed the door shut, tripped down the steps, and kept on her heels as they raced to the room with the trapdoor. Once inside, Morgan pulled the secret door shut behind them. With luck, the dead-heads would have no idea this room was here. It wasn't Morgan's favoured tactic to corner himself in the face of danger, but with so many of those things, and Henri to protect, there was no immediate alternative.

He tried ringing Sparks again. Then Lowry. Then Jurgens. None of them answered. Their silence brought on a sick feeling in his stomach. It didn't look promising – for the operation or for him and Henri.

Tapping the phone on his leg, he stared at the octopus on the bronze plate. They had seriously underestimated the capability of the enemy, believing that the major threat, at least in the short term, would come from Waite's army of the dead. Morgan knew Sparks or Lowry would have called for reinforcements by now, but he also knew it might take up to an hour for them to get here. And how many more soldiers' lives would be lost by then?

For a time, Henri had been shocked into silence, but safe in the sub-basement room she began raving. "I told you we needed more time! Didn't I? I told you! You wouldn't listen! Racing into this with all your guns and war toys … now see where we are! Trapped! We should have taken more time! I told you!"

Morgan kept his eyes on the bronze plate, playing out their options in his mind.

"Shut up, Henri. We're safe here. None of those things will find this room – unless you bring them here with all your shouting and carrying on."

She folded her arms. "How long do you suggest we stay here, hiding like scared puppies?"

He frowned at her sudden change of tone. "Would you prefer to be up there fighting?"

"I'd prefer to be doing something useful."

He held himself back from commenting on her usefulness to date, and instead went to the bronze plate, got down on all fours and placed his ear against it.

"It is what it is. You need to wait here till I make contact with some-body on the surface who says it's safe to come out."

Henri joined him at the trapdoor. "You're not thinking of going down there, are you?"

He tried to screen out her voice. It was important to concentrate, trust his instincts, and stop being sidetracked by the constant question-ing by this bookworm.

"You've got to be mad, Sam. You know what's down there."

Henri had the type of voice it was difficult to screen out.

"I have a mission to complete. If Orwell and Waite are down there, orchestrating all this, I need to stop them any way I can. It's my job."

He couldn't hear anything beneath the bronze plate.

"Everything most likely went through the barn," he conjectured. Thinking of the ghoul that had climbed out of the outside well earlier, and knowing how bloodthirsty the loathsome things were, he added, "Why would one be waiting here all this time when everything else went the other way? They can't be that smart. Or patient."

Turning to Henri, he asked her, "If you had longer, what would you have advised me to do?"

She was making little shakes of her head, staring into space.

"Henri."

No answer.

"Henri!"

She gave him a quick glance, then went back to shaking her head.

He jumped up and shook her arm. "Snap out of it, Henri! We don't have time for this!"

"Don't yell at me! I'm trying to think!"

He almost laughed. "I thought you were going into shock."

If Henri wasn't shocked before, she was now. "I'll give you shock, young man. Cheeky blighter … I've been thinking about something," she added belligerently, as if to counter his insinuation about her. "Legend has it the Great Old Ones controlled Tseg through mind control. Perhaps …"

Morgan nodded at her, urging her to finish the thought.

"Perhaps the magic that resurrected the dead works in the same way. If the wizards are killed, all this may stop."

It was only a straw to clutch at, a wildly improbable thought bubble, but it sparked in Morgan a glimmer of hope that at last they had a chance to stop this madness. He patted his rifle. "Good. Then that's our plan."

"It may not stop the ghouls or those tree things."

"Course not."

When she saw Morgan nodding at the trapdoor, she started backtracking. "Look, Sam, it's only a hunch. If we wait here for a rescue squad, I'll be able to research something more evidence-based. Back at the library."

"Your hunch works for me," Morgan said. "Trust your gut," he added with a twinge of melancholy.

Shaking thoughts of Cleo from his mind, he knelt by the tentacle switch and placed his finger on it. "Those two are down there; I know it. They think all these monsters they've set free will protect them, but they're dead wrong. They won't see me coming."

He could tell from Henri's vexed look that she wasn't convinced that going deeper underground, where the ghouls, zombies and other monsters came from, was the most sensible course of action.

"What if I'm wrong? It's been known to happen. What if we go to all this trouble to kill them and nothing changes?"

Morgan pressed the switch, got to his feet and watched with rifle raised as the trapdoor rose. To his great relief, the well was empty.

He looked at her. "Then, my dear Henri, at least we'll have two dead wizards who should have been snuffed out centuries ago. Right now, I'd be pleased as a pig in mud with that."

52

The spell

WILFRED DROPPED HIS bags at the altar, fell to his knees, pulled out the Necronomicon and opened it on the grass. Turning to a page he'd bookmarked with one of his business cards, he reached back inside the bag and pulled out a curved black horn. He smiled at the horn, weighed it in his hands, then leapt to his feet, stepped up to the altar and placed it on the edge of the pentagram.

After taking a few moments to relish the sounds of distant gunfire, he grabbed the backpack, took out a black conical vase and placed it on the grass. Then, one by one, he placed four more vases around the altar, each one aligned to a point of the pentagram. This done, he took out an oven lighter and went around lighting the wick inside each vase.

Throwing the lighter on the grass, Wilfred returned to the altar and examined the horn. It was a battered, ancient thing, marred by scratches and pockmarks. In colour it appeared black, but in fact it had no colour; looking at it was like looking into a black hole. The horn was etched with irregular lines and geometric shapes, apparently in a random configuration – but Wilfred knew better. He knew there was magic in those symbols, and he trembled with anticipation at what that magic was about to deliver. He sniffed it, like he'd done countless times before, and smiled at its non-smell, non-weight and non-colour – its alien ability to dampen all senses. There was life in the horn, life from its original owner, and it was this life that sucked in energy from whoever was holding it, and gave the object its power.

Positioning the horn at the centre of the pentagram, Wilfred pulled off his coat, threw it on the grass, and stretched his arms towards the sky. Staring into the dark clouds, feeling the pull of the wounds in his belly, the tickle of blood as it seeped from the newly-formed scabs, he cried, "Lord Azathoth! Stir from your eternal slumber and heed the call of your servant, Dhagdar! I beseech you: admit the dimensions to bleed the leviathan! And in your name shall chaos arise from order, and order from chaos! In your divine name! In the name of Azathoth!"

At his words, violet flames erupted with a roar from the vases. Billows of smoke rose into the air, undisturbed by the wind that was bending the grass and rustling the pages of the Necronomicon and blowing hair in Wilfred's eyes. The smoke spread out between the vases before settling gently to the ground, staining the grass purple.

Wilfred looked around with a wild expression on his face. The purple pentagram protected him from any would-be assailants. As long as he stayed within its bounds, no one could harm him; no one could so much as touch him; he would finish the spell. There was no stopping it; no stopping *him*.

Breathing fast, he retrieved the backpack, dropped it at his feet and reached into it again. This time he brought out a human heart wrapped with grey twine. Earlier, Wilfred had stuffed the atria and ventricles with a mixture of herbs and fungi, in the precise proportions instructed by the Necronomicon.

"Alas, poor Sebastian," he said to the heart with a misty smile. "You served me well. You sacrificed your life for a greater good, and at considerable cost to your person. May you rest at last in peace."

With reverence, he placed the heart at the top point of the pentagram. Then he reached into the bag and took out another.

ARIKA NOTICED THE smoke first. "There!" she cried.

Kane followed the line of her finger and spotted the violet haze rising above the scrub. "The road doesn't go that way, damnit." Jamming on the brakes, he turned to Dylan. "You know how to get up there?"

His brother shook his head.

"We'll walk," said Arika. "It's not far."

Kane frowned at Dylan. "You ready for this?"

Dylan gurgled.

"I'll take that as a yes."

ON THE SUMMIT of Mlal'orla, Wilfred opened his arms towards Jacob's

End.

"Lord Azathoth! In your name I break the five seals! In return I implore you: bleed the dimensions; grant me chaos; open the way for the Great Old Ones to transform this land of vile science and blasphemous human conceit in your divine name!"

He picked up the black horn.

"Enim Azathoth!"

With all the strength he could muster in his young body, he slammed the horn down on the first of the bound hearts.

As blood splattered across the altar, a rumble of thunder sounded in the clouds to his left.

Turning from Jacob's End, Wilfred squinted up at the clouds, his face creased with worry. He'd expected the response to come from the ocean, from the greyish, greasy water, the epicentre of the ring of creeping death, not from some point in mid-air. The sky was an unforeseen scenario, something he hadn't planned for. It worried him that the ritual had only just begun and already it was going awry, but then again, he reminded himself, wasn't that the nature of chaos?

Hearing nothing more, he raised the horn again.

"Enim Yog-Sothoth!"

He smashed the next heart.

KANE WAS RUNNING up the hill when the second rumble of thunder came. He was carrying Dylan like a baby, a baby that resembled a skinny, big-headed corpse swaddled in brown-stained bandages.

Arika, a few paces ahead, dropped to the grass.

Catching up with her, Kane saw why. At the hill's summit, Wilfred was standing with his back to them, a black spear-shaped object held above his head in both hands. Before him was a flat rock, sheared at an angle. It was the altar Dylan had described, and it was obvious even from this distance that the altar was stained with blood. Open on the grass behind Wilfred was the Necronomicon.

Placing Dylan on the ground behind a rocky outcrop, Kane touched Arika's arm and motioned her to stay put.

"Enim Z'garh Khrl'ur!" he heard Wilfred cry in his brother's voice, and glanced up in time to see him smash the black object down.

This time the action was accompanied by an ululating voice from the sky, a hollow cry of triumph or pain that shook every molecule in the air.

Staying low, Kane crept towards the Necronomicon, glancing around for any signs of Wilfred's accomplices. Wilfred was staring into the clouds, trembling with anticipation. As the voice continued its howling cry, he began grunting like an animal, the grunts rising in volume and turning into words: "Yes! Yes! Oh yes! Oh yes! Oh yes!"

Following the line of his stare, Kane froze. The grey clouds to his left were bulging – but not with the normal motion of clouds. They had a weird texture, a kind of bubbling plasticity, and inside them, like an embryo inside an egg sac, something dark and terrible squirmed and cried out as if demanding to be born.

Waving his bloodied arms at the clouds, Wilfred yelled something unintelligible.

Kane rubbed his eyes, then squinted up at the womb in the sky. He'd already guessed what the thing was: another Messenger. Wilfred was welcoming it with open arms, inviting it to join his infernal army in clearing the land of his enemies.

Taking advantage of the distraction, he scurried up, stepped over the purple ring and knelt by the Necronomicon. Closing the book quietly, he glanced up at Wilfred, then stepped back over the purple ring and crept back to Dylan and Arika.

Dropping the book on the grass, he flung it open, turned a few pages, and sighed with relief when he came to the picture of the seven-pointed star with the piercing eye in its centre.

"There you go," he said, pushing the Necronomicon closer to his brother. "Do your stuff."

Arika unwrapped the bandage from Dylan's decomposing hand and placed it on the page. "Focus," she said. "You can do this."

Kane nodded at her, while Dylan concentrated all his attention on the picture.

But when Kane looked over at Wilfred, he received a shock. The book wasn't working. Wilfred had turned away from the clouds and had picked up the black horn again.

"Faster," Kane urged. "Don't think about anything else. Just focus on getting back in your body. Come on, man, concentrate."

"Leave him be, Kane," Arika admonished. "You're the one breaking his concentration."

Dylan didn't react to either of them. He appeared to be in a trance, and when Kane looked again at Wilfred, he saw why. Wilfred had raised the black horn above the next heart, but he was hesitating – swaying and dipping his head like someone about to nod off.

Suddenly something seemed to click in his mind, and he whirled around and saw the Necronomicon was gone. With a cry of alarm, he looked up and locked eyes with Kane. His face twisted into a mask of hate.

Kane got to his feet, expecting Wilfred to cry out for help, or come running at them with the horn raised, or destroy them with a magic thunderbolt – and so he was surprised when he turned back to the altar, lifted the horn in the air and cried, "Enim Nyarlathotep!" The horn came down and smashed the fourth heart.

The cosmic voice rent the air. The clouds appeared to melt over the thing inside them, and a mass of writhing appendages now became visible. The thing, a mountainous black monster, hung suspended in the air, squirming as it struggled to escape the clouds that had birthed it.

Without stopping to check the progress of his creation, Wilfred lifted the horn above the last heart. But as he opened his mouth to utter the final words of the spell, he faltered. His hands lost their grip on the horn, it slipped from his grasp, bounced on the bloody altar and fell to the ground. Wilfred collapsed across the stone block.

Kane knelt beside Dylan, who was still focusing all his attention on the page. Glancing back at Wilfred, he smiled when he saw him trying to stand on wobbly legs. A moment later, and Wilfred was flat on his back on the grass.

"That's it! Let's go!" Kane cried, grabbing Dylan under the arms. He scooped him up and started running towards the altar, Arika following with the Necronomicon.

At a safe distance, they stopped.

"Dylan?" Kane said. "Is that you?"

His brother's blood-spattered body lay motionless. Kane tapped him with his boot, then kicked a little harder when there was no response. The shrunken body in his arms was unresponsive too.

"Kane!" cried Arika, pointing at the clouds.

Turning his gaze to the sky, Kane was relieved to find the monster dissolving into the clouds, its entry to this world checked by the unfinished spell. That's one disaster averted, he thought as the black shape faded to grey. No murderous Messenger to swoop down on leathery wings and vomit over us and suck up our liquefied remains.

At his feet, Dylan's body stirred. He gasped, his eyes opened, his hands grabbed at the grass.

Arika knelt beside him. He stared at her, blinked a few times, then with a groan pushed himself up.

"Arika. Am I …?"

She touched his shoulder. "Welcome back, Dylan."

Kane blew out a stream of air. The body in his arms squirmed and he glanced down. Wilfred was sneering at him.

"Gah!" he cried, and dropped him on the grass.

Joining Arika, he helped Dylan to his feet, and then each held an arm as they led him away from the altar. They sat him under a small tree, leaning his back against the trunk. Arika placed the Necronomicon on the grass, went to retrieve Dylan's coat, came back and draped it around his shoulders.

Kane asked, "Is that really you, Dylan?"

He nodded.

"I think I need more than that, chum."

"You're a dumb jock who doesn't deserve to get the girl," Dylan said with a crooked smile.

"Aha," said Kane, "that's the brother I know."

"Ow," he said, grimacing and bending forward in pain.

Kane lifted Dylan's bloody shirt, revealing bloody bandages wrapped around his torso.

When they removed them, they saw letters carved into his belly.

"What the hell is that?" Kane cried, eyes popping at the horrific wounds.

Arika squinted at the letters. "D-hag-dar. I think it says Dhagdar. Does that ring a bell, Dylan?"

"The bastard scarred me for life!"

"It's still bleeding. It must have been part of the spell."

"That psycho!" spat Kane. "Who does that kind of thing?"

"Someone who knows he can trade in a body for a new one if he damages it?" offered Arika.

Dylan carefully re-wrapped the bandages around his torso. "Is Wilfred …?"

They all looked over at the pile of dirty bandages and old-man clothes. Wilfred lay on his side on the grass, unmoving.

"Looks dead to me," said Kane.

"It's not the first time you've said that," Arika reminded him.

He pulled a face at her. "Dead or alive, he's in no state to steal your body now. Look at him. And look at you, kid. You're young again. We've got the book. He's done for this time, no doubt about it."

Dylan's face brightened. "Does that mean I get my inheritance?"

"You deserve it after all you've been through." He shook his head at Dylan's bloody shirt. "It'll help pay for the plastic surgery to get rid of those scars."

"What will you do with your new castle?" asked Arika.

Dylan grinned. "Two castles, remember. Do you want one?"

"I wouldn't mind a castle," she mused. "If you're giving them away."

"Would you prefer the Hungary one or the one in Austria?"

"Whichever is the smallest. I'm not much for housework."

As if spurred by their gloating, Wilfred stirred, dug his fingers in the grass, rolled onto his stomach and began dragging his rotting body towards the altar. When he got to the horn, he took hold of it with one hand and pulled himself up to the altar with the other.

Arika saw him first. Dropping her smile, she fumbled in her bag for her gun. But she was too slow. Before she could pull out the weapon, Wilfred gurgled, "Enim Cthulhu," and smashed the final heart.

The action sapped what was left of his energy, and he fell backwards. His head hit the ground with a dull thump.

This time the cosmic voice was so loud they had to cover their ears.

Climbing to their feet, they turned their faces in dread to the sky. The conclusion of the spell had reversed whatever was happening up there, and the black behemoth, with limbs thrashing and tentacles writhing, was now completing its inglorious entry into this world.

With the accretion of mass, it began slowly descending; then suddenly it slipped from the net of clouds and fell to earth with a ground-shaking boom. Roaring with the voice of a thousand wild animals, its mass of legs and arms and tentacles flying about madly, it soon found its bearings and pushed itself upright.

When it reached its full height, Kane stumbled backwards. The thing was the size of a small office block. It had limbs like a spider or ant or centipede, and tentacles like an octopus or squid or jellyfish, but its most distinctive feature was its human-like head, black as coal, bigger than an elephant, crowned with cilia that squirmed like snakes.

"Is that – a Messenger?" Kane asked, glancing at Dylan.

The black behemoth turned its face to the hill, as if it knew the altar was the source of its liberation. With narrow yellow eyes and lips thin and cruel, it regarded Kane, Dylan and Arika with an expression that suggested intense boredom. At the sight of the altar, its mouth opened and words thundered out: FHT'URH GWORRH CTHUT ESCHEK'TA!

They turned and ran.

Behind them, the thing continued its thunderous cries.

"Sounds like a chant," panted Arika. "May be part of the spell."

"Either that or it's really pissed off at being woken up," said Dylan.

Kane stopped suddenly. He'd remembered the Necronomicon, which they left on the grass in their haste to escape.

"The book. We forgot the damn book."

Dylan and Arika slowed to a walk.

"Leave it," Arika said, peering anxiously up the hill. "We'll go back and get it when that thing's gone."

But to Kane, leaving the book wasn't an option. Not after all they went through to retrieve it, and not with Dylan still vulnerable to any crazy who believed he could pick up where Wilfred Waite left off.

Arika read his mind. Pushing Dylan along, she said, "Hurry up, then. We'll see you back at the truck."

53

Outside

"WAIT, SAM. LISTEN."

Morgan, his boot on the first rung, paused.

"The shooting. It's stopped."

Henri was right. Morgan climbed out of the well. Part of him was relieved he wouldn't have to descend to the catacombs and face the wizards and their protectors without backup, but a bigger part was apprehensive at the sudden cessation of hostilities. It didn't automatically mean they won.

"Let's go," he said, motioning Henri to follow him up the steps.

He listened at the door. Nothing.

Pushing into the laboratory, he could see their pursuers hadn't breached the basement.

"So far, so good."

He ran lightly across the concrete floor and up the stairs, listened at the door, turned and shook his head at Henri. Holding his breath, he slowly opened the door, stuck his head into the hallway and looked around. There was no one there.

"Come on, Henri. Keep your eyes peeled."

Creeping down the hallway, they approached the front door. To his left, in the dining room, Morgan could see, slumped over the window frame, the man he shot earlier. In the parlour the window was smashed, but the glass was largely intact.

He approached the smashed window and was confronted by a horrendous sight: almost everything in the farmyard was dead.

Striding past Henri to the front door, he threw it open, raised his rifle, and marched out to the battlefield.

"Sam …" began Henri, coming up behind him.

Morgan gaped at all the dead soldiers, the mangled creatures from

Waite's army, the smouldering ghouls and other blackened heaps. The fungus creatures were the only living things in sight, a half dozen of them standing around chewing on dead bodies. Beyond the flattened gate were the vehicles, and he could see dead soldiers there too. He didn't immediately recognise anyone, but he knew some of the dead were his friends.

"What happened?" asked Henri, spinning around.

"You're the expert."

At that point, Henri spotted a lake of reddish-brown goo on the ground. "The Tseg!" she cried, pointing at it. "Destroyed! Look, Sam! Something must have happened to the wizards! The spell's broken! We won!"

"Does this look like winning to you?" Morgan shot back.

She adjusted her glasses. "I'm sorry, Sam, I didn't mean –"

"Maybe Sparks got them."

She was quick to agree. "Of course. That would explain where he went. He must have found a way down, found the wizards and killed them."

Morgan was desperate to believe her, but he knew too much about the army's tactics to hold out much hope that Lieutenant Sparks was alive. It didn't feel right. Then again, Henri had a point that the melting of the Tseg was a sign the sorcerers were dead, or at least incapacitated.

"Could be some of their own monsters got them," he pointed out. "We'll find out soon enough."

"There's protection spells –"

"What's that?"

Henri stared at him. "Protection spells? They're –"

"That rumbling noise."

She cocked her head. After a second, she heard it too. "I can feel it … coming up from the ground." She looked at him. "From the dungeons?"

Morgan crouched down. He could feel the vibrations in his boots, travelling up through his legs, could see the barn timbers trembling with every thud, but it felt like the vibrations were going *into* the ground, not coming up.

Looking over his shoulder, he froze. His tongue lodged in his throat.

Henri studied his face, as if reading what he was seeing in his expression. As he slowly rose, she turned, grabbed his arm and squeezed hard, though he scarcely felt it.

Crawling across the heath was a black monstrosity, the size of a four-storey building. It reminded Morgan of tree trunks and sea urchins and ant legs and jellyfish, all magnified and mashed together in a nightmarish form that made no sense. Leathery black tentacles waved in the air with a life of their own, while the branch-like legs propelled the behemoth forward with a motion that was totally alien. In its wake was death. Birds fell from the sky; plants wilted and dropped their leaves; the grass turned a greasy grey-brown – the same sickly non-colour that surrounded Jacob's End.

As the monstrosity approached the battlefield, its tentacles reached out, scooped up bodies and stuffed them into yawning mouths along the length of its body. Despite the frenetic activity of its tentacles, its yellow eyes, set in a strangely-human face, regarded everything with an air of apathy and disdain, as if it were already bored and disgusted with what it saw in this world.

"She's magnificent," Henri gasped.

To Morgan's surprise, she left him and began walking towards the thing. When he dashed after her and reached out a hand, she sprang away violently and started running like a sprinter.

Taking off after her, he eventually caught up, grabbed her arm and pulled her away, just as a gigantic black tentacle, appearing from nowhere, smashed to the ground at her feet.

The near miss broke the trance, and Henri's face quickly turned from rapture to fear. Realising the stupor could return at any time, Morgan took her under both arms and dragged her towards the farmhouse.

As they approached the portico, Morgan felt something wrap around his ankle, and the next moment his leg was pulled out from under him. With a grunt of alarm, he fell face down in the mud.

Spitting out dirt, he rolled over to find a black tentacle clamped around his ankle. Before he could pull the rifle off his shoulder, it lifted him off the ground and hoisted him into the air, and to his horror he was pulled past the enormous face with its yellow eyes and thin-lipped mouth towards a yawning, undulating hole in the thing's body.

Twisting himself up, Morgan managed to get his pistol out of his thigh holster. He raised it, aimed as best he could, and shot at the thing's face. The bullets bounced off its skin like rubber bouncing off rubber.

Desperate now, his head approaching the waiting mouth, he pointed the gun at the tentacle around his ankle and shot. This time the bullet entered the thing's skin, and the tentacle spasmed and released its hold on him.

As he fell, another tentacle whipped out and caught him by the same ankle. Morgan shot that one too, the tentacle let go, and he dropped through space and landed with a heavy grunt in the mud.

Winded, weak, white as death, all he could do was reach out a hand to Henri, who was standing at the farmhouse door, her face a mask of terror. As more tentacles grabbed him around the waist and arms and legs and lifted him off the ground, he felt a sense of relief and comfort that at least Henri was safe. It would be one less death he would be responsible for.

The tentacles carried Morgan through the air, and he suddenly became aware that his struggle to survive had captured the interest of the behemoth. This time, instead of dropping him into one of the waiting mouths, the tentacles raised him towards the giant face and dangled him in front of its slitted yellow eyes. For a while it looked him up and down with what seemed like fascination.

As the she-god stared, a warm tingle washed over Morgan. Her interest was giving him the kind of high he'd only ever experienced at university, when he experimented with ecstasy and felt an emotional connection to every person in the room. This was different, though: the elation wasn't coming from a chemical, it was flowing into him from the sublime creature that held him. She was a vision, a warrior, a conqueror of worlds, and she was interested in *him*, Sam Morgan. He was the favoured one of all, the sole focus of her attention out of everyone and everything in the vast universe, and he craved her lasting gaze and longed to crawl across her perfect tentacles and stroke her cool ebony cheek.

As his muscles relaxed and his mind wavered and his eyes went in and out of focus, it came to Morgan how rare it must be for the beloved to be challenged. This is what had warranted this unexpected and unwarranted favour, he was certain of it. She was a divinity, a supreme being, the Black Queen, and he was her servant, her protector, her obedient slave, to do with as she wished. His only desire was to worship her for all eternity, to beg for her glorious attention and become one with her perfection.

These were Morgan's last thoughts as his life was drained from him. Once he was nothing but a dry husk, the Black Queen opened her mouth, threw in his body, and swallowed him whole.

54

March of the Black Queen

WHEN KANE ARRIVED back at the truck, Arika was hanging out the window. She smiled with relief when she saw him.

Pulling open the driver's door, he jumped in and dropped Wilfred's bag at her feet. After handing her the Necronomicon, he turned and stared at the skinny, pale-faced, black-haired adolescent in the back seat. Wilfred Waite's success in unleashing a gargantuan alien monstrosity on the world did little to interrupt his joy at seeing his brother back in his own body.

"You okay?" he asked.

Dylan nodded.

Kane narrowed his eyes. "Say something Dylan would say."

"Where's my Mars Bar?"

"Okay. Welcome back, bro."

Glancing at Arika, he started the truck. "It went towards the farm-house. We need to work out what the hell it is."

Putting the vehicle into drive, he did a three-point turn and sped off down the hill.

"You didn't see Simon up there, did you?" asked Arika.

"No, no one."

She looked at her phone. "It's funny: he hasn't returned any of my calls."

Kane didn't think it funny. Simon was probably hunkered down in the catacombs, playing his deranged part in this mayhem.

"I hope for his sake he's back at the university," he said.

"Something's happened to him."

Kane kept his mouth shut. He didn't want to bring up Simon's unholy alliance with Wilfred again, but the only other reason he could think of for the radio silence was that Simon had dropped dead from old age. And he doubted Arika wanted to hear that explanation either.

"Is there anything in the book about the monster?" he asked.

Arika opened the Necronomicon on her lap. "Probably. How else would Waite know how to raise it?"

"Good point."

He tapped his fingers on the steering wheel. Speeding down the road, with time to think, he couldn't help but feel responsible for allowing the monster to complete its entry into the world. Was there some point at which he should have made a different decision and stopped this from happening? Had his preoccupation with saving his brother doomed the planet?

Arika was turning the pages of the Necronomicon.

"Found anything?" he asked.

"No." She bit her lip. "It must be in here. There's all kinds of monsters. This must be one of the bigguns in the pantheon." She twisted around. "Did you see anything like it?" she asked Dylan. "In the book?"

"He never really let me near it," Dylan said.

"He didn't mention any other god besides Yog-Sothoth?"

Dylan shook his head.

Kane waited for what felt like five minutes, and then said, "Found anything yet?"

Arika glanced up at the road ahead. "Where are we going?"

"Wherever that thing's headed."

"Okay. What do you plan to do when you get there?"

He raised his eyebrows. He hadn't thought that far ahead. "By that time, you'll have found a spell to send it back to whatever cesspit it fell out of."

Taking the hint, she returned to the book.

"Found anything yet?" he asked as they approached the site of the roadblock.

"No." She turned the page. "Wait! There it is!"

He pulled over.

Arika held up the book. The picture was titled, 'Q'assog-tha', and the monster was definitely the one they saw fall from the sky. She turned it around to show Dylan.

"Yep, that's it."

"Does it say how to kill it?" asked Kane.

She returned the book to her lap. "I don't recognise the language."

"Does it say how to kill any of those things at the farm?"

"Hardly any of it's in English."

"That'd be right."

"It's a good likeness. Whoever drew it must have seen the thing in real life."

"They lived to draw it so there must be a way to kill it."

"They didn't kill it," Dylan, who was leaning over the console, pointed out. "But they must have seen it to get the detail so right."

Arika flipped over the page. "It might have been a dream. The guy who wrote this thing was supposed to have dreamed it all. Doesn't necessarily mean Q'ass – Q'assog –" She turned the page back. "… Q'assog-tha was here."

"I've had some pretty horrifying dreams since all this began," said Dylan, leaning back.

Kane was contemplating the road ahead.

"Kane," said Arika, "we don't have a spell to stop it."

"Maybe we need to leave this to the army," Dylan suggested. "What can we do? They've got rockets and shit."

Kane sighed. He knew his brother was right, but he also recalled Arika's assertion that a supernatural problem needs a supernatural solution. What did the army – or the NSO, for that matter – know about sending giant aliens back to the hellhole they came from? He ran his hand over his hair. If they couldn't stop the monster themselves, the least they could do was give the book to Morgan and let him find a wizard or two to release its power.

He put the gear into drive. "Let's go see if we can convince those guards to let us through this time … now we don't have a living corpse stinking up the back seat."

They continued in silence down the road, Arika turning the pages of the Necronomicon, Dylan staring out the window at the passing fields. Kane half-expected to see fighter jets soaring overhead, shooting rockets and strafing the sky with machine-gun fire, but the day was curiously

calm. Part of him hoped the silence meant the monster was dead –
squashed by the Earth's gravity, suffocated by our air or slain by
microbes. Why else wasn't anyone shooting at it?

The roadblock soon came into view. It was abandoned.

Kane stopped the truck. "That's strange."

"Maybe the fight's over," Arika suggested.

"Then why are the barriers still up?"

No one had an answer.

Opening the door, he went up and began dragging the barriers to
the side of the road. Arika got out to help, and then they got back in the
truck and started off again.

"Hey, here's the Messenger," cried Dylan, who'd taken possession of
the book.

Kane glanced over his shoulder. "Show me," he said – and then
Arika yelled, "Kane!" and he swerved and slammed his foot on the
brake.

"Jesus Christ!"

During the distraction, he'd almost run down a woman in purple
slacks, mustard-coloured shirt and red-framed glasses, who came flying
out from a field and was now walking towards his window waving both
hands at him.

Kane opened his door.

"I'm Henri Appleby," she rushed to say, and then she spied Dylan in
the back seat. Her face blanched. Backing away, she pointed at him with
arm outstretched. "The sorcerer! He's got the book! He'll kill us all!"

Kane stepped out of the truck. "What do you know about the book?"

"Do you know who that is?" Henri demanded, still pointing.

"That's my brother, Dylan. What do you know about the book?"

"I'm a librarian."

It was like the punchline to a joke. He stared coldly at her.

"What's he doing with the Necronomicon?" she demanded.

"What business is it of yours?"

"You're Kane Gates, aren't you? You think he's your brother."

"How do you –?"

"He's one of the perpetrators of this massacre. Director Morgan said so. He showed me the surveillance photos." When Kane didn't react, she added, "Wilfred Waite. It's him. In the flesh. Don't be fooled by that stupid grin. He's a creepy old man in sheep's clothing!"

Kane glanced over his shoulder at Dylan, who was indeed smiling.

"That was all a misunderstanding. Now, what's your role in this?"

"Do you know Sam Morgan?" interrupted Arika, who'd gotten out of the truck and was walking up to them.

Henri looked at her. "I'm with the National Security Office. On assignment. But they're dead." A look of anguish twisted her face. "They're all dead."

Arika halted. "All of them?"

She nodded, and tears filled her eyes, steaming up her glasses.

"Sam Morgan too?"

Henri pulled out a tissue, took off her glasses, began polishing them.

"How do you know? – that … Mr Morgan is dead?"

When Henri didn't answer, Arika went back to the truck, climbed inside, and pulled the door shut.

"A monster ate him," Henri whispered to Kane.

"A huge black octopussy thing?"

She nodded.

Kane gulped. "Ate him? That's intense. What happened out there?"

"We don't have time for idle chit-chat. We need to get in contact with the NSO and call for reinforcements."

"That thing killed them all?"

She glared at him. "No. Only him. The other monsters killed everyone else."

"Waite's army?"

"I said we don't have time. We need to get the NSO out here."

Kane wondered whether she was right, that they should retreat and let the NSO handle it. But how long would that take? The monster could turn on Quorn and flatten the whole village in less than an hour.

"Can the Necronomicon help us kill that thing?"

Henri turned her glare to Dylan. "Waite should know. He brought it here; I assume he can send it back."

He shook his head. There was no point trying to explain about the body swap when they had a cosmic-sized monster to vanquish.

"So you don't know anything about all this?"

"Of course I do. That was my assignment with the NSO – to advise on magic and the paranormal."

"You can read the Necronomicon?"

"I've read copies – partial copies."

"Well, beggars can't be choosers. Where did that thing go?"

"That way," said Henri, pointing towards Jacob's End.

"Get in the truck."

"I'm not getting in with him!"

"Get in the truck, and you can ring the NSO while we chase down the alien."

"I lost my phone."

"You can use mine."

"I don't know the number. The only number I knew was Sam's. The others are in my phone."

"Just ring the number on their website."

"It's not that easy. Sam Morgan was head of a secret government agency. Let me think." She rubbed her neck. "Maybe Ames will be able to get through. I don't have his number, though."

Kane huffed in frustration. "We don't have time for this. Think in the truck."

"I'm not –"

"If you don't get in, I will pick you up and shove you in."

Henri took his measure, realised he could deliver on his threat, and climbed into the back seat. Pulling on the seatbelt, she sat as far away from Dylan as possible, while he smiled at her, enjoying his little moment of power.

"Take the book," Kane ordered as he started the truck. "See if you can work out how to get rid of that thing."

Dylan handed her the Necronomicon, and she frowned down at the picture of Q'assog-tha. "Ah, yes, I thought she looked familiar. This is a much more realistic rendition of her than the copies. Stay away from me," she demanded when Dylan leaned in for another look.

"There!" yelled Kane, startling them all.

Up ahead was Q'assog-tha, black tentacles waving wildly as she made her way across the fields.

"She's going the wrong way," said Dylan, "if she wants to destroy things."

"She'll figure that out when she hits the ocean," Arika said.

"If we're lucky she'll turn left. The nearest village is about half an hour away."

"That's not enough time for the NSO to stop her."

"How's it going back there?" Kane asked over his shoulder.

"I'm getting something," said Henri.

"Get it faster."

"Why are men so impatient?" She tapped the page with her finger. "There's something about Q'assog-tha being Cthulhu's sister … Oh, and mate. How dreadful."

"I don't care if it's the bride of Godzilla. Does it say how to kill it?"

"You can't kill a Great Old One. You can only send it back to where it came from."

"Holy shit!" cried Arika.

An attack helicopter had appeared from nowhere, racing towards Q'assog-tha, letting fly a missile. The missile hit its mark, exploding in flames and evoking a thunderous cry from the Black Queen.

"A chopper!" Kane cried excitedly. "Looks like they're not all dead."

"Won't do any good," commented Henri. "You can't destroy a Great Old One. They exist across multiple dimensions and will regenerate if they're injured."

"Thanks David Attenborough."

A second explosion sent Q'assog-tha into a rage. With alarming alacrity, she diverted to a nearby barn, rammed it with her gargantuan body, swept up the broken stones with a dozen tentacles and hurled them at the helicopter. Her aim was spot on: the stones collided with the chassis, smashed the window, flew into the blades. The damaged aircraft rose, spun a few times, turned on its side, and crashed to the ground.

Q'assog-tha rushed over and crushed the helicopter flat with great slams of her tree-like arms.

"Jesus," breathed Dylan, "I wonder how many people were in there."

"It's just the one," said Arika. "It must have been a survivor from the farm."

"They only had one," Henri confirmed. "But at least it means someone had a chance to phone it in."

Arika screwed up her face. "If you're right – and judging by the effect those missiles had on it – I'm not sure it'll make much difference how many there are."

"Maybe it'll be jets next time," said Dylan, "with higher firepower."

"A supernatural problem needs a supernatural solution," Kane said, and saw Arika's half smile from the corner of his eye.

The attack had given them time to catch up. As the truck drew close, Q'assog-tha started moving again.

"She's heading north of Jacob's End," said Dylan.

"Oh dear!" cried Henri, her back straightening. "Cthulhu. In his house at R'lyeh, dead Cthulhu waits dreaming."

"That's what Wilfred used to say," said Dylan.

"What does it mean?" asked Kane.

Henri leaned forward. "The great priest Cthulhu is trapped in an underwater city called R'lyeh, and according to ancient prophesy, one day he will rise up and destroy the world."

Arika went pale. "She's going to wake her brother."

"What's a Cthulhu?" asked Kane.

"Another Great Old One. Like Q'assog-tha. But Cthulhu is a High Priest."

"Don't tell me it's even bigger than that thing?"

"Not only bigger. Early last century there was a spate of madness across the South Pacific, and it's widely believed it was Cthulhu turning over in his sleep."

Kane snorted. "I don't get it."

"Cthulhu's consciousness can open windows to other dimensions," Henri explained. "If he awoke fully, his mind alone might be enough to plunge the world into chaos."

Kane had been following at a safe distance behind Q'assog-tha, but now he stopped the truck and turned to them.

"We need to get in front of it."

"What then?" asked Dylan.

"Then," said Arika, "our friendly librarian will tell us how to stop it."

Henri was running her finger along a line of text. "If you would all kindly be quiet, I may have a snowball's chance of delivering on your ridiculously high expectations."

Kane glanced around, searching for the best route to head off Q'assog-tha before she made it to the ocean. Nearby was a side road, little more than a track, that he knew was a shortcut to Jones Beach. The road would intersect with the Black Queen's current trajectory.

"Hold on."

Heading for the dirt road, he spun the truck's wheels and sped off.

Henri looked up from the Necronomicon. "I've got it!"

"What you got?"

She pulled off her glasses. "Q'assog-tha was summoned using the Black Ys-kar."

"The how's-it?"

"Ys-kar. It's a black spear that was part of the horn of a Supreme Being Cthulhu killed in one of his great battles. Apparently, the essence of Cthulhu still clings to it, which is what drew Q'assog-tha to it in the summoning spell."

"And? And?"

"And Ys-kar contains the poison of the vanquished god. If Q'assog-tha is pierced by it, the poison should make her existence in this world untenable. She should be sucked back to her own dimension."

Kane held the steering wheel steady as they sped along the rough track. "So we need to get close enough to stab her?"

"That's not quite all. To release the power of Ys-kar, we need a human sacrifice."

Anger stabbed at him. "Crap! Why is there always crap in the way? Bullshit! Crap, crap, crap!"

"It's the nature of magic. To make things hard."

He steadied his breathing, and gradually his anger subsided. This was a solution – perhaps an impossible solution, but it was more than they had five minutes ago.

"Okay, okay, we'll find a way round it."

Dylan regarded him coolly. "It's all academic if we don't have the horn."

Kane leaned down and reached into the bag at Arika's feet. "Does this look like the horn of a vanquished god?"

"Ah! Ah! Ah!" cried Henri, holding out both hands.

He gave the horn to Arika.

She stared at it in shock. "It's amazing," she breathed, holding it in her open palms. "It seems to have no weight or substance … or colour even."

"It's sucking the life from you," explained Henri, staring at Ys-kar with the eyes of a vampire.

Arika glanced at her, but didn't request an explanation. "So now," she said, stroking the carvings on it, "all we need is a human sacrifice."

Stopping the truck near a rise overlooking Jacob's End, Kane took Ys-kar from Arika and placed it back in the bag. Pushing open the door, jumping out, he threw the bag over his shoulder and raced up the incline. Arika and Dylan followed.

Q'assog-tha was making her way across the poisoned fields.

"She's moving further north of the bay," said Dylan. "We better hurry if we're gonna try and stab her."

"We need to work out how to make a human sacrifice," Arika reminded them.

"All those soldiers have died," Kane pointed out. "Won't they count?"

Dylan shook his head. "For a human sacrifice to work, there has to be intent."

Kane frowned at him. "I hate how my brother knows the correct way to do human sacrifices."

He stared at the building-sized mass of legs, arms and tentacles, an almost unstoppable force, raised by dark magic and intent on waking an even worse monster. He knew something drastic was called for to stop it, and he also knew he couldn't ask anyone else to do it.

"Look, guys, we don't have a choice. If she reaches the ocean, we've had it. We'll never stop her. The Cruelo dude will rise, and then … who knows what? The apocalypse most likely."

He frowned at Q'assog-tha, plotting a path towards her so they'd meet at a point well before the fields ended and the ocean cliffs began.

"Wait here," he said, getting up.

"Where you going?" asked Dylan as he took off.

Kane could feel their eyes on his back as he ran to the truck. Resisting the urge to look back, he jumped in the driver's seat, dropped the bag on the passenger seat, and fired up the engine.

As he backed up, Arika leapt to her feet. "Kane!" he heard her cry, but soon Arika and Dylan were receding into the distance, the truck heading towards Q'assog-tha.

All this time, Henri had been sitting in the back seat, her head buried in the Necronomicon.

"It doesn't say how or where you need to stab her, but it's the poison that needs to be administered, so I would guess it could be anywhere. It's probably best to aim for the body, though."

She glanced up, and noticed Kane was driving alone. Leaning forward, she peered into his face, which was pale and sweaty. Up ahead was Q'assog-tha, and they were driving straight towards her.

"Kane? What's happening?"

"So that's all you got? Stab her with the horn?"

"Where are the others?"

"Nothing about the human sacrifice?"

"That's all it says. Deliver the human sacrifice."

Holding her glasses steady, she turned and squinted out the rear window. "Where are the others?"

Kane ignored her.

Henri's eyes move from him to Q'assog-tha, and her face fell. "Um, Kane, perhaps you could pull over for a second and let me out."

"You're free to take the truck when we get there."

"Get where?"

"Where do you think?"

She shook the back of his seat. "Gates, you're mad. Stark raving. She'll see you coming. She'll have you for breakfast."

"Porridge, or bacon and eggs?"

Henri didn't seem to get the joke. "You'll be dead meat."

"What's with all the food references?"

"What do you think? Q'assog-tha clearly has a huge appetite."

"Aren't you a ray of sunshine?"

By this time, Kane had succeeded in getting them between the Black Queen and the ocean. Slamming on the brakes, pushing the gear into park, he pulled Ys-kar from the bag and jumped out of the truck.

"Get!" he yelled at Henri through the open door, and without stopping to see if she complied, took off towards Q'assog-tha.

Henri didn't wait to be told twice. Unfastening her seatbelt, throwing open the door, she rushed around to the driver's seat and jumped in. Kane had left the truck running, so she released the handbrake, peered over her shoulder and reversed at top speed. The truck leapt and bounced and banged over the rocky ground, throwing her about the cabin like a rag doll.

When she was a safe distance away, she braked, shoved the gear into park, and watched in shock as Kane ran up to Q'assog-tha.

Holding Ys-kar against his chest, face raised in defiance, he waited for her to approach. He looked like a mouse standing up to a dinosaur.

"Stark raving mad," muttered Henri.

DYLAN AND ARIKA ran up behind the truck. Their eyes were on Kane, and when he stopped, they stopped too.

"What's his plan?" gasped Dylan, fighting to catch his breath.

"I don't … I don't think he has a plan."

But Dylan knew his brother better than that. "Yes, he does. He's planning to die."

55

Duel

DYLAN WATCHED IN horror as Q'assog-tha advanced on Kane. She stopped and bent towards him, her tentacles reaching forward, her crown of cilia whipping about her head as if enraged by this puny human's challenge to her divine might.

"No," Dylan sobbed, his eyes streaming with tears. "Run, Kane. You need to run."

But Kane was holding his ground. Standing with legs apart and head raised, Ys-kar his sole defence against the might of the Black Queen, he stared up at her like he believed he had a hope in hell of winning.

Arika gripped Dylan's arm. She'd noticed something strange happening. Q'assog-tha, rather than attacking Kane, appeared to be studying him.

Her face, cool and composed until now, creased in impotent rage. TSUA-IARGH! she boomed, raising her head and pulling her tentacles back. Throwing herself to one side, she scrambled away from him.

"She's seen Ys-kar," Arika breathed, and without another word, took off for the truck. Dylan stood rooted to the spot for a few seconds longer, then took off after her.

INSIDE THE TRUCK, Henri was spellbound by the spectacle of Kane standing up to a god. Even more incredible was that the god was in retreat. But it was clear the Black Queen wasn't giving up. Circling around Kane, she was continuing her journey to the water, and barring a miracle, nothing was going to stop her.

"We're doomed," Henri declared, banging her head on the steering wheel. "Doomed."

Glancing up, she spied Dylan and Arika in the side mirror, running towards the truck. She watched numbly as their images grew larger, hardly registering them except as movement and colours.

With a deep sigh, she tipped the rear-view mirror and stared at her reflection. "Henri Appleby," she said to herself, "don't go trying to fool yourself." She smiled with self-pity at her red-rimmed eyes, the creases in her cheeks, the way her jowls drooped towards her flabby neck. It wasn't a pretty sight. She looked like she'd aged ten years in the past day. "Just look at you. How can you even contemplate it? You're not the hero type. You're just what Sam Morgan said you are: a scared, frumpish, owl-faced bookworm. It's all you ever were, and all you'll ever be."

Pushing up the mirror, sighing with the futility of it all, she moved the gear shift into drive, pressed her foot on the accelerator, and took off after Kane.

UP AHEAD, KANE was chasing after Q'assog-tha. She was moving across the terrain with surprising swiftness, heading for the cliff edge, her eyes on the ocean in which slept her brother Cthulhu, the high priest of other-worldly terror.

"Come back and fight, you coward!" Kane yelled as he stumbled over the rocky ground. "You're not a god, you're a stupid, scared, oversized squid!"

He waved Ys-kar in the air, challenging Q'assog-tha to a duel, but the Black Queen wasn't about to be distracted by a boy's cheap insults. She was faster and mightier than he, she'd fought battles with adversaries far stronger and smarter than anyone or anything on this planet, and he was losing the race to the water.

Discerning a rumble behind him, he glanced over both shoulders and was surprised to see Henri driving his truck at him like a madwoman, hurtling over the uneven ground, her forehead almost touching the windscreen.

She drove up alongside him, slowed the truck, leaned out the window and yelled, "Jump in! I'll get you closer!"

Kane gaped at the truck as if it were driving itself. His first instinct was to motion to Henri to stop so he could take her place behind the wheel, but he knew there was no time for that. Henri knew it too. She waited until he fell back, watched as he threw his body into the tray, then took off again at high speed.

Pushing Ys-kar under his armpit, Kane held onto the bar with both hands as the truck leapt over the rocky ground and skidded in the mud when Henri spun the wheel towards Q'assog-tha. Speeding past her, completing an arc, she slowed to let Kane jump out of the tray, then continued the arc.

Kane hit the ground running and charged at Q'assog-tha with Ys-kar raised. But once again the Black Queen was onto him. Her face steely with fury, she came to a sudden halt and shot out a single tentacle, which hooked around his calves and snapped away, pulling his legs out from under him. He fell, still clutching Ys-kar, landing painfully on one shoulder, his head bouncing on the grass.

Moving off, Q'assog-tha continued her trek to the ocean.

Henri, a safe distance away, thumped the steering wheel with both fists. "Damnit, Kane! Get up! You almost had her!"

Kane wasn't moving.

Putting the truck into gear, she drove up close and pushed open the door. "Kane! Wake up! You can still catch her!"

Her voice roused him, though his only reaction was to roll on his side and bring his knees up to his chest.

Putting the truck in park, Henri undid her seatbelt, clambered out and knelt beside him.

"You need to get up, Kane. She's getting away. If you don't stop her, we're finished."

Q'assog-tha was approaching the edge of the cliff.

"Oh no! No, no, no!" Henri cried, rigid with terror. "She's made it!"

Shaking Kane's shoulder, putting her mouth close to his ear, she yelled, "Get up, Kane! Get up, get up!"

Pushing herself to her feet, she watched as Q'assog-tha peered left and right, then up at the sky, as if trying to find her bearings. Now the ocean was in sight, she'd ceased her mad flight and was almost serene in her contemplation of the next stage of her mission.

As Henri stared at the black behemoth silhouetted against the tempestuous sky, a wave of emotion rose inside her chest, almost lifting her from the ground. The Black Queen had never looked more magnificent than she did right now: poised above the ocean, her eyes on the horizon, getting ready to fulfil her destiny by awakening her exalted brother.

The terror melting from her face, Henri gazed down at Ys-kar, as if noticing it for the first time. "This is yours," she said, and a single tear squeezed out of one eye and fell on the horn, disappearing in an instant.

Taking Ys-kar from Kane's hands, she began walking towards Q'assog-tha, holding it out as an offering. "You'll be needing this," she stated in a clipped, librarian's voice. "It will assist you in locating your brother."

As Henri neared Q'assog-tha, the Black Queen began making signs in the air with her branch-like arms. At the same time, the tentacles along her vast body curled and waved in a repeating pattern, as if executing a beautiful dance.

"Here you go," Henri chirped, holding out Ys-kar. "Use this in your spell. It's connected to your brother."

Suddenly, Q'assog-tha bellowed, CTHULHU LI'THAN R'LYEH! and in that instant the rapture in Henri's mind snapped. She stopped dead in her tracks, shook the fog from her head and gazed in awe at the colossal monstrosity that loomed before her. She could hardly believe she'd sauntered up to her enemy and almost handed over the key to the Earth's destruction. Standing so close to the monster that had sucked Sam Morgan dry and devoured countless other dead soldiers, she almost lost control of her bladder.

"She's not a god, she's a murderous devil," she lectured herself through clenched teeth. "She killed Sam. She wants to kill millions of others. She's evil and doesn't belong in this world."

With a burst of determination, Henri yelled, "Prepare to return to your cesspit hell dimension, you she-witch!" and threw Ys-kar with all her might.

The horn flew through the air and landed in a bush.

Q'assog-tha turned her head. A tentacle reached out, curled around Henri's waist, and cast her over the cliff.

HER FOES VANQUISHED, the Black Queen raised herself to her full height and began calling, CTHULHU LI'THAN R'LYEH! CTHULHU

LI'THAN R'LYEH! in her thunderous voice.

The noise roused Kane from his stupor. Pushing himself up, he rolled onto his knees and blinked the stars from his eyes. With a sideways glance at Q'assog-tha, he climbed to his feet and staggered to the truck, where he waited for Dylan and Arika to arrive.

"Are you okay?" Arika called out when they were within earshot.

"What did you think you were doing?" yelled Dylan, running up to him. "Are you stupid or something?"

Kane didn't know whether what he'd done was stupid, but he did know their only chance of vanquishing the Black Queen rested with Ys-kar. And Ys-kar wasn't about to wield itself.

"Haven't you ever wanted to be a superhero?" he returned, rubbing the back of his head.

Dylan was trying hard to catch his breath. "Not a dead one."

"You've read the comics. The dead ones always come back."

"I need you, you dumb, stupid jock. You can't go off being selfish and stupid like that. Where would I be if you're all dead and shit?"

Kane smiled at his brother's compliment-in-an-insult. A week ago he would have agreed with Dylan's contention that he'd be lost without him, but now he knew that whatever happened in the final battle with Q'assog-tha, his brother would be okay.

"You outsmarted a two-hundred-year-old wizard," he reminded him. "What do you need me for?"

"Um … to bug me, nag me, stuff God-awful salad down my throat … make my life a misery."

"I don't need you," interjected Arika, punching Kane's arm hard, "but I *have* gotten used to having you around."

Kane turned to her, surprised by the passion in her voice.

"Even if you *are* a dumb, stupid jock."

So you *do* like me, he thought with a burst of elation. I knew it! He could have kicked himself for not acting on his instincts earlier. Knowing he would have no other opportunity, he grabbed Arika's arms and kissed her hard on the mouth. She felt surprisingly warm and soft, and tasted sweet, like an orange. To his great relief, she didn't push him away.

When at last he pulled back, she stared him in the eye and said, "Okay, I do need you."

He smiled at her with tender regret, the rest of the world ceasing to exist in those few frozen moments. But the reality and urgency of the situation quickly returned, and his face hardened.

He glanced over his shoulder. Q'assog-tha was still performing her spell, bellowing, CTHULHU LI'THAN R'LYEH! over and over as her arms waved and her tentacles danced and her eyes scanned the watery horizon.

He dropped his hands. "If only we met in different circumstances," he mused – though he knew it was only these unique circumstances that had brought them together. Without the Messenger, their paths would never have crossed. Arika had no reason to visit Quorn, and Kane would never have gone anywhere near George University. More to the point, they had nothing in common besides stopping Wilfred Waite and Simon Orwell – and now Q'assog-tha. What kind of relationship could be built on such flimsy foundations? And even assuming it could, how would it ever last? The thought made him feel a little better. Any way you looked at it, this spark between them would never have gone anywhere.

The chanting suddenly rose in intensity, and the rhythmic motion of Q'assog-tha's tentacles gave way to a manic thrashing. U-ARGH! DIETSCHE FHT'URH! CTHULHU NA-AI K'THA! she screamed, leaning forward.

Kane saw Arika's eyes scan the ground and realised she was probably thinking the same thing he was.

"Do you think her brother heard her?" he asked, to distract her.

"Let's hope it's a locating spell, not an awakening one."

"If Cthulhu was awake, we'd probably have felt something by now," Dylan said.

"Good. That gives me time to finish this."

Dylan looked confused. "What's that supposed to mean?"

"You know what it means. I need to go."

"No, I don't know what it means. No one needs to do anything."

"Somebody has to stop her reaching the water."

Dylan sputtered and shook his head. "No, it's too late. That thing won't let you get close. You saw it. She'll kill you if you go back."

"I have to try, Dylan. You know I do. If she wakes that Coolio thing and they start Armageddon, it's the end for everyone."

"What about the human sacrifice?"

"I'm counting on that part being an old wives' tale. Or the dead soldiers might be enough. I'll just have to play it by ear."

Ignoring his brother's protests, he ducked inside the truck, pulled out the Necronomicon and handed it to Arika.

"Keep this safe," he said. "You'll need it if I don't come back. You're the only ones who can stop her."

Arika took the book from him. He was pleased to see her eyes stayed on him – a stark contrast to the other times she was near the Necronomicon, when she hadn't been able to take her eyes off it.

"Don't do it, Kane," pleaded Dylan one last time, grabbing his sleeve, pulling his arm towards him. "Let someone else be the hero."

"There *is* no one else." He glanced around, looking for Ys-kar. "There's only us. Only me. And I *will* come back; do you hear me? I'm a trained firefighter, and she's what? – some ginormous alien battle-queen god. No contest!"

His face grew serious. "I do need to ask one favour – just in case," he quickly added. "Can you please find January and tell her I'm sorry? I know I was unfair and immature and – well, a dick. Just say I'm sorry, okay?"

"You'll tell her yourself." Dylan threw his brother's arm away. "But yes, if it makes you feel better, I'll tell her."

When Dylan dipped his head, Kane said, "Listen, kid: Mum and Dad would have been proud of you. I am too. You've been amazing – strong and smart and – and I couldn't have asked for a better little brother." Taking him in a bear hug, he kissed his ear, then stepped away in embarrassment.

The chanting stopped. They turned their heads and watched as Q'assog-tha began her descent, walking down the cliff the way a lizard or a snail would, face first, clinging to the rock in defiance of gravity.

"I'll be back," Kane said in a bad Austrian accent.

With a bittersweet smile at Arika, he took off, retrieved Ys-kar and ran after Q'assog-tha.

At the top of the cliff, he paused and peered down at the black mass of sticks and tentacles. Q'assog-tha had reached the sand and was about to start her trek across the beach. Though his mind was screaming at him to stop and think, to back away from the edge and come up with some other way to stop her, Kane knew the die had already been cast, that everything in his life to this point had led him to this single decision, this single action.

"Here goes nothing," he said, and with a last glance back at Dylan and Arika, jumped.

Falling feet-first through the air, Ys-kar raised and ready, he landed with a grunt in the soft folds of Q'assog-tha's back. Her tentacles curled around him, and in the same instant a warming flood rippled through his body and a beautiful calmness entered his mind.

As the tentacles lifted him, he slammed the point of Ys-kar into her back.

The Black Queen roared, and Kane was hoisted high into the air. But it was too late. Ys-kar had penetrated her hide and its life force or poison, or whatever it was that gave it its power, had an immediate effect. The tentacles weakened, loosened their hold, and Kane slipped through them and dropped back into the folds of Q'assog-tha's body.

Flailing, he fought to turn over and get to his feet, trying to reach a position where he could jump down to the sand and run for cover. But his energy was flagging, and he was rapidly losing any desire to escape. Q'assog-tha's body was soft and warm, like his bed; it was a haven, the home he'd craved all his life, a place of safety and comfort, where Mike and Lauren and Oliver and Dylan waited to welcome him. They were happy and healthy, together at last, and together they would be impervious to any more harm or misery. Lying there, Kane felt an overpowering urge to curl up and sleep in the arms of his magnificent queen, the divine mother who could make this miracle happen, who, as a reward for his devotion, would return to him everything he'd lost.

With a sigh of pleasure, he closed his eyes and surrendered himself to her.

Meanwhile, Q'assog-tha continued dragging herself through the sand in a desperate effort to reach the sea. But she was weakening and slowing by the second, her tentacles turning a translucent grey. Her face wore an expression of surprise and hate and disbelief at the victory of this insignificant mammal.

At last she stopped, collapsed in the sand, and with a final raucous scream, faded into a colourless mass of protoplasm before melting into nothingness.

Dylan and Arika watched her defeat from the top of the cliff. After her disappearance, the sand and the sea went on as always under the dismal sky. Gelatinous brown waves lapped against the shore. Dead fish and seaweed in various states of decay dotted the beach. Kane and Ys-kar were gone.

56

Saving Kane

"H E'S NOT DEAD," Arika proclaimed, turning her back to the ocean. Dylan stood with hunched shoulders, his face and shirt stained with tears. "How do you know that?" he asked in a petulant boy's voice.

"Because it has to be true."

"The spell needed a human sacrifice. It wouldn't have worked without it. The monster disappeared, and Kane's gone."

"No one said the sacrifice meant Kane had to die. The condition could have been satisfied by Henri Appleby, or the soldiers in the chopper … Sam Morgan, even."

"Do you really think that?"

"He looked alive when Q'assog-tha disappeared, didn't he? He was moving. I saw it. I saw him trying to get up."

He peered at her from lowered brows.

"She hardly even noticed he was there," she went on. "So he was pulled back to her home dimension – alive. And all he had to do there was jump off her back and escape."

That was good enough for Dylan. He grabbed the Necronomicon from her hands and headed to the truck.

"We'll go back to the altar," he called out over his shoulder. "That's where the portal was opened, so we can do it again and get him back."

Arika opened her mouth to protest, then closed it. Of course it was futile attempting to open a portal when you had none of the materials or know-how needed to activate the magics, and couldn't even read the spell book – not to mention the insanity of re-opening a portal when you only just vanquished the deadly monster that dropped out of it the last time it was opened – but she also knew they couldn't stand around moping all day, or go home and just accept things were over. They had to *do* something. They had to believe they had some kind of control over Kane's fate, and at least give this a try.

"Okay then," she said, following him. "I hope Henri left the keys in the truck."

DOWN BELOW, HENRI stirred. She was lying on the beach, flat on her back, where she finished up after climbing halfway down the cliff, losing her grip, falling a short distance, then rolling the rest of the way down the slope.

Following her flight over the cliff, she hit a grassy outcrop and managed to grab onto exposed roots to stop herself dropping all the way to the sand. She remained there listening to Q'assog-tha's chant, pressing her cheek against the cliff face and holding on for dear life.

When the chant ended, she smiled in delight and turned her eyes to the heavens. Sure enough, the Black Queen was beginning her descent. She climbed past Henri on her way to the beach, at which time Henri left the safety of the ledge to begin the climb down the slope to join her.

By the time she rolled to a stop on the beach, Q'assog-tha was fading, fighting to pull herself along, her limbs and tentacles pushing the sand back more than propelling the gargantuan body forward. Winded, battered and bruised from the fall, all Henri could do was urge her adored queen along, like a cheerleader rallying a losing team. Then came the final defeat, the dissolution, and with it, Q'assog-tha's hold on Henri snapped for the last time. The Great Old One had been sent back to her own dimension, her power and influence gone. Cthulhu slept on, and the world was safe.

Getting up on her elbows, Henri looked around. She'd lost her glasses and everything was blurry, but she felt like a blind woman seeing the world for the first time.

"I'm alive!" she cried, falling back on the sand. "It's a miracle!"

For a while she lay staring at the clouds, mustering her energy and trying to make sense of what had happened. Ys-kar had worked. Obviously. Kane must have recovered. Or perhaps Arika did it. Whoever was responsible, they found a way around the human sacrifice.

"The soldiers; Sam; the helicopter pilot," she muttered: "they did it.

Well, Henri, your plan worked. Wait till I tell the Plenum about all this."

Sitting upright, she cried, "Oh my Lord, I just saved mankind!"

She glanced around.

"Where is everybody?"

BACK ON BIG Martha, Dylan carried the Necronomicon past the black vases and purple grass towards the altar. Wilfred was lying where he fell, a pile of old clothes and dirty bandages, his greenish-black skin showing where the wrappings had pulled away. Dylan gave him a wide berth. He couldn't bear to look at him, not even in his side vision, and the smell, which until recently had been his own body odour, made him want to puke.

"Yech, disgusting," commented Arika, holding a hand over her nose. She bent for a closer look. "He's melting."

Leaving the corpse, she joined Dylan. He'd opened the Necronomicon on the altar and was flicking through it. Now they were here, she was once again contemplating the futility of trying to rescue Kane. Wilfred had set up an elaborate spell involving human hearts – the smashed remains of which were all over the altar and the grass and Dylan's clothes. He'd slashed letters into his belly and wielded Ys-kar and done God knows what else to summon Q'assog-tha. All they had was the book.

But Dylan was undeterred. He'd been deep in thought all the way here, and now he turned to the page he believed would bring his brother back.

"Kane thought the starry eye thing might work as a wish-maker," he said, tapping the picture of an eye inside a circle of symbols inside a seven-pointed star. "We can wish him back and everything will go back to normal."

Arika was doubtful it would be that easy, but she wanted more than anything to be supportive. She turned it over in her mind. "You mean in the same way Waite's hold over your body was tenuous, and Q'assog-tha's presence in this world was the same, Kane belongs here, so we should be able to get him back using the power of the Necronomicon?"

Despite her scepticism, she could see her explanation had struck a chord with Dylan. Nodding excitedly, he placed his hand on the page.

Arika watched as his brow furrowed. After a few seconds of staring at the picture, he squeezed his eyes shut, like he was straining to make the impossible happen.

A full minute passed. Arika looked around. There was no sign of clouds transforming or human-like shapes appearing or Kane's voice crying out to them from another dimension. The day went on as before, grey clouds hanging low in the sky, a cold breeze coming in from the bay, flies buzzing around the blood on the altar – everything normal apart from the absence of Kane.

Suddenly a buzzard mewed, and Dylan's eyes shot open. He glanced around expectantly, spun in a circle, then visibly deflated. He turned his grief-stricken face to her. It seemed at that moment that all the world's misery was concentrated in that one sad look.

"Here," Arika said, "let me try. Maybe you're all magicked out. If this doesn't work, we'll go back to the uni and research everything we can on that monster. I'll get in touch with the best brains in the world, and we'll get Kane back. You have my word, Dylan. Even if it means travelling to that hell dimension and dragging him out ourselves."

She took Dylan's place at the altar and placed her hand on the picture. Setting aside her doubts, she concentrated her thoughts on Kane's face, on his muscular shoulders, on their kiss, on the feel of his firefighter's body pressed against hers; bringing all her memory and will to bear. Kane's soft lips, his slightly sour breath, the heat of his hands burning through her top – all the passion she ever felt in her life, focused on one moment, on one man.

"I can't feel anything," she said – and then something hard struck her behind her right ear. She fell sideways and crumpled to the ground.

Peering up, dazed and confused, she saw Dylan standing over her, holding one of the black urns.

"Dylan," she croaked. "What –?"

"I told you pathetic dust mites you wouldn't stop me."

Gasping, her eyes flew to Wilfred's corpse. Unbelievably, it was stirring. A wet gurgling sound bubbled up its throat.

With a wail, Dylan dropped the urn and grabbed his head in both hands.

"Arika, he's back! I was in that disgusting body. Oh my God! It was awful! The dead things. The abyss. Crawling out … rat-like things, with fangs and claws … The abyss. It wants me – I can't – No, no, no, no, no! I can't –"

The corpse gurgled again.

Dylan threw out his hands.

"Damn you, worthless cur! Fight me, will you? – supreme sorcerer and heir to New Earth? I should have throttled your scrawny neck when I had the chance!"

Suddenly he faltered, grabbed his head again and cried, "Arika! Help me! I can't hold on! He's too –"

The corpse raised its head. "– shtrong."

Arika leapt to her feet. "The book!" she cried at Dylan, before realising it was no longer him.

"*My* book," smiled Dylan with Wilfred's voice, and then he groaned again, and Arika could see the sorcerer was once again back in his corpse.

"Dylan!" she cried, taking him firmly by the shoulders. "Listen to me. Focus on my face. Don't think about anything else. Listen to what I say and screen out everything else. You've got to fight this." She steered him towards the Necronomicon. "Tell me about your parents; about the treehouse. Remember? – you used to play there. Kane told me. And I've been up there. With Kane. I've seen it. How did your father build it?"

He groaned and held his head.

"Dylan! Talk to me! The treehouse!"

When he went on groaning, she changed tack. "Okay, Dylan, tell me about Oliver, about your brother, Oliver."

He looked at her. "Oliver?"

"Oliver. Your brother, Oliver. Kane told me how he loved Donkey Kong."

"It was my fault," Dylan whined. "I shouldn't have left him. It was just for a second."

"It wasn't your fault, Dylan. It was an accident. Accidents happen all the time."

Taking his trembling hand, she stretched it towards the book.

"Dad blamed me," Dylan went on. "He said I –" His face froze. "Arika! I can feel it! He's pushing me out! Somebody's helping him. I can hear them. He's using their power. I can't hold on!"

The corpse began chuckling.

"Dylan! Keep talking!"

"Please, Arika! Don't let me go back in that thing! Please! Please!"

"Tell me more about Oliver, Dylan. And Kane. We've got to get Kane back. I can't do it without your help. You've got to fight this for Kane's sake."

"I can't hold on any longer," he whimpered. "He's too strong."

She turned to Wilfred's corpse. "You evil son-of-a-bitch!"

Pulling Dylan's hand, she placed it on the Necronomicon and leaned her weight on it. She was hoping the energy of the book would do the rest. But Dylan was falling to pieces. He wasn't mentally strong enough to concentrate his thoughts on the page, and he certainly wasn't strong enough to beat Wilfred's centuries-old will and determination.

As she stared in rage and disgust at the chuckling corpse, Dylan went on pleading, his voice growing weaker with each word.

Desperate, her mind in a whirling panic, she pulled Dylan's hand away, slammed the Necronomicon shut, turned, raised it high, and brought it down with all her might on Wilfred Waite's head.

His skull crunched sickeningly.

From behind came a thud. Dylan was lying flat on the grass.

Arika rushed to him. Lifting his head onto her thigh, she watched in terror as his eyes fluttered open.

"Dylan? Is that – you?"

Her heart was racing, her head pounding, and she felt vomit rising in her throat at the thought she might have just killed him.

He blinked at her. "Wilfred."

She gasped in shock, but the next moment he added, "I can't feel him anymore. Is he –?"

Arika slumped with relief. "Oh, thank Christ. Dylan, you almost gave me a heart attack there. Yes. Dead. For good this time."

"You did the spell?"

"I, er, found another use for the book."

She helped Dylan sit up, then pointed. He gaped at what remained of Wilfred Waite, his head squashed beneath the heavy, leather-bound tome.

When he didn't say anything for a while, Arika grew scared he was about to faint with shock, or accuse her of murder or reckless endangerment.

Instead, he curled his lip and said, "We should have thought of that in the first place." His eyes turned to the altar. "Now we need to figure out how to get my brother back."

57

The road to Whalen

AN OLD GREEN BMW turned into the dirt road, drove up slowly, and rolled to a stop before the closed metal gate.

The driver's door creaked open, a stonewash-jeans-clad leg emerged, and out stepped Kenny Snyder.

He stood for a few moments with his hand on the door, contemplating the distant ocean. The sun was bright in the sky and glinting off the waves like a thousand diamonds. The sea air blew in his face and tousled his hair, reminding him of his youth on the central coast, a misspent youth of loitering in beach car parks and concrete change rooms, stealing whatever wasn't bolted down. The memory felt like a thousand years ago. *I need a holiday*, he told himself. *Soon as this gig is over, I'm taking a week off and spending every day of it out there on the sand, sipping Piña Coladas and breathing in the fresh salty air, a universe away from the dead bodies with their foul stench, and the dank, dark rooms, and the freaks and fanatics telling me what I can and can't do.*

He turned his eyes to a battered sign that read, DEAD END. Private Road. Trespassers Prosecuted To The Full Extent Of The Law. Stooping to pick up a rock, he threw it at the sign, missed, and smacked himself in the face.

He was stooping to pick up another when he spotted in the corner of his eye an approaching car. Straightening, he turned and watched as it drove the dirt road towards him. It was a sleek yellow Alfa Romeo, with heavily-tinted windows and very black tyres. The car came up fast and stopped on the other side of the gate.

A man emerged, a tall, well-built man in his mid-forties, with short-cropped reddish-blond hair and blue eyes. He was wearing brown chinos, a white knitted jumper and chunky tan boots, the kind a tradesman might wear. Without acknowledging Kenny's presence, he strode up to the gate, unlocked it and threw it open.

"Got 'em all?" he called out, walking towards the BMW.

Kenny nodded enthusiastically. "Yessir. As many as I could get me hands on."

The man stopped and sneered at him. He appeared repulsed by what he saw. "What did I tell you? I said to get them all."

Kenny lowered his head and began picking at a dirty fingernail. Ignoring him, the man went up to the car and peered through the window. On the passenger seat was a jumble of books, some with faded cloth covers, some bound in leather. On the back seat were five cardboard boxes, and next to the boxes, as well as on the floor, lay scattered knives, whips, chains and ropes, along with an upended box that appeared to have tipped over on the way here. Everything looked like it had been thrown into the car in a hurry.

The man grunted and shook his head.

Kenny stepped around to the passenger side and opened the door. "I'm sorry, sir. Mr Livingston. It was dangerous work. The place was crawling with soldiers. I was lucky to get even these."

"What about Orwell's?"

"He just had one bookcase. The university was locked down, and I don't know where he kept the rest of his stuff."

"Well, find out."

"Yes, sir."

"And go back to the farm and get the rest of Waite's stuff. Before the damned NSO appropriates it all."

"Yes, sir."

"Do you understand? I want all of it."

He nodded.

"The bodies?"

Kenny leaned his arms on the car roof. "They're up for cremation at week's end. Six of them. I can cart them up on Sat'day. After the services are finished."

"You better. You know how he gets when he's hungry. You don't wanna have to take their place, do you?" He smirked at the thought. "Come on, help me unload this junk."

They transferred everything to the Alfa Romeo.

"Get out of here."

"Yes, Mr Livingston."

Jumping in his car, slamming the door, Kenny reversed and took off back to Quorn.

Corbin Livingston got back in his own car. Breathing through his mouth, he tried to blow the toxic filth of Snyder's memory out of his head. The man was a toad, an idiot, but somehow he'd managed to beat the great Wilfred Waite at his own game. He weaselled his way into the wizard's life, made himself indispensable, and then out-manoeuvred him to advance his own interests. Interests that now seemed to include Whalen. Corbin snorted. Snyder was a threat, a ticking time bomb, and would have to be dealt with – once his usefulness ran past its use-by date.

He switched on the engine and pressed the button for the radio. The reception wasn't great, but the signal was clear enough to pick out a man's voice, speaking with authority and self-assurance like he knew the answers to all the world's problems and desires.

"Forget the former things; do not dwell on the past," the evangelist preached. "See, I am doing a new thing. Now it springs up; do you not perceive it? I am making a way in the desert, and streams in the wasteland. The wild animals honour me, the jackals and the owls, because I provide water in the wilderness and streams in the wasteland, to give drink to my people, my chosen …"

"Hallelujah," responded Corbin, raising his hands from the steering wheel.

Releasing the brake, he drove in a tight circle and headed back the way he'd come. Passing a rusted, bullet-riddled sign that declared, Welcome To Whalen, he turned up the radio.

"But you have burdened me with your sins and wearied me with your offences," continued the evangelist. "I, even I, am he who blots out your transgressions, for my own sake, and remembers your sins no more."

"Sins no more," Corbin repeated, glancing at the books on the seat beside him.

"Borellus!" he cried, his face brightening. He reached out and caressed the tattered cloth cover. "Can't wait to get my hands on *you.*"

ABOUT THE AUTHOR

Dean Raven is a writer of dark fantasy, urban fantasy and horror. He is author of the Bringer of the Dark series, which tells the epic tale of the battle between two brothers and the primordial god, Kragn.

Dean lives in Melbourne, Australia, and has been a fan of fantasy, horror and sci-fi since he was a littlun, when his mum and dad let him watch slasher and zombie movies on Betamax and stay up all night for monster movie-thons.

Dean writes stories in which extraordinary things happen to ordinary people. Whether it's fantasy, horror or an urban fairy tale, you are sure to find the kinds of people you know and care about in Dean's works.

www.ingramcontent.com/pod-product-compliance
Lightning Source LLC
Chambersburg PA
CBHW060813120726
47909CB00006B/1910